PRAISE FOR THE REVEREND ANNABELLE DIXON COZY MYSTERY SERIES

"I read it that night, and it was GREAT!"

"I couldn't put it down!"

"4 thumbs up!!!"

"It kept me up until 3am. I love it."

"As a former village vicar this ticks the box for me."

"This series keeps getting better and better."

"Annabelle, with her great intuition, caring personality, yet imperfect judgment, is a wonderful main character."

"It's fun to grab a cup of tea and pretend I'm sitting in the vicarage discussing the latest mysteries with Annabelle while she polishes off the last of the cupcakes."

"Great book - love Reverend Annabelle Dixon and can't wait to read more of her books."

"Annabelle reminds me of Agatha Christie's Miss Marple."

"A perfect weekend read."

"I LOVE ANNABELLE!"

"A wonderful read, delightful characters and if that's not

enough the sinfully delicious recipes will have you coming back for more."

"This cozy series is a riot!"

THE REVEREND ANNABELLE DIXON SERIES

ALSO BY ALISON GOLDEN

Horror in the Highlands

THE REVEREND ANNABELLE DIXON SERIES

BOOKS 1-4

ALISON GOLDEN
JAMIE VOUGEOT

Published by Mesa Verde Publishing
P.O. Box 1002
San Carlos, CA 94070

ISBN-13: 978-1725997523

Edited by
Marjorie Kramer

"The greatest gift is a passion for reading."
Elizabeth Hardwick

To get two free books, updates about new releases, exclusive promotions, and other insider information, sign up for the Cozy Mysteries Insider mailing list at:

http://cozymysteries.com/annabelle

DEATH AT THE CAFÉ

Alison Golden

Jamie Vougeot

DEATH AT THE CAFE

BOOK ONE

Cover Illustration: Rosalie Yachi Clarita

Published by Mesa Verde Publishing
P.O. Box 1002
San Carlos, CA 94070

Edited by
Marjorie Kramer

NOTE FROM THE AUTHOR

The events in this book take place a few years before *Murder in the Mansion*, the next in the Reverend Annabelle Dixon series of cozy mysteries. It is set in London.

Death at the Café is a classic prequel to the other books, all of which are complete mysteries. They can be read and enjoyed in any order. I've made sure not to include any spoilers for those of you who are new to the characters. Any existing fans of Annabelle's escapades will still find plenty of fresh action and mystery, as well as a little background detail on some of the major players in the Reverend Annabelle universe. All in all, there is something for everyone.

I had an absolute blast creating this book – I hope you have a blast reading it too.

Alison Golden

CHAPTER ONE

NOTHING BROUGHT REVEREND Annabelle closer to blasphemy than using the London public transport system during rush hour. Since being ordained and sent to St. Clement's Church, an impressive, centuries-old building among the tower blocks and new developments of London's East End, she had come across every sin known to man – and a few new ones too. She had counseled wayward youths, presided over family disputes, heard astonishingly sad tales from the homeless, and retained her solid, optimistic dependability through it all. None of these challenges made her blood boil and her round, soft face curl up into a mixture of disgust, frustration, and exasperation. Yet sitting on the number forty-three bus to Islington, as it moved along at a snail's pace, was enough to almost make her take her beloved Lord's name in vain.

On this particular occasion, she had managed to nab her favorite seat: top deck, front left. It gave her the perfect position to view the different kinds of streets and the even more varied types of people. Today, however, her viewpoint afforded her only an even more teeth-clenchingly irritating perspective of a traffic jam that extended as far as the eye could see down Upper Street.

"I know I shouldn't," she muttered to herself on the relatively empty bus, "but if this doesn't deserve a cherry-topped cupcake, then I don't know what does."

The thought of rewarding her patience with the thing she loved almost as much as her vocation itself – cake – settled Annabelle's nerves for a full twenty minutes, during which the bus trundled in fits and spurts along another half-mile stretch.

The assignment of Annabelle, fresh from her days fervently studying Theology at Cambridge University, to the tough, inner-city borough of Hackney had been an almost literal baptism of fire. She had arrived in the summer, during the few weeks when the British sun combined with the squelching heat of a city constantly bustling and moving. It was a time of drinking and frivolity for some and heightened tension for others; a time when bored youths on their summer holidays found their idle hands easily occupied by the devil's work; a time when the good relax and the bad run riot.

Though Annabelle had grown up in East London, when it came to her first appointment as a vicar, her preference had been for a peaceful, rural village somewhere. A place in which she could indulge her love of nature, and conduct her Holy business in the gentle, caring manner she preferred. "Gentle" and "caring," however, were two words rarely used to describe London. Annabelle had mildly protested the assignment, but after a long talk with the Archbishop, who explained the extreme shortage of candidates both capable and willing to take on the challenge of an inner-city church, she agreed to take up the position and set about her task with an enthusiasm for which she had become noted.

Father John Wilkins, of neighboring St. Leonard's Church, had been charged with easing Annabelle into the complex role of a city-based diocese. He had been a priest for over thirty years, and for the vast majority of that time had worked in London's poorest, most difficult neighborhoods. The Anglican Church held far smaller sway in London than it did in rural England, comprised as London was of a disparate mix of peoples and creeds from around the world, each with their own beliefs. The only time Father John's church had ever been full had been a particularly warm Christmas Eve. Even then, the congregation had been composed of especially devout immigrants from Africa and South America, many of whom were not even Anglican but simply lived nearby.

Despite its lack of influence, London's churches found themselves playing pivotal roles in the local community. With plenty of people in need, churches in London became hubs of charity and community support. Fundraising events, providing food and shelter for London's large homeless population, caring for the elderly, and engaging troubled youths were their stock in trade, not to mention providing both spiritual and emotional support throughout the many deaths and family tragedies which frequently occurred.

The stress of it all had turned Father John's wiry beard a speckled grey, and though he knew his work was important and worthwhile, he had been pushed to his breaking point on more than one occasion. Upon her arrival, he had taken one look at Annabelle's breezy, cheerful demeanor and her fresh-faced and open smile before assuming that her assignment was a case of negligence, desperation, or simply a bad prank.

"She's utterly delightful," Father John sighed on the phone to the Archbishop, "and extremely nice. But "delightful" and "nice" are not what's required in a London church. This is a part of the world where faith is stretched to its very limits, where strong leadership goes further than gentle guidance. We struggle to capture people's attention, Archbishop, let alone their hearts. Our drug rehabilitation program has more members than our congregation."

"Give her a chance, Father," the Archbishop replied softly. "Don't underestimate her. She did grow up in East London, you know."

"Well, I grew up in Westminster, but that doesn't mean I've had tea with the Queen!"

Father John's complaints were shown to be premature, however, merely a week into Annabelle's placement. Her bumbling, naïve manner proved to be merely that – a manner. Father John observed closely as Annabelle's strength, faith, and intelligence were consistently tested by the urban issues of her flock. He noted that she passed with flying colors.

Whether it was with a hardened criminal fresh out of prison and already succumbing to old temptations or a single mother of three struggling to find some sense of composure and faith in the face of her daily troubles, Annabelle was always there to help. With good humor and optimism, she never turned down a request for assistance, no matter how small or large it was.

When Father John visited Annabelle a month later to check upon an incredibly successful gardening project she had initiated for young delinquents, he shook his head in amazement.

"Is that Denton? By the rose bushes? I've been trying to get him to visit me for a year now, and all he does is grunt. You should hear what he says when his parole officer suggests it," he said.

"Oh, Denton is wonderful!" Annabelle effused. "Terribly good with his hands. And a devilish sense of humor – when it's properly directed. Did you know that he plays drums?"

"No, I did not know that. He never told me," Father John said, allowing Annabelle an appreciative smile. "I must say, Reverend, I seem to have misjudged you dreadfully. And I apologize sincerely."

"Oh, Father," Annabelle chuckled, "it's perfectly understandable. You have only the best interests of the community and myself at heart. Let's leave judgment for Him and Him alone. The only thing we are meant to judge are cake contests, in my opinion. Mind those thorns, Denton! Roses tend to fight back if you treat them roughly!"

Progress in the service of the Lord was not matched by that of the London Bus Network on this occasion, however. The bus rolled forward and stopped once again, mere feet away from where it had started. Annabelle stood up to get a better view of the road ahead and scanned the long snake of traffic that extended in front of and behind the bus. She exchanged a shrug with a kindly-looking Jamaican man, grey curls tucked just underneath his porkpie hat.

"Fiddlesticks," she uttered, too exasperated to contain herself, "I'm supposed to meet someone."

"Aye," the Jamaican man replied in his heavily accented English. "The Lord moves in mysterious ways."

"Well, at least He moves, unlike this bus," Annabelle replied, sitting back down and clasping her hands.

After another ten minutes, the bus rolled forward a

little further, dejectedly opening its doors a full twenty yards ahead of the stop. Annabelle decided to walk the rest of the way and stepped off the bus into a crowd of people who all wore the same downtrodden expression of defeat.

Foregoing her usual laid-back, serene pace for one that would minimize the lateness of her meeting with her friend, Sister Mary, Annabelle marched down the high street, cassock flowing behind her, resolute about the cupcake and considering the benefits of buying a bicycle. It was to be the last time she and Mary would meet for a very long time.

Reverend Annabelle's and Sister Mary's lives had followed similar trajectories but for very different reasons. Mary had been born in the same year as Annabelle, in the back seat of the very cab Annabelle's father drove for a living. Having recently witnessed the birth of his own daughter, Annabelle's father was all too aware of how impossible it would be to get Mary's mother to the hospital on time. He had pulled up outside the nearest grocery store, and with the help of the shop owner who provided towels and water, delivered Mary himself.

With Mary's parents feeling deeply indebted to Annabelle's father for the successful birth of their child, the families – and thus the children – became lifelong friends. They soon grew into strikingly different figures. Annabelle grew tall and sturdy, with an ever-present smile on her face. Mary, on the other hand, was small and slim, with a delicate expression. It was, however, Annabelle's willingness and Mary's nose for adventure that caused the two girls to become fast friends until Annabelle left London to study at Cambridge.

Though Mary was slight, her five foot three looking even smaller next to Annabelle's towering frame, she had a habit of being at the center of things. Her first day at school ended prematurely when it turned out that an administrative error had registered her as a teacher, rather than a student. She passed her driving test with full marks, less for her ability to follow procedure and more for the expert precision with which she avoided an escaped bull that had found itself on the M25. Even the simple purchase of a second-hand coat turned into an event when Mary found plans for an undiscovered portion of London's underground tunnels sewn into the seams.

Wherever Sister Mary went, peculiar occurrences followed. Upon leaving school, she decided to study nursing at university. One day, she turned up to a fairly routine lecture on hospital procedures, only to find she had instead stumbled into a talk given by an order of nuns working in West Africa. Instead of discreetly leaving to double-check her planner, Mary stayed, captivated by the talk of exotic climates, dangerous but fulfilling work, and the devout purpose that the nuns exhibited. She had been raised a strict Catholic, and just minutes after the talk had ended, Mary had made up her mind – she would become a nun and go to West Africa. This unexpected turn of events, combined with her capacity for stumbling upon the unpredictable, is what led those around her to assign Mary her nickname, "The Accidental Nun."

This was to be their last meeting before Mary returned to Africa. As Annabelle drew closer to the café where Mary had requested they meet, she saw a gathering crowd of onlookers and felt her heart skip.

"Oh dear, Mary," she thought, "what on earth has happened this time?"

"Excuse me," Annabelle called, as she made her way through the crowd. Though there were many of them, they stood aside for her, partly due to the authority her cassock brought and partly because Annabelle was taller than most of them. "Vicar coming through!" she trilled.

When she broke through to the space inside the circle of gawkers, Annabelle saw what was at its center: a dead woman. She was sprawled next to an outside table, a waiter crouched beside her, barking out instructions for the crowd to stay back and let the paramedics through. The woman was young and beautiful, golden-blonde hair tragically splayed out against the dirty pavement. She was wearing a simple but well-fitting pair of jeans and an elegant jacket that would have given her the appearance of a trendy woman-about-town were she not lying on the grey concrete. Her slim, pretty face had high cheekbones, offsetting pale-blue, lifeless eyes that gazed into the sky, as if witnessing the flight of her own soul.

Two green-suited paramedics burst through the crowd with the swift and graceful purpose of a job done a thousand times. They dropped their bags beside the body and went to work, talking with the waiter who spoke continuously while shaking his head in disbelief.

Annabelle peeled her eyes away from the scene and noticed Mary, wearing her civvies rather than her nun's habit, standing on the other side of the crowd. Her hand was over her mouth, and she was visibly shaking. Annabelle's instincts told her something somewhat stranger than a simple, straightforward death had occurred. Mary had been in West Africa. She had studied nursing. When it came to tragedy, Sister Mary had seen it all, including death. For her to look so shaken would require something either incredibly awful or shockingly surprising.

Annabelle marched through the space toward the nun, whose eyes were so fixed upon the dead body that she barely noticed the Vicar until she grasped Mary in her arms and hugged her gently.

"Mary! Are you okay?"

"Oh, Annabelle," the Sister said, embracing her friend in return.

Annabelle patted Mary's back until she had calmed down enough to pull away and look her in the eye.

"What on earth happened?" Annabelle said, as she grasped Mary's arm and led her away from the crowd.

"It's awful, Annabelle," Mary said, sniffing back sobs. "She walked up to me. And then she just dropped down to her knees. Seconds later, she stopped moving. I don't know what happened, Annabelle. I really don't."

"Walking toward you?" Annabelle said, pulling an ever-handy pack of tissues from her pocket and handing one to Mary. "You knew her?"

"No," Mary said, just before blowing her nose into the tissue, "but I was to meet someone here, just before you came."

"Who?"

Mary gave her nose one last blow before speaking. "I've been in London for a month now, looking for funding. As hard as we work, the hospitals in Africa simply cannot cope without large amounts of money. I was meant to meet someone here who could help me. Just before you came along."

"The woman who is now dead?"

Sister Mary shook her head, too overwhelmed by the situation to think properly. "I don't know. We had only spoken over the phone. I don't believe so. I'm sure the person I spoke to was much older."

Suddenly, their attention was drawn by officious shouts to clear the pavement. Annabelle looked away from Mary's

small, pretty face to see police officers ushering the
onlookers away.

"Sorry, ladies," a nearby officer said, "would you mind
moving just a little further down the road? We're going to
have to tape the whole area. Thank you."

"Officer," Annabelle called, before he could turn away,
"this woman saw the death."

The bobby turned back and cast his eyes toward Mary,
who managed a mild nod from behind her scrunched-up
tissue.

"Detective!" he bawled, with a voice well-practiced in
commanding attention. He pointed at Mary. "Someone
here you need to speak to."

Seconds later, the two women found themselves joined
by a short, bulky man with a face screwed-up into a
perpetual expression of suspicion and frustration.

"Detective Inspector Cutcliffe," he said, as if even
pronouns were too indirect and time-wasting for him.

Everything about DI Cutcliffe was rough. Everything
from the heavy jacket he wore through all seasons to his angu-
lar, uncompromising jawline. There was a pool in his police
branch for whomever could make him laugh. It had run into
hundreds of pounds, and there still wasn't a winner despite
lowering the goal from "laughter" to "smile." Officers joked
that he had come out of the womb clenching his teeth, only to
immediately question the doctor's credentials. Colleagues
said that he asked more questions than a TV game show host,
and that he hadn't dropped a case since 1982.

They joked but never to his face. DI Cutcliffe was the
kind of detective who could do damage with a look. He was
the butt of many private jokes but the public recipient of
none. He also happened to be one of the most respected

detectives in London. He may have been a little harsher than he was fair, but he was fair nonetheless.

"Name?" he growled, his notebook and pen materializing from nowhere into his hand.

"Sister Mary Willis."

"And I'm Reverend Annabelle Dixon."

DI Cutcliffe's eyes darted between the two women beneath his perpetually quizzical eyebrows.

"Anglican?" he said, spearing the word toward Annabelle like a bayonet.

"Yes."

"And you're Catholic?" he said, pointing his pen toward Mary.

"Yes."

"How do you know each other?"

"We've been friends since... Well, forever," Annabelle said, looking at Mary who confirmed her statement with a vehement nod.

DI Cutcliffe shrugged away the line of enquiry before starting the next one.

"So you saw what happened?"

"Yes."

"Mind describing exactly how it went?"

"Yes. I mean, no, of course not. I mean, yes, I'll describe it," Mary stammered, finding the detective's flint-like tone much less inviting than Annabelle's. "I was waiting to meet someone. Here. At the café."

"The Reverend here?"

"Yes, but before her. Someone else. Someone I'd never met before."

The detective's intense look made it known he needed more.

"A... business colleague. Someone who was interested in funding my hospital in Africa."

"The dead woman?"

"I don't think so. I'd only ever spoken to my contact on the phone. I'm fairly certain it wasn't the woman...over there." She nodded toward the body on the ground. "The person I was supposed to meet was much older."

The detective nodded, accepting the answer for now.

"I noticed the woman, the dead one," Mary continued, "walking toward me. She was extremely close, barely a foot away from me. She seemed fine. Then suddenly she just dropped down, as if her legs had gone. Then..."

Mary began sobbing again, losing her composure as she relived the memory.

"Sorry," she said, to the expectant detective. "Then she just collapsed, fully. Flat on the ground."

DI Cutcliffe clenched his teeth as he mused over the description. "So she was looking at you. But you don't think she was the person you were going to meet?"

"No," said Mary. "I don't think so."

"But she was looking at you."

"Yes. No. Oh, I can't be sure, but I think so. Maybe I'm wrong. It was all so... fast. I thought maybe she had mistaken me for somebody else, or that she was a waitress, or wanted to ask for directions, or maybe an old friend... I don't know, Detective, I'm sorry. "

"I see," the detective said, scribbling something down so furiously Annabelle was sure he would rip the paper of his notebook. "So she walked up to you and then collapsed. Then what happened?"

"I screamed and jumped out of my chair. The waiter came over and checked on her. Then... a doctor came."

DI Cutcliffe's eyebrows raised themselves ever so

slightly. On a face more expressive, it would have barely been noticeable, on his, it seemed positively exuberant.

"You mean the paramedics?"

"No. A man who said he was a doctor. After I had screamed, people on the street turned to see what was going on. He came from the other side of the road and pushed through the crowd. That's when he said he was a doctor. He knelt over the woman and checked her pulse, then... I'm so sorry. I don't know. I was so shaken."

"Where is this doctor now?"

Mary looked around for a full five seconds. "I don't know. I believe he left. When I saw him tending to the young woman, I looked away, and when I looked back, he was gone."

"Could you describe him for me?"

Mary looked off into space for a while, squinting as if it would help her see further into her own memory. "It's difficult. I believe he was dark-skinned."

"Black?"

"No. Maybe. I didn't really see his face. He was dressed very strikingly though. He wore a dark suit. Tweed, perhaps. It looked very expensive. A waistcoat too. Brown leather shoes."

DI Cutcliffe let out a barely perceptible sigh.

"If I get a sketch artist, do you think you could describe him?"

Mary winced as she tried to extract further details from her memory. "I could try, but I'm sorry, I really doubt it. It's as if the more I try to remember him, the more I struggle."

"Just try to relax. It will come to you," the Inspector said.

"It's the strangest thing. At the time I thought I had seen him clearly, but I can't for the life of me recall..."

"You say you heard him say he was a doctor. Was there any kind of accent? What did he sound like?"

Mary bit her lip and looked away again as she delved into her memory. "Maybe... African? South American, perhaps? Actually I didn't notice any real accent. He sounded... like a typical Londoner, I suppose. If there is such a thing."

The detective stared at Sister Mary with eyes that seemed to excavate her mind, sizing up whether the small woman was hiding something. After a few seconds of this intense glare, he flipped to a blank page in his notebook, handed it to Mary along with a pen, and said: "Please write down your telephone number and contact details."

Mary willingly obliged.

"Inspector," Annabelle said, seizing the moment, "does this mean we can go now? Sister Mary seems incredibly shaken, and I'd like to take her somewhere she can gather herself."

The detective's small, dark eyes shifted to Annabelle's wide, bright ones. They darted quickly to her collar. He nodded as if allowing a great privilege. "You can go, but don't leave the city. I may need more information about this person you were meeting, as well as our non-descript 'doctor,' in the very near future."

Mary handed back the Inspector's notebook, and he handed the two women his card in exchange.

"If you remember anything, and I mean anything, then call me," he turned his penetrating gaze toward Annabelle. "I'm always willing to give the benefit of the doubt to Holy men – or women. Even though it's been known to backfire in the past on occasion."

Annabelle and Mary exchanged frightened glances as the Inspector turned on his heel and marched back to the scene of the crime. He was already barking out instructions to his officers. Annabelle found herself almost as shaken as her friend upon hearing the Inspector's last comment.

"Whatever could that be about?" she said, careful to remain out of earshot of any of the police personnel at the scene. "Come on, we'll go somewhere quiet and have a nice cup of tea and a slice of cake."

Mary nodded agreeably, allowing Annabelle to take her by the arm and guide her down the street.

"Annabelle," she said, in her soft voice, "could I trouble you for another tissue?"

"Of course," Annabelle replied, fishing around for the packet and handing it to her entirely. "Take the whole lot. You need them more than I do."

"Thank you," Mary said, pulling a tissue out and putting the packet into a pocket. "Oh!" she cried suddenly, as if a mouse had been waiting there to bite her on the finger.

Annabelle spun around to face Mary, and watched as she pulled out a small slip of paper.

"I completely forgot!" Mary exclaimed, in response to Annabelle's curious expression. "The woman who died. Before she collapsed – I mean, before she fell completely to the floor – she handed me this."

Annabelle's hands smacked into her cheeks in an almost childlike expression of surprise. She moved her lips silently for a few moments, as if unable to think of what to say. "Are you sure?" was the only thing that came to mind.

"Yes! I completely forgot in all the fuss. She had it in her hand and reached out to me. I took it, and she fell. It was almost automatic of me, I was so focused on her eyes. The life was visibly leaving them...."

"Well, what does it say?!" Annabelle said, as quickly as she could.

"I don't know," Mary shrugged, her friend's excitement confusing her.

"Well, open it!" Annabelle nearly screamed, her hands rolling over themselves in a gesture of hurried anticipation.

Mary stared at the small slip of lined notepaper that she held in her hand as if it were an incredibly fragile explosive. Carefully, she reached a finger into the crease and unfolded it. Annabelle watched wide-eyed and open-mouthed, her heart thumping.

Mary studied the contents for half a second, then gasped suddenly, her hand instinctively going to her mouth, causing her to drop the slip of paper itself.

Annabelle reached down to pick it up with cat-like reflexes, stood back up, and read it aloud.

"'Teresa is in danger'. And then there's a number."

Annabelle looked back at Mary, who was still clutching her hand to her mouth.

"Teresa is the woman I was supposed to meet!" Mary exclaimed. "What could it mean?"

Annabelle looked back at the note, as if the answer may have appeared upon it.

"Quick, let's go back and tell the Inspector," Annabelle said.

Mary nodded enthusiastically, and the two women ran back the way they had come. The café came back into view just as the Inspector was pulling away from the curb in his unmarked car, a police officer controlling traffic to allow Cutcliffe a route through the blocked lanes. She watched his car weave through the static vehicles and speed off down an empty side street.

"Fiddlesticks!" Annabelle cried out.

"What should we do now?" Mary said, her sobs and cries long gone with all the running and excitement.

Annabelle scanned the road, then marched toward a phone booth.

"Are you going to call him?" Mary said, as she struggled to keep up.

"No," Annabelle replied, a note of determination and purpose in her voice, "I'm going to call the number on the note."

Mary's voice raised itself a full octave. "But Annabelle! We don't know what is going on here! We should call the police."

"You're right, and there will be plenty of time for that. But first, we're not sure that this note actually means anything. We don't want to waste police time for something we could easily check up on ourselves – plus she handed the note to you. There would be no need for that if this 'danger' were something only the police could handle."

"I suppose you're right," Mary admitted.

"We'll just check, and then if we need the police, we'll hand this to DI Cutcliffe immediately. Besides, if someone is in danger, as this note implies," she said, picking up the receiver, "the closest person is sometimes more useful than the correct one.

ANNABELLE SHIFTED HER weight anxiously from one foot to the other as she listened intently to the phone ringing. Mary stood a few feet away from her, glancing from side to side up the busy street as if she were a lookout. It felt much like one of the many adventures they had enjoyed together as children. Perhaps it was the fact that they had not spoken for such a long time, Mary having spent much time in Africa, and Annabelle busy with her new position at St. Clement's Church. Suddenly, they were reprising the well-worn roles established in their youth; Annabelle taking the initiative, and Mary providing a willing, inventive counterfoil. The stakes, however, felt a lot more dangerous than a week's grounding this time around.

The rings abruptly ended, and Annabelle waved her hand gleefully at Mary.

"Hello?" came a scratchy but warm voice on the other end of the line.

"Oh, ah... hello! Ah... Is this Teresa?"

"Yes, I am Teresa," came the cautious reply. "Who is this?"

"Ah, this is Reverend Annabelle Dixon. I have with me Sister Mary Willis. I believe you know her."

"Yes. Indeed I do," the woman replied, a strange note of tension in her voice.

"Ah, well..." Annabelle stumbled over her words, wondering what she should say. The woman made no reference to the proposed meeting. She looked at Mary for a cue, but her open-mouthed look of anticipation provided none. "Well, we received a message that indicated you may be in danger. We'd like to come visit you as soon as possible."

"I see." Teresa said slowly, her voice still filled with a sense of wariness, before continuing after a short pause. "Well, yes. That would probably be for the best. My address is fifty-two Glentworth Street. Head directly north from Baker Street station. My apartment covers the second floor."

Annabelle nodded firmly at each sentence, as if the physical gesture would help her better commit the address to memory.

"Okay. We'll be there as quickly as possible. But please, be careful in the meantime."

"Goodbye," Teresa said after a second's hesitation, as if bracing herself for some immense challenge.

Annabelle slammed the receiver onto the hook and turned to Mary.

"So? What did she say?" Mary asked, her large, round eyes urging Annabelle for information.

"This is terribly strange," Annabelle said, scratching her neatly-bobbed hair. "She didn't seem fazed in the least, nor did she make any mention of the meeting with you. If the idea weren't so preposterous, I'd say she was even somewhat suspicious of me. Did she always sound so guarded to you?"

Mary pursed her lips as she thought. "No, not at all. From our conversations – though they were few – she seemed a very typical older lady. Warm, gentle, caring. Humorous, even."

Annabelle pitched her shoulders back and stood fully upright, like she always did before making a final decision.

"Then we should make haste, because the woman on the other end of that line is obviously afraid of something. Let's find out what it is."

And with that, Annabelle began her stern march once more toward the tube station, Sister Mary fluttering in tow like a ponytailed butterfly.

The two women made their way to the tube station and rolled through the turnstiles along with the mass of other fellow travelers. They reached the platform just as a train barrelled out from the dark tunnel and hopped on it.

Annabelle slumped into her seat as if it were a comfy couch at the end of the day, while Sister Mary sat down delicately and slowly, as if setting herself for tea.

"When I'm in Africa, I do so miss riding the tube," Mary said, displaying her unbridled positivity in spite of the macabre events of the morning.

"If it were up to me, I'd happily give the whole transport system away," Annabelle replied, gently kicking away an empty bottle that had rolled against her foot.

Mary giggled at Annabelle's rare grumbling. "However would you travel around London?"

Annabelle shrugged and smiled. "I'm beginning to think the best thing to do is stay at home anyway!"

Mary laughed gently, before her smile turned into the pursed lips of concern.

"I am terribly sorry for all of this fuss, Annabelle. It's a terrible shame that instead of catching up as we intended, we're going who-knows-where for what seems like an incredibly worrying purpose."

"Oh, tosh," assured Annabelle. "It's fine. I'm sure this is all perfectly reasonable and will be clarified as soon as we have a chat and a cup of tea with this Teresa. Perhaps you'll even get to finalize your funding."

"That would be very good," Mary nodded.

"Come on, we have to change trains here."

"Where are we going?"

"Baker Street."

"Home of Sherlock Holmes," Mary added, joviality returning to her voice.

"Perhaps he can help us with this confounding turn of events!"

They exited the train, navigated the tunnels and escalators that led them onto the Metropolitan Line, and waited patiently on the platform.

"Do you remember the time that we went to a Halloween party," Mary began, after a moment of thought, "you as Sherlock Holmes and me as Jack the Ripper?"

"But of course!" Annabelle said, happily looking into the distance as she brought the memory to her mind. "I had rather hoped you would go as Dr. Watson, instead."

"That would have been terribly boring," Mary said. "You took the costume entirely too seriously."

"I did not!"

"You did!" responded Mary. "You spent the entire evening – both the trick-or-treating and the party afterward at your cousin's – staring suspiciously at people over your plastic bubble-pipe, trying to 'deduce' who had committed the crime of taking a bite of your Halloween cupcake."

Annabelle laughed. "Well, perhaps I was a little overzealous."

"I've not seen your cousin Josh since he drove us to that concert."

"'The Jacksons'! Oh yes, I remember that well. You danced so wildly you nearly poked somebody's eye out!"

"How times change," Mary said, wistfully, as they stared into space.

As they waited, a man sitting on a bench tossed a free newspaper onto the seat beside him. Mary glanced over twice before mustering up the courage to walk over.

"Excuse me, are you finished with this paper?"

The man nodded curtly and turned his gaze back toward the darkness of the tunnel. Mary picked up the paper and walked back to Annabelle.

"I had forgotten how rude Londoners can be," Mary said in an almost silent whisper.

Annabelle shrugged sympathetically as the train rolled up to the platform. They entered a carriage and sat once again. Mary opened the paper and perused it solemnly, turning pages only after she had cast her eyes upon each headline at least once. Annabelle glanced curiously at her friend's intense focus.

"Are you always so interested in the news, Mary?" she asked.

Mary shook her head. "No. I'm just wondering if there's something here that could be connected to the woman who handed me the note."

Annabelle shifted her head, bemused.

"Such as?"

"Well, look here. A serial killer has been roaming the streets of Lewisham."

"That's nowhere near the café. And look here," Annabelle said, pointing to the top of the article, "it says he's been caught."

Mary turned the page, almost disappointed at her poor sleuthing skills.

"What about this! Russian spy poisoned in Notting Hill! She could have easily been poisoned!"

Annabelle leaned over the paper, scanned a few paragraphs, and then relaxed her brow.

"It says the actual poisoning happened last year – if it happened at all."

Mary turned the page again, deflated once more. Annabelle checked her watch while Mary continued to study the newspaper for clues.

"Shall I read you your horoscope, Annabelle?"

"Mary! You're a Catholic nun! You shouldn't be indulging in such poppycock!"

"Oh, it's just a bit of fun to pass the time."

"It's nonsense and dangerous at that if you take it too seriously."

"Don't be such a spoilsport!"

"I'm not!" Annabelle gasped, with mock offense. "Look at us. We have the same sign, and we're entirely different."

Mary smiled mischievously. "And we're also incredibly alike, wouldn't you say?"

Annabelle rolled her eyes in defeat. "Okay. Go on then."

Mary folded up the paper eagerly, as if better to read it, opened her mouth to recite the words, then lowered her brow in an expression of both shock and befuddlement.

Annabelle leaned forward, waiting for her to speak. "Well?"

Mary adjusted herself, before speaking in a slow, serious tone. "'Today will be a day of dramatic events. Stay alert, because somebody you know will be full of surprises.'"

The two women looked at each other for a few seconds, sharing their feelings of confusion. Annabelle broke the silence with a snort of derision. "Nonsense. That's so general, it could apply to almost anyone, or anything, on any day. Here's our stop. Let's go."

Though they were both already moving quickly through the busy London streets, the shock of the newspaper's words seemed to spur just a little more speed out of the two women. They exited the Baker Street station like a pair of scampering dogs, and after stopping briefly to ask for directions to Glentworth Street, maintained a quick pace all the way to the entrance of the large property whose address they had been given over the phone.

Annabelle pressed the bell eagerly, looking at Mary. When the door buzzed without a word from the intercom, she grabbed the handle and pushed quickly. Somehow, Mary managed to keep up with Annabelle's long strides up the stairs leading to the doorway of the apartment. By this time, they were out of breath from both the climb and the excitement but intent on their purpose of finally meeting the mysterious Teresa.

Mary raised her hand, fist ready to knock, but the door opened slowly before she could even begin, revealing a short lady who was no doubt the Teresa they had come to see. She was well-dressed in khaki slacks and an intricately-knitted cardigan in duck egg blue. The wrinkles on her face seemed well earned, and the deep brown of her eyes hinted at having seen many adventures. Her white hair was still thick enough to frame her face elegantly, and when she spoke, her voice had the strong, aged woodiness of a classical instrument.

"Hello. I've been waiting for you. Do come in," she said slowly.

"Thank you," Mary said, stepping into the house. Annabelle followed, politely nodding her appreciation at the invitation.

The apartment was lavish, and though it was open and large, everywhere the two visitors looked seemed to be filled with ornately-carved sculptures, powerfully evocative artwork, and ornaments of unimaginable shininess. Mixed among the relics and artifacts were crucifixes, elaborate carvings of the Virgin Mary, and diamond-encrusted plates that depicted scenes involving the saints.

They stepped carefully forward, as if in fear of spoiling what seemed like one of the most incredibly intimate and packed museum exhibitions they had ever seen. Teresa walked past them slowly, with a slight limp in her gait and led them toward a living room packed with just as many objects of delicate craftsmanship as the entrance.

"Please, take a seat. I've laid out some tea."

Though her instincts still told her that something was incredibly strange about both this elderly woman and the situation itself, Annabelle caught sight of the table and found a note of familiarity in which to ground herself. Laid there was elegantly sculpted china with detailed patterns painted tastefully upon each piece. Annabelle's eyes immediately focused upon a plate which held small, bite-sized pieces of cake that her connoisseur's eye could tell would be delicious. Whatever was causing the peculiar suspicions stirring in Annabelle's chest could wait.

"Oh, this looks delightful," Annabelle smiled.

Teresa held Annabelle's eyes as if judging her, a pleasant, if slightly reticent smile upon her face.

Once Annabelle and Mary had seated themselves, Teresa leaned over the table and began pouring tea. Though both the visitors would have liked to offer help, they were well aware of the customs such elderly ladies liked to uphold and chose to sit back.

"Please do try the cake," Teresa said, with a curiously tentative tone.

Annabelle glanced at Mary, and they each took one of the pieces from the plate. Mary nibbled the edge slightly, while Annabelle popped the entire thing into her mouth.

"Mmm!" Annabelle hummed, as she swallowed the creamy, soft texture. "Absolutely magnificent! Oh my!"

Teresa finished pouring the tea and set the teapot down.

"It's my niece's favorite. I call it 'Teresa's Surprise Cake'. She does so much for me, it's nice to repay the favor by baking one for her occasionally."

Annabelle was still sifting her tongue around her mouth, as if trying to capture every remnant of the extraordinary flavor. "Gosh! That might be one of the most scrumptious things I've ever eaten!"

Teresa raised an eyebrow as if she fully expected this reaction. Suddenly, her eyes widened slightly, and her smile was less tentative. When she spoke again, it was with an almost expectant sureness.

"I'm so glad you like it. I have some more in the kitchen. You're welcome to take some with you."

Annabelle's eyes lit up, all thoughts of danger and death had disappeared from her mind the moment she had tasted the stunningly tasty treat.

"That would be wonderful! Thank you ever so much!"

Teresa merely nodded her appreciation and left briefly

through a doorway Annabelle assumed led to the kitchen. She was still smiling so much at the thought of enjoying the cake once again (something she believed she had thoroughly deserved after the morning's events) that she barely noticed Mary's persistent nudging of her elbow.

"Annabelle!" Mary whispered, as aggressively as she could muster – which wasn't very aggressive at all. "You should tell her what happened! I can't! This is all too much for me."

"Yes, yes!" Annabelle said in similarly hushed tones, her friend's anxiety refocusing her thoughts upon the task at hand. "Don't worry."

Teresa returned clutching two zipped clear plastic bags with the cakes wrapped in foil visible inside them.

"I hope you don't mind," she said, "wrapping them up like this is all I could manage at short notice."

"Oh, of course," Annabelle said, gleefully taking the two bags and handing one to Mary. "They smell wonderful!"

"I call them 'Teresa's Surprise Cakes', because they have a very rare, very secret, ingredient."

Annabelle's eyes lit up as if in the presence of a fire-works display. "That sounds utterly thrilling! Doesn't it Mary?"

Mary nodded eagerly, but her face was still consumed by anxiety. Annabelle saw it, and her expression changed to one more appropriate for the subject she was about to bring up.

Annabelle and Mary watched carefully, as Teresa slowly moved to sit in her obviously favored chair by the open window.

"I like to sit here," she said, as if reading their thoughts, "and keep watch. I very rarely leave the house. My niece runs most of my errands."

"Oh," Mary said, "well, it's a wonderful house. I could find myself quite happily occupied among so many delightful things."

"Thank you," Teresa acknowledged. "My ex-husband was one of the greatest antiques dealers in the world. He dealt in only the most beautiful and rarest objects."

Though Annabelle was loathe to interrupt such an obviously pleasing reminiscence for Teresa – particularly with such dreadful news – her sense of duty rose within her.

"Teresa," she began, announcing her intent with her serious tone, "we believe you may be in danger. As I imagine you're aware, you were supposed to meet Sister Mary today to discuss funding, I believe. Instead, a person handed her a note that said you were in danger, along with your telephone number. A person who then died."

Teresa listened to Annabelle speak with a smile of knowing on her face until Annabelle uttered the last sentence, at which Teresa's smile turned into an expression of pure pain.

Teresa clutched the arms of her chair and looked wildly around her. She opened her mouth and closed it again, without speaking.

Then, in an act of apparent defeat, she slumped as if all the life and fight had gone out of her.

"I... know that I'm... in danger..." she said, as if woozy from the news. "I... know... something... danger—"

Suddenly, her smooth, firm voice began to crackle wildly, and her sporadic speech was accompanied by an increasingly wild swaying to and fro. Annabelle and Mary watched in rapt attention at the sudden and bizarre change in Teresa's manner.

Before one of them could even offer help, Teresa let out

one last broken syllable and clattered forward out of her chair onto the Persian rug beneath it.

"Teresa?" Annabelle gasped, before looking at Mary, who had resorted to her familiar pose of clasping her hand over her mouth. The two of them held each other's shocked gaze, until Mary's nursing instincts kicked in, and she sprang into action.

"Teresa, are you okay?" she said, as she knelt beside the fallen woman and gently pressed a hand to her shoulder. When she failed to receive a response, she looked once again at Annabelle, who stood up, cake still in hand, and looked around the room for some answer as to the woman's collapse.

With all the gentle, yet firm care of a well-practiced nurse, Mary lifted Teresa a little and placed two delicate fingers to the crease of her neck. Her lips pursed as her worst fears were confirmed.

"Annabelle! She's dead!"

"Are you sure?"

"The way she collapsed... It was almost exactly like the girl at the café today. I was just about to say som—"

Mary stopped herself abruptly, and her expression changed as she seemed to fumble for something in the woman's neck.

"What is it?" Annabelle asked.

Mary pulled out a tiny, hair-like sliver of something clear and sharp, just short of two inches long.

"It's... cold... Like a shard of ice," Mary said, twisting the fragment in her fingers as she searched for some explanation.

Annabelle stepped forward and leaned over her kneeling friend to get a closer look at the curious object.

"It appears to be melting," she said, before suddenly opening her eyes wide in terror.

Without thinking, Annabelle smacked the object out of Mary's hand with all the force of a heavyweight boxer.

"Ow! Annabelle!" Mary screamed, clasping her sore hand in her other.

"I'm awfully sorry, Mary, but a thought just occurred to me."

"What kind of violent thought would cause you to hit me!?"

"Check Teresa's neck," Annabelle said, stepping to other side of the woman and kneeling down. "Where you found that shard."

Mary cast one more scowl of hurt at her friend, before obliging.

"Well the skin is rather pockmarked anyway... But look here," she said, indicating the very side of Teresa's neck. "There's a little redness around this tiny dot. It's somewhat similar to a puncture wound."

As if surprised at her own words, Mary and Annabelle once again shared a look of horror. Annabelle took to her feet, turned her head toward the open window that the old woman had sat beside, and hurriedly gestured for Mary to get up.

"Come on, Mary! We have to leave immediately!"

Mary nodded her understanding of the situation and stood up quickly. They ran through the apartment without any of the care and delicacy they had exhibited upon entering. Suddenly, Annabelle almost slid to a stop before quickly turning back the way she came.

"Where are you going, Annabelle?" Mary called.

"The cakes!" she cried, emerging from the living room

seconds later carrying the two bags aloft. "We've left them behind!"

Once the two friends had scampered out of Glentworth Street and back out into the populated safety of Baker Street, Annabelle found a phone booth and called both the emergency services and DI Cutcliffe.

The detective told them to meet him outside the apartment in half an hour. He needed to investigate the area and ensure that it was safe for them to enter. Annabelle and Mary secreted themselves in a small café, clutching each other and casting glances around them as if surrounded by wolves. When the aforementioned time was up, they locked arms and slowly made their way once more into Glentworth Street. Their nerves jangled with a sense of danger until the sight of multiple police and ambulance vehicles afforded them a feeling of security.

As they drew close, joining the dozen or so onlookers who watched the covered stretcher being wheeled into the back of the ambulance, Cutcliffe appeared before them as if rising from the ground itself – pen and notepad already in hand.

"So, ladies," he said in his gruff voice, "you should know the drill by now. From the top, if you please."

Mary looked at Annabelle in the hope she would take the lead, which she promptly did.

"Mary received a note from the woman who died at the café earlier this morning," Annabelle said, pulling out the slip of paper and handing it to DI Cutcliffe. "One that said Teresa, the woman now in the ambulance here, was in danger. Along with a number—"

"You didn't think that was worth mentioning when I questioned you this morning?" Cutcliffe directed toward Mary, with more than his usual amount of intensity.

"I completely forgot about it! It was only when I later found the note that I remembered it!" Mary pleaded, exasperated and overwhelmed by both herself and the situation. "Oh Detective! Please, I know it sounds terribly negligent, but this is all happening so fast! I'm a nun, Detective. I am used to solemn worship. Slow, deliberate thought. All of this is much more intoxicating and confusing than anything I'm accustomed to!"

The detective's stern face remained still throughout Mary's speech, as if ignoring the content of her words, and instead studying her manner for clues.

"But you found the note, and instead of deciding to call me, visited Teresa yourself," he said, calm but forceful.

"When the note mentioned danger," Annabelle said, stepping in to offer some clarity on behalf of her stressed and frazzled friend, "we never interpreted it to mean immediate, fatal danger. Surely, it would have been easier to go to the police herself had it been so. Instead, the woman at the café handed it to Sister Mary, a nun. We had every intention of telling you, Detective, but we had hoped that we could discover more about the situation before placing the task at your door."

The detective shifted his eyes toward Annabelle, though his face remained pointed toward Mary, as if reminding her he was still suspicious of both.

"It was my idea, Detective, and I'm incredibly regretful about it," Annabelle added.

The detective offered a barely perceptible nod, before proceeding to scribble into his notebook in his angry fashion.

"So you visited the house, and then what?"

"She invited us in," Mary said, eager to answer a question that didn't depict her as worthy of suspicion, "and we sat down to take tea. We told her what had happened in the morning, and then she collapsed in almost the exact same manner as the girl at the café."

The detective raised an eyebrow so heavy it almost seemed to require effort.

"You didn't say anything to each other?"

"We exchanged pleasantries," Annabelle said, looking at Mary for confirmation.

"We complimented the apartment," Mary added.

The detective raised his other eyebrow suddenly.

"You complimented the apartment?"

"Why yes," Mary said, "it's full of wonder."

Cutcliffe jabbed his pen back over his shoulder, as if specifying the building. "That mess? You complimented it?"

"Mess, Inspector?" Annabelle said, taken aback both by DI Cutcliffe's apparently poor taste and his crude manner of expressing it. "How can you call a place so full of history, of beauty, and of rarefied artifacts a mess?"

"Quite easily," the detective responded, now displaying his own confusion. "When there's junk piled from the floor to the ceiling, and it looks like it hasn't been cleaned in a year."

Annabelle and Mary gasped. Reading their surprise, the detective continued.

"Are you saying that it wasn't like that when you arrived?"

"Not at all, Detective!" Mary exclaimed. "Why, it was utterly immaculate when we were there. We barely breathed heavily lest we knock something out of place."

The detective nodded, far more thoroughly this time, and scribbled so much into his notebook that he had to flip a page angrily, as if irritated that he was required to do so.

"Do you think somebody entered the apartment after us and wrecked it, Detective?" Annabelle asked.

"If you're telling the truth," DI Cutcliffe responded casually, as if it were still uncertain, "then that's precisely what happened."

"Who would do such a thing?" Mary asked.

"I have some ideas," the detective said dismissively, glancing back at his officers who were now cordoning off the area. "So she collapses, and then what?"

"I went to her, checked her pulse, and discovered that she was dead – I'm a nurse, you see," Mary added, initiating another bout of manic note-writing from the detective. "I found something very curious, actually. A thin shard of ice, embedded in her neck. We checked for a puncture wound and thought we found one."

"Hold on," the detective said, raising his hand. "You're saying there was a piece of ice in her neck? Like some kind of dart?"

"That's what I believe," Annabelle answered, "yes, Inspector."

"And where is this... ice dart now?"

"It was melting," Mary said, after a few seconds of thought. "I held it, but Annabelle knocked it out of my hand when we realized it may have been the cause of Teresa's death."

"I imagine it would have melted away by now, Inspector," confirmed Annabelle.

"Convenient," came Cutcliffe's reply, as he continued to write.

"Inspector!" Annabelle cried, when realizing the insinuation. "You do not seriously believe that we caused this horrible death, do you?!"

Cutcliffe noisily flipped to a new page in his notebook and raised his fearsome eyes to meet Annabelle's.

"I don't believe anything in my line of work. I just deal with facts. You have been at the site of two very similar deaths within the past three hours. The woman at the café died from poisoning, and I would bet a large chunk of my retirement fund that this Teresa died from the same poison."

Mary gasped. The detective handed his notebook and pen to Annabelle.

"This time I want *your* contact details and phone number, please," he said, firmly.

Annabelle reluctantly took the pen and the notebook, though she huffed slightly, hoping the detective would detect her annoyance. Cutcliffe just glared at her before continuing.

"You're telling me that an 'ice dart' that has 'melted away' was what killed one, or possibly two of these women. You're telling me that an apartment that looks like wild elephants ran through it was 'immaculate' and worthy of 'compliments' merely an hour ago. It's certainly not impossible, but it's definitely not probable either."

Annabelle handed back the pen and notepad. "But—"

"The most infuriating thing," Cutcliffe interrupted, "however, is that you withheld evidence. Not only did you hold back a critical piece of information, but you acted upon it yourselves."

"It was—"

The detective raised his square hand to silence Mary. "And to top it off, you're off buying cakes after witnessing the death of a defenceless old woman! What are they,"

Cutcliffe said, leaning over the bags Annabelle clutched in her hand, "chocolate?"

"We didn't—"

"I've heard enough. When I need to speak with you – and I most certainly will need to speak more with both of you – I'll be in touch. Until then, stay where I can reach you."

"I can't!" Mary cried. "I have to return to the rectory and then to Africa within a week!"

The detective shook his owl-like head with resolute refusal. "That's not going to happen. Like it or not, both of you are embroiled in what seems to be a double-murder case, and I've already stretched the limit of my leniency by not throwing you into a cell until we've answered more questions than we've asked."

Annabelle opened her mouth to offer a reply, but by the time she had thought of something to say, the detective was already heading back toward the apartment entrance, directing orders to his constables.

Annabelle and Mary sat beside each other in silence on the way home. If the earlier part of the day had brought to mind fond memories of their schoolgirl adventures, their second meeting with DI Cutcliffe had reminded them of the inevitable scoldings when things went too far. They stared into space, forlornly clutching their – now, rather pathetic-seeming – clear bags containing Teresa's cakes.

"What are you thinking?" Annabelle said, after almost half-an-hour of quiet contemplation of her wrongdoing. It was the same phrase she had always used as a kid, when breaking a long silence between herself and Mary.

"I'm thinking about how to explain this all to the Mother Superior. I'm thinking about how many people I'll have to inform that I may not be back when I said I would and thinking about how disappointed they'll be when I tell them I didn't get the funding," Mary said, as slowly and as considerately as a night-time prayer.

Annabelle cast a determined look at her cake, her eyes narrowing.

"What are you thinking?" Mary asked.

"I'm thinking about how we're going to solve this case," Annabelle replied.

Mary stiffened and turned to Annabelle, all steadiness disappearing from her voice.

"Solve the case?! We can't solve the case!" she screeched.

"Whyever not!?" Annabelle said, adamantly. "We are two smart, confident women of God."

"But we're already under suspicion!"

"All the more reason we need to fix this terrible situation! The Inspector obviously didn't believe us with regards to the ice dart and the destroyed apartment, but we know that it's true. And that means we're in a much better position to uncover the real murderer than the Inspector is. If we don't, then we may find ourselves being put on the block for lack of a better suspect!"

"Oh Annabelle," Mary said, slumping back into her seat, "you're going to get us into an even bigger mess!"

Mary tentatively agreed to meet Annabelle for lunch the next day, circumstances allowing. Annabelle pocketed her cake, exited the train, and made her way back to St. Clement's Church, her thoughts still with her friend who would have a lot of explaining to do when she returned to the rectory where she was staying.

When Annabelle entered the imposing, awe-inspiringly crafted doors of the large church, she heard the satisfying clink of tea cups in the kitchen to the side. She entered the small kitchen to find Cecilia Robinson, church secretary, cleaner, and expert tea-maker.

"Hello, Reverend," she said, in her cheery Manchester accent. "You must have had a busy day. I've not seen you at all. Tea?"

"The words 'yes, please' have never felt so insufficient," Annabelle said, taking off her coat and placing it on the coat rack. "Oh," she squealed suddenly, fishing around in her sizable coat pocket. "I've got cake."

"Don't bother," Cecilia said, "Mrs. O'Dwyer brought some of the cherry cupcakes you like this afternoon. You know what they're like; soft as snow when she's just made them, and hard as rock the morning after."

Annabelle caught sight of the pile of cherry-dotted crumbling magnificence Cecilia placed on the small table and completely forgot about Teresa's Surprise Cake.

"Just when I was beginning to question my faith," Annabelle joked.

Cecilia tutted a mild disapproval. Though she had a dark past, Cecilia had rebuilt her life around the Lord, and she was now in possession of a devout faith that put even a lot of priests to shame.

Annabelle took the mug of milky tea that Cecilia handed her and picked out what she deemed the largest cupcake.

"Father John is in the back, Reverend. You should see him as soon as possible."

Annabelle questioned Cecilia with her eyes, her mouth fully occupied with the cupcake.

"Apparently the Catholic Bishop has called twice today,

asking about you," Cecilia continued. "I spoke to Father John a little while ago. He said, "if she's not returned in an hour, I'll call the Bishop back myself!""

Annabelle chewed slowly, swallowed, and pursed her lips.

"Is something wrong, Reverend?" asked Cecilia, receptive to Annabelle's look of deep concern.

"Yes," replied Annabelle.

"What is it?"

Annabelle held the cupcake aloft, as if to inspect it in the light. "I believe Mrs. O'Dwyer has begun using tinned cherries."

THE OFFICE OF St. Clement's church was Annabelle's pride and joy. It had originally begun life as a room for the incumbent reverend to change clerical garments, gain some respite, and to store things. Over the years, however, numerous priests had added to and refined the room's purpose, finding its size and the large window that overlooked the giant sycamore trees in the church's grounds an enticing place to spend time. A bookcase added here, an oak desk there, some leather seats, an expertly carved prayer stand, and the room was now a fully-fledged office, from which a priest could conduct all manner of affairs.

As Annabelle stepped inside the warm and inviting room, Father John pulled his head away from his Bible and leaped up out of the office chair.

"Annabelle! Where on earth have you been?" he exclaimed, as she allowed her body to drop into the inviting couch next to the desk.

"Oh, Father," Annabelle replied, still new enough in her position that she referred to him by his title, despite his protests. "I have just experienced one of the most eventful days I believe I've ever had."

"I've been trying to reach you, Annabelle – and indeed, I've been waiting for you here – for the entire day. I do wish you would take your phone with you when you go out."

"I assure you, Father, I only intended to be away for an hour or two. I left my phone here as I hate interruptions. Cell phones are terribly rude."

"Well, this is exactly the sort of circumstance in which they're also 'terribly' useful," Father John chided, as he stepped around the desk and paced the floor in front of Annabelle. "Bishop Murphy – he of the Catholic Church, no less – has called multiple times. He left a message."

"What did he say?"

Father John shrugged curiously. "He'd like to speak to you. He sounded very insistent. I believe it has something to do with whatever bother you managed to get into today. You were with Sister..."

"Mary."

"Yes, Mary. It's likely he'll want to speak to her, too."

Annabelle sighed.

Father John pitched his trouser legs up slightly as he leaned back slowly against the desk, folded his arms, and looked at Annabelle with the patience of a sympathetic parent.

"What happened today? Tell me everything."

Annabelle shook her head and took a deep breath. She figured out where to start and began. The meeting with Mary, the identical deaths, DI Cutcliffe's penetrating questions, Mary's despondency at explaining it all, they all tumbled out. When she had described every event in full detail, she looked up at Father John's confused face, and asked, "What should I do, Father?"

He scratched at his short, well-pruned beard as he considered the question.

"That's an astonishing story," he said, slowly. "To witness not just one death but two? In the space of a few hours. It's incredible. You can hardly blame DI Cutcliffe for being suspicious."

Annabelle smacked her thighs in disappointment at the Father's dispiriting but fair appraisal.

"But I know DI Cutcliffe well. He's a good detective. He wouldn't have allowed you to leave if he suspected you as much as you think he does, though it's possible he may just be trying to give you enough rope to hang yourself," the senior cleric continued.

"Would he really do that?"

"As I said, he's a good detective, and part of the reason for that is because he works somewhat unconventionally."

Father John cast a thoughtful look at Annabelle that made her jaw clench.

"What is it?" she said, curious to discover whatever thoughts had caused him to look at her like that. "What are you thinking?"

Father John gestured with his hand, as if using it to form his thoughts into speech. "Now don't be offended, this is just an idea I find myself unable to shake. It's the most obvious question that springs to mind."

Annabelle's eyes narrowed, trying to decipher where the Father was leading her.

"This Sister Mary," he said, slowly, "how well do you actually know her?"

"Just what are you insinuating?!" Annabelle gasped, her hands shooting to her hips. "Mary and I have been friends since we were babies almost! Why, she was born in the very taxi my father drove!"

"Yes, yes," the Father acknowledged, trying to calm Annabelle's offended reaction. "You've told me that before. But you haven't seen her in a while, correct?"

"Two years, but if there's one person in this world I would trust, it would be Mary. She's one of the kindest, gentlest, most beautiful human beings I've ever had the good fortune to meet!"

Father John nodded toward Annabelle, as if taking her comments sincerely. He began to pace a little.

"I'm sure of it. You're a very good judge of character, Annabelle. It's just…"

Annabelle watched the Father walk up and down, her head following his path as if observing a very slow tennis match.

"Well," he continued, "the whole encounter seems shrouded in strangeness. Arranging to meet a woman she'd never met before, who didn't even show up; a meeting arranged merely half an hour before yours."

"She's been very busy since she arrived in London," Annabelle said firmly, as if objecting in a court of law.

"She 'forgot' to give Cutcliffe the slip of paper, only showing it to you later. And as far as you've told me, it was she who discovered the ice dart in Teresa's neck."

"That's pure coincidence! She was trying to help!"

"Was there a moment when you weren't looking at both Teresa and Sister Mary? A split-second, even?"

Annabelle opened her mouth to utter an instinctive confirmation before remembering something and closing it again.

"What was it?" urged the Father.

"Well, there was one moment, when Teresa had offered us the cakes, during which I spent a few moments…"

Father John waited, before saying: "Yes?"

"...my eyes were closed – I was fully engaged in the enjoyment of the cake, so I didn't have my eyes on them all the time. But that doesn't mean anything! This is an entirely preposterous idea, Father, and I'm gravely disappointed in you for even thinking it!"

"I'm just considering the possibilities, Annabelle," Father John said, in a voice devoid of malice. "I assure you, DI Cutcliffe won't be nearly as merciless once he's conducted his preliminary investigations."

"I suppose," Annabelle uttered, reluctantly.

"A nurse – no doubt well acquainted with concoctions that can kill as well as heal – who has recently returned from Africa, where various poisons are still frequently used in hunting. It's all rather incriminating, even if not reality."

"But why, Father? Why would Mary do anything like this?"

"You said yourself that she was in need of funding. Perhaps she felt murder was the only way to get it – or perhaps the entire idea of funding her hospital in Africa is a pretence for something else."

Annabelle stood up angrily, and once again she thrust her hands onto her hips.

"I would sooner send myself to the gallows than believe Mary is guilty of such things! She is innocent in every sense of the word! All you've done, Father, is further convince me that it is imperative that I find the truth behind what went on today and do it quickly!"

Father John looked at Annabelle's stance of rock-like steadiness and smiled, impressed.

"I must say, your faith in your friend is extremely noble, Annabelle. But it's always worth remembering that blind faith can lead us as wildly astray as easily as it can fortify us."

"It is not faith, Father. I know her to be innocent."

"Very well. Then you should consider the other possibilities."

"What are they?" Annabelle asked, loosening her arms and settling down once again into the couch.

"Well, in my experience, such closely timed, similar deaths, are usually gang-related. Or at the very least, some kind of family feud. It seems coordinated enough for that, but an old lady... Look, we could sit up all night creating conspiracy theories and motives. What you need right now is a good night's rest. We can talk about this again tomorrow. In the meantime, the one thing you must do, Annabelle, is co-operate with the police. Trust DI Cutcliffe to do his job. He rarely gets it wrong, and if, rather like your cake, there are further layers to this, he'll be sure to uncover them. You could even bring the matter of your faith in Sister Mary's innocence up with Bishop Murphy when you speak to him. He's a smart man, and if things do get a little... heated for your friend Mary – or yourself – then you'll need his help."

"Thank you, Father," Annabelle sighed, soothed by his assuredness and authority. "I don't know what I would do without you."

Father John smiled at her and shook his head. "And I don't know what I'm going to do *with* you."

Since moving to London, Annabelle would wake up and ensure that until she had settled down for breakfast, she would not let the onrush of the day's errands and planned activities into her mind. Instead, she would use the calm respite of her early morning routine to mentally contemplate her privileged position, to refine her sense of magnanimous faith, and to reflect upon her personal growth.

On the morning after the terrible events surrounding Mary, Teresa, and the young woman at the café, however, Annabelle found herself making an exception. She brushed her teeth purposefully, dressed in expectation of any and all surprises, and ate a hearty breakfast that she hoped would give her the fortitude to handle the day's investigation.

Her first task was to call Bishop Murphy. She gathered her composure, braced herself for addressing such an influential and important figure, albeit in a different branch of the church, and made the call. Rather anticlimactically, the Bishop was not available, but Annabelle was reassured by the kind voice of the secretary on the line that she was welcome to call back later.

With some time left before her lunch meeting with Mary, Annabelle had a brief, pleasant conversation with Cecilia as she arrived to perform her morning duties before setting off on a walk. She even remembered to take her cell phone, and upon placing it into her pocket, was reminded of the cake that remained there. She decided to keep it on hand, having just eaten breakfast, and in anticipation of another long day gallivanting around town.

After confirming her meeting with Sister Mary, who sounded more rather than less stressed after her night of sleep, Annabelle set off. They had agreed to meet in Soho, the densely packed district in the very heart of London. It was extremely busy throughout the day, meaning it should be safe, while still being far from the sites of the two murders. There was also a rather enticingly colorful tea shop about which Annabelle had heard some positive things.

Annabelle stepped off the bus. She smiled as she felt the

warmth of the sun on her face and witnessed the pleasing scene of a London street in the middle of the day. It was difficult to feel the proximity of evil in such delightfully uplifting surroundings, however much she reminded herself to stay alert. She strolled along the pavement with a smile on her face, enjoying the surprised reactions of Londoners for whom a smiling pedestrian is as alarming as a crazy one, and reached the tea shop feeling full of verve and wonder.

She stepped inside to the sound of the doorway's tinkling doorbell and nodded a happy hello to the proprietor behind the counter. After scanning the tables, she noticed the politely raised hand of Mary, who was seated at the very back clutching an orange cup. She was wearing her habit, though she still carried the same handbag she had the day before.

Annabelle gestured for Mary to wait while she bought herself an Oolong tea and a chocolate caramel bar, then carried it to the table.

"Mary! How are you?" she said, after they had exchanged a quick embrace and settled into comfortably old-fashioned chairs.

"I feel awful, Annabelle," she muttered from beneath her downturned face.

"Did you tell everyone what happened?"

"I told them I had to stay in London a little longer than I had intended, but I didn't say precisely why. Oh Annabelle, I couldn't! I was far too frightened of what they might think of me."

"I'm sure it'll turn out fine."

Mary shook her head. "So much depends on me, Annabelle. People are dying daily from easily curable diseases and afflictions in West Africa. We work almost around the clock with minimal resources, to put every penny toward the drugs and treatments that allow people to live. Even small donations allow multiple people to stop suffering. There are so many people in need, however, that we really need a lot of funding. That was my task. That's why I'm here. And instead, I'll return penniless!"

Mary seemed almost on the verge of tears as she finished speaking. Annabelle placed a hand over her friend's and rubbed it supportively.

"Don't worry, Mary. We'll get to the bottom of this. I promise."

Mary looked into Annabelle's eyes. "Oh Annabelle, you don't still want to... "investigate" this, do you? We're in enough trouble as it is."

"Well actually, I think I might be on to something," Annabelle said, leaning forward to grab her friend's full attention. "Do you recall what the Inspector said about Teresa's apartment? Shortly after we had left it?"

Mary thought for a few seconds, before latching on to what Annabelle was referring to.

"About it being in complete disarray?"

"Yes!" Annabelle exclaimed.

"It was rather strange..." Mary agreed.

"There must have been someone else who entered the house after us, who then proceeded to turn the place into the ransacked mess that the Inspector discovered."

"The person who killed her, perhaps?" Mary said, becoming entranced by Annabelle's enthusiasm.

"Very possibly. Likely, I would say. They must have killed Teresa with the intention of entering her apartment."

"But why? I don't understand what someone would get from destroying such a beautiful home."

Annabelle wagged a finger and smiled sneakily. "What if they were looking for something?"

Mary placed her palms on the table and glanced around, finding herself almost as deep in conspiratorial thought as Annabelle. "One of her artifacts, perhaps! There must certainly have been some priceless valuables among those pieces."

"Precisely," Annabelle added, pleased to find her friend joining in with her deductions.

"But why kill her while we were there? Wouldn't it have been much easier to do it beforehand, or at least wait until we had left? Then the thief could have easily taken what he – or she – wanted from the apartment, and nobody would be any the wiser. Did they not know we were there? Could that have been merely an extraordinary coincidence?"

Annabelle nodded, then looked at her tea concentrating deeply. When she looked back at Mary's face, she wore deep frown lines on her brow.

"I believe that wasn't a coincidence," she said, deliberately. "I don't see how they couldn't have known we were there. We were clearly visible through the windows."

"Then why not wait until we had left?"

"Mary," Annabelle said, using the tone of her voice to prepare her friend for a statement she wished she didn't believe as much as she did, "I believe somebody is trying to frame us. More accurately, I believe they're trying to frame you."

Mary's hand was barely quick enough to her mouth to smother the loud, shrieking gasp she emitted. Tea drinkers from the surrounding tables whipped their heads around to see the source of the high-pitched noise. Annabelle turned and smiled toward them.

"It's alright," she assured, "she's just never tasted chocolate caramel bars before."

She turned her head back to Mary, who had now managed to calm herself enough that she was able to pull her hand away and speak.

"Frame me? Why would anybody seek to frame me of all people?"

"That's one of the questions that's been troubling me since I woke up," Annabelle replied."

"And who would do such a thing, anyway?"

"That's the other question," Annabelle said, confirming her lack of further answers by taking a sizable bite out of her own sweet treat.

They sat silently, sipping their tea and considering the irritatingly perplexing questions that hung in the air between them. Every once in a while Mary would frown at her own thoughts, until finally sighing sorrowfully at her inability to conclude them. Annabelle could feel the deep worry and intense strain that her friend was under as keenly as if it were her own.

"Oh Annabelle," Mary said, eventually, "where will this all end? I don't see how I'll ever get out of this pickle. At best, I'll return to Africa late, disgraced, and without any of the funding that I tried so hard to get. At worst... I daren't think about it, but if I am being framed, then I won't just be punished, I'll bring huge amounts of shame to the work my fellow nuns are doing all over Africa, perhaps the entire Catholic Church!"

"I'm sure it won't be as bad as you believe."

"I cannot share your optimism, Annabelle. Can you imagine what the papers would say if they found out? A nun? Accused of murder – and possibly stealing? It would probably make the front pages! The indignity!"

Annabelle sipped her tea. She wished that she could calm her friend's worries, but to deny them would be a lie.

Mary was right. If the newspapers did find out, the ensuing mess would be dreadful for everybody involved.

"What should we do now?" Mary said, eventually.

Annabelle nodded as she placed her tea cup down gently, as if she too had been considering the very same question.

"There's one person who can help us."

"Who?" Mary quickly said, eager to follow any avenue that could lead her away from her sticky situation.

"Bishop Murphy. Apparently he has already heard about this spot of bother we find ourselves in. He left me multiple messages yesterday and is keen to speak with me. I would imagine he'd like to speak with you too."

"Yes. He called after me too, but I had hoped to delay meeting with him until... well, until I had rather more positive news."

"Let's hope that Bishop Murphy can provide us with that positive news himself," Annabelle said, pulling her cell phone from her pockets.

"I should mention something before you call," Mary said, placing a hand over Annabelle's phone.

"Yes?" Annabelle said, raising an eyebrow.

Mary squirmed a little before speaking. "The Bishop may not be as sympathetic toward me as you might expect. You see..."

Annabelle's eyebrows and ears pricked up at this somewhat peculiar tone in Mary's voice.

"He and Teresa knew each other. I'm not sure, but I believe they were friends. She was a well-known contributor to the Catholic Church. It was the Bishop himself who suggested I seek her out in order to gather resources for my hospital. He is probably gravely concerned about her death, not least because of my involvement – or I should say – suspected involvement."

Annabelle considered her friend's words briefly, but carefully. She pushed away the unthinkable thought that popped into her mind and proceeded to smile good-naturedly as she sought out the Bishop's number in her phone.

"All the more reason to get him on our side as quickly as possible," she declared, bringing the phone to her ear. "Let's just hope that his judgment is as capable as his faith."

The two women set off as soon as Annabelle had arranged a meeting with the Bishop's secretary, who had assured them that Bishop Murphy was anticipating their meeting greatly.

Bishop Murphy's home was in the heart of Kensington, one of London's oldest and wealthiest boroughs. With its clean, tree-lined streets, and the well-maintained fronts of its vast and diverse homes, it was an area that drew the kind of people who enjoyed the distinctive flavor of London life while still requiring the peaceful repose of quiet streets and luxurious homes more often situated in suburbia.

For the first time since they had met again, Annabelle and Mary felt relaxed as they strolled through the safety and the beauty of the area's spotless streets. They walked arm in arm, just as they had as children in search of their next adventure.

"This is it," Annabelle said, as they stopped outside the address given to her by the Bishop's secretary.

"Oh my!" replied Mary, as she craned her head back to take in the full majesty of the Bishop's abode.

They were standing in front of a tall, four-story Victorian structure, though it displayed none of the typically Victorian austerity, with vast, arched windows and double doors almost as large as those of Annabelle's church. The white-stone walls of the building were purer and brighter than any other on the street. A dense array of colorful flowers lined the gravel path up to the door, as inviting to newcomers as they were to the bees and butterflies that frolicked among them.

"Have you ever been here before, Annabelle?"

"No, though I'm incredibly curious to see what it's like inside. If it's half as striking as it is outside, we're in for a treat."

"You go first, Annabelle," Mary said, as if daring her friend.

"Off I go!" Annabelle chuckled breezily, before opening the gate and leading the way up the large steps toward the big, brass knocker.

CHAPTER FOUR

SECONDS AFTER ANNABELLE had confidently and firmly struck the knocker, the door was opened by a young woman dressed demurely in a grey pencil skirt and white blouse. With her black, perfectly coiffed hair, her dark eyes, and dusky skin, Annabelle assumed she must be of Spanish or Italian descent. She smiled, revealing a set of perfect teeth, as white and as strikingly large as the front of the building.

"You must be Sister Mary and Reverend Annabelle," she said, in husky voice with an accent that Annabelle couldn't quite place. "Please come in."

"Thank you," the two women responded, stepping carefully inside.

Suddenly, they felt as if they had stepped into some kind of portal, for the large entrance hall was more like that of a castle or stately mansion than a home tucked into a corner of Kensington. A thick, red carpet sat in the middle of the marble floor. To one side, there was a small, tidy desk and to the other, patterned carpeted stairs chased up the wall toward the second floor. Doors led in all three directions from the entrance, guarded by plinths upon which various busts stared blankly forward, like an unimpressed audience.

"Golly!" cried Annabelle, as she stepped onto the soft carpet and craned her neck to see the religious artwork hung high upon the walls. "It looks larger inside than it does outside!"

"How impressive!" Mary added.

The dark woman retained her smile and clasped her hands in front of her.

"This property has actually been owned by the Catholic Church since shortly after it was built in 1822. It has been used for a multitude of purposes over the years, mostly involving visits from various Catholic officials abroad. Pope John Paul II was rather fond of stopping here when he traveled to London. Currently, as you know, it is predominantly being used by Bishop Murphy, as both his main place of residence and that from which he conducts his London-based affairs."

"It's almost inconceivable that such a place would lie behind what seems to be a simple Kensington home," Mary said.

"It's interesting you should say that," the dark woman replied, retaining her upright, prim posture. "The building once had a far more elaborate – and rather striking – exterior. However, two years ago, Kensington council introduced a set of initiatives to help retain the harmony of the neighborhood's appearance. Although this building was protected by various laws pertaining to matters of religious and historical importance, Bishop Murphy agreed to have the façade redesigned so that it was more in line with the area's aesthetics.

"Though it seems small from the outside, there are actually twelve large rooms in the building, along with three bathrooms and a sizable kitchen. There is also a large cellar in which items of value and significance are stored and occasionally displayed to select visitors."

"How interesting!" Annabelle said, turning her head to the woman for the first time since she had entered.

"My name is Sara," the dark woman said, unclasping her hands to shake Annabelle's and then Mary's. "I'm Bishop Murphy's secretary. He's expecting you. If you'll just hold on a second, I'll let him know you've arrived."

Once, when they were children, Mary and Annabelle had been called to the headmaster's office together. As they had taken the solemn walk toward his extremely private office, they realized that it could only mean one of two things. One, they were to receive a commendation for the recent, well-designed, soda-bottle-rocket project they had conducted in science class. Or two, they were about to be punished for said soda-bottle-project's destruction of the science classroom's ceiling, as well as the clothes of everybody in the room at the time. As they waited for the Bishop, they shared the same mixture of foreboding and excitement.

Sara stepped lithely toward the desk, leaned over it, pushed a button on a panel, and spoke briefly with the Bishop.

"He'll be down immediately," Sara said, flashing her fashion magazine smile at the visitors once again.

"Thank you," Mary said.

Though Bishop Murphy was renowned for his warmth and his inviting nature, the two women felt as if they were preparing for an occasion with all the glamour and pomp of a visit from the Queen. Mary brushed a little dirt from her friend's cassock, to which Annabelle nodded a curt "thank you."

Soon, they heard the sound of well-heeled shoes upon marble steps, as Bishop Murphy came down the stairs. The sense of being in the midst of a special event only increased as they watched the slow, descending emergence of his polished, elegant shoes, then his tailored suit, his tall, athletic build, and finally his dashing, combed-back hair.

Though he was well into his fifties, Bishop Murphy had all the vigor and sharpness of a man half his age. Were he not a relatively high member of the Catholic Church, many would have described him as having a "roguish charm." Instead, they referred to his "energetic dynamism" and "sparkling personality."

"Hello," he said in an Irish brogue as warm and as satisfying as good malt whiskey. He stepped toward the visitors keenly, his hand already outstretched.

"Hello, your Excellency," Mary said, shyly, wondering how such terrible events could result in something as honorable as a meeting with the Bishop.

"Good to see you, Sister Mary," the Bishop replied. "And yourself, Reverend. It's always nice to meet someone from a different church — especially someone as well-respected as you."

"Oh," Annabelle blushed, shaking her head at the compliment.

"Really," insisted the Bishop. "I've heard a lot about how much wonderful work you've done already in East London. And still so young! You've certainly got a lot of promise, Reverend."

Annabelle sought and failed to find appropriate words to respond to the handsome Bishop's compliment. Instead, she looked downward bashfully and mumbled a mild "thank you."

"Shall we go to my office?" the Bishop asked, turning

toward a door on the balls of his feet, much like a ballroom dancer.

Annabelle and Mary followed closely behind, stepping through the door that the Bishop held open for them.

If the entrance hall felt like that of a palace with its marble floors, plinths, and red carpets, then the Bishop's office felt like that of a grand library. Everything inside seemed to be carved from the richest and sturdiest woods, from the bookshelves that covered almost every wall to the heavy desk and seats upholstered in green leather.

"You must be tired," he said, nodding toward the chairs in front of his impressive desk. "Take a seat, and we can have a little chat."

Mary and Annabelle sat down, while the Bishop took his own seat in a slightly more modern, but no less luxurious, office chair.

"Sorry, I completely forgot – I'm so eager to talk with you! – would you like something to drink? Water? Tea? Juice?"

"No, thank you," Mary replied.

"Water would be lovely," Annabelle said.

Bishop Murphy nodded, held down a button on his intercom, and uttered a brief but polite request of Sara. Then he sat back, touched the pads of his fingers together forming an arch, and smiled sympathetically.

"So... It seems like both of you have had a lot of adventures this past day or two."

"Indeed," Annabelle said, after glancing at Mary. Though it ought to have been her – Mary being a nun and all – who spoke to the Bishop, Annabelle knew her friend would be feeling rather nervous and decided to take the lead until Mary herself was comfortable enough to talk.

"So what's been going on?" the Bishop inquired.

There was a knock at the door, after which Sara entered carrying two bottles of water and two glasses. She laid them out in front of Annabelle and the Bishop, then left quickly. Annabelle looked at Mary, whose face still wore an expression of mild astonishment at the Bishop's presence, and then began talking.

Though Annabelle gave a detailed summary of the events which had occurred the previous day, she refrained from inserting any of her own conjectures, as well as Mary's own concerns, preferring to wait until the Bishop had offered his own objective judgment. Once she was done, she took her glass again and sipped.

"Hmm, that's quite a dramatic turn of events," the Bishop said, scratching his grey hair in puzzlement. He switched his glance between the women a few times. "What do you make of it all?"

"I have some ideas," Annabelle said, "but I was rather hoping to hear yours."

"Well," the Bishop began, "I wanted to see both of you for two reasons."

Annabelle and Mary leaned forward slightly.

"First, I'd like to apologize."

"Whatever for!?" Mary exclaimed, suddenly bursting into life.

"You know very well, Sister Mary," the Bishop replied. He looked at Annabelle. "I'm not sure if Sister Mary told you, Reverend, but I was the one who put her in touch with Teresa."

"Yes," Annabelle replied, "I was aware."

"I knew Teresa personally. She was a wonderful member of the church. She was also fabulously wealthy, as you saw for yourselves. Her ex-husband dealt in some of the rarest artifacts and relics the world has ever seen. Since she had provided funding for the church in the past, and being particularly fond of nuns – Teresa persistently tried to get her niece, the young woman who died at the café, to join the sisterhood – I thought it would be a simple matter for Mary to approach her with respect to her need for funding."

"It was a wonderful idea, Bishop, and I'm grateful for your help," Mary assured him, as if the Bishop himself had suffered the consequences.

"No, don't thank me. I misjudged the situation entirely. I should have known something like this could happen."

"How!?" exclaimed Mary, almost leaping out of her seat. "Who could have killed Teresa? Why would anyone do such a thing?"

The Bishop paused for a long moment, staring intently at Mary.

"That's the second thing I brought you here for," he said, slowly. "I think I may know the 'why', though I'm still trying to figure out the 'how'."

Annabelle gasped, Mary's hand covered her mouth.

Slowly, the Bishop filled his glass with water, picked it up, and placed it on the other side of the desk, in front of Mary. As if in a trance, she took it and sipped. The air felt thick with anticipation, so much so, that when the Bishop began to speak again, his words seemed to reverberate around the room, sending chills down the spines of the two women.

"Teresa recently came into the possession of something extremely valuable, sought after by every collector and appreciator of fine things the world over."

Annabelle and Mary leaned forward, mouths open, just as they had done as young girls when an adult would read them a captivating story for the first time.

"What?" Mary said.

The Bishop eyed her so keenly, Annabelle suspected that he was trying to read her thoughts.

"The 'Cats-Eye Emeralds'."

In the pause that followed, Annabelle and Mary glanced at each other. They had no need to speak. They could read each other's stunned, confused, and fascinated thoughts intuitively.

"They are called this," the Bishop continued, "because they are of such high purity and cut with such expertise and precision, that when it is dark, they seem to sparkle even more brightly – such is their ability to catch even the dimmest of light. Their history is shrouded in mystery. There are suppositions that they were cut by one of the greatest lapidarists of the sixteenth century, but nobody is sure. In fact, for the past century or so, nobody has had any idea where these emeralds even were, or if they even really existed. Until last week.

"Teresa's ex-husband held an exhibition of his rarest objects here, in London, merely six days ago, among which were the emeralds. Though it was a private and extremely exclusive exhibition, there is not a collector worth his salt who hasn't been voraciously inquiring about the emeralds. Eventually, their inquisitions were answered. They were to be given to Teresa, who could do with them what she willed. Nobody knows why."

"But," Mary interjected, "no matter how nice they are, they're not worth more than the lives of two women!"

The Bishop leaned back into his chair, an agreeably disappointed look upon his face.

"Of course," he said, "but don't underestimate the desire attached to these things. People commit greater sins for mere wealth daily, and the Cats-Eye Emeralds are something almost entirely beyond wealth. They're the definition of priceless."

"So you think somebody committed the murder in order to steal the emeralds?" Annabelle asked.

"I don't think it," the Bishop said, "I know it."

He shifted his eyes once again between the women.

"I spoke with DI Cutcliffe, as soon as I heard of Teresa's death. I informed him of the situation regarding the emeralds, after which he searched her apartment. They were gone."

"Oh dear!" Mary cried, breaking the tense quiet that surrounded the sobriety of the Bishop's information with her high-pitched squeal. "This is terrible!"

The Bishop looked toward her, then toward Annabelle, for explanation.

"Bishop Murphy," Annabelle said, inching slightly out of her seat to offer a comforting hand on Mary's knee, "we are in need of your help."

The Bishop raised his thick eyebrows.

"Mary was to return to Africa within a few days," Annabelle pleaded, "along with the funding she had hoped to acquire. This awful mess has scuppered all of her plans, however. Inspector Cutcliffe wishes her to stay, and possibly even suspects her, as preposterous as that is."

"Of course," Bishop Murphy mused.

"Surely you can help her, if not with the investigation, then at least within the Church." Annabelle looked to her friend, who was staring into her lap, trying her hardest to suppress sobs. "She's concerned that her reputation will be in tatters, not least because she'll have to return without the funding she came for."

"Yes, I see," the Bishop said, deep in thought.

"And... Well..." Annabelle stammered, finding it difficult to say what she was thinking. The Bishop raised his eyebrows once again in a gesture of open, fair curiosity. "Well, you were the one who gave her Teresa's number..."

"Meaning it was my fault?" Bishop Murphy replied with wry humor.

"Gosh, no!" Annabelle protested. "I simply meant that you know more than anybody else how unlikely it is that Mary stole the emeralds. Perhaps you could also put in a word with the police?" Mary shot Annabelle a surprised glare, begging her not to be so forthright. "I mean, of course, if it's not terribly bothersome for you. I understand this is a big request and— "

Bishop Murphy chuckled and raised his hand for Annabelle to stop.

"Yes, of course. I did bring you here to apologize anyway, and it is, in a way, entirely my fault. This is not the first time somebody has gone after Teresa's riches and gotten away with it. I'll make some calls and ensure that you get back to Africa in time, safely, and that no mention will be made of this unfortunate affair."

Mary's stifled sobs disappeared with the quickness of a rainy day turning bright.

"Really?" she exclaimed, her eyes as astounded and as brilliant as a child's on fireworks night.

"You're a nun in the Catholic Church. It's remarkable that the thought would even occur that you'd be involved – let alone a suspicion. I take that as a personal affront. I'm just sorry that this has wrecked your plans for funding, but I'll make some calls regarding that too at the first opportunity."

"Oh, Your Excellency! That's so... benevolent of you! I'm... speechless!" Mary said, looking toward her friend. Annabelle smiled warmly at the disappearance of the frown lines and clouded eyes that had plagued Mary's expression. "I wish there were some way in which I could repay you."

The Bishop brushed the request aside. "You repay the Catholic Church greatly with the work you do in Africa. It is something of which we are all immensely proud."

Mary smiled, her hands in her lap, but her knees jogging with excitement.

"I feel as if the world's weight has been lifted from my shoulders!" she said to Annabelle.

Annabelle beamed Mary's smile back to her as neatly as a reflection, before a slight pause for thought.

"It does make one wonder," she said, thoughtfully, "as to who actually stole the emeralds and killed Teresa, as well as the other woman, her niece."

Bishop Murphy nodded. "Lauren Trujillo was her name, a wonderful young woman. She had taken good care of Teresa in her later years. As for who could have done it, I've been thinking very hard about it myself."

"It's almost as if the entire thing was constructed to place Mary at the center of events. As if someone were framing her," Annabelle said.

"It has certainly placed an incredible amount of suspicion upon her. I'm rather surprised Cutcliffe allowed her to roam London without further questioning," the Bishop agreed.

"Yes," agreed Annabelle. "I've been racking my brain about it since the moment it happened. Who would frame someone for a murder? Particularly when it would have been easier to murder Teresa and steal the emeralds before we had even arrived."

"Somebody close enough to Teresa to have suspicion immediately cast upon them," Bishop Murphy added.

"Precisely!"

"That's a keen mind you have there, Annabelle. I've not been disappointed in the high praise I've heard about you. I will make some phone calls and see what I can find out. In the meantime, you should probably try to protect Mary from any further plans this person may have. Keep her safe and sound. Out of harm's way."

"I most certainly will," asserted Annabelle.

"Thank you once again, Your Excellency. I am extremely indebted to you."

The Bishop waved Mary's compliment away shyly. "The least I can do. For now, let me see what I can dig up about this business – as well as your funding."

Annabelle and Mary stood up, said their goodbyes, and left the Bishop, who was already picking up the phone and dialing fervently.

Sara flashed one more headlight-bright smile as they left, and they made their way down the sunny streets of Kensington. Mary was almost skipping with joy, while Annabelle smiled and laughed at her friend's overflowing delight.

"Oh Annabelle, finally, we can relax! Let's go to Kensington High Street, it's been so long since I've seen it."

"Me too," said Annabelle, before reluctantly frowning. "Shouldn't we do as the Bishop says, however, and stay somewhere safe?"

"But I've not been in London for over a year! And I'll probably not return for a while either. With all this fuss, I've barely had a chance to enjoy it. This is the first time we've been able to spend some quality time together. Come on, I'll buy you something."

Annabelle locked arms with Mary, and said: "You've convinced me!"

Though like many areas of London, it had changed

much over the years, Kensington High Street still played host to many of London's most discerning – and richest – shoppers. Filled with one-off boutiques, antiques dealers, and some of the finest chocolate and bakery shops in the whole city, Annabelle and Mary found themselves easily occupied simply window shopping.

Now it was Mary's turn to lead Annabelle, as she flitted from shop to shop as randomly and as gleefully as a bumble bee in spring. As good as her word, she even bought Annabelle a bag of exquisite fudge, which Annabelle sneakily ate as she tried to keep up.

"These ornaments are astonishing!" Mary said, leaning over and peering into an antique shop window.

"Mmm," Annabelle replied.

Suddenly, Mary stood upright and turned toward Annabelle with a pale-faced look of chilling terror.

"I know," Annabelle said, nonchalantly, "these prices are shocking."

"No!" Mary said, grabbing Annabelle's arm and shaking her. "I saw him!"

"Who?"

"The man in the tweed suit. The doctor. The one who ran across the street when Lauren collapsed in front of me."

Annabelle spun around, scanning the street.

"Where is he?"

Mary looked around herself slowly, frightened by the prospect.

"I saw his reflection in that silver mirror."

Annabelle turned back toward her friend. "I'm sure it wasn't him. How could you have seen him so clearly in a mirror so small? It's just your mind playing tricks." Mary drew close to Annabelle, clutching her tightly. "Ow! That hurts!" she said.

"Let's go, Annabelle. Please."

"Okay, okay. The tube station is nearby. Here, have some fudge to calm yourself down."

Though Mary scanned her surroundings as they entered the station with all the intensity and thoroughness of a tourist, she could not find the man again. They boarded the tube, and she found herself relaxed in the safety of the carriage.

"See?" Annabelle said. "We would have seen him if he was following us."

Mary didn't reply. Annabelle noticed that she wasn't looking back at her. She followed Mary's eyes to the window at the back of the carriage. Standing in the carriage two behind theirs was a man in a tweed suit.

"That's him," Mary said coldly, her face a mask of stilled fear.

Annabelle jostled through the people to get to the window and take a closer look. It was difficult to see clearly through the crowd of the intervening carriage, not least because the curvature of the rail tracks brought him in and out of view. He was a slim, tall man, with dark skin but with features which didn't seem entirely African – much as Mary had described him.

Annabelle turned around.

"Are you sure that's him?"

Mary simply nodded and grabbed Annabelle's arm tightly once again.

"We're safe, he can't do anything to us."

"What if he's just waiting for the right moment?" Mary said in a shaky voice. "We have to call the detective."

"I agree, but you know there's no phone reception on the tube. Let's try something. I saw it in a film once. Just do as I say."

Mary nodded.

As the train rolled to a stop at the next station, Annabelle ushered Mary toward the door, keeping her eyes on the carriage she had seen the man in. The doors opened with a sharp hiss, and Annabelle stepped out of the train clutching Mary's arm. They stood in front of the doors of the train as people pushed and pressed past them, Annabelle's eyes searching through the marching crowd of commuters for sight of the tweed-suited man. At the very last moment, with the expert timing of someone intimately familiar with London's transport system, Annabelle shoved Mary back onto the train and jumped in behind her. The doors closed, and the train started pulling away.

Mary glanced around her, checking for any sign of him. "Did he get off? Is he still here?"

"I don't know," replied Annabelle, "but I don't see him. Yes, I think he's gone."

Mary allowed herself a brief sigh of relief. "Let's just go somewhere safe."

"I'll take you to my church. We'll call DI Cutcliffe on the way."

Shaking with nerves but somewhat eased by Annabelle's firm presence, Mary allowed herself to be taken all the way to Old Street Station, where they left the train and made their way up the escalators to the many exits.

As soon as they emerged into the bright daylight, Annabelle pulled out her phone and foraged in her pockets for the card that DI Cutcliffe had given her.

"Blast! I've lost the Inspector's number!" she said.

"No need," uttered a rough voice behind her.

Annabelle and Mary spun around and saw DI Cutcliffe standing feet away, two of his officers standing behind him as if flying in perfect formation.

"Detective!" Mary explained, with relieved surprise.

"We have to tell you something, Inspector."

Cutcliffe raised a broad hand to stop them. "There will be plenty of time for that," he said, in an even firmer, more authoritative, and antagonistic tone than the one he usually used. Annabelle and Mary looked at each other curiously.

"Mary Willis. Annabelle Dixon," he continued, as his officers stepped forward. "I am arresting you on suspicion of murder and burglary. You do not have to say anything. But it may harm your defense if you fail to mention when questioned anything which you later rely on in court. Anything you do say may be given in evidence."

CHAPTER FIVE

ANNABELLE STARED IN disbelief as one of the officers stepped forward, gently pulled Mary's hands away from her face, and placed her in handcuffs. The other officer placed his hand around Annabelle's wrist, but instead of complying absently as her friend had done, Annabelle furiously shook away his grip.

"This is utterly, astoundingly, unbelievably preposterous!" she shouted incredulously. "What on earth are you thinking, Inspector?!"

DI Cutcliffe snorted derisively.

"I don't know what I was thinking earlier, allowing both of you to walk away from two separate crime scenes. My instincts were wrong on this one."

Once again, Annabelle shook away the young officer's attempt to place her in cuffs and shot him a glare so defiant that he looked to the detective for advice. Cutcliffe merely scowled and nodded for him to try again with more force.

"And what, may I ask, has caused this sudden turnabout? This incredible bout of folly, Inspector?"

Cutcliffe didn't balk from the indignation in Annabelle's tone.

"The right information, at the right time, from the right person," he said, cryptically.

Annabelle stared back in disbelief. The young officer moved forward, hoping to catch Annabelle in this stunned moment. Instead, Annabelle's eyes squinted, and her almost perpetually gentle, caring face stiffened into a look of determination.

And then she ran.

The Inspector had seen many strange things in his decades of service, from an elderly lady who suffered from dementia eventually turning out to be the head of a crime syndicate, to a man who stole shop mannequins by carrying them outside as if they were his girlfriend. The sight of a five foot eleven, sturdily-built, and typically bashful vicar, sprinting out into the street, cassock flying behind her, was an entirely new occurrence, however. She had all the ferocious acceleration and natural grace of a gazelle. He watched for a few seconds, frozen by the complete strangeness of seeing Annabelle weave between moving traffic, before setting off himself.

"Take her to the station!" he commanded the officer next to Mary, before turning to the other. "You come with me!"

By the time DI Cutcliffe and his fellow officer had set off, Annabelle had already made it to the other side of the street. She bombed forward with long, powerful strides and a stiff back, screaming polite requests as she ducked and dived through the dumbfounded crowds.

"Excuse me!"

"Sorry!"

"Move, please!"

"Vicar coming through!"

Cutcliffe and his companion did their best to keep up with Annabelle, but after a minute of full-on sprinting, Cutcliffe doubled over to catch his breath.

"You okay, Chief?" his officer asked.

"Has she been drinking holy water or something?! How the hell is she so fast? Get after her!"

The officer immediately broke into a sprint, with Cutcliffe huffing and puffing behind him.

"Stop that woman in the dog collar!" he screamed.

Annabelle reached a corner that led into a marketplace, swung her head from side to side with all the perspicacity of a guard dog, then burst forward once more between the market stalls of fruit and vegetables. Shoppers and stall owners, their heads snapping from side to side as if watching race cars at a race track, looked on in awe as the galloping vicar, followed by the policemen, raced past them.

Though the detective, and indeed, the onlookers themselves were surprised by the Reverend's extraordinary pace, Annabelle herself was not. As the tallest girl in her year for most of her school life, Annabelle had developed a slight self-consciousness about standing out. She stood with a slight hunch or a bended knee to lower herself and always preferred sitting rather than standing when around her group of friends. When it came time to do sports, however, Annabelle relished her large physique. Field hockey, long-distance running, netball, or volleyball – Annabelle took to them all like a duck to water and gained plenty of self-confidence in the process. Though it wasn't long before her love of cakes outweighed her love of winning matches, the endeavors of her youth had left their mark, and she retained a natural athleticism she could call upon when the situation demanded it.

As the chase continued, the young officer cleverly cut a corner by sidling between two market stalls and gained some ground on the runaway Reverend. After a few more yards of sprinting, he had her in his sights and was ready to catch her as soon as the opportunity presented itself. His plan became unnecessary, however, as suddenly, Annabelle flew through the air as if she were an angel spreading her wings about to rise toward the heavens, her arms outstretched in front of her.

"Geronimo!" she screamed, as she clattered into the mass of shoppers like a bowling ball into skittles.

The officer quickly darted back into the street and ran through the crowd toward the fallen vicar, followed seconds later by DI Cutcliffe.

Annabelle was sprawled on her stomach on the pavement, surrounded by shocked observers with barely a closed mouth among them.

"What the hell are you playing at!?" cried the Inspector once he had caught up. He leaned over the cassocked figure.

Annabelle rolled over onto her back, revealing the person she had crashed into and had been lying on top of – the dark-skinned man in the tweed suit.

"This is the man you want, Inspector!" she gasped between heavy pants. "The 'doctor' from the first murder!"

Roughly an hour later, DI Cutcliffe and his fellow officers marched Annabelle, Mary, and the mysterious tweed-suited man toward the reception desk of the nearest police station.

Mary walked soberly, her head down, mouthing a silent prayer, while the strange doctor walked gracefully, with his head high and an indiscernible expression on his face.

Annabelle, in contrast, had not stopped pleading her cause from the back seat of the police car and was still vocalizing her astonishment at the situation.

"...terrible lack of judgment on your behalf, Inspector. Utterly baffling. I had you down as a good egg, someone with some common sense and decency. But this is just... well, it's simply... I'm just completely speechless! I cannot find the words to describe the sheer absurdity of this far-fetched attempt to frame us. It's inconceivable, and yet here I am – in handcuffs! Crikey! Of all the—"

"Fill in the forms, please," the desk sergeant said sternly, making her voice loud and forceful enough to break Annabelle's rhythm of speech. Mary promptly picked up a pen and began diligently giving her information. Annabelle, after a few more haughty sighs, did the same. The doctor, however, stared blankly ahead.

"Please fill in the forms, sir," repeated the desk sergeant. Then, when the doctor showed no sign of responding, the sergeant turned to the Inspector. "Does he speak English?"

Cutcliffe shook his head in confusion. "I have no idea."

The desk sergeant turned back toward the man. "Empty your pockets," she said, slowly and loudly, in the manner frequently adopted by the British when talking to those who don't speak English. She made a gesture to indicate the action, at which the man raised his eyebrow slightly.

"Your pocket," the Inspector said, pointing toward the man's pockets.

The man gave a look that could have meant understanding but could have just as easily been defeat before reaching into his pockets and putting items on the table.

"That goes for all of you," the desk sergeant said toward Annabelle and Mary.

The Inspector watched closely as all three began to pat

and pull objects from their clothes. The doctor was quickest, simply placing a wallet, a watch, a basic phone, and an incredibly detailed silver box about the size and shape of a cigarette case neatly on the desk in front of him.

The desk sergeant eyed the case suspiciously before picking it up and opening it.

"Nice cigarette case," she said, bringing it to her nose and sniffing it. Her expression twisted into one of confusion when she could find no smell – of drugs nor tobacco – and she brushed a finger along the velvet insides of the case. "It's wet. Why is the inside of this cigarette case wet?"

The doctor retained his blank stare.

A moment after she had asked the question, Annabelle's eyebrows rose so high and so suddenly that they almost flew off. "The ice dart!" she exclaimed. "That must be where he kept the ice darts!" she repeated, toward the Inspector this time.

Cutcliffe nodded dismissively. "Sure. Empty your pockets."

The desk sergeant, DI Cutcliffe, and possibly the doctor, found themselves watching with strange fascination the number of objects Annabelle and Mary had managed to secrete upon themselves despite their religious attire. Mary's barely noticeable leather handbag seemed to hold enough for her to travel for days. Passport, paperwork, two purses (one for pocket change, one for notes), a card holder, a disposable camera, rosary beads, postcards, fridge magnets she had picked up for her friends in Africa, a Bible, some hard-boiled sweets, and finally, the clear bag which contained the foil-wrapped cake given to her by Teresa.

Annabelle's treasure trove was no less impressive. After pulling out her own Bible and taking off her watch, she proceeded to place upon the table her cell phone, bus pass, notebook, pencil, a pocket bag of wet wipes, mints, an empty bag of fudge, lip balm, purse, keys, various crumpled receipts and sweet wrappers, then finally, her own see-through bag of cake.

"Are we done?" the desk sergeant asked, with more than a little sassiness. "We'll have to dispose of the foodstuffs, I'm afraid."

After putting most of the items in boxes, she gestured to Annabelle and Mary's similarly-wrapped bags of cake. "Mind telling me what those are?"

"They're cakes," Annabelle retorted, picking hers up from the desk and tearing through the clear bag. "And if you don't mind, I'd rather you didn't dispose of them. They were gifts from a very kind old lady."

As Annabelle unfolded the foil, revealing the remark-ably well-preserved cake, the desk sergeant shot DI Cutcliffe an alarmed look, as if to ask whether it was really acceptable for Annabelle to eat cake under such circum-stances. Cutcliffe replied with a shrug and a defeated shake of his head.

"Let them eat cake," he said, with dry, rough humor.

The desk sergeant, who by this point had indulged the arrestees far more than was typical for her, pursed her lips and continued to pack and mark the boxes. While she did so, DI Cutcliffe persevered with completing the doctor's forms. For his part, the doctor was still staring at some distant spot on the opposite wall. With this backdrop, her frustration over the turn the day's events had taken showing clearly on her face, Annabelle defiantly and slowly brought the succulent cake to her mouth and took a large, haughty bite.

"Ow!" she cried, suddenly, spraying cake all over the desk and clutching the side of her jaw.

Everyone's heads turned to see crumbs clatter every-where with a loud tinkling sound. Their eyes shot from Annabelle's pained expression to the scraps that had scat-tered across the desk – among which were two marble-sized gems that caught the light brightly despite the sugary remnants that still clung to them.

Annabelle slowly lowered the rest of the cake from her mouth, placed it upon the table, and broke it apart, revealing another four gems.

"The Cats-Eye Emeralds!" she said, mumbling through the tooth pain she was now experiencing. "Teresa baked them into the cakes!"

Promptly, the desk sergeant brought Mary's cake from its box and tore the wrapping. After pulling it apart on the desk as Annabelle had, sure enough, she found another six of the brilliant jewels.

Cutcliffe snorted. "I have to say, Reverend. This is one hell of an act you've put up here, but you're only confirming what we already know. You'd have been better off letting those cakes go into the rubbish."

"But I had no ide—"

"Put her in a cell and the doctor in another," the Inspector commanded the young officer who stood to the side. "Mary, come with me. It's time you told me the truth."

DI Cutcliffe was a formidable interviewer. He was not the most adaptable nor even the most perceptive. Some said his technique was even rather old-fashioned. But he was by far the most detailed, and by an even further stretch, the most determined inquisitor any unfortunate reprobate was likely to meet. After ten minutes of questioning Mary, without any further information gained, he began to get tough. When that didn't work, he began to pace furiously up and down in the interview room, searching for the key that would cause Mary to tell the truth. When that only seemed to make her cry, the Inspector began to worry.

Cutcliffe hated two things more than anything in the world – criminals and the sound of women crying. When the two things came in one package, DI Cutcliffe grew extremely exasperated.

"Look, Mary," he said, after giving her enough time to stifle the sobs and wipe her face, "you've told me the same story about a dozen times over. You can cry all you want, but I know it isn't the truth."

"It is!" Mary said, the shake in her voice indicating that she was close to breaking down once again.

The Inspector sat at the table, leaned forward, and struggled to contort his face into the nicest, warmest, and friendliest expression he could muster.

"Look at it from my perspective, Mary. You're asking me to believe in an almost insane number of coincidences, flukes, and mishaps. First you're claiming that Lauren Trujillo died right in front of you, having gone to meet you, but that you have no knowledge of who killed her or how. You claim you 'forgot' to hand me a crucial bit of evidence, and then when you realized, you instead acted upon it yourself because it seemed the smartest thing to do. Then, Teresa dies in a room with only you and the Reverend with her, but you again claim you have no idea how or why. Her apartment is found trashed immediately afterward – but you say this was done after you left. You then take her emeralds away, hidden in a cake, and you still say you had no idea they were there. Now, just think about how that sounds. That's a hell of a lot of convenient accidents."

Mary looked up, her eyes red and her nose runny from crying. She laughed despairingly and mumbled softly: "That's my nickname."

"What is?"

"The Accidental Nun."

The Inspector processed this comment, sighed deeply, then stood up to leave the interview room, still shaking his head.

"Sir?" the young officer who had been waiting outside said. "Did you find out anything?"

"She's either the greatest liar I've ever encountered," DI Cutcliffe replied, "or she's telling the truth."

"But she can't be telling the truth, sir. If she didn't do it, who did?"

Cutcliffe looked into his young officer's eyes.

"It's a good thing we brought in two suspects. Though I was rather hoping I wouldn't have to question Reverend Annabelle."

"Why's that, sir?"

"She can talk even faster than she runs."

A few minutes later, DI Cutcliffe and his fellow officer entered the interview room which held an Annabelle deep in thought.

"Inspector!" she said after a pause, almost failing to notice him in her state of contemplation. "I've been meaning to speak with you for ages now!"

Cutcliffe exchanged an 'I told you so' look with his accompanying officer.

"This is PC Montgomery. He'll be sitting in on the interview."

"Of course," Annabelle said graciously, as if allowing permission.

The policemen took their chairs, and Cutcliffe proceeded to start the tape machine and give the formal details of the interview. When he was done, he turned his attention to Annabelle and spoke in a voice filled with authority.

"So, Reverend Annabelle, we've placed you at both crime scenes, we've discovered that you concealed evidence, and we've caught you with the emeralds. This is an open-and-shut case, frankly. All you have to decide now is how easy you want this to go for you."

"I'm beginning to form a theory," Annabelle replied, completely oblivious to the Inspector's accusatory tone. "The pieces don't make much sense on their own, but when you put them all together, they fit as perfectly as, well, a jigsaw."

"You have a theory, do you?" the Inspector sighed.

"Oh yes."

"Does this theory still involve ice darts and emeralds used as cake ingredients? Or is it something more plausible, such as mind control? Invisibility cloaks, perhaps? Transfiguration, even?"

"I know you suspect me, Inspector," Annabelle said, smiling wryly as if this were a tense game of Scrabble and not an interrogation, "but if this were an 'open-and-shut' case, as you say, then how do you explain the doctor following us?"

"He could have been anyone!" the Inspector said quickly. "A random passer-by who was unfortunate enough to land in – or be landed upon by, I should say – this mess."

"Not a random passer-by at all, Inspector," Annabelle said, raising her finger as if scoring a point. "He fits the description Mary gave you at the first crime scene exactly. Tweed suit. Tall. Dark-skinned and with strange features."

"Annabelle, this is London. It has a population of over nine million people. I could tell my officers to go out and find me an albino in a pink dress, and they would probably find one before teatime."

"It's still strange that he was right there in the vicinity at the time of the arrest, don't you think?" Annabelle replied. "And though you scoff at the ice dart theory, what could be stranger than an empty cigarette case that is wet on the inside, even though it has not rained for days now? I'd also fashion a guess that the toxicology reports on Teresa indicated a poison was inserted directly into her bloodstream, perhaps via a needle or possibly by dart rather than orally, the method by which you assume we would have killed the two women."

"There's still a grey area surrounding how you poisoned both of them," the Inspector said. "And the toxicology reports are inconclusive."

"But Inspector—" PC Montgomery interjected, before a sharp jab in the ribs curtailed his speech.

Annabelle smiled at this vague answer.

"If I'm not mistaken, Inspector, your reasoning is that we murdered Teresa, turned over her apartment in order to find the emeralds and then proceeded to bake them into a cake in order to carry them around discreetly."

"Precisely," Cutcliffe scowled.

"How, Inspector, would we have had the time to bake such a delicious cake, with those complex, rich flavors, in such little time? There were two hours, if that, between the time we left you at the first crime scene and our meeting at the second. You can check the closed circuit television cameras at the tube stations to confirm that it took us roughly an hour to arrive at Teresa's apartment."

"That gives you plenty of time," Cutcliffe responded.

"If anyone who likes to bake heard you say that, Inspector, they would laugh. Laugh, I tell you. That cake has thick layers of cream which have been slowly mixed with fine melted chocolate. It has flecks of almonds that have been slightly toasted to bring out their flavor. It had to have been cooked slowly at a low heat to retain that incredible, flaky moisture. Two of the finest chefs in the world could not bake such a cake in under three hours, at the very least!" Annabelle's voice rose as if she were enunciating a theatre monologue. "There is only one answer to that question, Inspector. The cake was baked before we got there!"

"Maybe so!" the Inspector said, angrily slamming his palm upon the table, uncomfortably aware that his theory was starting to unravel. "But you still stole it!"

"Why would we upturn the entire apartment to look for the emeralds if we knew they were in the cake? We would have simply taken it from the kitchen," Annabelle said, before slamming her own palm on the table. "Where cakes should be!"

"This is insanity! We're here to interview you, Reverend! Not the other way around!" DI Cutcliffe shouted, standing up from his seat sharply and pacing as he did when exasperated. "This is a case involving two deaths and a theft amounting to millions of pounds, but you're here talking about bloody cakes!"

PC Montgomery hunched further over, focusing all his attention onto his fidgeting hands that lay in his lap. He had expected a routine cross-examination, not to be caught in the collision of two such blustering firebrands as DI Cutcliffe and Reverend Annabelle.

"You're a Catholic man, aren't you, Inspector?" said Annabelle.

"What the hell does that have to do with anything?"

"That's why you gave Sister Mary the benefit of the doubt on more than one occasion," Annabelle said firmly, "and that's why..."

The two policemen looked toward Annabelle as she trailed off abruptly.

"What?" PC Montgomery ventured, in a quiet, shaky voice.

Annabelle looked to the side, as if deep in thought again. Her face changed, and she nodded to herself as if struck by a stunning revelation. She turned her face back toward the Inspector with eyes full of righteous purpose.

"That's why you trust the Bishop implicitly."

Slowly, DI Cutcliffe took his seat again, and spoke in a low tone, directing the full power of his voice and his attention toward Annabelle.

"What are you implying, Annabelle?"

"I would bet the entire value of those emeralds," Annabelle said, not balking from the severity of the Inspector's tone, "that it was the Bishop who told you to arrest us today. And who told you precisely where we would be."

DI Cutcliffe's eyes narrowed with pinpoint focus upon the Reverend.

"So what if it was?"

"It should be obvious, Inspector," Annabelle said, slowly. "The Bishop is behind it *all*."

"THAT'S A BOLD claim," Cutcliffe said, after taking a moment to make sure Annabelle had really said what he thought she had. "I underestimated you. You really did top the ice dart theory. If you're trying to get off on insanity claims, you're certainly doing a good job, though."

"Like it or not, Inspector, it's the truth," Annabelle said, raising her chin in defiance.

"I don't suppose you have any evidence to back up your claim."

"Oh I do. It's all right under our noses. "

The Inspector raised his eyebrows in disbelief, unable to find words to respond to something he found so extraordinary.

"I've been thinking about our meeting with Teresa since it happened," began Annabelle, displaying a focused curiosity. "She said she liked to sit by the window in order to keep watch. Not to 'look outside' or to 'see people', but to 'keep watch', as if on guard. As she died, she was in the middle of saying that she'd learned something, about knowing she was in danger."

"Could be meaningless turns of phrase," Cutcliffe said.

"But put them together with the fact Teresa had baked the emeralds into a cake. And add the fact that her niece had decided to tell Mary about Teresa's danger with a note rather than communicating it verbally. After all, she had the note already written before she was suddenly struck down.

"It all points to someone powerful, someone able to listen in on conversations, observe Teresa even in her home. Someone as powerful as the Bishop, with spies, accomplices, a large network, and employees, presumably like the 'doctor'."

"I'll indulge you for a moment, and agree that it sounds like somebody was watching them. Teresa's niece obviously felt some sense of insecurity to write that note. But why the Bishop? There's no connection."

"Think about it, Inspector. The Bishop has known everything from the start. On the day of the murders, I received multiple calls from him at the church. He told Mary and me that he called you after he had learned about Teresa's death. From whom would he have learned about the murder so quickly, if not the killer himself? And wasn't it he who told you where to find us just now? I'm guessing he gave you a clever excuse as to how he knew, but how did he know where we were if the tweed-suited man were not working for him and following us on his orders?

"Consider this, Inspector, if Teresa were in danger, why would she contact Mary and myself for help? Why not the police? Or indeed, why not the Bishop himself, if they were as friendly as he claims?"

"Maybe it wasn't serious enough."

"Or maybe she knew that nobody else would believe her."

The Inspector sighed and looked to his officer, who seemed at a loss.

"Okay. So Teresa was in danger. Why not leave? Why stay in her apartment?"

"I believe there are two reasons for that Inspector. First, Teresa very rarely left the house. She had a limp when we saw her and mentioned that her niece performed most tasks for her. Secondly, I don't think even Teresa realized the depths to which the Bishop would sink. She wanted to guard against theft of the emeralds and had no idea the Bishop, or rather, his assassin, would be willing to kill for them."

DI Cutcliffe put his hands on the table. He was visibly struggling with what Annabelle was saying. It did make sense, but it was still too far-fetched for him.

"So these... 'Cat Emeralds...'"

"Cats-Eye Emeralds," Annabelle corrected.

"'Cats-Eye Emeralds," the Inspector repeated, "why give them to you? Why not give them to her niece to stuff somewhere safe? Why not put them somewhere meant for valuable things? A bank deposit box or a museum vault?"

Annabelle nodded at the legitimacy of the question. "I think Teresa wanted very much to help Mary, no matter how corrupt she believed Bishop Murphy to be. Perhaps she thought that the Bishop would never have suspected one of his own, certainly not someone as innocent as Mary. Teresa knew that her niece was being watched. She also knew that whoever had the emeralds would be in grave danger unless the person themselves were beyond suspicion and carrying them unwittingly. So she decided to give them to Mary directly and in such a way that she herself would not realize it until she was at a safe distance.

"Had she not died so suddenly, I am positive Teresa would have given us instructions – no doubt cryptic – on what we were to do with the emeralds or the 'cakes', I should say. Perhaps she would have told us to meet someone else who could help sell them, or maybe even warn us against contacting the Bishop or people within the church."

There was a few moments of silence as the Inspector leaned back and scratched his head furiously while he turned over this new information in his cluttered mind. Eventually, he sighed deeply, shook his head, and said, "I'm sorry, Reverend. It's not enough."

"What do you mean?" Annabelle replied pleadingly.

"It's not enough for me to do anything. I'm not going to bang on the Bishop's door and start throwing accusations around based on some discrepancies. I'm sorry."

Annabelle pursed her lips in an expression of rebelliousness.

"Then let me talk to the Bishop!" she said resolutely.

Cutcliffe chuckled incredulously. "That's not going to happen!"

"It's the only way!" Annabelle persisted. "Right now, the Bishop still believes that I am in possession of the emeralds. The entire reason he made you arrest us was a last-ditch attempt to discover where we had hidden them. If you let me call him now and tell him that I'm willing to cut a deal, I can assure you he'll do exactly what I tell him."

"This is ridiculous!" Cutcliffe bellowed. "Do you expect me to allow you to go and talk to the Bishop and bother him with these crazy ideas of yours?"

"I'm willing to stake my entire reputation on this, Inspector. You can listen in while I talk to him, and if it does turn out that he's innocent, I'll sign any confession you like," Annabelle said, excited by her own idea. "Without any trouble," she added, making a gesture as if zipping her mouth shut.

Cutcliffe chuckled darkly at the bizarre turn the interview had taken.

"You do realize," he said, with just a small note of defeat in his voice, "that what you're asking me to do is highly illegal as well as absolutely insane."

"I believe her," PC Montgomery blurted out suddenly. Cutcliffe and Annabelle turned to him, having completely forgotten that the meek constable was still in the room.

Annabelle smiled triumphantly at the Inspector, who wiped a broad hand over his face. He glanced for a few moments at the unyielding expression on the Reverend's face and then at the equally adamant expression of PC Montgomery. Slowly, he pressed stop on the tape recorder, ejected the tape, and put it in his pocket.

"Go make sure the coast is clear, Montgomery. We'd better leave from the rear entrance," he said in a low voice. "I'm going to be saying Hail Marys for the rest of my life."

Barely ten minutes later, the three of them were zooming back across London in the detective's unmarked car toward Kensington. Annabelle had made the call to the Bishop's office requesting a meeting. She had not said much else apart from a sly reference to "a deal." Unsurprisingly to her, Sara claimed that Bishop Murphy was immediately available.

"I can't believe I'm doing this," DI Cutcliffe said to

himself once he had parked the car in a discreet parking spot a little way down the road from the Bishop's house.

Annabelle shifted nervously in her seat. She was breathing deeply, feeling both incredibly exhilarated and increasingly nervous.

"Now listen to me," Cutcliffe said, "these are the rules. Don't, whatever you do, mention anything about me. If this blows up, I don't want anyone to know I'm the one who allowed a cake-obsessed vicar from East London to conduct a sting operation to entrap a bent Bishop."

"Oh, of course, I mean—"

"And get him to talk." the Inspector interrupted. "Get him to confirm what you're saying. We need him to incriminate himself or to at least explain some things that we can turn into evidence."

"Yes," Annabelle said, almost literally biting her tongue.

"And..." Cutcliffe looked from Annabelle to Montgomery and back again, "don't be nervous. I don't usually say this kind of thing to suspects, but I wouldn't be here if I didn't think you were on to something."

Annabelle seemed to relax somewhat at this display of trust from the detective, however meager it was.

"Thank you, Inspector. I won't let you down."

"I hope not. Okay. Call my phone, then put yours on speaker. We'll mute ours so you don't hear us. I want you to say a few words once you've walked down the street, then turn toward us. If we can hear you well enough we'll give a thumbs up. If we give a thumbs down, come straight back to the car, and we'll figure something else out. Once the Bishop has said enough, we'll enter. If we don't like what you're doing, we'll enter and arrest you again. If it turns unsafe, we'll enter. Got that?"

Annabelle nodded. "Yes."

"Okay. Time to go. Call my phone."

Annabelle promptly pulled out her phone, rang Cutcliffe, and then placed it on speaker. She gave one last nod to the Inspector and Montgomery, who nodded back with looks of nervous pride like parents reluctantly sending their child off on their first day of school, full of support but knowing that it was solely up to the child now. Annabelle exited the car, looking around, and began walking down the street.

"Um... Ah... Oh, I'm terrible at things like this. I feel like a madman talking to myself in the street. Ah... Is that okay?" Annabelle said, turning back to see the Inspector give a thumbs up. "Okay. Good. Well, off I go. Oh, I suppose I should stop talking," she said, turning once again to see the Inspector give another thumbs up. "Yes. Well... Good."

Annabelle walked slowly toward the Bishop's house, up the path to the brass knocker, and paused. She shook her limbs, set her posture, and fixed her expression into one of casual nonchalance, tossing her hair back for good measure. Then she knocked.

The door opened to Sara's smile, which seemed fixed in the same position in which Annabelle and Mary had left it.

"Hello, Reverend," she said in her still unplaceable accent. She stepped aside and gestured Annabelle inside. "Bishop Murphy is waiting for you in his study."

"Ah, good," Annabelle said, as casually as she could.

She strode toward the study door, placed a hand upon the door knob and looked back at Sara.

"Please go right in," Sara said.

Annabelle took a deep breath and opened the door.

"Reverend Annabelle!" Bishop Murphy said, standing

up from his desk and walking around it to greet her. "A pleasant – and somewhat unexpected – surprise!"

He shook Annabelle's hand, while she looked away dismissively.

"Yes," she said, "I suppose."

The Bishop returned to his chair while Annabelle took hers opposite. She crossed her legs in what she thought would be an elegant movement of ease and grace, but found it such a terribly uncomfortable position that she quickly shuffled her legs to uncross them.

"So what brings you here, Reverend?" Bishop Murphy asked with a wry smile.

"Well, I have something that you want. And I want to see how far you'll go to get it," Annabelle said, enjoying the demureness of her own tone.

The Bishop raised a curious eyebrow.

"Oh gosh!" Annabelle exclaimed suddenly. "That sounds awfully flirty, doesn't it? Well, I don't mean that!" she laughed, awkwardly. "I'm talking about the emeralds, I mean. The Cats-Eye Emeralds. I'm saying that I have them, and, well..."

Annabelle trailed off in a series of stammers and snorted laughs, while the Bishop watched her sardonically.

After a moment's consideration, the Bishop spoke.

"What makes you think that I'm interested in the emeralds?"

Annabelle gulped. Was the Bishop going to pretend he wasn't? Did he know what was going on?

"Well," Annabelle said, regaining some of her composure, "you said that the emeralds were exhibited very privately and that only prominent collectors were even aware they had been found. For you to have known that meant that you were likely one of those collectors yourself.

Sara told us when we visited about your own 'private' exhibitions in the cellar beneath this very building."

The Bishop laughed gently. "That's true. I do have a rather excellent collection of artifacts. That doesn't necessarily mean I'm interested in the emeralds, however."

Annabelle shifted uncomfortably once again. A note of doubt entered her mind. She gazed around the study, as if some support could be found there but knew that she was on her own. Now or never, she thought.

"I must be mistaken then," she said, placing her hands on the chair's armrests to push herself upright, "I had thought you would be interested in a deal. I suppose I'll just find someone else. Someone with better taste."

"Sit down, Vicar," the Bishop said, dropping his smile and replacing it with a mean sneer. "Of course, I'm interested."

Annabelle sat back down.

"But how do I know you have them? Can you prove it?"

Damnit! The emeralds were at the police station. Annabelle should have asked DI Cutcliffe to give them to her as a negotiation tactic. She met the Bishop's eye once again and laughed strongly.

"Do you really think I'd bring them here? Ha! I've seen how far you're willing to go for them, Bishop, and I was rather hoping to have my tea tonight in one piece!"

The Bishop's sneer grew into his sly grin once again.

"Clever. But I'm not sure what you're implying, Reverend. I'm simply an interested collector."

"Tosh!" Annabelle exclaimed, once again losing her decorum. "We both know that you've gone out of your way to get your hands on those emeralds!"

"Do we?"

"When your 'inquiries' about the emeralds were

rejected, you decided to steal them and make Sister Mary take the blame. You even told us that somebody had stolen from Teresa previously and 'gotten away with it.' How would you know that unless you were the very person who had stolen from Teresa before?"

"Teresa was a friend of mine. She told me."

"I believe that about as much as I believe that you tried to help us!"

The Bishop chuckled to himself at the memory of how easily he had double-crossed Annabelle and Mary.

"So you put Mary in touch with Teresa and waited for the perfect opportunity to steal the emeralds with Mary as the prime suspect. You underestimated the two women, however. Teresa, possibly suspecting something, arranged for her niece to meet Mary in a public space, and Lauren realized she was being spied upon. She wrote a note to hand over to Mary. You panicked and told your assassin to kill Lauren before she could reveal anything. However, Lauren still managed to hand over the note. The assassin even searched Lauren for it, but he found nothing."

"An interesting perspective," the Bishop smirked.

Annabelle waited for him to say more, and when he didn't, she continued.

"The perfect chance soon presented itself, however, when Mary and I went to Teresa's house. At the first opportunity, your assassin killed Teresa with us next to her. Now he simply had to wait for the police to take us away or for us to leave so that he could enter and take the emeralds easily. The good news was that we left immediately, the bad news was that we had taken the emeralds with us."

"You know," the Bishop said, examining his nails casually, "one thing puzzles me. You seemed so unaware that you had the emeralds upon you, I almost believed it. You are clever enough to lie, but Mary... she's far too honest to have deceived everyone this well."

Annabelle grinned. "The truth is, we didn't know. Teresa baked the emeralds into a cake which she gave us."

The Bishop set his eyes upon Annabelle in an expression of pure disbelief. "Are you joking?"

"Not at all, Bishop."

"Ha!" he exploded. "That's precisely the sort of cunning thing Teresa would do. She was almost as wily as me – almost."

"Your assassin searched her apartment and found nothing, meaning that we had taken the emeralds. At a loss, you tried the direct approach, calling us to arrange a meeting and discern what we were doing."

"You seemed entirely ignorant of the entire affair when we spoke," the Bishop added. "I did suspect that Teresa had somehow given you the emeralds or at least a clue as to where they were."

"At the time, we didn't even know we had them," Annabelle said.

"Leaving me with two choices: To kill you and hope that you had them, or to follow you until I found out more."

"But if you killed us and we didn't have them, you'd have lost the only chance of getting them."

"It was a conundrum, to be sure," Bishop Murphy said. "But there's one thing I never told you. Those emeralds originate from West Africa. I was sure Teresa wanted Mary to have them so that she could sell them and fund her hospital there. A sense of justice and charity was always her big weakness. It's the very reason her ex-husband was so generous as to give them to her. I was certain you had them. I just didn't know where."

"But you were confused by our meeting, when we didn't seem to know anything about them."

"Confused, yes, and you were getting a little too close to the bone. You suspected that somebody was framing Mary, and you knew that I was the one who had put Mary into contact with Teresa. Not only did you have the emeralds I wanted, but you were a day or two away from incriminating me. If it were just Mary, as I had planned, I wouldn't have been afraid, but you," he pointed a finger toward Annabelle and looked down it, as if aiming a gun, "you were sure to cause me a lot of trouble."

"So you called DI Cutcliffe and told him that you were suspicious after speaking to us, in the hope he would find out what we didn't even realize ourselves."

The Bishop opened his hands in a gesture of mock-apology. "I'm good with Cutcliffe. Once he discovered the emeralds, I could have easily persuaded him that they were my property, or at least I would have a head-start on knowing what the police would do with them once they took them from you. Better in police custody than the unpredictable hands of two religious women who didn't even know what they had. Which makes me wonder, Reverend, how are you sitting here with me, when you should be locked up about now?"

Annabelle squirmed in her seat.

"I blamed Mary," Annabelle said, though she found it a struggle to even say the words. "She was, after all, intended to take the blame for the murders your assassin committed, wasn't she?"

The Bishop laughed heartily. "Very clever, Reverend. Very clever indeed. You are as merciless and as sly a player of games as I. You will make a very intriguing Vicar, I should imagine. Now," he said, slapping his hands upon the table, "let's talk numbers shall we?"

Annabelle balked. Though he had insinuated plenty, the Bishop hadn't actually confessed to anything. Was this enough for DI Cutcliffe? Was it too late? She searched for something she could say which would force him to reply with a definitive answer, but the Bishop was intently waiting for her answer to his question.

"Ah... Well... What are the lives of two women worth?"

"You tell me, Reverend."

"Um..." Annabelle tried to think of a number that didn't sound too preposterous. "Ten million pounds?"

The Bishop's face slowly twisted into an amazed smile, before breaking out into such a fit of laughter that he almost fell backward from his chair.

"Ten?! Haha! Ten million pounds?!" he bellowed, wiping tears from his eyes. "Oh dear!"

"Is that too much?" Annabelle asked meekly.

The comment instigated another, larger fit of laughter from the Bishop.

"Stop! Stop it! Haha!" he wailed, struggling to calm his loud uproar into controllable giggles. "Annabelle! Ten million is less than I spend on travel in a year! I had two women killed in cold blood for these things! I pulled in favors with a respected detective. I got myself involved with suspected criminals! I risked my own neck! You think all that is worth a measly ten million? Ha! Why, I'm almost insulted!"

"Twenty million?" Annabelle blurted.

"Ha!" the Bishop cried. "I'll give you fifteen million and a piece of advice – get somebody better to do your negotiating in future."

"Fifty! Fifty million!" yelled Annabelle, as the door burst open with a loud crash.

Bishop Murphy leaped out of his chair and onto the balls of his feet with the agility of a cat as DI Cutcliffe and PC Montgomery ran into the study. They each took a side of the room and cornered him behind his desk, where PC Montgomery grabbed his hands and placed him in cuffs.

"What's going on here?!" Bishop Murphy cried.

"You're being arrested under charges of murder and theft, Bishop," Cutcliffe said, grimly.

"You do not have to say anything. But it may harm your defence if you fail to mention when questioned anything which you later rely on in court. Anything you do say may be given in evidence," added PC Montgomery, almost gleefully.

"Surely not one hundred million?" Annabelle said, still caught up in her bidding war.

"Cutcliffe!" the Bishop shouted. "You're not going to let this happen, are you?"

"Unlike you, Bishop, I'm compelled to act when I hear a confession."

Bishop Murphy turned his head toward Annabelle, his eyes snake-like with their ferocity.

"You! You tricked me!"

"Come on, Bishop, we've got a lot to talk about down at the station."

PC Montgomery dragged Bishop Murphy away as he snarled and squirmed under his grip, leaving DI Cutcliffe and Annabelle alone in his study.

The Inspector sighed before patting Annabelle respectfully on the shoulder.

"You did a fantastic job, Reverend. The Bishop is a hell

of a slippery customer. Too slippery for his own good, some would say."

"Thank you, Inspector," Annabelle said, dizzy from excitement and adrenaline. "I'm just glad it's all done."

"I'll put a call through to release Mary from custody. Do you want to come back to the station to meet her?"

"That would be good, Inspector. I need to pick my things up as well."

"Of course," the Inspector said, beginning to leave.

"One more thing, Inspector," Annabelle said, causing him to turn and raise his eyebrow. "You didn't throw away the rest of Teresa's cake, did you?"

EPILOGUE

"'FURTHER THEFTS REVEALED *in ongoing Bishop Murphy case.'* Ooh! Look at this, Cecilia, there's an entire two-page spread of all the things that man has stolen over the years."

Annabelle spread the paper over the kitchen table as Cecilia turned away from the steaming Beef Wellington she was carefully slicing.

"Oh my! There's more gold there than in the Tower of London!" she said, as she saw the wide variety of shiny trinkets and ancient artifacts. "Whatever did he want with so much jewelry? To wear it?"

Annabelle giggled gently before continuing to read. "'The Bishop's closest accomplice is still unnamed and refuses to talk. It is believed, however, that he has been involved in at least four other thefts on the orders of the Bishop.' Isn't that astonishing?"

Before Cecilia could answer, the heavy clomping of Father John's boots sounded in the church hallway. He entered the kitchen, inhaled deeply, and smiled at Cecilia.

"The church's best kept secret strikes again! This smells delicious, Cecilia."

Mary entered close behind Father John and uttered her agreement. "It smells utterly splendid! Hello, Cecilia, Annabelle."

"Mary! I was just reading the day's report on the case. Have you seen this?" Annabelle said, holding up the paper as Mary and Father John took their seats.

"Oh Annabelle, I've had just about all I can handle regarding the entire affair," Mary replied.

Father John shot her a quick look of confusion. "Have you not heard the news, Mary?"

Mary's nonplussed gaze told the Father she hadn't.

"Hand me that paper, would you, Annabelle. Now, let me see," he said, noisily turning pages. "Ah! Here it is. *'Albert Trujillo, who lives in São Paulo, Brazil with his family, was astonished to discover that following the death of Teresa Nortega's niece, his sister Lauren Trujillo, he was the next in line to inherit her incredible collection of jewels, including the Cats-Eye Emeralds. In a statement given to journalists two days ago, Albert Trujillo announced that he believed that it had been his aunt's intention that the emeralds be sold. He further stated he would be heeding the calls to follow her wishes and put the jewels up for auction at Sotheby's in London. The funds will be donated in their entirety to the Saint Baptiste hospital of West Africa, where one of the nuns involved in Bishop Murphy's capture and arrest currently works.'"*

Mary gasped, her hand shooting to her mouth.

"Why, that's wonderful!" Annabelle said delightedly.

"You'll be a hero when you go back to Africa," Cecilia added, as she brought the plates of sliced meat and vegetables to the table.

"I don't... That's incredible... Is it really true?" Mary stuttered.

"Says so right here," Father John added, handing the newspaper back into Annabelle's eager hands. "Come on, plenty of time for talk, let's eat now."

Cecilia sat and, with everyone silent, Father John blessed the food. A rapturous chorus of cutlery and happy hums began as the delicious first bites were taken.

"Expected to go for one hundred and fifty-seven million pounds!" Annabelle shouted, suddenly. The others looked up. "I was going to sell them for ten!"

Mary, Father John, and Cecilia exchanged confused glances, before turning their attention back to Annabelle.

"Oh, never mind," she said, tossing the paper aside and tucking in to the juicy meat and gravy.

They ate heartily, satisfying not just their appetite for wonderful food, but also for pleasant company and comfortable chatter. The warmth and fragrance of the meat course was followed by the sweet, fruity aroma of Cecilia's juicy jam turnovers. Not a single person at the table wasn't enraptured.

Even Mary, who found herself in a state of shock at the wonderful news of finally receiving more than she could ever have hoped for regarding the funding, allowed her attention to be taken by Father John's intelligent humor and Cecilia's down-to-earth warmth and companionship.

Once their hunger had disappeared and the atmosphere had settled into satisfied afterglow, Annabelle took a long sip of water and addressed Father John.

"Father, I have something I've been meaning to talk to you about."

"Oh? Well, of course. What is it?"

"Well," Annabelle began, taking time to think about her

words, "this is a truly wonderful church. And you are undoubtedly the best person I could have had to help me during my first assignment as vicar. I've loved every moment of our work here, and despite all the fuss and difficulties, I would not exchange these experiences for anything."

Father John sighed deeply. He was old enough and wise enough to know what was coming.

"But I find myself yearning for the green fields and the seasonal changes of life in the country," Annabelle continued. "When I thought about what it would be like to practice, I always envisaged serving a small, rural community. Though I grew up here, in East London, I feel somewhat misplaced now, as a Reverend."

"Annabelle," Father John said, "I thought you would be misplaced here too, honestly. When I first saw you, I thought the work would eat you alive! Having worked with you as much as I have, I can say without a doubt, however, that I can think of nobody finer, nobody more accomplished, with whom I'd rather work. You've performed miracles in your parish. You've reached people many of your predecessors had given up on. You've grown the congregation at a time when every other church in London is struggling just to maintain their numbers. Why, I believe I've learned more from you than I've helped you."

"Thank you Father, I appreciate the kind words," Annabelle smiled. "I'm sorry to be saying this, as I will dearly miss you and Cecilia and indeed the community. But—"

"Say no more," Father John interjected, raising his hand. "I understand, Annabelle. Let me talk with the Archbishop, and I'll see what I can do. I can't guarantee anything, and almost certainly not soon, but I'll do my best."

Annabelle felt touched by Father John's kindness and smiled with gratitude.

"Annabelle, are you really thinking about leaving?" Cecilia said, the sorrow of the idea clear in her eyes.

Annabelle shrugged apologetically.

Father John raised his glass of red wine, prompting the others to do the same.

"Let's not think of this as cause to be sad, but rather, cause to be glad that we had Annabelle for as long as we did," he said. "Let's take this chance to be grateful for this breath of fresh air in the smog of London and wish Annabelle a pleasant journey through her inevitable adventures, wherever she goes!"

The others needed no cue to affirm the sentiment. "Cheers!" they shouted in unison, over the clinking of their glasses.

REVERENTIAL RECIPES

CONTINUE ON TO CHECK OUT THE RECIPES FOR GOODIES FEATURED IN THIS BOOK...

CHERISHABLE CHERRY BLOSSOM CUPCAKES

For the cupcakes:
½ cup (1 stick) butter
4 egg whites
2 cups flour
1 ½ teaspoons baking powder
½ teaspoon salt
¾ cup whole milk
⅓ cup maraschino cherry juice
1 ¾ cups sugar
1 teaspoon vanilla extract
½ teaspoon almond extract
Maraschino cherries with stems (decoration)

For the frosting:
1 cup (2 sticks) butter, softened
4 cups powdered sugar
3 tablespoons maraschino cherry juice
½ teaspoon almond extract

Preheat the oven to 350°F/180°C. Line cupcake tins with paper liners. Allow butter and egg whites to stand at room temperature for 30 minutes.

In a medium bowl, sift together flour, baking powder, and salt. In a separate bowl, whisk together the milk and cherry juice until combined. In a large mixing bowl, beat butter with an electric mixer on medium to high speed for 30 seconds.

Add sugar, and vanilla and almond extracts to the butter. Beat until combined. Add egg whites, one at a time, beating well after each addition. Alternately add flour mixture and milk mixture, beating on low speed until just combined. Spoon mixture into each paper liner, filling them about ⅔ full.

Bake the cupcakes until a toothpick inserted into the center comes out clean, about 20 to 25 minutes. Leave to cool completely.

To make the frosting, in a large mixing bowl, beat butter until smooth. Gradually add two cups of the powdered sugar, beating well. Gradually beat in ⅔ of the maraschino cherry juice and all of the almond extract. Beat in the additional powdered sugar slowly.

If necessary, add the additional juice one teaspoon at a time until frosting reaches a spreadable consistency. Top cupcakes with frosting, and add whole cherries for decoration.

Makes approximately 24 cupcakes.

CHERUBIC CHOCOLATE CARAMEL BARS

For the base:
5 oz. butter
½ cup sugar
1 ½ cups flour
4 oz. dark chocolate, broken into pieces, for topping

For the filling:
½ cup butter
½ cup sugar
2 tablespoons Lyles golden syrup
14 oz. can condensed milk

Preheat oven to 350°F/180°C. To prepare the base, cream the butter and sugar together in a mixing bowl. Work in the flour with a wooden spoon or electric mixer. Press into a greased 12 x 9-inch baking tin, and bake in oven for 15 to 20 minutes or until shortbread base is golden in color. Remove from the oven, and leave to cool.

To prepare the filling, put all the ingredients in a

saucepan and heat gently until the sugar has dissolved, stirring occasionally. Increase the heat, and boil the mixture for five minutes, stirring continuously. Remove from the heat, leave to cool for one minute, then pour onto the cooled shortbread base. Leave to set.

Melt the chocolate in a small, heatproof bowl over a pan of hot water. Spread over the set filling. Mark into portions, fingers, or squares, and leave until quite cold and set before removing from the tin. Cut into pieces.

Makes 18-20.

JUBILICIOUS JAM TURNOVERS

For the pastry:
8 oz. flour
¼ teaspoon salt
5 oz. (1 ¼ stick) butter
1 oz. lard
½ cup cold water

For the filling:
Approximately 1 cup strawberry or apricot jelly

To finish:
Milk
Sugar

Sift the flour and salt into a mixing bowl. Add the butter and lard in walnut-sized pieces, and rub into the flour. Add water a teaspoon at a time until you can press the dough gently together with floured hands. Roll out on a well-floured board into a long thin oblong shape with a floured rolling-pin, keeping the edges as straight as possible with a palette knife.

Fold this oblong strip into three with the open edge facing you. Turn the dough a quarter turn clock-wise, and roll out to an oblong shape again. Repeat this folding and rolling process three times more, turning the dough a quarter turn each time it is folded. Fold into three, wrap in cling wrap, and chill in the refrigerator for 30 minutes.

Preheat the oven to 400°F/200°C. Line two baking sheets with parchment paper. Roll out the chilled dough very thinly into a square shape. Cut into 4-inch squares. Put two teaspoons jelly just off center on each square of dough, leaving a margin. Dampen the edges with water. Fold the dough over the jelly to form a triangular shape, and press the edges together to seal. Brush with a little milk, and dredge with sugar.

Place on baking sheet. Bake in the oven for 15-20 minutes or until the pastry is puffed and golden-brown. Keep an eye on them as they cook quickly.

Makes approximately 12 turnovers.

TERESA'S SURPRISE CAKE

For the cake:
1 ¾ cups flour
1 teaspoon baking powder
¾ teaspoon baking soda
¼ teaspoon salt
½ cup (1 stick) unsalted butter, softened
1 ⅓ cups extra-fine sugar
½ cup + 2 tablespoons unsweetened cocoa powder
1 teaspoon almond extract
2 large eggs
2 oz. unsweetened chocolate, melted
½ cup water
½ cup milk

For the mousse:
8 oz. semi-sweet chocolate
½ cup (1 stick) unsalted butter
⅔ cup heavy whipping cream
4 large eggs
6 tablespoons extra-fine sugar

2 tablespoons water

For the frosting:
1 ¼ cups heavy whipping cream
½ cup (1 stick) unsalted butter, softened
1 teaspoon almond extract
¼ cup powdered sugar

For the ganache:
4 oz. semi-sweet chocolate, chopped
½ cup heavy cream
3 tablespoons light corn syrup
1 tablespoon palm shortening
½ teaspoon almond extract

For decoration:
2 tablespoons slivered almonds

Preheat oven to 325°F/160°C, and position rack in the center of the oven. Prepare a 9-inch round cake pan by lining the bottom and sides with parchment paper and brushing lightly with oil. Melt the chocolate in a small heat-proof bowl over a pan of hot water. Allow to cool slightly. Sift the flour, baking powder, baking soda, and salt together in a bowl and set aside until ready to use.

In a large mixing bowl, cream butter, then add sugar, almond extract, and cocoa powder with an electric mixer until well blended. The appearance will be grainy and lumpy. Gradually add eggs, one at a time, mixing until each is incorporated into the mixture. Add melted chocolate to creamed mixture, and blend it in so that the batter is smooth.

Heat the milk with the water until hot to touch (not boiling). Set aside. Add the dry ingredients to the mixing bowl with the butter, sugar, chocolate mixture. Slowly fold in, then mix until completely blended. With your electric mixer on slow, pour in the hot milk and water. Increase the speed to medium to completely mix everything together. If it is too stiff, add water a tablespoon at a time to get a soft but not loose cake batter consistency.

Pour the batter into the prepared cake pan and place in the preheated oven for 40 minutes, or until a wooden toothpick inserted into the center comes out clean. Allow to cool completely before removing it from the baking pan. Once cooled, wrap the cake with plastic wrap and place in the fridge until completely chilled (about 1 1/2 hours).

While the cake is cooling, prepare the chocolate mousse. Melt the chocolate and butter together in a small heatproof bowl over a pan of hot water. When the mixture is completely smooth and glossy, scrape into a large bowl and set aside.

In a clean bowl, mix the heavy cream until it comes together and whip lines are slightly visible. Place in the fridge to keep chilled.

Heat eggs, sugar, and water in a small heatproof bowl over a pan of hot water. Whip until frothy and warm to the touch. Pour the mixture into a clean bowl, and mix on high until the mixture is very thick, smooth, and nearly white in color, about 8-12 minutes.

Scoop about 1/3 of the egg mixture into the melted chocolate and butter, and using a folding motion, lightly blend. There will be streaks of light and dark in the mixture. Add the rest of the egg mixture to the chocolate, carefully folding until a fairly uniform tone. Lightly fold in whipped cream. Place the mousse in the fridge until it is solid and the cake is ready to assemble.

To assemble the cake, very lightly spray a 9-inch spring form pan with oil and line it with parchment paper. Remove the cake from the fridge and using a very long, sharp knife, slowly slice through its middle to create two layers of equal size. (A serrated, sharp, bread knife works well).

Carefully place one layer into the bottom of the spring form pan making sure it is snug. Remove the mousse from the fridge, and spread half of it over the cake layer, making sure to even it out to the edges. Add the second layer of cake, and place it over the mousse. Gently press.

Spread the remaining mousse over the second cake layer, spreading to smooth it out on top. Place the cake in the freezer for at least 4 hours. If you are making this one day in advance, once the top of the cake is firm to touch, cover it in plastic wrap.

While cake is chilling, prepare almond buttercream frosting. In a bowl, beat the heavy whipping cream until holds its shape in peaks. Chill. In a separate clean bowl, cream softened butter, sugar, and almond extract until smooth. Combine the chilled cream into the almond buttercream mixture. Chill until ready to use (at least 1 1/2 hours).

Once the cake and mousse layers are chilled, the cake is ready to be frosted. Prepare the cake plate you will serve the cake on by lining it with pieces of parchment paper to be removed after frosting. Remove the spring form pan from the freezer.

Run a thin knife smoothly around the edge of the pan to help release it. Remove the cake from the pan and peel off the parchment paper from its bottom. Place the cake on the prepared cake plate. Spread the top and sides thinly with the chilled almond buttercream frosting. Place in the refrigerator while the chocolate ganache and decoration are prepared.

To make the ganache topping, heat the heavy cream, corn syrup, and palm shortening in a pan until just below boiling. Stir to blend, then pour the mixture over the chopped chocolate. Allow to sit for two minutes, then mix well until everything is smooth and glossy. Add the almond extract, and stir well.

To use immediately, remove the cake from the refrigerator, pour the ganache over the surface of the cake, and with an offset spatula, quickly smooth across the surface of the cake, allowing some to dribble down the sides. Place the cake back in the fridge.

If making the ganache ahead of time, place in the fridge in a covered container. When ready to use, heat in the microwave to bring to a pourable consistency and proceed as described above.

To prepare the toasted almond decoration, place almond slivers in a heavy, ungreased skillet. Stir continuously over medium heat until golden brown. Cool for 30-40 minutes.

Remove the cake, and put the toasted almond slivers along the edge of the finished cake, pressing in gently. This decoration gives the cake a delightful finish and elegant, nutty flavor.

Notes:

It is suggested that, for best results, this cake is made a day prior to serving, otherwise, allow at least six hours to make and assemble cake. Make sure the cake has ample time, at least 30 minutes, in the fridge to thaw before serving. Use a warm knife to slice through.

Serves 16-20.

All ingredients are available from your local store or online retailer.

You can find links to the ingredients used in these recipes at http://cozymysteries.com/death-at-the-cafe-recipes/

A Reverend Annabelle Dixon Mystery

MURDER AT THE MANSION

Alison Golden

Jamie Vougeot

MURDER AT THE MANSION

BOOK TWO

Cover Illustration: Rosalie Yachi Clarita

Published by Mesa Verde Publishing
P.O. Box 1002
San Carlos, CA 94070

Edited by
Marjorie Kramer

CHAPTER ONE

T HE ONLY THING Annabelle didn't like about driving her royal blue Mini Cooper was that she couldn't see how pretty it looked against the lush English countryside. In her mind, the various green hues of the fields, trees, and hedgerows provided the perfect backdrop for her petite blue bullet of a car. She would always picture herself zooming along like an actor in a lavishly produced, British television drama with an audience of millions. Happy ending guaranteed.

Annabelle loved driving. She loved driving almost as much as she loved cakes, and that was saying something. Annabelle's enthusiasm for sugary treats was as well-known in the village of Upton St. Mary as was her easy-going yet steadfast character. Going for a spin in her Mini with its go-faster stripes followed by a cup of tea and a slice of cake was her idea of a perfect summer's afternoon.

She whipped the terrier-like motor through the gentle inclines of the Cornish countryside and found it impossible not to smile. Upton St. Mary was very much the kind of village in which people often smiled for no apparent reason.

She was coming up to her third year as vicar of the small but dedicated community, yet the elegantly built stone walls, the unfurling landscape of green hills, and stout trees still took her breath away.

Though she had grown up in the hustle and bustle of working-class London, daughter of a street-savvy cabbie and a friendly but reserved cleaning lady, she had always dreamed of finding some grand version of idyllic peace. A place filled with beauty, calm, and goodness. After her troublesome teens, her soul found it in the glow of the Lord, and her body found it in this quaint little village tucked into a beautiful corner of the county of Cornwall, at the very end of England. Even the frequent rains and chilly winters couldn't spoil this very British Garden of Eden for her.

The villagers themselves, though many had spent their entire lives here, were just as appreciative of Upton St. Mary as their entranced Reverend. Many of their pastimes and traditions involved enjoying the good-naturedness of their neighbors and their delightfully well maintained cottages. Residents also loved nothing more than an open-air crafts fair or competition in which the patient, studious members of the community could display their talents in gardening, knitting, pottery, and – frequently to Annabelle's delight – baking. Much attention and discourse was directed at every local issue in the name of retaining the village's rustic charm. Whether it was a problematic pothole or a controversial building extension, the traditional and proud villagers had very strong opinions and voiced them at every opportunity.

The strictly-held traditions of the village, coupled with the speed at which gossip traveled through the close-knit community, meant that Annabelle's introduction as vicar had been greeted with reticence by some and concern by others. "A female vicar? In Upton St. Mary? What on earth will we do!?" said one particularly worrisome voice. "It's a slippery slope. Today a female vicar, tomorrow the tea shop will convert to a coffee bar!" said another.

But Annabelle was not the type to be fazed. Though her tall frame and somewhat large figure gave her an ungainly and jovial air, her dedication to church matters was unparalleled. She dealt out sermons with devotion and strokes of well-appointed humor and galvanized more than a few reluctant churchgoers to participate with her abundant, positive energy. She was never too busy to lend a hand here or an ear there. Her willingness to strap on her wellies and get stuck in with the farmers just as easily as she could comfortably chat with the ladies of the tea shop, navigating discussions with decorum and grace, was irresistible. She quickly became the presence villagers wanted at their bedside when ill and the first port of call when a village-wide dispute needed to be resolved fairly and with tact.

Her predecessor had been male, a distinctly hairy male, and relations had been all quite straightforward. However, Annabelle's appointment had put the villagers in a quandary. How should they refer to the female Reverend? Was her gender to be a cause for impropriety and social faux-pas? "Father" had long-been the customary term, and now that was out of the question. Much discussion ensued on the subject until Annabelle herself put an end to it with her typically tactful decisiveness. The villagers were to call her "Vicar" or just plain "Annabelle." With their concerns addressed, everyone went about their merry way.

Yes, Annabelle had become a widely accepted and to some, a much-loved boon to the village. The fact that her dog collar was wrapped around a distinctly feminine and surprisingly elegant neck had now been forgotten (or at least ignored) by those who were perhaps a little slower to embrace the new ways of the world. She had settled into the gentle, quiet pace of life a village church position afforded with good humor and grace – making it easy for the villagers to accept her.

Annabelle eased her Mini onto the tightly woven, cobblestone streets that indicated the village's center and gave a jolly wave to Mr. Hawthorne as he passed by on his daily, morning bike ride. He was a mischievous gentleman of fifty, who told tall tales of his youth in the local pub. While he claimed to ride his bike every morning "for the constitutional benefits," it was an open secret in the village that he rode to a secluded spot in which he could enjoy the pleasure of his tobacco pipe away from the prying eyes of his disapproving and critical wife.

Annabelle reached a small house on the outskirts of the village, as cute and prim as its inhabitant, stopped the car, and got out. The sun was just beginning to sprinkle a dappled yellow light on the village, and Annabelle took a deep breath of crisp, fresh air. She detected a faint whiff of something sweet and warm, briskly locked the car door, marched to the front of the house, and knocked cheerily.

After a few moments, the door opened by the tiniest of slivers, revealing a pair of deep blue eyes and pinned-back grey hair.

"Good morning, Vicar," said Philippa, opening the door and quickly hurrying back into the house.

"Good morning, Philippa," said Annabelle, wiping her feet on the doormat and following her through the cottage. "Why do you insist on opening the door in that manner? I feel like a door-to-door salesman. I'm sure you're not expecting anybody else."

"Better safe than sorry," said Philippa, leading the way

past her paper-filled desk and into the kitchen.

"Oh, these look scrumptious!" squealed Annabelle, catching sight of the range of cakes Philippa had laid out on the kitchen table.

Philippa smiled, took the teapot, and began pouring tea for the Vicar.

"I'm trying something new this season. I thought I might experiment with nuts a little. Walnuts, almonds, that sort of thing. I thought it might give me a better chance of standing out at the fair this year."

"Mmm," mumbled Annabelle, already chomping on a particularly rich and utterly delicious cupcake, her ravenous appetite winning the battle over ladylike reserve. "Your baking always stands out, Philippa."

"Thank you, Vicar," Philippa chuckled, "but there's some stiff competition in Upton St. Mary. I even considered a baklava at one point. I do love them. They remind me of my youth and a trip I took to Greece."

"Baklava? I haven't the foggiest idea what that might be."

"You'd love it. It's an incredibly sweet pastry drenched in honey, with nuts. *Very* continental," winked Philippa, with a mischievous tone.

"Well, I say jolly well go for it!" Annabelle exclaimed, putting down the cake reluctantly and sipping at her tea.

"Oh, I couldn't, Vicar."

"Why ever not?"

"Think of the outrage!"

Annabelle considered the point for a moment before nodding. Upton St. Mary was welcoming to new people but not nearly as benevolent to new ideas.

"I see we have company," Annabelle said, gesturing toward the corner of the room. Biscuit, the church's ginger tabby cat was sitting demurely by the door, lazily gazing at the two women while licking her lustrous fur.

"She dropped by last night and stayed here while I prepared the attendance and donation reports for the church. That cat visits more places around this village than you do, Vicar."

Annabelle chuckled and reached down to urge the cat toward her. "Here, Biscuit! Here, girl!" Biscuit continued to gaze at her nonchalantly. Spurned by the feline and feeling a little foolish, Annabelle turned to Philippa and asked: "Did you feed her?"

"That cat is a complete mystery, Vicar. I put some food out for her last night, and I don't believe she took more than a mouthful."

"Hmm."

"The strange thing is that she's still putting on the pounds."

"Well, I suspect half the village is probably feeding her," said Annabelle, picking up the cupcake again. "Lucky girl!"

"Indeed. Well, cats are fortunate in that they don't need to worry about such things," Philippa said, disguising the comment by bringing her teacup to her face for an uncommonly long time.

"Philippa!" the Vicar said.

"Now, Reverend, I only say this out of concern. None of us are getting any younger. It would be a shame if you struggled to find a young man because of that sweet tooth of yours."

Annabelle tried to protest but found her mouth full of succulent walnut cupcake and instead decided to put it down indignantly and furrow her brow.

"And if the rumors about the Inspector are true..." Philippa continued.

"Philippa!" the Vicar said again sternly, to which the elderly lady raised her hands in apology.

The two women sat in a silence that grew more tense by the second, gently pierced by the occasional clink of teacup on china, their eyes fixed upon the large window that looked out onto the deep woods behind Philippa's cottage.

"What rumors?" said Annabelle, unable to hold her curiosity any longer.

"Well," said Philippa with a twinkle in her eye, gleefully embracing the opportunity to indulge in her primary passion – gossip, "as you know, Dorothy's sister-in-law has a son who works in Truro in a baker's shop just a couple of streets away from the police station. He was the one who told us that the Inspector was probably married, but that was always just hearsay, we were never absolutely sure. And everybody who knows Dorothy's sister-in-law is well aware of the time that she claimed—"

"Philippa, please. If it will take us the entire morning, I'd rather move on to another topic."

"Sorry, Vicar. Well, essentially, Inspector Nicholls is single again. Now might be your chance. Oh, you would make such a lovely couple, Vicar. He's such a dashing young man. Terribly smart. A vicar and a police inspector. It would be like something from a novel!"

Annabelle sighed. "I appreciate your concern, Philippa, but I'm in no rush to begin courting, thank you."

"Whatever you wish, Vicar," Philippa said, barely concealing a wry smirk, "though you may find yourself with some competition in the near future."

Annabelle furrowed her brow again. She hated the gossip and rumor-mongering that passed for conversation with Philippa, yet the wily church secretary had a talent for piquing her interest.

"Are there people coming to the village?"

"You're aware of the new person who was going to move into the large country house in the hills by Arden Road?"

"I'm aware of the rumors, yes."

"Well, he's here, and he's already causing quite the stir."

"Really?"

"Why, yes. Apparently he's been inviting all kinds of women into the house since he moved in, just a few days ago. Can you *imagine*, Vicar? It's extremely concerning. Those sorts are ten a penny in London," Philippa said, growing visibly irate, "but *here?* This is the last place to find... that kind of person. People say he doesn't even have a denomination!"

"Calm down, Philippa. I'm sure he's a perfectly nice man. This is all conjecture. People running wild with their imaginations."

"I hope so, Vicar. I really do."

"What is he doing here?"

"That's just it. Nobody knows. What if he intends to open some sort of... Well, to put it in the devilish terms it deserves... a brothel, in the village!"

"Philippa, please. I wish you wouldn't allow yourself such ridiculous flights of fancy."

"But Reverend, to invite not one, but multiple women to—"

"Look, I'll pay the gentleman a visit today. It's likely that people have been so carried away with gossiping that they have forgotten to welcome our new resident. Let me speak with him and set everybody's fears to rest."

"That sounds like a good idea, Vicar. Perhaps you're right."

"Do you happen to know his name?"

Philippa pretended to ponder a moment before saying,

"I believe it's John Cartwright. Yes, yes, that's it."

"Very well. I shall speak to Mr. John Cartwright myself. Extend the hand of neighborly friendship, as it were. In the meantime, I do hope you can refrain from indulging in these fantastical stories, Philippa. They don't help anybody."

"Oh, I will, Vicar," said Philippa, and though Annabelle knew she meant it, she also knew that Philippa would find it hard to resist.

Be it gossip or cakes, some things were beyond certain people's control.

Annabelle left Philippa's house with a nagging feeling in the back of her mind. Nothing good ever came from gossip, and as if offering a stark contrast to Upton St. Mary's idyllic scenery, the rumors that occasionally spread rapidly around the village tended toward the extravagantly fearsome. Though Annabelle was only too aware of this fact, she could not shake the worry that tainted the clear, pure atmosphere of the emerging morning. What *was* the elusive stranger doing in Upton St. Mary? Could there be any truth in the concerning rumors? It seemed unlikely, thought Annabelle, but even a stopped clock is right twice a day.

After revving up the perky engine of her blue Mini and waving cheerily at Philippa, who turned quickly back into the house to continue with her church bookkeeping duties, Annabelle whipped the car around and carefully trundled on toward the church, mindful of both the early hour and the speed limit.

Pushing her disquieting thoughts away, Annabelle decided to pay a quick visit to the Wilshere family, who had just returned from the hospital with their new baby. They were a jolly kind, the sort of people who had worked the land and served the good folk of the village for generations. The parents, Mitchell and Michelle, were both rotund and bubbly, and with puffy cheeks prone to flushes, they were much like babies themselves.

Being that this was their firstborn, the parents were still doting nervously over the new baby boy when Annabelle arrived. She cooed and cuddled the baby, and the parents exchanged looks of pride when the baby smiled at the Reverend as she held him. Annabelle politely declined their appeals to sit and have tea but left feeling serene and content from the warmth and good humor of the happy-go-lucky Wilsheres.

She continued on toward the church absent-mindedly, enjoying the hypnotic greens and browns that passed by her windows. As she did so, she found herself thinking of the Inspector. Single again? Maybe she should pay him a little visit. Just to see how he was getting on. It had been a while since they last spoke, and he really had looked rather handsome when she had last seen him....

Annabelle buried the thought by remembering John Cartwight. She really should discover the intent of this newcomer and nip all the rumor-mongering in the bud before it was assumed he was some terrible monster and found himself confronted with pitchforks at dawn. She chuckled to herself at the thought and took the long and winding Arden Road up toward the newly-occupied expansive estate in which she hoped to find him.

It had been a very long time since Annabelle had last visited the estate. There were, in fact, a few such large properties of its kind at varying distances from the village, though not much was known about the owners. Most of them popped up in the village or at community events just frequently enough to keep rumors at bay. They tended to be older sorts from distinguished families, left to enjoy the serenity of their abodes as their offspring ventured into the metropolitan cities of the world to seek out their fortunes (or squander it, as some rumors suggested).

This particular property had always been shrouded in mystery. Annabelle had heard it referred to by some of the older villagers as Woodlands Manor, presumably due to its peculiar position tucked deep into a thickly wooded area. While many such properties were sought after for their magnificent views and the isolated peace of such a mellow and sleepy part of the world, this secretive and secluded estate had garnered little attention. Until now.

Annabelle eased her car off the smooth surface of Arden Road and onto the grassy, overgrown path that led blindly into the trees. The stiff, firm wheels of the Mini jostled over the ground, giving Annabelle a good shaking, until she emerged a few dozen yards later into an expanse that made her squeal, "Crikey!"

The grounds of Woodlands Manor were immaculate. Vivid green lawns extended away in front of her, pressing up against the wild woods like some vast oasis of the desert. Delicately pruned hedges and tastefully arranged patches of irises, roses, and petunias threw elegant splashes of color onto the grounds like an expert painter's canvas. A gently curving gravel path extended deep between the guiding hedgerows, leading the way to the Elizabethan mansion that stood proudly aloft, as though surveying the beauty of its surroundings.

Annabelle eased the car forward slowly, taking in the impressive scene that surrounded her. Why on earth would such a well-preserved estate be tucked away beyond view of everything around it? Had these astonishingly lavish grounds always been here? She rounded a large fountain that stood tall on the open area facing the property, parking the car in front of the stone steps that led to its gigantic oak doors. Upon exiting, she allowed herself one more look at the incredible sight of the mansion grounds, spun on her heels, and marched in her determined manner up the steps. After a couple of enthusiastic whacks of the heavy iron knocker, the door was opened by a young, attractive woman in jeans and a t-shirt. She had golden blond hair that framed her pretty face nicely, and thin, sharp lips that lent her musical voice an upbeat tone.

"Hello?" she said, curiously, before noticing Annabelle's collar, "Oh. How may I help you?"

"Good morning," Annabelle said in her most cheerful voice, "I'm Reverend Annabelle Dixon. Of St. Mary's church in the village. I recently learned that someone had moved into this magnificent property, so I wished to extend a welcome."

"I see. That's very kind of you, Reverend," the girl said, set at ease by the Vicar's open manner. "I'm afraid Sir John is unable to meet you at the moment, however."

"Oh?"

"Yes. He has just begun his daily meditation."

"Really?" Annabelle said, considering this information. "Well, taking the time to reflect is very important and difficult to find these days. Do you happen to know when he will be available?"

"He is not to be disturbed for another hour yet. If you are able to return then, I'm sure he'd love to chat with you."

"Wonderful," Annabelle said, clapping her hands together, "I shall call upon you in an hour. Thank you very much."

"You're welcome, Reverend. I'm sure Sir John will greatly appreciate your visit."

"I look forward to speaking with him. Well, it was very nice to meet you. See you shortly!"

The girl nodded and closed the door as Annabelle jogged down the steps and settled into her Mini. As she urged the car around the fountain and back along the satisfyingly crunchy gravel toward Arden Road, she thought about what the girl had said. *Sir* John Cartwright? Philippa had not mentioned anything regarding a knighthood. Could this elusive stranger really be a knight of the realm?

The sheer size and stature of the property would certainly fit but knights tended to have reputations that preceded them. This "Sir" had arrived with little fanfare or foreknowledge. It was, thought Annabelle, possible that the title had been self-adopted. It would not have been the first time a person of wealth had done so in order to gain social standing and acceptance into the circles of aristocracy. Members of such classes were above checking credentials, making it surprisingly easy to pass oneself off as a person of nobility. But if he really were a knight, how had he achieved such a title? And what of the women that had allegedly been invited to Woodlands Manor? The girl who had greeted her was rather young. She had seemed perfectly nice and respectable, yet Annabelle felt she had detected a note of reticence. She had not even offered her name....

"Oh, stop it, Annabelle," the Vicar chided herself when she got home. She parked the car and entered the wonderfully gothic church she called her own. "You're getting as bad as Philippa. You'll be grabbing a pitchfork yourself, soon."

She busied herself with church duties for a while, before the phone rang.

"Vicar?"

"Yes, Philippa?"

"I've completed the reports."

"Wonderful! Thank you ever so much, Philippa."

"Of course, Vicar."

"Was there anything else?"

There was a pregnant pause before Philippa spoke again.

"Well, I'm dreadfully ashamed to bring it up..."

"What's the problem?"

"It's just that I like to know my portion sizes. Waste is a terrible sin, after all."

"I'm not sure I follow you, Philippa."

"Well..."

Annabelle waited for a few moments before urging the church secretary again. "Do tell me, Philippa. You'll have me awfully worried if not."

"Well, it's the cupcakes."

"The cupcakes?"

"Yes."

"What about them?"

"The walnut cupcakes. The ones I laid out this morning."

"Yes, I know."

"How many did you eat? Oh, I'm so ashamed to ask."

Annabelle struggled with her memory for a moment, then said: "I believe I had two. Yes. That's it. I certainly had two."

"No more than that?"

"No. Definitely just two. Why?"

"You're sure you didn't have three, Vicar? I feel so embarrassed to ask. Do forgive me."

"I recall our chat perfectly, Philippa. I had two cupcakes – one with each cup of tea."

"I see," Philippa said, trailing off into a note of disappointment.

Annabelle sighed, and quickly checked her watch.

"Was there anything else Philippa? I really must be off."

"No, no. That's all, Vicar," Philippa said, her dismay apparent.

"Very well. I'll speak to you later today then. Thank you very much for the reports."

"Of course, Vicar. Thank *you* very much."

Annabelle pondered the call for a few moments before remembering her appointment at Woodlands Manor. She rushed out of the church and back into her car. It was turning out to be a rather eventful day, and it had barely begun.

Once again, Annabelle headed out to the discreet lane that led through the trees and into the luscious grounds of Woodlands Manor. Just over an hour had passed since her last visit, and her curiosity had only grown in that time. She found herself chomping at the bit to see this mysterious newcomer for herself; this meditating nobleman, the source of so much conjecture in Upton St. Mary.

She spun the Mini around the fountain, bringing it to a stop with a confident flourish of the brakes. She climbed out and marched up the steps to the intimidating doors. They were so tall that even Annabelle, with her five foot eleven inch frame, felt tiny in their presence. She thumped the knocker again and stepped back.

The youthful face of the blond girl appeared as she opened the door and smiled as she recognized the Vicar. She was just about to speak when she was interrupted by a wild, bloodcurdling scream, echoing down through the mansion from somewhere above. The gentle smiles of both women froze and then disappeared. Their expressions turned to horror as their eyes locked, and they found themselves stunned, shaken, and shocked by this absolutely beastly sound.

CHAPTER TWO

T HE GIRL BROUGHT her hand to her mouth in horror, gazing at the Vicar with eyes that were wide with fear. Annabelle, on the other hand, sprang into action. She pushed past the young woman and ran into the foyer with a speed and agility she had retained from a youth spent on hockey fields. She scanned the large entrance hall, looking for anything suspicious, then leaped up the stairs, two at a time, into the passageway of the second floor.

In times of emergency, Annabelle's clumsy charm and humble self-deprecation would give way to a keen wit and sharp reflexes. Within seconds of reaching the ornate surroundings of the second floor, a door at the end of the passage caught her attention. Its handle was slightly more elegant than those of the other doors, and it was framed by two perfectly preserved Ming vases on intricately carved pedestals. She assumed this was the master bedroom – and home to the source of that terrifying scream. She rushed toward it. The blond girl scampered close behind her, as if the Vicar were a shield that would protect her from whatever lurked behind the door.

"Fiddlesticks!" Annabelle said, as she grabbed the door handle and discovered it was locked.

"I'll go get the keys from the cloak room," the blond girl said, her voice no less musical for the shaky fear that permeated it.

Annabelle turned to her and nodded her approval, at which the girl ran down the passage and spun so quickly onto the stairs that a last-minute grab at the bannister was the only thing that stopped her from tumbling head over heels. Loathe to wait, Annabelle grabbed the door handle once more and leaned into the door, expecting nothing but resistance. Much to her surprise, the door moved, slightly at first, before the antique door handle's weak mechanism gave way, allowing the door to swing wide open under the force of Annabelle's weight.

The scene that confronted Annabelle was nothing short of astonishing. The room, much as she had expected, was large and elegant. A wide, antique bed sat against the far wall, and to one side there was an oak desk. On the other side of the room, three large windows that reached up toward the high ceiling, and down to within a foot of the floor, allowed a pale light to fill the room.

The middle window was wide open, and beneath it lay the spread-eagled body of a man Annabelle assumed to be Sir John Cartwright. A single arrow was stuck deep within his chest, cleanly piercing his loose shirt and protruding from his heart like a macabre signpost. Annabelle rushed toward the prone figure, and quickly placed her fingers to the man's neck. She waited for a few moments, just for confirmation, but Annabelle knew she wouldn't discover a pulse. In her short time as Upton St. Mary's vicar, she had seen the passing of many, almost as many as had been born, and she had developed what she considered a spiritual instinct about such things. She had known the moment she had opened the door that Sir John Cartwright was no more.

She knelt solemnly beside the old man's body, crossed herself, and clasped her hands in a quickly-mumbled, sincere prayer for the "dearly departed." Once she was done, she opened her eyes and stood, feeling oppression in the silence that always seemed to follow the end of a human life. Though in her duties as a servant of the Lord, Annabelle was accustomed to death, she had never seen anything as shocking as this. She realized this was almost certainly murder, and thus, death of a vastly different kind to the natural and godly kind of passing that Upton St. Mary was commonly home to.

She looked around the room once again, seeking further signs of foul play. She gazed out of the open window at the dense woods that wove themselves into the hills at the back of the mansion. Where was the girl? Annabelle wondered, remembering the young woman's promise to fetch the keys to the master room. Surely she would have found them by now? In the shock of discovering the dead body, Annabelle had almost forgotten the young female's presence. With a deepening sense that something curious was afoot, she set out to look for her.

A few minutes later, Annabelle was confident she had searched almost every spot in the grand house that the girl could have gone to. She hoped that the girl's disappearance had merely been fear getting the better of her. Perhaps she had caught a glimpse of the body as Annabelle prayed, the morbid surprise causing her to cower in some corner. However, after searching the major rooms of the expansive house, Annabelle resigned herself to the truth – the girl was gone.

Cautious of wasting any more time, she fumbled for the number in her cell phone and called the local police constabulary.

"Vicar! Been a while since I heard from you!" said the chirpy voice on the phone.

"I noticed. Your presence is sorely missed in the congregation."

"Um, well, yes. Busy, you know..."

"Never mind. Something serious has occurred. I need you to come as quickly as possible. I'm at Woodlands Manor, the estate by Arden Road."

"That doesn't sound too good," the Constable said. "I'll be on my way as soon as I'm done with –"

"Now, Constable," she said firmly.

Annabelle could almost hear the look of surprise her brusqueness caused.

"What is it?"

"Murder, Constable. A man is dead."

There was another pause, in which Annabelle could hear him slam his cup down and stand up from his desk.

"I'm on my way."

Constable Jim Raven was well into his thirties, but the constant glint in his brown eyes, as well as his boyish, cheeky grin, made him appear much younger. It was a well-known joke that he'd only become a police officer in order to avoid getting into trouble himself. He was the type to join children in a game of street football or take a little longer than was strictly necessary ensuring everything was in order at the local pastry shop. The truth be known, his *laissez-faire* approach to police work would have had him reprimanded almost daily, were it not for the scarcity of criminal elements in Upton St. Mary. It also helped that Jim Raven was an incredibly effective police officer.

With a wink and a joke, Jim could diffuse even the most hostile of disputes, and his breezy, infectious manner could persuade the most stubborn residents of Upton St. Mary to see the funny side. Children of the village would even confess their transgressions to him like an elder brother. If there were a traffic accident or pub fight, Jim could be relied upon to resolve the situation in an amicable exchange of verbal agreements, handshakes, and gentle chidings. However, Constable Jim Raven had never had to deal with murder before.

He jumped into a police car and sped away from the station, forgetting even to put his siren on until he had completed half the journey. To Jim, sirens had proven more useful when giving villagers a funny fright or for children to play with as he gave them a lift home, than for actual police work. He reached the fountain in front of Woodlands Manor and screeched to a stop. The tires of his small police car slid across the gravel, giving the Constable a guilty sense of drama and excitement. He turned off the sirens, and leaving the flashing blue light on, got out of the car and fixed his hat firmly onto his head.

Jim entered the open entrance of the estate to find Annabelle sitting on an upholstered bench beside the staircase. Her face was fixed in an expression of intense thought and concentration. The two knew each other very well, having frequently crossed paths amid the daily affairs of the village. Their shared love of laughter had instigated many a rumor to flare up regarding a possible romance although there was a slight incongruity in that the police officer, at only five feet five inches, was towered over by Annabelle who had a full half foot on him. It made them an odd couple when in close proximity – not least when Annabelle wore heels. Eventually, the stark contrast between Annabelle's diligent and sharp mind and Jim's perpetual seeking of mischief forced even the most persistent of matchmakers to give up.

As he saw Annabelle sitting there, Constable Raven braced himself for a long story. He knew the Vicar well enough to be aware of how she could regale events in full detail, with elaborate and expressive language, many digressions, and only when she was fully ready. This time, however, Annabelle simply stood silently and led the way up the staircase. Jim followed behind, growing increasingly nervous at the absence of talk.

Annabelle reached the master bedroom with the Constable close behind. She stepped aside to reveal the still figure of Sir John Cartwright. Within seconds, Jim had turned around and put his hand over his mouth, leaping toward the private bathroom. After examining the inside of the toilet bowl more closely than he would ever have liked, splashing water onto his face, and returning to the bedroom, the Constable found Annabelle standing in the doorway, surveying the scene as if looking for something she'd forgotten.

"I'm sorry, Vicar. This is the first time I've ever seen a dead body."

"It's alright, Jim."

"It just caught me by surprise, is all."

"Of course."

"And I've had this stomach bug for days, anyway, you see. I shouldn't have had that fry-up this morn—"

Annabelle turned to the Constable. "Don't worry, Jim. I won't tell anybody else unless it's absolutely necessary."

Jim smiled. "Thank you, Vicar. Much appreciated."

He turned slowly to look at the body again, fortifying his stance and tightening his stomach this time. "Is this how you found him?"

"Yes," replied Annabelle, still deep in thought.

"We should be careful to preserve the crime scene."

"Absolutely. I do hope that there weren't any clues in the bathroom, however."

Constable Jim Raven's smooth-shaven cheeks went red with embarrassment. "I don't think so," he said bashfully.

"Hmm, me neither," muttered Annabelle.

"I'll go radio for Inspector Nicholls," said Jim with an air of finality. "He'll need to come all the way from the city." He pulled his radio from his lapel and returned to the passage.

It was Annabelle who found herself blushing now.

Forty minutes later, Inspector Mike Nicholls strode into the bedroom along with two other officers of the Truro police branch. Annabelle forgot what she had been saying to Constable Jim Raven as she noticed the graceful confidence with which the Inspector walked. She noticed how he scanned the room with sharp, piercing eyes, his broad, powerful shoulders shifting nonchalantly beneath his trench coat. She wondered if he had chosen the cut of his suit to bring out the commanding posture of his height or if it was just a happy accident. She gazed at the grizzled stubble that accentuated his strong bone structure and couldn't help imagining what it might be like to run a hand across his–

"Good to see you, Constable," the Inspector said, shaking his hand vigorously, "and you, Vicar."

Annabelle applied all the strength she could find to keep her knees from failing to do their duty.

"Oh, yes," was all she could muster.

"The pathologist should be here any second now. Mind telling me what happened?"

"Well, the Vicar here called me about a—"

"I heard a man had moved into the village," interrupted Annabelle, raising her hand to silence Constable Raven and sidling over to place herself at the center of the Inspector's attention, "a Sir John Cartwright. There was some gossip about him among the villagers."

"What kind of gossip?" asked the Inspector.

"Oh, nothing out of the ordinary, Inspector. The typical kind of paranoid fantasy and nonsense. Why, you'd be surprised at how fertile some imaginations can be when seeds are planted."

"I understand. Please continue, Vicar."

"Of course. You're a busy man, Inspector. I appreciate your sense of focus. Well, as the Vicar, I decided to pay the gentleman a visit so that I could welcome him to the community. You know, it's dreadfully important to get to know the people you work with, Inspector. I make it a habit of mine to spend time with those who I feel may need it."

The Inspector smiled, then gestured for Annabelle to continue. All memories of the horrendous crime had gone far from her mind in his striking presence.

"About two hours ago, I dropped by, and was greeted at the door by a young girl."

"Where is she?" said the Inspector, looking around the room.

"She left."

"Can you describe her?"

"Blond hair, to the nape of her neck. Blue eyes. Early twenties, I should say. Attractive – I suppose."

"No name?"

"No. She told me Sir John was busy meditating and would not be available for a further hour. I left and returned almost exactly one hour later. The young girl opened the door once again, and a moment later there was the most chilling scream from within the property."

"The dead man?"

"I believe so. I ran into the house, conquering my fear in order to discover the reason for the horrendous sound. I am not one who departs during times of danger or crisis, Inspector," said Annabelle, looking fixedly into the Inspector's eyes, as if trying to communicate telepathically the subtext of her speech. "Eventually I came up to the bedroom," she continued. "The door seemed locked at first, and the girl who had been here said she would find the key. She left, but I managed to open the door, only to discover *this,*" Annabelle gestured toward the dead body, "truly horrifying scene."

The Inspector exchanged a quick glance with Constable Jim Raven, who had been edged ever so slightly further to the side during Annabelle's recital of events.

"It's always a shock to see a dead body."

"That's very perceptive of you Inspector," Annabelle said, slowly.

"Especially when it's a case of murder, as this appears to be."

"It must take such strength to face this kind of horrible

brutality. It takes a man with real fortitude and conviction to do so in the name of justice."

"I suppose. It's my job, really, Vicar."

"So stoic, so noble, so—"

"Ah, Harper!" exclaimed the Inspector as a raven-haired woman entered the bedroom. As he turned to greet the pathologist, Annabelle quickly suppressed the petty irritation she felt at the newcomer, who had seized the Inspector's attention away from her so easily.

Harper Jones had been one of the most exemplary physicians in the north of England before moving south to the sunnier climes of Cornwall to marry the owner of a local bicycle shop. A strict believer in leading by example, her extensive fitness regime and dedicated diet had afforded her an appearance far younger than her forty-seven years. She still warranted stolen glances from men half her age. Her silky-black hair cascaded around her sharp features, which included a pair of hazel eyes that seemed to probe and investigate everything in their path.

"Inspector," she said, curtly nodding a perfunctory greeting to the assembled group, barely breaking her stride as she made her way to the victim's body. "Vicar. Jim."

Without ceremony, Harper dropped her doctor's bag beside the corpse and knelt down. The Inspector stepped toward the open window, with Annabelle shuffling closely behind. As the pathologist began probing the body, fumbling in her bag for various instruments to take measurements, the Inspector flipped open his notebook and began scribbling.

"Vicar..."

"Yes?" said Annabelle, rather more hastily than was warranted.

"How long ago would you say you heard the scream?"

Annabelle checked her watch. "Almost exactly an hour ago. I found the body, prayed for a minute or two, then I took a short while to look for the girl. Constable Raven arrived about ten minutes later, and a few minutes after that he called you. All in all, I suppose just under twenty minutes went by between our discovery and the call to you. You arrived around forty minutes later, making an hour."

"I see," said the Inspector, directing his attention further across the large room. Annabelle watched him with rapt attention as he stood in front of the window, holding his pen to simulate the arrow's trajectory. She noticed a police officer scanning the grounds at the edge of the woods outside. She looked back at the Inspector and noticed his brow was filled with lines of frustration.

"Is something wrong, Inspector?"

"Hmm, I can't figure out why he's lying where he is."

"Oh?"

"The arrow is embedded deep enough in his chest to indicate a hell of a lot of force. That kind of whack should have sent him farther back than it did. Unless he was leaning out of the window..."

Annabelle looked from the body, to the window, and back to the Inspector's irritated expression, before coyly saying, "Might I offer an idea?"

The Inspector looked up from his notebook. "Of course, Vicar."

"I mean, it's probably nonsense," Annabelle chuckled, "I'm sure it's just a silly idea, and I'm just wasting your time. I probably shouldn't even be bothering you right now."

"No, no. Go ahead."

"Well, he was meditating, so he was probably sitting cross-legged just in front of the window. His legs are crossed at the ankle. If he had been standing – and this is just a wild assumption, please ignore me if I'm being terribly ignorant – I would imagine his legs would be splayed out a little more."

"Hmm," the Inspector mumbled, tapping his pen against his lips.

Annabelle continued, spurred by the excitement of having the Inspector's full attention. "The window reaches low to the ground so his head and upper body would have been visible from the ground outside, even while sitting. The arrow is embedded rather high on his torso too, in the part of the body that would have been visible from outside were he sitting at the time. It seems entirely plausible to me. Perhaps... Maybe... Forget I said anything, it's probably ridiculous."

After a few moments of pondering, pen-gesticulating, and note-scribbling, the Inspector looked at Annabelle with a warm smile.

"I think you're most likely correct, Vicar. Some keen observation skills you have there."

Annabelle felt all the blood rush out of her legs and into her cheeks. There were times she wished she could loosen her collar, and this was certainly one of them. After some struggling due to the dryness of her throat, she managed to utter a high-pitched "yes" and decided against anything more ambitious.

The Inspector went back to his notebook, leaving Annabelle to gaze at his strongly defined jaw. Before her reverie could take over completely, Harper suddenly stood up between them and said: "He died well over an hour ago. Much before you heard that scream."

The statement, as were so many of Harper's, was brief, to the point, and threw the entire logic of the situation out of alignment.

"That doesn't make any sense," the Inspector said.

"No, it doesn't," Annabelle agreed.

Harper shrugged the statement off. "I'll need everybody out of here. My assistant is on his way and will take the body away. I'll confirm the time after an autopsy."

Harper turned around and walked away, giving instructions to the medical assistant who stood by the door. The crowd of police officers that had amassed inside the room shuffled away down the steps and out onto the gravel in front of the large house. There were now several cars parked at all manner of angles around the fountain, including an ambulance. Annabelle, being one of the last to exit, lost sight of the Inspector. She frantically searched for him as multiple police officers got in their cars and drove away.

"Inspector! Inspector!" she called wildly, as she discovered him about to get into his unmarked Ford Focus. She half-ran, half-walked toward him as daintily as she could, but so quickly that she was badly out of breath upon reaching him.

"Yes, Vicar?"

"Is there... anything... I can do... to help?" Annabelle gasped, in as ladylike a manner as she could manage.

"I'm not sure, really," the Inspector grumbled dejectedly. "There's not much to go on and a lot to find out. I get the impression we've only seen a small portion of whatever's happened here."

"Really?"

"It doesn't get much cleaner than an arrow shot from outside the building. No bullet to match, no gunpowder sprays, no fingerprints. No sound, even. We've got no witnesses right now. I had my men search the house top to bottom, as well as most of the surrounding grounds, just in case our "mystery man or woman" was hiding somewhere. Nothing. The only people I can place are you, the girl, and the dead man. On top of all that, the scream happened *after* the man was dead, which I can tell is going to make me rack my brain for days. We're definitely a long way from solving this one."

"Could the scream... really have happened... after the murder?" Annabelle said, gulping as much as she could to gain her breath.

"If Harper says so, then that's definitely the case. She's as reliable as rock, Harper Jones is. As much as I wish she weren't, in some cases."

"What will you do now, Inspector?"

"Well, we need a suspect. And you're the only one I can think of right now."

Annabelle found herself lost for words. Inspector Nicholl's face was deadpan.

"Ha! Relax, Vicar," the Inspector chuckled. "Just a joke. You're far too saintly for any of this business."

"Oh," breathed Annabelle, seconds away from blacking out entirely. "Good one."

"Actually, there may be something you could do for me after all."

"Whatever it is, Inspector. I'll do it. Just say the word."

"Well, you mentioned some rumors that were flying around regarding the dead man."

"Yes."

"There's probably nothing to them, as you said, but just to be on the safe side, it might be worth knowing what people thought about him. We'll see what we can find out about his past, but sometimes people believing a rumor is as good a motive as the real thing. I know a lot of people confide in you, Vicar, so perhaps you could get a feel for what people were saying about him. There might be something there."

"Of course, Inspector. That makes perfect sense."

"If you hear anything, just let me know."

"Likewise. Please contact me if you find anything, Inspector."

They exchanged smiles, and the Inspector opened the door of his car and got in. In the reflection of the door mirror, Annabelle caught a glimpse of herself, sweating profusely, her hair a mess of tangles, and her cassock askew from all the running. As the Inspector revved his car around the fountain and drove away, she gritted her teeth and said, "Oh, bother!"

CHAPTER THREE

ANNABELLE MARCHED BACK toward her Mini, exchanging a brief "hello" with the SOCO team that were still going to and fro around the property. It was barely noon, yet the good Vicar had seen more drama that morning than she usually did in an entire month. The sun was high and bright, though the air remained crisp and cool. It was just calm enough to hear the songs of birds that danced from branch to branch. Annabelle geared the Mini and set off. A good drive always soothed her, but her mind was tied into too many knots for her to relax just yet. Questions jabbed at her like troublesome thorns, and the words of the Inspector echoed along the fringe of her thoughts; *"We've only seen a small portion of whatever's happened here."*

Murder was the last thing Annabelle had ever expected to occur in Upton St. Mary. Previously, the greatest scandal Annabelle had encountered in the placid and quiet village had been the alleged theft of Mr. Maitland's prize-winning marrow. Those had been dark days indeed, with accusations flying in all directions. It had been one of the most divisive events in Upton St. Mary's recent history, with the question, "So who do *you* think took Mr. Maitland's marrow?" being whispered tersely at many a dinner table.

After days of investigation and questioning, Annabelle finally cracked the case. She gathered the concerned villagers after her Sunday sermon and outlined her discovery. She had sifted through a turn of events – part coincidence, part negligence, and part farce – and deduced finally that the nearly-blind Mrs. Niles had mistaken the marrow for a misshapen pumpkin and taken it home from the county fair, whereupon she promptly cooked it into a soup that turned out peculiarly sour. Her sleuthing had put the gossip to rest finally, but it was a chapter of the village's history best forgotten, in her humble opinion.

Sir John Cartwright was no missing vegetable, however, though in much the same way, Annabelle felt duty-bound to solve his mystery. This was her village now, her congregation. As a servant of the Lord, it was her responsibility to root out evil, just as it was to praise the joy that was abundant in her chosen corner of the world.

Despite her determination, however, Annabelle struggled to make sense of the incident. She relived the events multiple times in her memory, talking to herself as she drove toward the church in order to find some sense of logic. Unfortunately, she simply couldn't find it. Everything seemed to happen in the wrong order and for no reason. The scream *after* the death. The girl, who had exhibited no indications of malice, even inviting the Vicar in a second time but who disappeared immediately afterward. Even the method of death itself was unseemly. Annabelle had never even heard of someone being killed with an arrow, let alone seen it with her very eyes.

And finally, Sir John Cartwright himself. A man

shrouded in mystery, who was barely known in the village to which he had recently moved. A man who had received visits from mysterious women, and, if the rumors were to be believed, fancied himself a brothel owner. A man whose dubious title of "Sir" drew many questions. And what had been the blond girl's relationship to the old man?

Annabelle reached the churchyard and spun the Mini into her regular parking spot with far less precision than usual, such was the tangled nature of her concentration. As she got out of her car, Philippa called her from the church steps.

"Vicar! Vicar!"

Annabelle walked toward her, straightening her cassock and palming down her hair.

"Hello, Philippa. I take it you've come to bring the reports?"

"Yes, Vicar, they're on your desk." Philippa's expression grew more concerned as Annabelle drew closer. "Oh, Vicar, you look dreadful! Has something happened?"

"Thank you, Philippa. For the reports, that is. Yes, actually, something terrible has indeed happened."

"Oh, well, let's go to your cottage. I'll make you a nice cup of tea and perhaps some sandwiches. I'm sure you haven't eaten anything yet."

"That would be wonderful, Philippa."

"And you can tell me all about it."

The church of Upton St. Mary was the centerpiece of the small village, with a size far larger than its small congregation required and a spire that reached higher than any other point for miles around. It was a Gothic building, constructed from large, grey slabs of stone that had braved centuries of England's most turbulent weather with stalwart stoicism. Its arched windows contained some of the most intricate and awe-inspiring stained glass in South West England, and just beneath its heavenward spire, sat a huge bell, as big as any man, with a tone so rich and powerful, it could be heard in fields far beyond Upton St. Mary's borders.

Annabelle would still sometimes gaze at the imperious structure and the equally impressive oak trees that framed it. She often wondered how many generations of people had gathered there, how many children had been raised in its vast shadow, and what an important part it had played in the lives of Upton St. Mary's humble, but no less complex, history. To one side of the church, curving all the way to the back, lay the extensive cemetery with its gravel path weaving between the tombstones. There were benches along the path, where those of a more peaceful disposition would rest in order to contemplate the solemn surroundings. On the other side of the church, among orchids and well-maintained flowers, many of which had grown from buds and cuttings gifted by enthusiastic gardeners in the village, sat the white-walled cottage that Annabelle called home.

It was a small abode, with red window and door frames and a thatched roof that, despite requiring plenty of maintenance, Annabelle adored so much she had squealed with delight when learning this would be her place of residence. She had wasted no time at all in turning the wonderfully twee cottage into her own and had cultivated a surrounding garden that, though it couldn't compete with the best of Upton St. Mary's, was a source of great pride.

Both within and without, the home soon became a testament to the humor, care, and diligence of its owner. Cheerful, ceramic gnomes stood proudly among the Bellflowers,

Sweet Williams, and Hollyhocks that distinguished it as a traditionally English garden. Beside this, a well-maintained cherry orchard complemented Annabelle's colorful flowers perfectly and was the site of her beehive, which she tended daily.

Inside the charming little cottage, gaudy knick-knacks and souvenirs sat atop handmade shelves and dressers alongside her religious iconography. One needed only a brief glance at the soft, inviting sofa and matching armchairs with their colorful, wool-textured cushions, to find evidence of the Reverend's open, humorous personality and deep love of her home. Her extensive book collection, covering almost an entire wall of the living room, was a constant surprise to newcomers, who found it difficult to believe the energetic, ever-moving Vicar was capable of sitting in one place long enough to read a book. While there wasn't much room to entertain, Annabelle loved the intimate, cozy warmth of her little house by the church, as did her frequent visitors, who weren't deterred in the slightest by its somewhat limited space.

As she went through to the kitchen, Annabelle was pleased to discover that Philippa had prepared a pot of hot tea and numerous sandwiches for her on the table. Annabelle's focus, however, went first to the cupcakes that Philippa had brought with her.

"Sit down, Vicar. You could do with a rest."

"Thank you ever so much, Philippa. It's been a terribly eventful morning."

"Whatever happened?" asked Philippa, pouring the tea as the Vicar bit into a sandwich with zeal. Annabelle's mother had always told her sandwiches before cake, and she had always listened to her mother.

"There's been a death."

Philippa balked, causing hot tea to spill upon the grained wood of the oak table.

"Oh dear, I'm sorry, Vicar," she said, materializing a cloth in her hand almost instantaneously and wiping away the spill. "May I ask who?"

"John Cartwright. *Sir* John Cartwright."

Philippa's eyes widened, and her mouth dropped open with surprise. She halted her wiping and slumped down onto a chair.

"Heavens!"

"Yes, under very peculiar circumstances as well, I'm still in utter confusion as to how it happened."

Annabelle watched as Biscuit stepped through the cat door, her green eyes fixed upon the table, and hopped up onto a shelf. She curled her tail around her feet and watched, as still and delicate as the ornamental figure of Christ beside her.

"Allow me, Philippa," the Vicar said, as she swallowed the last of her sandwich and poured some more tea into her cup. "I haven't told you the most incredible detail yet."

Philippa leaned forward, as if fearful she might miss the Vicar's next words.

"Sir John Cartwright was murdered."

Philippa sat back suddenly, as if thrown, and sighed. She looked incredulously around the room as if an explanation lay somewhere in the Vicar's accumulation of bric-a-brac.

"Are you sure, Vicar?" she managed to say eventually.

"Fairly certain, yes."

"How ghastly! I don't believe we've ever had a murder in Upton St. Mary. It's *unimaginable*."

"I saw his body with my own eyes," Annabelle said, her hand hovering between a second sandwich and a cupcake, before settling reluctantly on a sandwich.

Annabelle continued to recount the events of the morning in as much detail as possible, with all the skill of narration her sermons were lauded for. Even this though wasn't quite enough for Philippa, who prodded and poked with questions large and small. With all the curiosity and tenacity of a police dog, Philippa diligently went over all the inconsistencies of the Vicar's story, confirming each detail multiple times, and asking the Vicar's opinion throughout.

"What of the girl?"

"You say she was young?"

"Did you notice any differences in her appearance the second time you saw her?"

"How did the scream sound exactly?"

"There was no sound after that?"

"How long did it take you to reach the bedroom?"

"Did you notice any vehicles on the way there?"

"How large was the house?"

"What was John Cartwright wearing?"

"Were any of the police officer's acting suspiciously?"

Once Philippa had exhausted both her questions and the Vicar, she allowed Annabelle to take a cupcake and eat it in peace. They both sat, enjoying a few moments of silence, as they considered the situation in the warm, comfy ambience of the Vicar's kitchen.

Annabelle finished the cupcake, wiped the crumbs from her lips delicately, and broke the silence, "Please don't concern yourself with this, Philippa. It's in the capable hands of Inspector Nicholls now, and I'm sure he'll find the awful creature who committed this sin eventually."

"Yes, Vicar," Philippa said, gazing at her teacup absently, "but I was just trying to remember something."

"Yes?"

"Who in the village is a capable archer?"

"That was just one of the many questions I was hoping to answer soon," replied the Vicar, standing up from the table and fixing her cassock in the mirror hung beside the window. "Regardless, let's put this horrid affair aside for now. Life goes on, even in the presence of death. Tomorrow's Sunday, and all this fuss has given me no time at all to prepare."

"Yes, Vicar. I'll leave you to it. I've yet to call the carpenter about that rickety pew."

"Oh. That's not been fixed yet?"

"Unfortunately not, Vicar," Philippa said, picking the china up from the table and arranging it neatly beside the sink. "Ah, Vicar?"

"Yes?" Annabelle said, turning around.

Philippa picked up the tray of cupcakes and presented them to the Vicar. "You know, you're welcome to take cupcakes whenever you wish."

Annabelle shot Philippa a look of confusion, then chuckled in bemusement. "Why, yes, Philippa. Of course."

"I mean, there's no need to hide your love of cakes from me, Vicar!" Philippa said, laughing nervously.

"Don't worry, I won't. Whatever is the matter, Philippa?"

"Oh, nothing, Vicar. I just think, perhaps, you're a little stressed. Nothing to be concerned about. For now."

Annabelle looked with an expression of deep befuddlement at the table as she sought to make sense of her secretary's strange behaviour. On a day that seemed full of odd and unusual occurrences, however, she decided to reserve her critical faculties for the more concerning matters at hand. She bid Philippa a cheery farewell and made her way to the church in order to work on her upcoming sermon.

Just as she expected, news of Sir John Cartwright's death spread throughout the village rapidly and with fervor. Though she would have confided the extraordinary events to her ever faithful friend anyway, Annabelle was aware of the added benefit to be gained from Philippa's tendency to spread news quickly. Indeed, she had often joked that Philippa was faster at spreading both information and misinformation than the internet. Just as the Inspector would no doubt use his sources and databases to his advantage, Annabelle would use hers, the village's own little Hermes, messenger of the heavens, Philippa. She was certain that many of the rumors flying around about the newly arrived knight were poppycock, but if there were some kernel of truth in them, then news of his death would bring it to the fore.

As she expected, fueled by the absence of excitement that typically accompanied the sleepy Cornish weekend, the news spread to every corner of Upton St. Mary. Within a matter of a few hours, almost every resident had not only heard the news, but had also come up with a motive, a full backstory for Sir John, and even solved the murder.

"These rich types are all the same," grumbled a voice from the back of the local pub, "always involved in something shady. Drugs, theft, you name it. They get involved in anything they can up there in the city. Then, when they're getting close enough to getting caught, they come down here, bringing all that trouble with them."

"Come on," pleaded a younger, less cynical voice at the bar, "there are lots of rich folk around Upton St. Mary. None of them are involved in anything shady."

"Yeah, but I never liked that John Cartwright anyway."

"You never even met him!" came the reply, causing rowdy laughter around the pub.

"Exactly. Show me an Englishman who moves to an area and whose first order of business isn't to visit his local pub, and I'll show you someone shady," replied the old grump, to which everyone's laughter turned into murmurs of begrudging agreement at his distinctly British logic.

Elsewhere, a couple of young mothers sitting on a bench watching over their children were just as opinionated.

"Good riddance, I say."

"Helen!"

"Well, I'm sorry, Julia, but do you really want a weird old pervert like that living this close to Upton St. Mary? Building a brothel here, of all things?"

"Well, I don't really think that's what he was doing."

"Of course it was!"

"You really believe that?"

"Why not? Everyone knows Cornish girls are the prettiest in England. We're close enough to the cities to keep it convenient and just far enough away to keep it secret. This is the perfect location for a brothel! And Woodlands Manor is all tucked away behind those trees. Why would you choose to live there if you weren't doing something shameful?"

"I suppose."

"No doubt about it. No doubt at all."

"It's not that what worries me though. The really scary thing is that there's a killer right here in Upton St. Mary. Can you imagine? How could someone *do* that? Kill someone in cold blood. It sends shivers up my spine."

"Are you talking about the werewolf?" came the chirpy voice from beside the two women.

"Tommy! Don't creep up on us like that!"

"Sorry, mum."

"There's no werewolf. Don't talk nonsense."

"There is. The one that killed the old man."

Julia and Helen exchanged glances.

"Who did you hear that from?"

"Eddie told me. He said the werewolf ran into the old man's house, and slashed him – like this! He was so strong, that he left his claw sticking out of the man's chest. And the blood was going everywhere – like this!"

Tommy mimicked spurts of blood shooting from his chest like geysers, falling to the ground as he did so and tossing himself around in a manner that demonstrated he was thoroughly enjoying himself.

"Come now, Tommy. There are no werewolves around here. People would have seen them."

"Not this one. This one is clever. He disguised himself as the Vicar!"

And so it went, in a game of Chinese whispers played in a similar fashion in similar villages around the world since the dawn of news itself. In some reports, the murderer was a Robin Hood-type figure who ransacked the home of the evil brothel keeper and distributed his ill-gotten gains to those in need. In others, the murderer was a cold-blooded killer who had conducted the act with calculated malice and who would strike again unless the village of Upton St. Mary barricaded their windows and doors against the fearsome predator. Scenarios of every sort were put forth, and the lack of available knowledge allowed a wide range of theories to flourish. After all, Sir John Cartwright had been an unknown entity in the village while alive and was now very much a stranger in death.

Sunday rolled around, and with it, the Holy Communion. Despite giving a particularly grave service and a sermon that focused on what the proverbs had to say about gossip and the judgment of neighbors, Annabelle still found herself fielding plenty of inquisitive remarks as the congregation sidled down the well-worn steps of the church.

"It is terrible, what happened, is it not, Vicar?"

"I do hope you were not too shaken, Vicar. I would not know what to do had I been in your shoes."

"These are dark times. I do hope this horrid business blows over shortly."

Annabelle clasped their hands and reciprocated their well wishes, revealing none of her inner turmoil in deciphering the mystery. Though outwardly she displayed her typically good-humored demeanor, her mind had been twisting and turning the events of the previous day around like a curious Eastern puzzle box, seeking a point at which she could find the unlocking mechanism and reveal the truth held inside.

Once the last of the lingerers had made their way out of the church gates, Annabelle sighed deeply and joined Philippa inside the church.

"That was a good service, Vicar. Just what the village needed," Philippa said, as she swept the aisle of the church.

"I don't suppose it'll have much of an effect, Philippa. From what I've gathered, it seems much of the village is engaged in hearsay too fantastical to bear any truth."

"Oh, I wouldn't be too sure of that," Philippa remarked ominously.

"Well, anyhow. I need to take my mind off this for a while. It's been tugging at my thoughts since I came back from Woodlands Manor. I'll be with the bees in the orchard if you need me."

"Yes, Vicar. Don't worry yourself. It's a lovely day to be outside."

Annabelle left the church, changed into her gardening shoes and protective helmet, and began tending to her bees. She enjoyed her hobby greatly, consistently filled with wonder at the brightly-colored insects' incredible combination of wild abandon and perfectly symmetrical order. It also gave her an excuse to talk about her thoughts. She'd always found bees a most satisfying audience.

"Just look at you all! So ordered, so focused. Truly God's creatures. If only human affairs were so simple and clear. Well, I suppose it's my own fault for fancying myself some kind of detective. I should just leave this whole mess to the professionals. My clerical teachers always said I needed to remember when things should be left for higher powers to deal with. So, enough! From now on, if I'm of no use, I'll abstain from anything to do with this. That's all I—"

Suddenly, Annabelle caught a glimpse of a non-descript blue Ford Focus pull into churchyard and park beside her Mini. She had only to see the merest glimpse of the Inspector's brush-like hair before she scampered out of her garden to greet him.

"Ah, Reverend!"

"Inspector! So lovely to see you!"

"And you," he said, casting his eyes over her outfit.

Annabelle snorted a laugh as she frantically pulled off her gardening gloves in order to shake his hand.

"I hope I wasn't interrupting you."

"Oh, not at all. Never, Inspector. I was just tending to my bees," Annabelle said, surprised to discover her voice was muffled, then remembering that she was still wearing her bee-keeping helmet. She removed it quickly, and tossed her hair into place in a manner she hoped was not too glamorous for a vicar.

"You keep bees?"

"Yes. It's a silly hobby, I know, but it passes the time."

"I don't think it's silly. I think it's rather interesting, actually."

"It is, isn't it?"

They smiled at each other awkwardly for a few moments before the Inspector said, "I was just on my way to the crime scene, so I thought I'd drop by and see how you were doing. You seemed a little... flustered, yesterday."

"Oh, well. I wasn't at my best," laughed Annabelle, "I'm much better now. Thank you for asking, Inspector."

"Actually, I thought you seemed to take it rather well. The last time I spoke to someone who had discovered a dead body, they were covered in their own vomit."

Annabelle laughed so loudly, that Philippa appeared in the doorway to see what all the fuss was about. Annabelle, catching sight of her, promptly flicked her hand in a peculiar gesture intended to get Philippa to return inside, a gesture she hoped the Inspector wouldn't notice.

"Are you okay, Vicar?"

"Yes, Inspector. I think I have a bee sting on my hand."

"Oh, let me see."

As the Inspector took Annabelle's hand, the Vicar struggled to retain consciousness as once again her knees barely held her up. Philippa, who was still standing in the doorway, saw what was happening, and cheekily winked at Annabelle. The Vicar responded by mouthing the word "Shoo!" as aggressively as she could without catching the attention of the Inspector.

"I can't see anything, but I suppose they don't swell up until much later."

"Precisely, Inspector."

The Inspector looked around at the churchyard, nodded his appreciation, and then looked toward Annabelle. "Well, I suppose I should let you get back to your bees."

"Inspector, have you made any progress? Have you looked into Sir John Cartwright's background, at all?"

The Inspector's face stiffened. "Yes."

"And was there anything peculiar about him? I ask, because, he's still very much a mystery to many of the village residents."

"Well, I wouldn't normally say this to a civilian," said the Inspector, leaning toward Annabelle conspiratorially, causing her to breathe more deeply, "but he was actually quite well known to the police in London."

"Oh?"

"Apparently, he had been under suspicion for a few years, though never charged, of running a high-class – if you can call it that – escort agency."

"Golly gosh!"

"Indeed. Not the sort of thing you would usually hear about in a place like this."

"No... I mean, yes... I mean..."

"Vicar?"

"Remember the rumors I told you about?"

"Of course."

"Well, that's almost exactly *it*. I thought it was utter nonsense. People watching too many television shows, but I suppose there was some truth to them."

"Truth to what? I'm not following, Vicar."

Annabelle took a deep breath before continuing. "People were saying all manner of things about him, much of it complete poppycock. But one of the things that kept cropping up was this idea that he had moved into Wood-lands Manor with the intent of turning it into a brothel."

"I see," said the Inspector, nodding gently.

"I suppose someone had heard about his past, and that's where the gossip began. But I never expected there to be any truth to it. It seems so implausible."

"Well, Vicar, when you've done this job for as long as I have, you learn just how unbelievable the truth can turn out to be."

"But a *Sir?* Is that how he made his fortune? Prostitution?"

"I doubt it. My guess would be he fell into it. A respected member of high society. Trusted. He's the guy you'd want to buy from, if you're into that sort of thing. He saw a gap in the market and decided to fill it, as it were," the Inspector said, nonchalantly, before holding his hand up in apology. "Sorry, Vicar. I don't mean to sound crude."

"Oh, of course not," giggled Annabelle, "I may be a person of the cloth, but I'm not a prude. Uh, I mean... Not that I approve of such things... Well, the paying part. That's the part I disapprove of... Not the..." Annabelle stammered, before deciding to stop digging by getting back on topic. "Do you think that he was really planning to open some kind of brothel here in Upton St. Mary, then?"

The Inspector sucked air through his gritted teeth. "Perhaps. If he was, we could pretty much pin a motive on every member of the village. On the other hand, if you were looking to make a fresh start, I can't think of many other places that would be better than Upton St. Mary."

"Indeed."

"Did you hear anything else interesting about the dead man?"

"I don't think so. A story about a werewolf getting him."

The Inspector laughed, which sent Annabelle's heart aflutter once again. "Like I said, I never rule anything out!"

They chuckled together for a few moments, before the Inspector reached into his large trench coat and pulled out a folded piece of paper.

"Well, since you're officially a member of the investigation team now..."

"Really?" exclaimed Annabelle, with all the naivety of a pre-pubescent girl.

"Just a joke," the Inspector carefully assured her.

"Oh."

"But since you're so interested in the details, you might want to know that I received the autopsy report this morning," he said, handing Annabelle the sheet of paper. "Nothing surprising. He was in good health, as you'd expect from a man who meditates. Died from a lacerated lung and heart failure brought on by a puncture wound. It does confirm the time of death, though. Just as Harper predicted, he died well before you found him. So that's the easy explanation gone; that the scream came from Sir John himself."

Annabelle perused the medical information, nodding her head to make it seem like she understood the arrangements of numbers, abbreviations, and terminology.

"I see," she said, after a full two minutes, handing the sheet back to the Inspector.

"Well," sighed the Inspector, with an air of finality, "I've dilly-dallied long enough. I should be off."

"Of course, Inspector. Sorry for keeping you."

"No problem. You've given me more help than you realize. Be careful, Vicar."

The Inspector got into his car, and waved at Annabelle as he backed out of the driveway and sped through the church gates.

"See you soon!" shouted Annabelle, when he was already long gone.

She turned on her heels, ready to return to her bees, and found Philippa standing right in front of her, a wry grin breaking the wrinkles that crisscrossed her face.

CHAPTER FOUR

THE WOMAN WHO sat in the second-floor tea room of the Athenaeum hotel in London projected an aura of movie-star glamor and refined taste. Her cream-colored pencil skirt accentuated both the slim contours and incredible length of her crossed legs, which were tipped by a pair of pastel blue, high-heeled shoes. Above her loose-fitting grey blouse, her delicate neck was turned demurely toward the window, and her emerald eyes peered indifferently down her thin nose at the London traffic. With her blond hair pinned upward into a tight bun, she cut a statuesque and manicured figure, as precisely engineered and as effortlessly timeless as the leather upholstery and thick, regal pillars of the luxurious tea room. She extended her long, slender fingers, picked up the sculpted teacup, and brought it to her crimson lips with the grace of royalty, sipping silently before replacing the cup with a gesture both casual and quick.

As if sensing her presence, she cast her eyes toward the entrance of the room and saw another woman enter. Though not as slim or as tall as the seated figure, this new woman walked with just as much elegance, seeming to glide over the soft carpet in black shoes that perfectly comple-mented her bright red dress. She eased herself into a leather chair opposite the woman in the cream skirt. The two of them exchanged the wry smirks of acknowledgement only friends of many decades, and frequent meetings could. The newcomer had a dark complexion. Her brown, almond-shaped eyes and black-brown hair that cascaded in waves around shoulders led many to the assumption of Latin heritage. She tossed her head gently, with the haughty nobility of a racehorse, causing glimmers of light to shake and settle along the silky curves of her mane.

"Did you come to take tea," said the first woman, nodding subtly toward the ample cleavage revealed by the second's red dress, "or to seduce it?"

"Inner beauty is of no use," replied the other, "unless you reveal it on occasion."

As their smiles grew, the woman in the red dress gestured a waiter over. He was a smartly-dressed man in his twenties, well used to the meticulous manner and strong personas of the Athenaeum's élite clientele. But even he found his sense of confidence and propriety diminished in the presence of such formidable and sharp women. Though their easy demeanor and natural class belied the fact they were in their forties, they were no less filled with a dangerous and pointed energy that was scary to those who couldn't match their wits. After taking her order, he spun on his heel and returned to the bar as quickly as he could, lest they notice his sense of embarrassment.

"You may wish to order something a little stronger, dear Sophie. Something unpalatable has occurred. I'm still strug-gling to digest it myself," the first woman said, picking up a newspaper from the table and handing it to the woman in the red dress. After shooting her a quizzical glance, Sophie took the newspaper and read it in the pale morning light that seeped through the thick panes of the window. Once she had read the column, she tossed it upon the table and looked at her companion.

"John Cartwright is dead?" she stated, in disbelief.

"Murdered. By an archer."

"It's positively Shakespearean."

"It's why I prefer knights to be in shining armor."

"Do archers really exist?"

"In abundance. I am a persistent target of darting glances."

"If knighthoods can still exist in this day and age, I suppose archers can, too."

"Despite chivalry being dead."

They giggled gently as the waiter brought Sophie's order, and after a quick nod of assurance, was sent back on his way.

"This is a cause for concern though, Gabriella. What of our investment?" asked Sophie, bringing her voice down a notch to indicate the seriousness of her inquiry.

"I was just considering it," replied the demure woman, tapping her elegant fingers against the chair's armrest anxiously. "Our first aim should be to recoup our finances."

Sophie nodded, then shook her lustrous hair and pressed a finger against her thick lips.

"The situation is still very much unknown, however. No suspect. No conviction," Sophie uttered.

"Indeed. Not to mention peculiar. Especially for such a quaint and traditional place as Upton St. Mary."

"In which mild-mannered residents are no doubt in a state of unrest and confusion at this alien occurrence," Sophie quipped, drolly.

Their eyes lit up as they simultaneously sipped from their tea cups. After a few moments, Gabriella's lips formed a dry smile.

"I do believe we are, as ever, thinking the same thing, my dear Sophie," said Gabriella, in the sparkling tone she used whenever something mischievous was on her mind.

"That such dramatic affairs of murder and conspiracy are better left to a pair of keenly devilish women, than the gentle, kind – and thus ill-suited – people who reside in that Arcadian corner of the kingdom known as Cornwall?"

"And that this pair of inquisitive – and no doubt refined – coupling of talents would be best served in their endeavors by entering the sleepy village stealthily and under cover."

Sophie's eyes widened, and she leaned forward in glee.

"Are you suggesting, dearest Gabriella, a little game of dress-up?" Sophie said, playfully slapping her hands against her knees.

"You know too well, Sophie, that I need only the slightest excuse."

"It would certainly allow us to ease into the daily machinations of village life and discover everything we can from the colloquial gossip."

"Absolutely. I don't see a more efficient manner in which we can extract our investment without drawing unwanted attention to ourselves," Gabriella said, in a mockingly serious tone.

"And which type of sheep's clothing should we adorn ourselves with?"

"Why, it's obvious, is it not? Two wealthy women, visiting a deliciously British village, invading the privacy of others in the spirit of haphanded curiosity."

"Tourists!" they said, in near-perfect unison.

They laughed heartily together. Sophie's musical and rich laugh offering a pitch-perfect counterpoint to Gabriella's delicately high-pitched giggles. Once the humor of the moment had died down, Gabriella said: "That brings me to ask: Where shall we claim to be tourists from?"

"An interesting question," replied Sophie, pursing her lips as she considered the options. "Germany?"

"Darling, my fashion sense is far too good. How about Italian?"

"I certainly have the look," said Sophie, gesturing toward her thick, dark hair, "but I struggle to imagine why an Italian would be interested in any other place on Earth."

"True," replied Gabriella, "Australians, perhaps?"

"I don't drink nearly enough," Sophie said, "and I'd prefer not to wear a backpack everywhere. Russian, maybe."

"No, no. The aim is to *deflect* attention, not attract it."

"Americans?" Sophie put forward, cautiously.

"Too stereotypical. Besides, people would assume we've just been waylaid on the way to Paris or London."

"Well, how about French?"

Gabriella pondered for a few moments, before turning back toward Sophie and nodding slightly.

"Yes. I do speak French, after all."

"It would provide the perfect opportunity to utilize our wardrobes," Sophie added.

"And establish our credentials as exotic femme fatales."

"Good," Gabriella said, with finality, "it's settled."

"*Allez!*"

Try as she might, Annabelle could not take her mind off the murder. Since the Inspector had driven away, leaving her with plenty of startling new information, she had tried to keep her hands and mind busy. She thrust herself heartily into her typical weekend routine: tending to her bees, studying the scripture, and doing her very best to persuade Biscuit to play with her. Unfortunately, she failed miserably – both in distracting herself and in provoking Biscuit's interest.

"Oh, do come on, Biscuit! Look! I've bought you a brand new toy! Surely you're tempted to at least sniff it," she said in a sing-song voice, dangling the scratchy ball in front of the ginger cat's thousand-yard stare. "It's even got catnip in it!"

"There's no playing with that cat," came Philippa's voice, as she gathered her coat from the doorway, ready to leave, "she does everything on her own terms."

"Come on, girl! Don't be shy!" persisted Annabelle.

"I'll see you tomorrow, Vicar," Philippa said, as she closed the door behind her.

"'Bye, Philippa!" Annabelle turned her attention back to the orange tabby in front of her.

"No? Perhaps if I just leave the toy in front of you," Annabelle said, placing the ball between Biscuit's tiny paws. "I'll just go into the other room and leave you to investigate it."

Annabelle stepped across the living room, left the room, and stamped her feet a few times to simulate walking away. She counted to ten, then peeked slowly around the doorway, hoping to find Biscuit joyfully pawing at her new purchase.

Instead, Biscuit turned her head toward the Vicar with an expression Annabelle interpreted as extremely condescending.

"That's it!" she exclaimed, grabbing her hat and gloves.

"You're no entertainment at all. I'm off. I'm sure I'll be of more use to the Inspector than I will be to you."

She threw on her favorite red and black-checkered coat and grabbed her keys.

"Oh, and Philippa is right, you are becoming terribly fat!" she said in a huff, as she left the house, locked the door, and marched toward her car.

Annabelle drove without pleasure, her hanging questions regarding the murder intensifying. She liked things to be clear, ordered, proper – and so far nothing about the horrific death of Sir John Cartwright was as she liked it.

The stormy weather of her thoughts was so intoxicating, that as she pulled in to the long driveway of Woodlands Manor, she almost failed to notice the car heading in her direction. As it drew close enough for her to discern its driver, her mood quickly cleared.

"Hello, Inspector!" she said, as they pulled up close to each other and rolled down their windows.

"Hi, Vicar. Surprised to see you here."

"I just thought I'd drop by to see if a visit might jog any important memories I might have forgotten in all the fuss."

"Good idea," the Inspector nodded, "but the house is all locked up now. We've been looking over the crime scene again. The SOCO team have been and gone, I'm the last to leave. I might come back tomorrow, but I don't really see a reason to at present."

"Have you discovered anything new?" asked Annabelle.

The Inspector sighed. "Nothing too extraordinary. Apparently the arrow that killed the dead man didn't come from an ordinary bow."

"Oh?"

"It came from a crossbow of some sort."

"Oh dear. Those things are the devil," said Annabelle.

"Yeah. It also somewhat throws off our projections regarding where the murderer shot from. Crossbows are more accurate than simple, straightforward bows, meaning that the shooter could really have been standing anywhere."

"That's incredibly strange," mused Annabelle.

"How so?" the Inspector asked.

"Well, archery with a typical bow and arrow is a fairly well practiced sport in this area. It would make some amount of sense to assume that was the weapon. But I've yet to see a crossbow used anywhere in the locality."

The Inspector chuckled grimly. "It seems like this case just gets harder rather than easier."

Annabelle decided to keep her thoughts to herself and bid the Inspector farewell. He rolled his window back up and drove off, leaving Annabelle to close in on the fountain that was by now becoming rather too familiar for her own taste.

As she got out of the Mini and began making her way around the house, Annabelle mulled over the idea that she had refrained from telling the Inspector. Archery was a popular pastime in and around the village. As a predominantly male-dominated pursuit, archery skills were often passed down from father to son, a popular excuse for some male bonding between generations as much as between old friends. It was unlikely that somewhere along the line, the community of close-knit archers had suddenly embraced the crossbow – a much more brutal and ugly weapon, which required none of the finesse or skill of the traditional bow.

It was entirely possible, of course, that someone in the village had taken up the more effective, machine-like crossbow, but Annabelle had never come across it. She had visited almost all of the homes in the village, seen many a proud huntsman display his fine weapons in pride of place on a mantel or wall frame, and observed the camouflage-clad hunters rambunctiously set off for a day of hunting bearing their weapons across their backs. Not once had she seen one of them use, own, or even mention a crossbow, however. The conclusion she came to was an unnerving one; the murderer must have come from outside the village.

As she turned a corner and found herself behind the house, in the area that the murderer must have been near or nearabouts, Annabelle looked back toward the house and was struck by yet another revelation. The murderer may not have planned it! Annabelle noticed that all the windows, including the one at which Sir John was meditating when he was killed, were now closed. The windows presented an obvious obstacle to a successful murder attempt. No matter how thunderous a shot from a crossbow, the trajectory, as well as the power, would have been too unpredictable for the murderer to have shot through a closed window. That meant that the murderer *needed* the window to be open in order to carry out the killing.

While it was possible that the murderer knew of Sir John Cartwright's penchant for meditating in front of open windows, a slightly chilly day, or the type of brief rains England was known for would have caused him to close the window and set the murderer's plans askew. Perhaps the murderer had visited the site day after day, in anticipation of the perfect circumstances – Sir John's eyes-closed meditation, an open window, and no onlookers. But Annabelle found the scenario of forethought and planning unlikely, given that Sir John had only resided in Woodlands Manor for barely over a week.

It wasn't concrete, but Annabelle felt like she was beginning to find the slimmest of threads to follow. She had been reluctant to tell the Inspector her idea for it was merely a belief. As a vicar, however, she knew how powerful belief could be. Annabelle turned her attention to the unkempt ground where the dense woods met the manicured lawns at the rear of the house. She stepped carefully forward, intently searching every peculiar stone and suspicious mound for something tangible. After searching for a whole hour and feeling the oncoming chill of evening, Annabelle turned back toward the front of the house. Despite the fruitlessness of her search, she left resolved to come back, a stirring hope that with enough effort she would find the key to this puzzle.

Over the next few days, Annabelle returned to the large manor house several times. She came equipped with a set of binoculars and a moleskin notepad in which she scribbled everything of note. Before her second "expedition," she called Harper Jones and quizzed the talented pathologist for everything she knew. After the briefest of explanations, Harper was surprisingly forthcoming with enough details to fill an entire page of Annabelle's notebook. They were all technical and complicated, however. Math had been a favorite subject of Annabelle's, but even she struggled to understand more than half of the calculations and measurements Harper offered her. Despite this apparent obstacle, Annabelle prevailed. As she traipsed through the woods, armed with a flask of tea under one arm and her binoculars in the other, she tried her very best to triangulate where the murderer had fired that fatal shot from.

Though she was on the trail of a cold-blooded killer, Annabelle could not hold herself back from enjoying her surroundings. She delighted in the bird songs and stately beauty of the trees. She found herself stooping constantly to observe a patterned butterfly or a spider weaving an intricate web between two logs. She felt herself relax and focus in the presence of God's creation. Apart from a slight scare when something rustled hurriedly in some nearby bushes, the hours she spent in the woods were good for her soul, if not her investigation. While she felt that she was getting somewhat closer to the truth, Harper's calculations still proved too abstract for her, and she eventually left, slightly disappointed but no less determined.

The next day, Annabelle once again packed her binoculars and her notebook and took a small detour on her way to Woodlands Manor. Mr. Squires was one of the keenest archers in Upton St. Mary and one of the most trustworthy people Annabelle knew. He was an older gentleman who always wore clothes of deep farmer's green. He possessed a thick, grey mustache that lent him the air of an old wartime general and when he invited Annabelle into his office, she saw it was adorned with old leather-bound books and watercolor paintings of various hunting scenes. After begging his discretion, which he assuredly gave, Annabelle showed him Harper's calculations and the dimensions of the scene of the crime.

For a little over an hour, Mr. Squires regaled the intently observant Vicar on archery, crossbows, and the distance-power ratios you could expect from various weapons. He troubled to give her full explanations of all the factors involved including wind, weights, the kind of arrows used, and the skill of its user. His explanations were most comprehensive and Annabelle left Mr. Squires extremely grateful, feeling that she knew more than she ever needed or intended to know about the centuries-old pastime.

When she found herself back in the woods, Annabelle

applied everything she knew, taking great care to incorpo-rate all the information she had gathered from both Harper and Mr. Squires. After carefully cross-checking her notes multiple times and making many fine adjustments, she finally found herself standing a few dozen yards away from the edge of the woods. She was on a mild incline, surrounded by a handful of trees that hid her almost completely but also afforded a clear view – and a straight shot – into Sir John Cartwright's window.

"This has to be it!" she exclaimed to herself as she checked her calculations once more, ensuring there were no mistakes. "It certainly *feels* like a murderer's spot." Some-thing about the spot was secretive and sinister. It was an area of the woods that would be perfect if one wanted to be hidden. Annabelle felt a shiver run up her spine. "Don't be silly, Annabelle."

Then came a sound. It was a rustle, of the kind Annabelle had heard the day before, and which she had assumed to come from a small woodland animal. Standing there, where a few days previously one person had ended the life of another, the sound took on an ominous weight. Annabelle crouched down to the ground, as silently as possible, her ears alert. Once again, the bushes rustled. Annabelle's blood rushed through her body, and she gripped her flask tightly with one hand, and in the other, her crucifix.

Annabelle turned around slowly, looking for the cause of the sound. As she rotated almost a complete circle, the sound came once more from directly behind her. Only this time, it didn't stop. Annabelle spun back around so quickly that she slipped on the soft soil and tumbled backwards. She shut her eyes and screamed as the rustling grew so loud it was now mere inches away from her. "Our father, who art in heaven, hallowed be thy na –" Annabelle muttered, quickly and quietly, until she felt something press against her leg and opened her eyes in horror. "Biscuit!"

"Meow," came the cat's sardonic reply.

Annabelle reached out and stroked the cat's head, as if unable to believe the source of her terror was none other than the church cat. Biscuit, in an atypically forthright gesture, pressed her head against the Vicar's hand.

"What on earth are you doing so far from the church? We're almost two miles away!"

Annabelle picked the cat up and cuddled it to her chest. Biscuit licked her face, causing Annabelle to double-check that it was, actually, Biscuit.

"I do believe all this drama is driving me quite mad and more than a little hungry. I'd like one of Philippa's cupcakes so much I can already smell it," Annabelle joked, as she placed the cat on the ground, stood up, and brushed off her slacks.

After a few moments of adjusting her clothes, picking her notebook up from the dirt and tucking it away into her pocket, Annabelle clipped her flask to her waistband and looked around at the sodden dirt of the area.

"I suppose we'll have to look for clues together now, Biscuit," she said, as she concentrated her eyes upon the area.

Unfortunately, the heavy rainfall of the previous night had flattened and soaked the earth, leaving only the markings and footprints Annabelle had made herself. As she carefully walked back and forth, desperately seeking something that could cast some more light onto the secret of the murderer's identity, her heart began to sink.

"Oh, Biscuit. I'm starting to think all of my efforts have been for naught," Annabelle sighed, deflated, "though I suppose the Inspector will be interested in knowing where the murderer was when he fired the shot. Don't you, Biscuit?"

Annabelle glanced around, failing to see the ginger cat.

"Biscuit? *Biscuit?*" she said, rushing forward.

She turned her head once more and noticed the tabby cat crouching next to the two trees through which the arrow must have flown. Annabelle turned her attention toward the ground, taking one last look in search of clues.

"I need the bathroom myself, actually," Annabelle said, looking upwards at the encroaching darkness. "I think it's time we went home. Come on."

Biscuit, however, was not yet ready to leave the murderer's den. The ginger cat began pawing at the ground, spraying clumps of dirt in order to disguise her scent, as cats are wont to do. Annabelle waited patiently for the cat to finish. She looked once again toward Sir John's window, then back at the cat. Suddenly, she noticed something small and whitish-brown sticking out of the earth that the cat had uncovered.

"What's this? What have you found, Biscuit?" she said, gently nudging the cat aside and pulling the cigarette butt from the ground. She rubbed the dirt away and peered closely at it. Upon realizing that the discovery was a mere cigarette butt, Annabelle's shoulders slumped in disappointment. A moment before tossing it away, however, she began to wonder. In her now numerous trips to the woods, she had not noticed litter of any kind, let alone cigarette butts. The hunters of the village were as proud of the woods as their wives were of their homes, and they did their utmost to preserve its immaculate condition. Biscuit had also uncovered the cigarette butt in the *precise* position that the murderer would have stood. It was a spot unsuitable for hunting anything other than a certain Sir John Cartwright.

Annabelle studied the cigarette butt further, noticing how fresh and clean it looked. It certainly didn't bear the worn look of something that had been in the rain for longer than a week, and unless Inspector Nicholls' officers had snuck off into the woods for a sneaky smoke, she concluded it may very well be the murderer's. She placed the butt carefully into her pocket, picked Biscuit up, and strode purposefully back toward her car. The thread was getting stronger.

It was almost dark by the time the Vicar pulled up beside her home. The village by night was a serene place. The lights of the cottage windows twinkled as sporadically as the stars in the clear night sky above. With the exception of the raucous bouts of laughter and occasional music from the pub, the air hung so silently that you could hear the owl calls for miles. Annabelle got out of her Mini, quickly followed by Biscuit, who disappeared into the shadows to conduct her nightly affairs. Annabelle entered the warmth of her kitchen.

"A cup of tea and bed for me," Annabelle said, with a gentle sigh. It had been a long day.

Just as she was removing her coat, however, the phone rang. Annabelle closed her eyes, groaned, and picked up the receiver.

"Hello?"

"Hello, Vicar."

It was Philippa.

"It's rather late, Philippa. Is something wrong?"

"Not at all, Vicar," she said, a little too brightly. "I just wanted to see how you were."

"Oh. Well, thank you. I'm rather pleased, actually. I believe I've gained some intriguing insight into the murder."

"Now, don't concern yourself so much with this. It's a job for professionals. You already push yourself so hard."

"I appreciate your thoughts, Philippa. Really, I'm absolutely fine. I'll rest well and good once the murderer has been found."

"I'm sure you will, Vicar. I'm sure you will."

"Thank you, Philippa. Is that all?"

"I was reading this thing, Vicar," Philippa said, causing Annabelle to roll her eyes. This conversation was not going to end soon, she felt.

"What thing was that?"

"It was about kleptomania. Do you know what that is, Vicar?"

"I'm not terribly sure I do, Philippa," replied Annabelle.

"It's a disease. A psychological confliction. It's where someone is compelled to steal things. For no other reason than to steal them. And then lie about it."

"That sounds dreadful," exclaimed Annabelle, her confusion growing, "but why ever would you ask me about that? Do you know someone who has this... *affliction?*"

"Oh... Ah... Yes. Maybe I do."

"That's awful. I'm deeply sorry to hear that."

"What do you think I should do, Vicar?"

"Well, stealing is a sin, of course. But if this... *person* is doing so because of an affliction, well, I should think the most Christian thing to do would be to extend our compassion and to forgive."

"Hmm," said Philippa, "I had a feeling you would say that."

"Would you like me to speak to the person?"

"No, no, Vicar. That would be rather difficult. Thank you. That's all."

"Okay. Well. See you tomorrow, and sleep tight."

"You too, Vicar."

Annabelle hung the phone up, and wondered why she sometimes found investigating a murder more straightforward than talking to Philippa.

CHAPTER FIVE

TIME PASSED BY in the village of Upton St. Mary much the same as it always had, filled with simple pleasures and satisfyingly dependable routines. But talk of the murder showed no sign of abating. With much of the village still in the dark as to the nature of the killing as well as the killer, the joys of speculation still had plenty of mileage. Annabelle told the Inspector of what she had discovered, taking a guilty sense of pleasure from his vocal gratitude. When she handed him the cigarette butt found at the location from where the killer had likely fired his fatal shot, Inspector Nicholls was almost lost for words. Philippa had always told her that "the way to a man's heart is helping him do his job better!"

The Vicar had detected a sense of reticence on behalf of the Inspector, however. It had been almost two weeks since the murder, and he was beginning to worry about the trail going cold. If Annabelle was right, and the killer was not from Upton St. Mary, then he (or she) would have had plenty of time to get away. DNA test or not, the longer they went without a clear suspect, the harder it would be to discover the killer's identity. Unfazed by the Inspector's pessimism, Annabelle was certain that the key to the murder was just within reach – and when her Sunday service rolled around, she was proved right.

The open-top Jaguar's slinky curves reflected the trees and hedgerows that whipped past as it hurtled down the country lanes toward Upton St. Mary. At the wheel, her hair flowing magnificently behind her, was Sophie, joyfully guiding the car. The long form of Gabriella was stretched out in the passenger seat, an arm nonchalantly hanging out of the window and another clutching her purple beret to her head.

Sophie drove the car around what looked like the ruins of a castle and brought the car to a slow stop in order to allow a farmer and his sheep across the road. She winked at the farmer, causing him to raise his eyebrows and smile as he urged the sheep forward.

"Such a spiritual part of the world, isn't it?" she said, as she watched the happily bleating sheep.

"Unquestionably," replied Gabriella, "I've often considered taking a home in the country."

"*You?*" exclaimed Sophie, in a tone of utter surprise. "I find it difficult to imagine you living anywhere but within ten miles of Harrods."

"Harrods won't go anywhere. London is always nearby, wherever in the world you are."

"And what, pray tell, would a lady of such sophistication and fine tastes actually *do* in this rural paradise?"

Gabriella gazed upwards in a gesture of deep thought. "I'm sure I could make my own entertainment. If it's good enough for the Queen, it just might suffice for me. The clean air and local produce would be wonderful for the skin, too."

"And who should I call upon for tea when you are gone?"

"Oh darling! I'd take you with me of course. I shall probably require a milk maid!"

"How incredibly cheeky of you!" grinned Sophie, as she put the car in first gear and drove away.

Eventually, the two women arrived in the village of Upton St. Mary, and like travelers of old, were almost magnetically drawn to its highest, most visible, point – the church spire. As Sophie swept the car up the tightly-packed village streets, they noticed the crowd of smartly-dressed people heading toward the church's old iron gates.

"I do believe we're in time for communion," Gabriella said.

"A church service? But we've only just arrived!"

"Why not? Churches are the pillar of such small communities. I cannot think of a better way to ingratiate ourselves into the daily life of the village."

Sophie raised a curious eyebrow at her friend. "You may be better suited to the country life than I suspected."

Though Upton St. Mary was used to tourists and visitors of many kinds, the two women, with their fine clothes and haughty dispositions, drew more than a few conspicuous glances and whispers. They took their places at the very back of the church and proceeded to mouth the words to the hymns and listen intently to the captivatingly refreshing lady vicar.

Once the service was finished, they milled around with the rest of the congregation, finding themselves ushered outside with the rest of the sizable crowd. Expecting to engage with whoever was curious enough to ask them who they were, they were surprised when the Vicar herself made a beeline for the newcomers.

"Hello! I'm the vicar of St. Mary's. Do call me Annabelle. It's always nice to receive new visitors."

"Oh," fumbled Sophie, "Bonjour."

"French?" Annabelle said, before pressing a finger to her lips as she tried to remember the French classes she took at school. "Let's see. *Ma Francaise c'nest bien pas, mais je comprend un petit peu.*"

Sophie panicked at the assault of unfamiliar words and looked desperately at Gabriella to save her.

"We speak English," Gabriella said, giving her voice a slight French accent. "It's okay, Vicar."

"Oh, good!" Annabelle said, clapping her hands together. "I haven't spoken French since I was a young girl! Such a beautiful language, though. I take it you are both tourists?"

"Yes. Zisiz se troof," Sophie spoke in an accent so forced it sounded more like a speech impediment than French. "Ve are ze tourists. Zeriz no miztake."

Annabelle turned her head, casting her perplexed gaze at both of the women. Sophie glared at Gabriella, begging her to save the moment.

"Yes, well, tourists with business to do," Gabriella said, confidently.

"I see," mused Annabelle. She found herself growing suspicious of these two bizarrely obtuse women, one of whom spoke in an accent that was unlike any she had ever heard and the other far too self-assured to be a tourist, the like of which Cornwall hosted on an ongoing basis. "I take it you've just arrived?"

"Yez," Sophie said.

Annabelle had to know what these women wanted. Even if it wasn't connected to the murder, she had been cautious and watchful of everything since it had happened.

"My house is just over there. I insist you join me for a spot of lunch. I'd like to do everything I can to make your visit a pleasurable and memorable, one."

"Thank you so very kindly, Vicar," said Gabriella, urging her friend toward the house.

Fifteen minutes later, after the congregation had dispersed to their homes, the two women found themselves sitting around the table watching the Vicar pour hot cups of tea for them.

"I'm terribly sorry, but I didn't catch your names," Annabelle said.

"Francoise," Gabriella said, with as much French musicality as she could muster.

"S... So... Simone," Sophie stammered, with a sense of relief afterward.

"Welcome to Upton St. Mary, Francoise and Simone," Annabelle said, cheerfully.

Philippa burst into the room carrying plates of food. "I've prepared some sandwiches for your guests, Vicar," she said. "I've also had to make some more cupcakes," she added, looking at Annabelle as she said so.

"Wonderful," said Annabelle, oblivious to Philippa's pointed behaviour.

Sophie picked at a sandwich, took a bite, and said, "Magnifique!"

After they had begun sipping delicately at their tea and nibbling on their sandwiches, Annabelle casually questioned the two women.

"I would be more than happy to help you enjoy the treats of Upton St. Mary in any way I can."

"Thank you, Vicar."

"Oh, zis cat is adorable!" Sophie said, as Biscuit rubbed her body against her boot.

"That's Biscuit. She's actually very temperamental," Annabelle said, barely hiding the annoyance she felt that Biscuit was giving more attention to these strangers than she ever did to her.

"Que belle!"

"Perhaps I can help with this business concern you have," Annabelle said, trying to bring the conversation back on topic.

Gabriella glanced at Sophie.

"Yes. Indeed," Gabriella said. "As a vicar, you are most probable to help."

"Anything I can do," Annabelle said, warmly.

"Well, we learned of a friend's demise in this area. We wanted to pay our respects to the family if they were here?"

"I see," Annabelle said. "I'm sorry for the loss. Who was the poor soul, if I may be so bold to ask?"

"Zir Jean Cartwright," Sophie said, the abrasiveness of her accent changing the name "John" into its French counterpart – "Jean."

The shock of hearing the name caused Annabelle to spill the tea she was in the middle of bringing to her lips.

"Oh dear!" she sputtered, as politely as she could. "I do apologize!"

Annabelle excused herself and ran toward the kitchen, where Philippa was busy tidying up.

"Philippa!" she whispered, as excitedly as volume would allow.

"Yes, Vicar?"

"They're here about Sir John!" she said, pointing toward the door that led to the dining room.

Philippa dropped her tea towel on the counter and turned all of her attention toward the excited Vicar.

"Really?"

"Yes!" Annabelle said, nodding furiously. "They say they're French tourists, but there's something awfully queer about them."

Philippa ran toward the door and pressed her ear to it.

"What are you doing?"

Philippa put a finger to her lips to shush the Vicar, then gestured for Annabelle to join her.

Annabelle tip-toed to the door, and carefully placed her ear against the wood of the door.

"...respects? We would do better if we found that Poppy Franklin, first."

"Poppy Franklin?"

"You know! The impossibly young girl that John had lived with in London. There was a rumor he brought her here with him."

"But she was young enough to be his daughter!"

"She definitely wasn't old enough to be his friend!"

"Well, if she's here, I'm sure the Vicar will take us to her."

"I hope so. The Vicar seems like a bright sort."

"Your accent wouldn't fool her even if she wasn't."

"Oh shush, so long as we get to check out our investment..."

Annabelle nearly leaped back from the door. Philippa pulled back as well.

"Did you hear that?" mouthed Annabelle, struggling not to squeal her surprise.

"I knew there was something terribly wrong with that Sir John. Fancy that, a girl young enough to be his daughter."

"Oh Philippa, that's beside the point. These women aren't French at all! They're investors!"

"It's all very fishy."

"I should get back in there before they suspect something."

"Please be careful, Vicar."

Annabelle opened the door theatrically, in order to give the women enough time to prepare their Gallic act for her once more.

"I've just had a little chat with Philippa, the church secretary," she said, as Philippa followed her into the room. "She would be more than happy to make the arrangements for your stay. There's a delightful bed and breakfast nearby that offers everything you could possibly need."

"Oh, zat is kind, but ve do not need zis treatment."

"Please, I insist!" Annabelle said. "There's no point coming to Upton St. Mary if you can't appreciate our hospitality!"

Just before the two strangers left the Vicar's home, Annabelle pulled Philippa aside and said, "Make sure nothing they say goes further than your ears. This could be the key to the entire case."

"Oh, of course, Vicar. I won't tell a soul," Philippa assured her, before trotting off to lead the women to their temporary abode.

As Annabelle waved them off merrily, she remembered that Philippa had a crochet club meeting the next day. Annabelle sighed wearily. Her secret probably wouldn't last beyond Philippa's second row of chain stitch.

The man who sat in the interview room was tall and lean.

His leathered face held an expression of extreme distress. His hair was fair and thinning on top. He wore a tweed waistcoat and checked shirt with the ease only wealthy landowners could possess. Inspector Nicholls entered the room with a self-assured stride, took a seat opposite the man, and laid a file on the table in front of him.

"What is this? What is —" the man said, before the Inspector held up a finger to silence him.

The Inspector pressed a button on the tape recorder that had been placed on the edge of the table, and said: "Inspector Mike Nicholls, interviewing Harry Cooper. Sunday the fourteenth of September, two thirty-four PM."

The fair-haired man stammered but found his throat too dry to protest.

"You are Harry Cooper, correct?"

"Yes."

"You own the property known as Woodlands Manor, situated just off Arden Road, near the village of Upton St. Mary."

"Yes. Well, I did own it," he said, nervously. "I don't anymore. I sold it."

"To whom?"

"Sir John Cartwright. Why are you asking me this? You know this, surely?"

"Sir John Cartwright was murdered. Did you know that?"

"Yes. Of course. It was in the papers."

"Were you in or around the property on the day of the murder?"

"No! Absolutely not!"

The Inspector leaned back in his chair and looked at the suspect opposite him. The man was red-faced and fidgeting anxiously. He was clearly panicked, and the Inspector assumed he had never been placed under suspicion of any kind before.

Nicholls had conducted many interviews and knew with intimate familiarity the best approach. Suspects such as Harry Cooper were already on edge before a question had been asked. The question was, was it due to fear or guilt? Usually it took the right kind of pressure, applied with expert timing, to get to the truth. Thanks to Annabelle, however, the Inspector had a trump card.

"Do you smoke, Mr. Cooper?"

"Yes."

"You used to smoke at Woodlands Manor when you owned it?"

"Yes. Well, my wife never liked it, so I would smoke on the grounds."

"So you knew the grounds well."

"Of course. They were mine."

"You would know where you could be seen and where you couldn't. Where the secret places, locations you could enter unseen, were?"

"Well, yes."

"And you say you haven't been there since Sir John Cartwright moved in?"

"Well, no. I never said that. I've visited him."

"At Woodlands Manor?"

"Yes."

"And you smoked while you were there?"

"Yes. I did."

"Inside the property?"

"No. Outside, like I did when I owned the house."

"Why?"

"Well, John didn't like smoking either. He was very into health and fitness, as you'd expect."

The Inspector paused for a second.

"Why would I expect that?" he said.

"He was going to turn the property into a health spa."

Inspector Nicholls leaned further back in his chair and looked at Mr. Cooper, considering the information he had just given him. A few hours ago, the SOCO team had discovered Cooper's DNA on the cigarette Annabelle had found in the trees at Woodlands Manor. It seemed like a lock. Cooper was the man. He had been standing precisely at the spot where the arrow had been fired, and the cigarette butt proved that he had been there recently. He had visited Sir John frequently enough to know his movements, to plan his attack. And having sold him Woodlands Manor for an undoubtedly large sum of money, Inspector Nicholls was sure he could find some motive there – a deal that big usually came with one.

And yet, something wasn't right with this sweating, terrified person on the other side of the interview table. He was either very clever or very unfortunate. The inspector hadn't told Harry about the DNA and had given him the perfect opportunity to cover his tracks. But Harry hadn't taken it. He had just admitted to being at the property and smoking there.

"Inspector," said a voice from behind him, interrupting his thoughts. Nicholls turned to look into the face of Police Constable Chambers. "Phone call for you, it's urgent."

"More important than an interview?"

"It's the Vicar of Upton St. Mary," the officer replied.

"Okay," the Inspector said, stopping the tape recorder and getting up out of his chair.

Chambers led the Inspector to his desk and handed him the receiver.

"Annabelle?"

"Hello, Inspector Nicholls," came the Vicar's distinctly chirpy voice.

"I'm glad you called. I was just interviewing the man whose cigarette you found. A Mr. Harry Cooper."

"Oh, do you think he did it?"

"I don't know. I get the impression it's more complicated than it seems. He was actually the owner of Woodlands Manor before Sir John Cartwright bought it from him."

"That's very interesting."

"What's more interesting is that he believes Sir John was going to turn it into a health spa."

"Do you believe that, Inspector?"

"Actually, Vicar, I do. Sir John Cartwright may have been involved in criminal activities over the past decade, but he actually made his name in the field of leisure and fitness. I believe he bought Woodlands Manor for a fresh start rather than to turn it into a brothel, but that doesn't mean others will agree with me. It could still be our motive. The person who killed Sir John may have believed the rumors and not liked the idea of Woodlands Manor being turned into a brothel."

"There's someone else you should probably talk to about that," said Annabelle.

"Who?"

"Poppy Franklin. Sir John was living with her in London, and she may have come with him to Upton St. Mary."

"The blond girl you saw?"

"Most likely."

"Hold on, Vicar," the Inspector said, before turning to PC Chambers and asking him to run a check on the name. There was a pause while he waited for the results to come up on the computer screen. "She's actually supposed to be on parole. Was jailed a few years ago for petty theft, let off with a light sentence because her then-boyfriend had coerced her into it. Hmm... What do we have here? Seems like she was employed by John Cartwright shortly after leaving prison."

"Oh my!"

"I'll put a call out. We'll find her as soon as we can. Once again, Vicar, you have come to the rescue."

"Oh, think nothing of it. I only want to help," Annabelle said.

"I'm going to owe you once this is done."

"Well, there is one thing, Inspector."

"What is it?"

"I'd really like to take a look inside Woodlands Manor once more. I know it's a crime scene, but I'd only need a few minutes. I have a theory..."

"Think nothing of it, Vicar. The SOCO team has finished up there, so it's just locked up and gathering dust. Constable Jim Raven has the key. I'll have him drop it off to you."

"Oh, that's ever so kind of you, Inspector! I suppose I will owe you as well," Annabelle said, coyly.

Annabelle could not bear to wait any longer. She sat at the kitchen table, head resting on her hand, her other hand drumming against the table anxiously. Gazing out of the window that looked up the church driveway, waiting for Constable Jim Raven's police car to pull up alongside her house, she allowed her mind to wander over her conversation with the Inspector. She hadn't told the Inspector about the two female investors, thinking that it might be more prudent to wait patiently and learn more about them. Currently, she knew little more than what she had heard from the other side of the kitchen door but things were beginning to fall into place. The arrival of the "French" investors and the revelation that the cigarette had been smoked by Woodlands Manor's previous owner had thrown up a whole host of new questions. But they had also provided plenty of answers.

With Philippa keeping a close eye on the two women and Inspector Nicholls on the hunt for Poppy Franklin, Annabelle was left to muse over the one question with which she had been struggling. Who had screamed when she had knocked on the door a second time? Her mind had conceived of and ruled out dozens of possibilities, from the idea that it had been an animal (it hadn't, Annabelle knew very well what animals sounded like), to some kind of "death groan." Harper herself had dismissed this as ludicrous when Annabelle posited the idea to her. Annabelle was so wrapped up in her questions that when the good Constable rolled into her driveway she afforded him only a distinctly British balance of politeness and briskness before setting off on her way.

As soon as she got there, Annabelle entered the manor house and slowly made her way up the stairs to the master bedroom. Had she been any less focused on every detail of the impressive building, she might have been frightened. Entering a large, empty house that had been the scene of a murder was something only the very brave or the very determined do. Annabelle's curiosity had given her an abundance of both.

She entered the room that had played at the edges of her mind for weeks and was surprised. It seemed larger than it had previously when her focus had been dominated by the shocking figure of Sir John's body on the floor. Now that her eyes allowed her to study the room, it felt lighter and a lot more spacious. After looking over the room for any object that could have made the sound, such as an unseen speaker or discreet TV, Annabelle decided to investigate the other rooms on the second floor. Though she was concentrating on her goal of finding the secret to the "bedroom screamer," Annabelle still found herself taken aback by how beautiful the house was. There were roughly a dozen rooms of all shapes and sizes shooting off from the second floor passage, from elaborate, luxurious parlor rooms filled with antiquities to tastefully arranged bathrooms with wonderfully preserved fittings.

Annabelle cooed her appreciation at the wonder of the house, then refocused herself on the goal at hand. She re-entered the master bedroom and stood precisely where the body of Sir John Cartwright had been brutally slain.

"Right. Let's see."

It was, of course, entirely plausible that the scream had come from another of the many rooms on the second floor. Yet Annabelle's intuition would not let her consider it. The scream had been shocking, quick, aggressive. It sounded primal, like death itself. Not until she had entirely ruled out the possibility of the scream occurring in the master bedroom would Annabelle allow herself to consider the alternatives.

"How would the screamer leave the room so quickly?" Annabelle whispered to herself.

The first possibility was, of course, the window. But upon opening it and looking down across the face of the building, Annabelle dismissed the idea completely. Not only was the drop leg-breakingly long and the outside wall slippery and steep, but also the ground surrounding the building was lush with bushes and fauna. Even if the screamer had made his way down the wall safely, he would surely have left noticeable signs of his descent.

The other escape route was the bedroom door, and though there had been a few seconds between the scream and Annabelle reaching the staircase, enough time for the person to enter one of the other rooms, the door itself had been locked. Annabelle studied the locking mechanism of the door closely. It was old and well-worn. She remembered how it had given way when she had applied pressure to it. Stranger still, she discovered that when the door was slammed shut, it would lock itself – such was the weakness in the ancient mechanism.

For a brief moment, Annabelle thought she had cracked it but then realized that should the screamer have slammed the door upon his hasty escape, she would have heard it. Even in her heightened state of fear and excitement rushing up the stairs, she wouldn't have missed the sound of the slamming door. As exemplified by the scream itself, sound traveled very well in the large house. Annabelle felt frustrated and deflated. Perhaps she would never figure it out. Then she noticed the bathroom door.

She opened the door expecting to find something impressive, and yet was still stunned by what she saw. The master bathroom was huge! Larger even than her living room! She stepped onto the marble flooring, marveling at the extravagance on display. Along one wall, there were two vast sinks with a framed mirror set into the wall above them. In one corner, a shower stall big enough for four people ascended from the marble flooring to the high ceiling. In the center of the bathroom, in the dappled light that poured in through the frosted window, was a porcelain and cast-iron bath set upon four elaborately engraved feet.

Once Annabelle had regained her breath, she scanned the walls and discovered exactly what she had expected. Another entrance. She marched toward it, cast one last longing look at the opulent bathroom, opened the small, plain door, and went through it. Annabelle found herself in a slim, barren passage, far more rough and dirty than any other part of the house she had seen.

"A servant's entrance," she said to herself. "This must have been how they transported household items to the masters of the house."

Annabelle imagined how many people must have scurried up and down this bare-walled passage, loaded with buckets of hot water for the bath or coal for the parlor's fireplace. She explored it carefully, opening doors that poked into various rooms of the house, many of which she hadn't even noticed when exploring the house from the other side. Eventually, Annabelle found herself descending rugged stone steps that seemed to delve even deeper than the house itself. Sure enough, the cold, blank walls of the house's secret passage gave way to the textured stone of a vast coal cellar. Though there was barely any light, the Vicar continued onwards through the thick, dusty air and long forgotten cobwebs. Somewhere to her right, she could see a vague glow, and she let it guide her out of the coal cellar and down a long tunnel where wooden rafters held up the stone.

The glow grew larger and larger with each of the Vicar's careful steps, until she recognized it as a large entrance. She put some haste into her gait and was astonished to find that the entrance emerged all the way out in the woods!

"This must be where coal and firewood deliveries were

made," she said. "The perfect getaway for the mysterious screamer. I'm sure to find a road nearby."

She left the stone tunnel behind, breathed in the cool, clean air, and was struck by a strangely familiar smell. Once again, Annabelle focused her senses and walked slowly forward in search of information – only this time it was her nose guiding her, not her curiosity.

The smell intensified, and Annabelle could not shake the sensation that this was something she knew well. Something that she liked. It reminded her of her kitchen. Of tea. Of...cupcakes! Annabelle looked down at the ground and saw, barely a few yards away, a stash of stale, nibbled-upon cupcakes, in precisely the same shape as the walnut delights Philippa had made earlier. The Vicar picked the freshest one up and sniffed it. There was no mistake. The cake was one that the church secretary herself had made.

"Surely not! This is from the very batch she made today!" She prodded at the remainder of the pile. "And these at the bottom must have been made weeks ago – on the day of the murder!" Annabelle said, finding the words she was saying too incredible to understand. "I don't believe it! Philippa is involved in this!"

As her blue Mini rolled into the driveway of the church, Annabelle noticed a light on in her house and wasn't sure if she was pleased or afraid of confronting Philippa just then. She parked the car, breathed deeply, and stepped inside.

"Hello, Vicar," Philippa said, as she wiped her hands on her apron. "I was just washing the church bowls. I'll be done in a jiffy."

"Actually, Philippa," Annabelle said, in a solemn tone, "I'd like to speak with you."

"Oh," Philippa said, noticing the seriousness of the Vicar's speech, a tone she reserved for bad news alone, "I see."

Annabelle took her coat and gloves off and put them away while Philippa took off her apron. They took their seats around the kitchen table, facing each other, and sat down with a sense of ritual and purpose.

"It's time, isn't it, Vicar?"

"I'm afraid it is," Annabelle said.

"I've been meaning to bring this up for a long time. I just didn't want to cause a scene."

"I understand, Philippa. It's difficult for me too."

"I just didn't want to cause you any problems, Vicar."

"Philippa!" Annabelle gasped. "It's you I'm worried about!"

"That's kind of you."

"Well?"

Philippa sighed, readjusted herself in her seat, and spoke slowly. "I know about the cakes."

"You know how they got there?"

"I don't know where they are. But I know what happened to them, yes."

"Wait a moment," Annabelle said, growing slightly confused. "You don't know where they are?"

"Well, I imagine you ate them, Vicar."

"Philippa! Why would I eat old cupcakes that have been left outside in the rain?!"

"Why would you leave them outside in the rain?!" Philippa exclaimed, in the exasperated voice she usually only used when the church accounts failed to add up. "Oh, Vicar, you don't even know when you're doing it!"

Annabelle tried to speak but found herself so confused she didn't know what to say.

"What are you talking about exactly, Philippa?"

"About the cupcakes, Vicar!"

"What about them?"

"You steal them!"

Annabelle slumped back in her chair. She had never been accused of theft in her life and certainly not in as strange a manner as this.

"Why on earth would I steal cupcakes, Philippa?"

"The thrill of it. The excitement of the chase. The feeling of getting away with it. It's that kleptomania I told you about! Oh, I know it's not your fault, Vicar. You can't help it. I see you eat one or two, but then three are gone! You probably stash it in your pocket when I'm not looking. Maybe you feel guilty about eating so many. I don't know. I'm just glad it's out in the open now!"

Annabelle could not help but smile at the insanity of the accusation. Partly because Philippa's conviction removed any doubt that she was involved with the mystery screamer's escape into the woods.

"I can assure you, Philippa, I do not steal cupcakes."

Philippa sighed deeply again, as if in the presence of a child caught red-handed but too stubborn to admit guilt.

"If not you, then who?"

With the perfect timing of a grand entrance of which only cats are capable, Biscuit sidled through the cat door, slinked her way toward her bowl, and began lapping up water noisily.

"I believe we won't need to find a suspect. The suspect just found us."

"Biscuit?" Philippa said, incredulous. "That's impossible!"

Annabelle waved her finger as if pointing at her thoughts. "Actually, it makes perfect sense, the more I think about it. I did find her out in the woods a few days ago, where the stash of cupcakes was. You said yourself that she had stopped eating, and whenever you bring those cupcakes out, Biscuit seems to make a timely entrance."

"That's incredible!"

"What's incredible is the fact that this is the second mystery I've solved today!"

CHAPTER SIX

ANNABELLE SLEPT UNEASILY and woke up in a huff. She washed, dressed, and made herself a small breakfast that she ate pensively at the kitchen table, muttering things to herself and scaring Biscuit with her self-engrossed gestures. Much had happened. There was no doubt that the case was progressing. However, the one element that had bothered Annabelle the most since the very start was still a complete mystery. Who was the secret screamer? She suspected that the Inspector had perhaps assumed there wasn't one, thinking instead that Annabelle had been caught up in the moment. While it was understandable – Sir John had already been murdered, and the arrow's trajectory placed the killer *outside* the building – it was also frustrating. Annabelle *knew* what she heard.

Annabelle glanced at the clock and realized that she had been lost in her breakfast reverie for a little over an hour. She tidied up the plates and decided to get out of the house. Her preoccupation with the case had left her with many calls to make, and she was determined not to let them wait any longer. Unfortunately for her plans, however, the phone rang just as she was about to leave the house.

"Hello, Annabelle speaking."

"Hello, Vicar. We've found Poppy Franklin," came the Inspector's commanding voice.

Annabelle was not only delighted to hear news about the case, but also mildly irritated that once again, her more mundane routine was going awry.

"Good! What did she say?"

"We interviewed her this morning. She seems to fit the description of the blond girl who met you at Woodlands Manor."

"Oh, I assumed that already," Annabelle said. "But why did she run?"

"Well," the Inspector began, "she said she didn't want to be accused of Sir John Cartwright's murder. Says she came back up the stairs when she heard you had opened the door, caught a glimpse of the dead body, and just ran for it."

"It is possible..."

"Possible and likely. Turns out she knows how to use a crossbow."

"Inspector!" Annabelle said, as his insinuation became clear. "I didn't mean that. You don't really think she committed the murder, do you?"

"She knew Sir John very well. Claims that she was just a 'friend,' but it's obvious there was more going on between them. She knew how much he was worth, and I'm willing to bet that such a close 'friend' would be well taken care of in the will."

Annabelle mused for a second, recalling the sweet young face of the blond girl at the door. She knew that she should never judge a book by its cover, but Annabelle trusted her instincts when it came to people, and Poppy's innocence seemed as clear as day to her.

"I just don't believe it, Inspector."

"Look, Vicar. She confirmed that Sir John Cartwright was building a health spa, even mentioned some of the other investors by name—"

"Investors?" interrupted Annabelle. "What were their names?"

"Oh... Ah... Let me see... A Sophie and Gabriella. Couldn't give us last names, but apparently they put quite a lot of money into the property. Why do you ask, Vicar? Do you happen to know them?"

"I may have heard some rumors," Annabelle said, wanting a little more time to investigate the mysterious "tourists" and still unsure of their names herself.

"Anyway, we'll be holding Poppy for twenty-four hours. If nothing happens by then, we'll let her go but keep a close eye on her. Between her and Harry Cooper, though, I think we have enough to make a case."

There was a long pause. So long, in fact, that the Inspector followed up by saying, "Are you alright, Vicar?"

"Yes, yes," replied Annabelle, instinctively. "Bye, Inspector."

"Bye, Vicar. And take care. Stop worrying about the case. Now it's up to us to take it from here."

Annabelle placed the handset down and held her hand there for a long time, biting her lip. She left the house, got into her car, and began driving. She was not happy. At the time when the whole, horrid affair had occurred, Annabelle would have been satisfied with offering whatever help she could. Now, she felt responsible for many aspects of this case. It was she who had discovered the name of Sir John Cartwright's companion, Poppy Franklin, and it was she (with the help of Biscuit) who had found the cigarette that implicated Harry Cooper. Now, either one of them – maybe even both – would feel the force of the law upon them.

Something within Annabelle stirred when she considered this. It wasn't quite right. In fact, it felt entirely *wrong*. In a rare, sudden example of reckless driving, Annabelle slid her Mini into a sharp U-turn – nearly knocking Mr. Hawthorne off his bike.

"Sorry, Mr. Hawthorne!" Annabelle shouted out of the window behind her, as he watched, with jaw open, the ever-unpredictable Vicar take the road that led to Truro.

Annabelle marched into the Truro police station with all the enthusiastic vigor of someone who had a job to do and who was jolly well going to do it.

"Hello, Vicar!" Constable Rose, the desk officer said, cheerfully.

"Hello, Officer. I'm here to see the Inspector."

"He's just this way. Follow me."

When Inspector Nicholls saw the Vicar approach his desk, he rubbed his eyes and took another sip of coffee, assuming the late nights and stress of a perplexing murder case were causing him to hallucinate.

"Hello, Inspector," Annabelle said, affirming that she was not, in fact, a mirage.

"Vicar, is something the matter? We only just spoke."

"Yes, Inspector. I must speak with Poppy."

The Inspector studied Annabelle's face for a sign that this was a joke.

"Are you serious? With all due respect, Vicar. I can't allow just anyone to speak to her."

"I understand that, Inspector. But I sincerely believe she is innocent, and I'd like to prove it."

"What makes you think she's innocent?"

"Faith, Inspector."

The Inspector sighed deeply.

"I'm going to need more than that, Vicar. However much I'd like to use faith in my police work, it doesn't work like that."

"Inspector," Annabelle said, putting some steel into her voice and placing a firm hand on his desk, "I have helped you at every stage of this investigation. It is not arrogant of me to say that I have discovered and provided you with some of the most crucial pieces of evidence in this case. I'm asking you to sincerely consider my trustworthiness, diligence, and abilities before you dismiss my request."

The Inspector sighed again and looked over at the Constable beside him, who raised his eyebrows in support of the Vicar's statement.

"I do appreciate everything you've done, Vicar. But I've interviewed her already. I don't want to put more pressure on her unnecessarily. She's already shaken up. I don't see what you could ask her at this stage that would help."

"You asked her whether she knew how to use a crossbow."

"Yes, I did. And she said she knew."

"Did you ask her *where* she learned how to use a crossbow?"

The Inspector rubbed a finger across his pursed lips, then stood up, and grabbed a key chain from his desk.

"Okay. I'll give you five minutes," he said, then turned to the Constable who was listening intently, "and don't you tell anyone I did this."

Inspector Nicholls led Annabelle to the cell, opened the door, and allowed Annabelle to step inside.

Poppy looked vastly different from the perky, pleasant girl who had breezily chatted with the Vicar on her arrival at Woodlands Manor. She sat on the hard bed, hunched over and clutching her sides, as if protecting herself from harm. Her cheeks were flushed, and her brown mascara streaked lightly on her cheeks. She had been crying and still wore an expression of utter turmoil.

"Vicar?" she whispered, squinting through the reddish puffs of her eyes as if she couldn't believe it.

"Poppy? Oh dear," Annabelle said, sitting beside the girl and putting an arm around her.

She allowed Annabelle to clutch her to her chest, welcoming the warmth of someone caring. She struggled not to break into tears again.

"Why... What are you doing here?" she muttered, as she pulled away from her embrace to see the Vicar's sympathetic face.

"I'm here to help you. But I need you to answer something for me."

"What? Anything, if you can get me out of here."

"I need you to tell me who taught you how to use a crossbow."

Poppy looked away from the Vicar, as if the question had slapped her across the face.

"I can't."

"Poppy..."

"No. I'm sorry."

This was it, Annabelle thought, this was the key. It had been merely an incidental thought before, but Poppy's reaction confirmed it was the answer.

"Poppy, they won't be able to accuse you of the murder,

but they will almost certainly accuse you of being an accessory to murder. You're the only person who's admitted to knowing how to use a crossbow. You were in the house when the murder occurred. You ran from the scene of the crime. Whomever you're protecting, you'll pay a big price for doing so."

"No," Poppy stuttered, through sobs. The Vicar pulled a pack of tissues from her pocket and handed them to the shuddering girl.

"You're innocent, Poppy. I know you are. You did nothing wrong. That's why this is difficult for you to take. Tell the truth, and set things right."

Poppy looked up from the scrunched up tissues she held to her nose and into Annabelle's compassionate eyes.

"Go on," Annabelle urged.

"William...Will," Poppy said suddenly, as if it were an uncontrollable reaction. "Will Conran. He's a friend of mine – an ex-boyfriend. We grew up together. We've known each other since we were kids."

Annabelle rubbed Poppy's back. She could see the relief flooding through the younger woman's slim body, as if purging a poison she had held inside for a very long time.

"He's always been an archer. He's always used crossbows, since he was a teenager. Goes hunting regularly. Sometimes he'd go on several trips a week."

"You think Will might have shot Sir John?"

"I don't know for sure, but I think so."

"Why?"

Poppy's sobs grew a little louder, and it took a while for Annabelle to calm her down enough to speak again. When she had, Poppy turned to the Vicar, and gathering all the strength she had, said,

"Because I left Will for Sir John."

The next few hours were a flurry of activity and noise. Once Annabelle had given the Inspector the name, he put all of his men on the tail of William Conran. With the call sent across police stations nationwide, it took barely an hour before they tracked Conran to Reading, just south of London. The Reading police were sure to secure the suspect and bring him to the local station, so it was just a matter of Inspector Nicholls driving there to question him. He threw on his distinctive trench coat and made for the police station exit.

"You coming, Vicar?" he asked.

Annabelle, who had been milling around the station, caught up in the excitement while swapping questions with Inspector, found herself utterly befuddled.

"Me?"

"Do you see any other vicars around here?"

"You want *me* to come with you to Reading to interrogate the suspect?"

"Why not? As you said, Vicar, you've been involved each time we've made a breakthrough. Either you're very good at this or extremely lucky. Either way, I'd rather have you with me than not."

Annabelle grinned at the Inspector's words. She would have hoped for nothing more just a couple of weeks ago.

"Of course, Inspector. Lead the way."

Annabelle found herself carried off toward Reading police station along with various members of the police force. As the convoy of police cars set off into the early evening light with a flurry of squealing sirens and flashing lights, Annabelle found herself giddy with childish excitement. This was a change of pace from the county fair! They arrived as it was getting dark. Though the larger, busier atmosphere of the station made Annabelle feel slightly intimidated and a little over her head, she prepared herself to accomplish what she had set out to do since the beginning – discover the truth.

With assurance and professionalism, the Inspector exchanged a few words with the Reading officers and was soon led toward the interview room that held Will Conran. Annabelle followed close behind, her self-confidence quickly being sapped as she realized the immense seriousness of what was happening.

Conran was in his mid-twenties and as much a picture of youth and attractiveness as Poppy. With his chiselled jawline and sparkling blue eyes, Annabelle couldn't help but notice what a perfect match they were – or at least, had been. Such a good-looking young chap would have no problems meeting a new girl, Annabelle thought, so if he were still to care about Poppy after all that had gone on, it must be a very deep love.

"Why's the Vicar here?" snarled Conran.

"New justice system," the Inspector said, gesturing Annabelle toward a seat opposite. "If you're guilty, she'll damn your soul straight to hell."

"Guilty of what?" Will barked.

"You know what," the Inspector growled back.

"I have no idea what you're talking about."

The Inspector leaned toward Annabelle and whispered in her ear. "You might want to come back later, this is going to take some time."

Annabelle looked at the Inspector, than back at Conran.

"Poppy is in utter pieces!" Annabelle exclaimed loudly, taking both of the men by surprise. "She's in a terrible state!"

The Inspector put his hand on the Vicar's arm to calm her down, but her eyes were locked with Will's.

"Poppy's just a friend..."

"She's more than a friend," Annabelle replied, with as much piercing aggression as she could muster.

"Not for a long time," came Will's reply, but there was a shakiness in his voice that hadn't been there before. The Inspector retracted his hand, noticing the effectiveness of the Vicar's tactics.

"So you don't care about her?"

"I... I care about her as much as she cares about me. So no."

"If she didn't care about you," Annabelle continued, lowering her voice to deliver the blow, "then why would she protect you?"

"She... protected me? From what?"

"It took her this long to give us your name in connection with the murder of Sir John Cartwright," the Inspector chimed in.

Will shook his head.

"I didn't do anything. If Poppy's protecting anyone, it's herself."

The three of them sat in silence for a few moments.

"Well," Annabelle said, with deflated exasperation, "if you didn't do anything, then Poppy is off to jail for a very long time."

Will's eyes widened. Annabelle stood up slowly, as if the interview had been concluded. Reading what she was doing, the Inspector followed suit.

"Wait!" Will said.

Annabelle and the Inspector froze, casting their eyes toward Will.

"You... You can't arrest Poppy for this. You know she wouldn't hurt a fly."

"We can, and we will," the Inspector replied. "She knew how to use a crossbow. She was at the scene of the crime. And she was close enough to John Cartwright to benefit from it. Weapon, location, and motive. It'll run a lot further in court than your character profile of her."

Will slumped over the table, his head in his hands.

"Okay," he mumbled.

"What was that?" the Inspector asked.

Will raised his head.

"Okay. I'll talk."

Annabelle and the Inspector took their seats again, and the Inspector gestured for Will to start speaking.

"Me and Poppy grew up together. She was sort of my childhood sweetheart. We were together all through our teenage years. I loved her more than anything, but I made a lot of mistakes. Took her for granted."

"You made her steal for you," the Inspector said.

"Yeah. Don't get me wrong though, Poppy wasn't an angel herself. She liked nice things, expensive things. Clothes, make-up. You know how girls are. I got into shoplifting, and I got her to do it too. It's easier to get away with it when you look as innocent as she does.

"But then we got nicked. We'd already been caught a few times, but this time, it was big. We were actually breaking into a store. I ended up doing a lot of time. Four years. Poppy got one because her lawyer said I forced her to do it."

"And that made you bitter," the Inspector prodded, again.

"No. That's not what made me bitter," Will said, his eyes alive with anger and regret at his memories, "I would have done two extra years if it meant Poppy did none. But I expected her to wait for me. To support me. To appreciate what I had done for her all through our time together. Instead..."

Will looked at the wall, unable to face his own pain.

"She found John Cartwright," Annabelle said, as softly as she could.

Will slammed his fist against the table.

"Can you believe it?! An old pervert more than twice her age! She was only meant to work for him a bit, doing some stupid maid stuff in one of his fancy houses in the city. I knew he was after her from the start, but she wouldn't listen. Then the next thing I know, she's all, 'I can't live this life anymore, visiting you in jail, scratching a living as an ex-con. We both need a fresh start.'"

"That's when she came to Upton St. Mary?" asked the Inspector.

"Yeah."

"And you followed her?" Annabelle asked.

"Yeah," Will said, quietly, "When I got out of prison, I went straight down there."

"Okay," the Inspector sighed, "then what?"

"I wanted to learn a bit about what they were doing there. Eventually I found out that Cartwright had bought the house from Harry Cooper. I found Cooper drunk in the pub one night. We got talking. It seemed like he hated John Cartwright nearly as much as I did."

"Why?"

"I don't remember exactly. Something about selling him the house at a discount, so that he would have a share of the health spa... Yeah, that was it. Harry and a pair of crazy old women apparently. All invested in the health spa. Harry was really worried that John was going to swindle him somehow and kept spying on him."

"How would he spy?"

"Well, he knew the property. He would go there sometimes to watch the house. Check up on him I guess. Make sure that everything was going to plan. He said he could see right into Cartwright's bedroom from one spot. He told me about a secret entrance to the house, the coal cellar shaft in the woods."

"The spot you killed him from."

Will glared at the Inspector. "I already told you. I didn't kill anyone."

Annabelle and the Inspector exchanged looks.

"So you're saying Poppy killed him?" the Inspector said.

"I'm not saying anything," Will sneered.

"That's the same thing."

Will broke into a pained smile. "You wouldn't pin this on Poppy. You know she's innocent."

The Inspector smiled back – Will was playing hardball, and that was the Inspector's favorite game.

"You've been to prison, Will," the Inspector said. "You know how many innocent people there are in there. Sir John was a knight of the realm, so I'm not putting his death in the 'unsolved' section – *somebody* has to go down for his murder."

"But not Poppy..."

"Look," the Inspector said, leaning forward menacingly, "I've been on this case for over two weeks now. Everyone in this room knows you did it. But if you don't talk, Poppy's the closest thing to you I've got."

Will was breathing heavily, glancing around the room as if looking for an escape route. He had been backed into a corner, and he knew it. The Inspector saw that he was breaking down and urged him on.

"So you were at the location in the woods."

"Yeah," Will mumbled, dropping his head, "Harry told me it was a good spot for hunting. Lot of pheasants and even some rabbits in that area. So I went hunting."

The Inspector snorted. "Don't try and tell me you killed him by accident."

"I'm telling you I went hunting. Yeah, I wanted to see the house for myself, maybe catch a glimpse of Poppy, but I was there to hunt."

"So how does that end up with you shooting him?"

Will looked around him once again, trying to muster some more defiance, but when his eyes met the sympathetic face of the Vicar, he knew he had lost.

"I saw him with Poppy. They walked around the house. Talking and laughing, just like I used to do with her. I couldn't believe it.... Couldn't believe how he acted like she was his. Putting his arm around her. Touching her. It made me furious. It still does."

"So you shot him?"

"I just sat there, getting madder and madder. I felt like I was going to explode. I never hated anyone so much as I hated him. Then he opened the windows, and he just sat there, right in my view with that smug look on his face, as if he was looking right at me. It was like it was meant to be. I had the crossbow in my hand, and he was right there. His eyes weren't even open."

Will swallowed hard before continuing.

"I shot my crossbow, and then I just froze, staring at the window he had just been at. Then I just started running. I hadn't seen if I had killed him, and I needed to make sure. I needed to see it with my own eyes. I knew Poppy would be in the house, but I just wanted to see *him*, make sure he was dead. I found the coal cellar entrance just where Harry had described it and ran through into the darkness beyond. I don't know how, but I ended up in a bathroom, a big, fancy bathroom.

But then I heard a car crunching on the gravel outside. I stopped running. I wasn't sure what to do, so I waited. I waited a long time. I heard the car drive away but still I stayed where I was. I felt like I was going insane. I was trying to calm myself down, but I had to know if I'd killed him. Just as I was about to go through the door of the bathroom to look, the car came back! So I just went for it. Through the door and into the bedroom. The old man was spread out on the floor with an arrow through his heart. He was as dead as the crows I used to shoot when I was a kid. When I saw his body, I was so angry, so glad, so pumped-up, I yelled my head off.

"Then I heard something downstairs, loud footsteps, like someone was running up the stairs. I ran back outside the way I came, through the coal cellar, and didn't stop until I was back in Reading."

Will looked at the Inspector one last time, then slumped back in his chair, as if physically exhausted by the confession. It was over, and the tension in the room dissipated, leaving nothing but regret and sorrow for the lovelorn murderer.

The Inspector rose to his feet and tapped Annabelle on the shoulder to do the same.

"You'll be going to jail for a very long time, Mr. Conran," he said.

"I know," Will mumbled. "But at least Poppy will be free."

Annabelle looked at the condemned young man with deep sympathy.

"You know, you could have won her back. She still cares for you. If only you hadn't..."

"I know that now," Will said. "But it's too late."

The Inspector shuffled Annabelle outside. She looked distraught. The Inspector placed a hand on her shoulder gently.

"Such an awful tale!" Annabelle said.

The Inspector nodded slowly. "I guess Sir John wasn't the only victim of a broken heart. William Conran killed because he had nothing to live for without Poppy. Now he'll spend the rest of his life in jail, reflecting on that one moment of passion-induced madness. Even if Poppy still loved him, he'll never get to live the life he wanted with her because of this – and that's the most severe punishment of all."

EPILOGUE

I F THE GROUNDS of Woodlands Manor were beautiful before, those of the newly-refurbished Woodlands Manor Resort & Spa were spectacular. Annabelle and Philippa gasped with wonder as their Mini made its way up the driveway in a procession of cars.

"They've worked wonders!" Philippa said, pointing at the grass tennis courts to one side.

"Oh look! A pool!" Annabelle exclaimed.

It had been a mere six months since the tragic events at Woodlands Manor, yet no remnants of the earlier dark circumstances were apparent in its magnificent reinvention. Annabelle slowed the car to a halt just in front of the entrance.

"Oh!" she exclaimed with surprise when her driver side door was opened.

"Ma'am," said the red-suited valet.

Philippa and Annabelle exchanged appreciative smiles before clambering out of the car. The valet took Annabelle's keys and gestured to the side of the house.

"If you'll just follow the path, Vicar, you'll find the other guests."

"Thank you," Annabelle said, slightly embarrassed by the courteous treatment.

"I could get used to this," Philippa said, as they made their way along the indicated path.

They found themselves at the back of the house and discovered lines of buffet tables arranged under a large, brightly-colored marquee, a prudent necessity on even the sunniest of days in England, due to the whimsical unpredictability of the British weather. Around the tables gathered a large crowd composed of both Upton St. Mary villagers unaccustomed to such extravagance and well-heeled spa patrons unaccustomed to such villagers.

As they stepped toward the crowd, two women emerged with open arms.

"The guests of honor!" Sophie said, delightedly.

"How wonderful to see you!" Gabriella added.

After many enthusiastic hugs and greetings, Annabelle said, "It really was wonderful of you to invite the villagers to the opening."

"Oh, but of course! The villagers are the reason we decided to take on this project," Gabriella said.

"That and Gabriella having grown rather fond of the organic produce," Sophie said.

"Speaking of which, I insist you try these chia seed and coconut macaroons," Gabriella said, gesturing toward the table. Annabelle and Philippa took one each.

"I've never heard of chia seeds," Philippa said.

"They are going to be *huge*," insisted Gabriella. "I hear they have them for breakfast in California. In smoothies. The health benefits are marvellous, darling."

Annabelle and Philippa took tentative bites, disguising

their reactions with all the reserve and politeness that has been the staple of British life for centuries.

"Oh. They're very interesting," Annabelle said, munching purposefully through the sticky treat.

"Oh, and do try this chamomile tea," Gabriella urged, pouring two teacups full of hot yellowy liquid and offering them to the guests.

Once again, Philippa and Annabelle exchanged glances, sniffed at the aromatic beverage and sipped tentatively.

"It's very different from English tea," Philippa said, who struggled to contort her expression into something resembling pleasure.

Gabriella smiled with pride.

"So, I take it you're here to stay?" Philippa asked.

"Indeed we are," Sophie replied.

"The French tourists have become British residents," joked Gabriella.

"You won't miss London?" Annabelle asked.

"Well," Sophie began, "some would say that the appeal of fast city life is unmatched. But, as I think you know well enough yourself, Vicar, adventure and excitement can crop up in the strangest of places."

Annabelle and Philippa spent a delightful couple of hours mingling with Upton St. Mary's newest residents from London and sampling the breath-taking delights of the Woodlands Manor Resort & Spa. They then got back into the blue Mini (brought conveniently to them by the valet, of course), and made their way to Philippa's house.

For the first time since the grim events at Woodlands Manor, Annabelle allowed herself to enjoy the simple pleasure of driving away from the house through Cornwall's vibrant countryside, unfettered by troubling thoughts of mystifying murders. They reached Philippa's home and made their way to the kitchen.

"Cup of tea, Vicar?"

"Oh, yes. That's just what the doctor ordered."

"Chamomile?" Philippa said, before breaking into a small giggle.

"I think I'll stick to tradition for a while, Philippa," Annabelle smiled back. "Milk and sugar, please."

Philippa brought the pot to the table and then opened the oven to reveal a tray of deliciously aromatic, freshly-baked cupcakes.

"Heavens!" the Vicar exclaimed. "Those look wonderful!"

"They're almond, Vicar."

"They smell absolutely scrumptious!"

"Thank you. I decided against making a baklava."

"Why so?" Annabelle said, trying to restrain herself from grabbing the cupcake too ferociously.

"We've had enough drama in Upton St. Mary this past while."

"Meow," Biscuit said, announcing her arrival to the two ladies. The ginger cat stepped lazily to her favorite position by the door, her eyes keenly focused on the cakes.

"Don't worry, Vicar," Philippa said, noticing the cat, "I'm keeping my eye on that cat. She won't be stealing any more of these cupcakes. She's on a strict diet of chicken bits and fish now. She could do with losing a few pounds herself."

"Philippa!" Annabelle said. "What are you inferring?"

"Well, Vicar, since you've reacquainted yourself with the Inspector recently..."

"Oh," Annabelle interrupted, "our relationship is strictly professional."

"Yes, Vicar. Sorry," Philippa said, winking at Biscuit. "Though I daresay you impressed him – in a professional capacity, of course."

Annabelle focused on sipping her tea and eating her almond cupcake. The two ladies were silent for a few moments, enjoying the peace and pleasure of the atmosphere, a silence only broken by the occasional chirping of a spring bird outside.

Annabelle swallowed the last of her cupcake and sipped once again from her teacup. She started to reach for another cupcake, before pausing halfway. She considered for a moment, before catching Philippa's eye.

"Oh, go on, Vicar. You deserve it," Philippa said, with a smile.

REVERENTIAL RECIPES

CONTINUE ON TO CHECK OUT THE RECIPES FOR GOODIES FEATURED IN THIS BOOK...

WICKED WALNUT CUPCAKES

WITH MAGNIFICENT MAPLE BUTTERCREAM FROSTING

For the cupcakes:
¾ cup (1½ sticks) unsalted butter
1 cup soft brown sugar, packed
1 cup sugar
3 eggs
3 cups flour
1½ teaspoon baking powder
¼ teaspoon salt
1¼ cup whole milk
1 teaspoon vanilla extract
Walnut butter (see recipe)

For the frosting:
¾ cup (1½ sticks) unsalted butter
2 cups powdered sugar
Walnut butter (see recipe)
½ teaspoon molasses
½ teaspoon maple extract

1 teaspoon vanilla extract
2-3 tablespoons water
½ teaspoon walnuts, finely chopped

For the walnut butter:
1 cup shelled walnuts
2 tablespoons butter
3 tablespoons water (as needed)
Dash salt

Preheat the oven to 350°F/180°C. Line cupcake tins with paper liners. To make the walnut butter, mix all ingredients in food processor until well blended. Add water to make the consistency creamy, like mildly chunky peanut butter.

To make cupcakes, cream butter and sugars until light and fluffy. Beat in eggs one at a time. Add sifted dry ingredients, and slowly blend in milk. Stir in vanilla extract and fold in six tablespoons of the walnut butter. Reserve remainder of butter for frosting. Spoon cupcake batter into paper liners, filling them about three quarters full.

Bake the cupcakes until a toothpick inserted into the center comes out clean, about 20 to 25 minutes. Leave to cool completely.

For the frosting, cream together unsalted butter and sugar. Gradually add remainder of walnut butter, molasses, maple extract, and vanilla extract. Add water, one tablespoon at a time, until mixture is fluffy and creamy. Top cupcakes with frosting, and add finely chopped walnuts for decoration.

Makes approximately 30 cupcakes.

BEATIFIC BAKLAVA

1⅔ cups sugar
1½ cups water
2 teaspoons rose water
2 teaspoons orange blossom water
⅔ cup honey
2 cinnamon sticks
2 (5-inch x ½-inch) strips orange peel
2 cup (2 sticks) butter, melted
1 cup chopped walnuts
½ cup chopped pecans
½ cup chopped almonds
1 teaspoon ground cinnamon
½ teaspoon ground allspice
15 phyllo pastry sheets frozen, thawed

Stir 1⅓ cups sugar, water, rose water, orange blossom water, honey, cinnamon sticks, and orange peel in saucepan over medium heat until sugar dissolves. Increase heat and bring to boil, stirring continuously for 10-15 minutes or until consistency is thick like syrup. Remove from heat, and chill until cold.

Preheat oven to 325°F/160°C. Line a 13 x 9 x 2-inch metal baking pan with parchment paper, and brush with a little of the melted butter. Mix walnuts, pecans, almonds, cinnamon, allspice, and the remaining ⅓ cup sugar in a medium bowl.

Fold one sheet of phyllo pastry in half to form a 12 x 9-inch rectangle. Place folded sheet in prepared pan. Brush with melted butter. Repeat with four more folded sheets, brushing top of each with butter.

Sprinkle half of nut mixture over the top of the pastry. Repeat with five more folded sheets, brushing the top of each with butter. Sprinkle remaining nut mixture over the top. Add five more folded sheets of pastry, again brushing the top of each with melted butter.

Using a sharp knife, make seven diagonal cuts across the phyllo pastry, cutting through top layers only and spacing cuts evenly. Repeat in opposite direction, with cuts crossing in the middle to form a diamond pattern. Bake in the oven until golden brown, around 30 to 40 minutes.

Strain white foam, cinnamon sticks, and orange peels from syrup. Spoon 1¼ cups syrup over hot baklava. Cover and refrigerate or dispose of remaining syrup.

Cut baklava along lines all the way through layers. Cover and let stand at room temperature for four hours before eating. Can be made one day ahead. Do not wrap, or it will become soggy. Best if served individually. Can be chilled.

Makes approximately 30 pieces.

CHASTE CHIA SEED AND COCONUT MACAROONS

1 egg, beaten
¼ cup sugar
¾ cup shredded coconut
1 tablespoon chia seeds

Preheat oven to 350°F/180°C. Put the egg in a mixing bowl. Beat the sugar into the eggs with a fork, then stir in the coconut and chia seeds. Press the mixture, a few spoonfuls at a time, into a small eggcup, then turn upside down and tap out onto a baking sheet to form small rounds.

Bake for about 20 minutes or until golden-brown. Remove from the oven and leave to cool for a few minutes before transferring to a wire rack to cool completely.

Makes 7-8.

ANGELIC ALMOND CUPCAKES

WITH ABUNDANT ALMOND BUTTER FROSTING

For the cupcakes:
1 ½ cups flour
1 ¾ teaspoons baking powder
1 cup white sugar
½ cup (1 stick) unsalted butter, softened
2 eggs
1 teaspoon vanilla extract
2 tablespoons almond butter
1 cup vanilla flavored almond milk
1 pinch salt

For the frosting:
½ cup (1 stick) unsalted butter, softened
1 ½ cups powdered sugar
2 tablespoons almond butter
½ teaspoon vanilla extract
2 tablespoons water (or as needed for consistency)
¼ cup almond slivers

Preheat the oven to 350°F/180°C. Line cupcake tins with paper liners. In a bowl, sift together the flour and baking powder.

In a separate bowl, using an electric mixer, cream together the sugar and butter until well blended. Beat in the eggs, one at a time, and stir in the vanilla. Gradually beat in the flour mixture, slowly adding in the almond milk, almond butter, and salt. Make sure all the ingredients are well blended. Spoon mixture into each paper liner, filling them about ¾ full.

Bake the cupcakes until a toothpick inserted into the center comes out clean, about 20 to 25 minutes. Leave to cool completely.

To make frosting, sift powdered sugar and beat together with butter. Add almond butter to sugar and butter mixture. Add vanilla extract. Add water, one tablespoon at a time, until mixture is fluffy and creamy. Top cupcakes with frosting and add almond slivers for decoration.

Makes approximately 16 cupcakes.

All ingredients are available from your local store or online retailer.

You can find links to the ingredients used in these recipes at http://cozymysteries.com/murder-at-the mansion-recipes/

A Reverend Annabelle Dixon Mystery

BODY IN
THE WOODS
Alison Golden
Jamie Vougeot

BODY IN THE WOODS

BOOK THREE

Cover Illustration: Rosalie Yachi Clarita

Published by Mesa Verde Publishing
P.O. Box 1002
San Carlos, CA 94070

Edited by
Marjorie Kramer

CHAPTER ONE

I T HAD BEEN a tough week for young Master Douglas "Dougie" Dewar. It had begun with him tearing his school uniform during a particularly ambitious tree-climbing adventure, continued with reprisals about his over-active imagination from his teacher Miss Montgomery, and reached its peak when Aunt Shona discovered he had been trying to rustle sheep by training none other than the church cat, a ginger tabby named Biscuit.

How could they blame him? He had been in Upton St. Mary for only four months since his mother had sent him there from their home in Edinburgh, and he still found the village and the vibrant countryside surrounding it full of possibilities.

He would trek the rolling hills armed only with a trusty stick and an insisted-upon sandwich, imagining himself a brave adventurer on a quest to find a wise, old wizard. He would swing from tree branches like a wilderness warrior, announcing his presence with a signature yell, determined to save all of civilization, reaping world domination as his prize. And he would creep through the dense forest, envisioning it as some deep, exotic jungle on a strange new planet, while encountering delicate, well-camouflaged wildlife that demonstrated all the curiosity and nervousness of timid alien visitors.

For Dougie was not just energetic and rambunctious of body, but of mind as well. When he wasn't scampering through the rolling countryside in search of adventures, he was poring over pages of the most astonishing and outlandish tales he could find, stoking the fires of his imagination before he lived out his fantasies against Cornwall's glorious pastoral background.

Oh yes, it had been a tough week indeed, but it had also been an incredibly fun one.

Now it was Friday, and the glorious feeling of being on the precipice of the weekend's adventures had Dougie running wildly through the forest on his way home from school. After his mishap earlier in the week, Aunt Shona had insisted he change out of his uniform when he got home before embarking on his adventures. It was a small price to pay, thought Dougie, as he darted, jumped, and swerved around the various tree trunks. But he wasn't home yet.

"No more school," he shouted, as he deftly switched his weight from one foot to another to avoid slipping on a tree root. "No more Miss Montgomery!" As he kept on running, he ran through his weekend plans. "I'll meet the boys to play football tomorrow, and then Aunt Shona promised me a trip to the bookstore. Gonna get the next in the 'Reptiloid Hunter' series. Woo-hoo!"

His imagination ran wild with excitement. He ducked his head and pictured himself a spaceship shooting through an asteroid field. He skipped off a bank and fancied himself on a flying carpet. He spread his arms and turned sharply like a fighter jet, his school satchel sailing behind him like a tail.

Just as he was about to bank sharply again and release another barrage of missiles, however, Dougie found himself genuinely floating in mid-air, his feet up behind him. For a split second, he almost believed he was flying.

"Oof!" he grunted as he landed on his chest atop the tough late summer soil.

Dougie bounced back up almost immediately, his youthful exuberance overwhelming the sharp pain in his elbow and the winded sensation in his chest.

"Oh no! I'm going to be grounded for a week!" he cried as he looked down at the dirt and grass firmly embedded into his school uniform. Cautiously, he checked the spot where the stinging sensation was coming from on his elbow.

"Noooooo!" was all Dougie could muster. He had been well-schooled in the art of politeness and not even being alone in the middle of the woods was enough for him to forget his good manners and utter anything ruder – however much the frayed tear on his blazer warranted it.

He spun around, his pained expression turning to one of anger. Whichever tree root was responsible was going to get it. He took a few steps toward the spot at which he tripped and scanned for the offending object.

The thin, bar-like protrusion which jutted out of the ground at a low angle was not like any tree root Dougie had ever seen. In fact, he had never come across anything remotely like it on his treasure hunts across the forest. He knelt and brushed some of the dirt away.

As he uncovered more of the thin, white oddity, Dougie's heart seemed to sink lower, until it turned a somersault. He knew what this was. They had studied the human skeleton just last week in class.

Dougie's mouth opened slowly as he stared at the bone, his mind searching for another, less terrifying prospect. Suddenly, he found himself out of all other potential explanations and incredibly afraid. He hopped to his feet and sprinted toward Aunt Shona's cottage – only this time he was trying to stifle his imagination rather than explore it.

"The boy's fine," Shona Alexander assured her sister on the phone, "he's a little scamp. With a boy like him you only need to worry when he's *not* up to something... Oh, of course he misses you. He asks after you every chance he gets... He's still so distracted by the excitement of a new place... You've got enough to worry about right now with the chemo, Olivia, just let me take care of Dougie for now... Oh, wait, I think I hear him coming in. I'll get him to call you later, okay? Bye, Olivia."

Shona placed the receiver down gently and turned around.

"That was your mot—"

"Aunt Shona!"

Shona and Dougie stared at each other, each bearing an expression of absolute horror.

"Good Lord, Dougie! Look at you!"

"There's a.... There's... It's... I don't know why it's there!"

"Is that a rip? Turn around! Turn around, now! Oh dear Lord..."

"No, Aunt Shona... I saw a... It was right there!"

"What was?"

"A... It looked like... There's a... There's a dead body in the woods!"

"Oh, there'll be a dead body in the woods, alright, if you don't explain to me how you made a mess of yourself when I specifically told you not to go running about before coming home to change."

"Really, Aunt Shona! There's a bone sticking out!"

"Sticking out of where?"

"Out of the ground! I tripped over it!"

Shona placed two hands upon her hips and circled Dougie as if inspecting a car she was considering buying. She shook her head as she noticed every stain, assessing how much time it would take to get each one out.

"You really do have quite an imagination. I hope you realize this means you won't be playing soccer this weekend, young man!"

Dougie stamped his foot impertinently and cried out desperately. "I don't care about the football! There's a dead body in the woods!"

Bizarrely, Shona found Dougie's first statement more surprising than the second, and when she saw the earnestness in the boy's face, she realized that he meant both of them sincerely. Dougie certainly attracted more than his fair share of trouble, but if anything, it was his open, impulsive nature that drew him to it, rather than his proclivity to spin tall tales.

"Sit down," Shona commanded the boy, as she pulled out a chair and sat on it. "Tell me exactly what happened."

Inspector Mike Nicholls was in no mood for games and hadn't been for a while. He had grumbled and complained his way through each workday for over two weeks, and yet his fellow officers had grown none the wiser as to the cause.

Nothing out of the ordinary had happened, and the incidents they had dealt with were remarkable only in their consistency and mildness. Even the weather hadn't been so bad. Yet not even a cup of tea could be served to the Detective Inspector without vociferous criticism about its sweetness or lack thereof. He did not hold back expounding on any other grievance he found pertaining to the cup in question, either. The tea might be too hot, too cold, too strong, or the wrong kind of brew entirely. Officers within his vicinity were liable to receive spiked comments about their manner or work ethic, and even those not present would be noted for their absence, the reasons for which were undoubtedly nefarious in the Inspector's newly negative outlook.

So when the call came from Constable Raven that drove the Inspector to leave the city for the countryside immediately, the officers of Truro police station breathed a sigh of relief before drawing straws to decide who would go with him. Constable Colback drew the short one.

After a long trip, during which Inspector Nicholls articulated his grievances on topics as wide-ranging as long car journeys, people wasting police time, the declining standards of police ceremonies, and the road manners of his fellow drivers, he and his bedraggled constable met the local village bobby, Constable Raven, outside Shona Alexander's house.

"Hello Inspector! Long time no see," said Constable Raven, more cheerily than the grave circumstances demanded.

"I have a forensic team on standby, Constable," the Inspector responded curtly. "So I sincerely hope this is not a waste of time."

Picking up on the Inspector's unusually stern tone, Raven stood upright.

"I don't think so, Inspector. Ms. Alexander and Dougie, her young nephew, sound very concerned."

"How old's the boy?" the Inspector asked.

"I believe he's eight, sir," Raven replied.

"Wait a minute, Constable," Nicholls said, a dark cloud passing over his face. "Are you telling me that I've just put all my other duties aside, made a formal request for the forensic team to enter the area, and driven for almost an hour, based on the story that a schoolboy told his aunt? You didn't check the site yourself?"

Constable Raven struggled to disguise his gulp. He was an informal but effective officer, though diligence and rigor had never been his strengths. Under the intense glare of the Inspector, he suddenly wished they were.

"I didn't want to disturb the scene, Inspector. I thought it right that you be here to witness it first."

DI Nicholls winced, opened his mouth to say something, decided against it, and walked up the pathway to Shona Alexander's door, leaving Constables Raven and Colback to exchange sympathetic glances.

"I'm Detective Inspector Nicholls," he said to the blonde woman who opened the door, "I believe you are Ms. Shona Alexander and this lad is Dougie Dewar?"

"Yes, thank you for coming, Inspector."

The Inspector crouched, bringing himself to eye-level with the freshly-washed boy who clung to his aunt's trouser leg.

"What did you see out there, boy?"

After a few seconds, Dougie gathered up the courage to speak.

"There was this bone. An arm bone, sticking out of the ground. I tripped on it and got mud and dirt all over me."

"How big?"

Dougie raised his hands and held them about four inches apart. Nicholls looked around to cast another stern glare at Constable Raven.

"Now are you sure it wasn't a twig? A strange stick, or maybe something plastic?"

Dougie shook his head, too intimidated by the Inspector's direct, unyielding approach to speak.

"A lot of animals have bones, you know. Tell me why you think this was a human bone? An arm, you say?"

"I studied the skeleton at school last week. It has a curve like this," Dougie said, proudly tracing his finger along his forearm, "and another bone next to it like this. That's what it looked like."

Nicholls sighed deeply.

"Well, let's get to it then. The young lad can show us the path and tell us about it on the way."

The detective stood up and began walking back down the path, followed by Dougie and his Aunt Shona. As he passed Constable Raven, he glowered once again and said:

"I hope this kid's knowledge of anatomy is better than your knowledge of police procedure, Constable. For all our sakes."

The sky was turning a dark shade of orange as the five figures approached the long shadows of the woods. Though the days still bore the pleasant warmth and brightness of summer, the sharp decrease in temperature as the sun set over the hills indicated that the warm season was about to be chased away. There was a little crunch in the rustle of leaves underfoot, and the fervent greens that rolled away in all directions began to wane into shades less vivid as encroaching hues of brown and yellow made themselves apparent.

Though Dougie was meant to lead them, he shuffled along beside his Aunt Shona, clutching her hand, while Inspector Nicholls strode forward, setting a brisk pace. Constables Raven and Colback brought up the rear, chatting a little and scanning the surroundings purposefully when they thought Nicholls was watching.

DI Nicholls turned to Dougie as they passed through another clump of trees and began to navigate the deepening shade of the dense forest. Dougie, still rather intimidated by the Inspector's intense silence, raised his arm and pointed ahead, a little to one side. Nicholls nodded once and continued onwards determinedly.

"There!" Dougie squealed suddenly. "That's where I fell! So the bone is..."

Everyone watched the boy's finger trace a trajectory in the air until it pointed to a spot on the ground. Dougie stepped back and pressed himself up against Aunt Shona's trouser leg once again.

DI Nicholls almost leaped toward the spot Dougie had indicated, followed closely by the two constables. They gazed at the strange protrusion for a few seconds, musing over its unusual shape.

"Take the woman and the boy to the edge of the forest, Colback. It's a little way over. You can meet the forensic team there if we need them. Constable Raven?"

"Yes sir?"

"Help me dig it out a little – carefully."

"Yes sir."

As Shona walked after Constable Colback, pulling Dougie away and holding his head so that he couldn't look back, Nicholls and Raven pulled away at the dirt from which the bone emerged. After almost ten minutes of clawing at the ground, growing increasingly impatient, they unearthed what was unmistakably a human elbow.

DI Nicholls pulled out his phone.

"Colback? Call in the forensic team, and bring them over. Tell them we've confirmed it."

Within the hour, night had fallen swiftly and Upton St. Mary had become shrouded in darkness. Drivers on the lazily curving country lanes had to depend on their headlights to see, and the quaint cottages and houses were apparent only by the warm glow coming from their windows and visitor lamps. Few people were outside, most choosing to enjoy the comfort and warmth of their homes, but for those who were, the sky was clear enough for moonlight to help them along their way.

Tonight, however, there were vibrant additions supplementing Upton St. Mary's nighttime illuminations. Multiple police cars had parked by the wall of trees at the woods' edge, their blue lights casting ominous blinking shadows across the forest floor. A little deeper in the woods, powerful lamps, set up by the forensic team, cast a piercing white glare over the scenes of crime officers as they carefully excavated and examined the forest floor. Police officers circled the area, scanning for clues or merely making their way through the unlit portions of the woods, directing their flashlight beams erratically like they were roving spotlights.

There would be gossip in the morning for sure, thought DI Nicholls, as he marched back toward the woods from Shona Alexander's house. He had really needed that cup of tea, but his lengthy conversation with Dougie and Shona had not revealed much. The boy had been more concerned with the mess he had made of his uniform, while his aunt seemed to live an incredibly isolated life at the big stone cottage, sentimentally named "Honeysuckle House." Despite living for fifteen years in Upton St. Mary, the closest she had come to giving him a lead was information concerning a land dispute that had been resolved eighteen months ago.

"Damnit!" Nicholls exclaimed into the dark night as he stubbed his boot on a large rock, almost stumbling head over heels. "Bloody rock!"

"You should have a torch," came a distant voice.

Nicholls looked up and was blinded by a powerful beam.

"Get that light out of my eyes!" he cried, angrily.

The beam was lowered, and as his eyes adjusted once again to the darkness, Nicholls saw the svelte figure of Harper Jones emerging from a cluster of trees.

"Sorry," DI Nicholls growled, as she drew closer, "I didn't realize it was you, Harper."

Not many people could elicit an apology from the Inspector, but Harper Jones demanded a certain respect, not least because she was one of the most brilliant pathologists in Britain and thus the Inspector's best hope for making some sense of the dead body in the woods.

Harper reached the Inspector and dropped her flashlight to her side. Even in the dim light, the Inspector could make out Harper's attractive face and upright bearing from the slivers of fading light that outlined her sharp features.

"This body's been here a while," Harper announced rather obviously, never one for small talk.

"How long?" the Inspector asked.

"We'll definitely need some time to figure it out. We're

still excavating it as carefully as possible, but my guess is that it's been buried there for well over a decade," she said.

"A decade?!"

Harper nodded, the moonlight skipping along her wavy hair. "Judging by the tissue quantities and the large number of roots that have grown around it. It's why the excavation still has some way to go."

Nicholls scratched his stubble and looked off toward the rhythmic blue glow being cast over the road.

"Is there anything else you can tell me?"

"Not much," Harper replied. "The body is in a fetal position, but that could mean anything. Defending against an attacker, huddling for warmth, disposal into a small hole – I don't know. That's your job."

Nicholls sighed deeply.

"We're never going to close a case this cold."

"There is one request I'd like to make," Harper said, maintaining her cool, assertive tone of voice despite her slight alarm at the Inspector's level of pessimism so early in the case.

"What's that?"

"I'd like a second opinion on this body. There's a lot of damage. It's difficult to ascertain what may be suspicious and what is the effect of decay, root growth, or simply the person's health in life. If I'm to make any judgments, I'd like the opinion of a forensic anthropologist."

"Do you have anybody in mind?"

For the first time, DI Nicholls detected a slightly regretful expression on the face of Harper Jones. He immediately dismissed it as a trick of the light, but Harper's somewhat wistful tone caused him to reconsider.

"Yes, actually."

"Okay. Well, bring them on board. I'm willing to pull in anyone who can help."

"That's good," Harper said, turning her head toward the road, "because I believe you're about to gain another ally."

Nicholls turned his head just in time to see a royal blue Mini Cooper pull up neatly behind a police car.

They watched as the large, unmistakable frame of Reverend Annabelle Dixon stepped out of the car and strode over to a nearby officer. After exchanging a few words, the constable gazed across the open stretch of land and pointed them out.

"Oh great," muttered Nicholls as Annabelle waved cheerily and began striding toward them, her smile visible even in the darkness. Harper raised her torch to reveal where they were, causing Annabelle to squint and stumble backward in its blinding glare.

"Don't be proud," Harper said quietly, as she turned back toward the woods. "The Reverend is a smart cookie – and you're going to need all the help you can get with this one."

DI Nicholls gazed at the looming figure of Annabelle coming toward him, arms in full marching mode. When she got close, she took one step too many and clattered into him.

"Oops!" she said, unconvincingly. "Terribly dark, isn't it?"

"I'm afraid I'm busy, Reverend."

"Whatever's going on, Inspector?"

"I can't tell you. It's police business and classified. The one thing I can tell you is that you'll have to move along."

Disregarding the Inspector's dismissive tone, Annabelle decided to keep probing.

"It looks serious," she remarked, turning her head

toward the bright lamps of the forensic team. "I hope nobody was hurt."

Nicholls remained silent.

Annabelle was rather fond of the Inspector, more than a little fond if the rumors were to be believed, but she found his silence somewhat rude and unfriendly. Not least because she had only recently helped the Inspector solve a particularly tricky case. Nonetheless, Annabelle, her big, warm heart nearly always bursting with generosity, was determined, happy even, to place the blame for the Inspector's grumpiness on his long drive from Truro.

"Do you know whose body it is?" asked Annabelle, matter-of-factly.

The lines of DI Nicholls' frown were so deep that they were visible even by the faint light of the moon.

"Who told you there's a body?!"

"Nobody!" Annabelle responded jovially. "I simply noticed the forensic team working busily away. There are only two things I can think of that would demand so many people be plugging away at the ground – the discovery of treasure or a dead body. And you don't need so many policemen to unearth treasure!"

Annabelle laughed easily, unable to notice the Inspector's scowl in the darkness.

"I'll hope you're not planning to go around telling people there's a dead body in the woods, Reverend."

"Heavens, no! But I don't imagine it'll be a secret for long."

"Why's that?"

"Well, this road gets rather busy in the morning. It's one of the main commuter routes. You'll have plenty of rubberneckers spreading gossip before most people have had their morning coffee!"

Nicholls sighed defeatedly. He hated gossip, especially when it involved a case of his and even more so when it involved a case as open as this. Once it started, he would be stumbling upon more red herrings than one would find in a mystery novel.

"Goodbye, Reverend," DI Nicholls said, decisively.

"Bye, Inspector!"

Both of them took a step in opposite directions before DI Nicholls looked back.

"Reverend? Your car is that way."

"Oh I know, Inspector. I'm still on my daily rounds and thought I'd pay the good Ms. Alexander a visit."

Nicholls considered trying to dissuade the Reverend, but he knew her well enough to know it was a lost cause. He nodded grimly and headed back toward the forensic team.

Annabelle was not immune to the Inspector's bizarrely downbeat manner, and she could only surmise that whatever – or whoever – was buried in the woods behind Honeysuckle House was a cause for great concern. If anyone knew what was happening, it would be Shona Alexander, her bouncy young nephew being the only one who frequented those woods daily.

She walked briskly closer to the welcoming light of Honeysuckle House's decorated windows. Pots of herbs and aromatic flowers were neatly arranged beneath them. As she opened the wooden gate to Shona's wildflower garden, she noticed Constable Raven coming in the opposite direction.

"Constable Raven!"

"Oh, hello Reverend. Strange to see you out this late."

"It's not that late, Constable. The days are simply getting shorter."

Jim Raven looked up at the sky.

"I suppose you're right. It's going to get cold soon, I'd better get my boiler fixed."

"Constable," Annabelle said, seriously. "What is all this fuss about in the woods?"

Constable Raven shook his head slowly. "I'm sorry, Reverend. I'm under strict orders from Detective Inspector Nicholls to keep this as secret as possible."

"I had a feeling you might say that. But it must be something rather concerning to have the Inspector so worked up."

Raven allowed himself a wry smile. "Are you referring by chance to the chief's foul mood? I'm afraid that's got nothing to do with the case. He's been acting like he swallowed a wasp for weeks now."

"Why?" asked Annabelle, leaning forward with keen interest.

Raven shook his head.

"Constable Colback tells me nobody in Truro has the faintest idea what's bothering him. It's an even bigger mystery than the body in the woods. Ah—"

Raven stuttered, looking for something to say that would distract Annabelle from his slip of the tongue. Annabelle chuckled.

"Relax, Constable. I had already figured that out."

Raven's shoulders dropped a full inch, deflated. "It's nice of you to fib, Reverend, but I shouldn't have said that."

"Forget about it, Constable," Annabelle said, stepping past him. "I'll see you about the village, I expect."

"Yeah," muttered Constable Raven, still shaking his

head at his own stupidity. "You're not planning to ask Ms. Alexander about this, are you?"

Annabelle smiled. "I was actually planning to ask her how she was managing to keep her basil so vital at this time of year, but I expect this will be a rather unavoidable subject."

Constable Raven nodded as if receiving bad news, before turning around and making his way out of the garden and back toward the crime scene. As he went on his way, he decided that his spilling the beans was no fault of his own. It was Reverend Annabelle. She simply had a very sharp knack for uncovering secrets.

CHAPTER TWO

ANNABELLE RUNG THE doorbell and almost immediately heard Shona Alexander's Scottish brogue grow louder as she made her way to the door.

"I think this is quite enough for one night. I've already fallen behind on my chores. I've got an unbelievably muddy school uniform to mend, and — Oh! It's you, Reverend!" Shona's flustered face appeared at the door. Her expression had quickly turned to one of relief when she saw who was standing there. "I'm sorry, Reverend, I've just been run ragged by all these policemen and their questions. There are only so many times you can tell people that you don't know anything before you start going mad."

"I understand, Shona. Are you alright?"

"I'm fine, Reverend," Shona sighed. "I just need a little peace and quiet."

"Is Dougie holding up?"

"Oh, that little rascal," she said, gesturing the Reverend inside and closing the door, "he's indestructible. He was shaken more by the Inspector than the body, I think."

Annabelle nodded ruefully as she entered the kitchen and took a seat at the table. Shona picked up the kettle.

"Tea?"

"That would be lovely," cooed Annabelle.

"How are things at the church?" asked Shona as she sat down.

"They're ticking over smoothly," Annabelle said, "which is all you can really ask for. I think Philippa has been rather bored lately, honestly. The church accounts don't make for riveting reading at this time of year, not during the quiet time between the summer fête and the harvest festival. I'm sure she'll have plenty to talk about tomorrow though, once the news spreads. What about you?"

"Och," Shona said, waving the comment aside. "I've got more than enough to occupy my mind these days."

Annabelle noted the sadness in Shona's liquid-blue eyes. She was an attractive woman, though she had never married. After spending her formative years in Scotland, she had moved down to the south of England in order to pursue her passion for painting and pottery. Her family had been wealthy, and supportive, yet the young Shona Alexander was keen to strike out on her own. She had moved to Honeysuckle House, a property her family had owned for generations, full of excitement at her impending independence. But after years of only moderate success in her artistic endeavors, she had settled into a life of quiet routine; the odd exhibition in Truro, taking on the occasional commission, and more recently, the task of caring for her nephew.

Shona had always lived a life of her own design, but in recent years she had felt a lack of something profound, something larger than herself that she could dedicate herself

toward. Her sister's illness had only added to her morose-
ness, and though the arrival of Dougie had offered plenty to
occupy both her mind and hands, it had also reminded
Shona of what she had been missing: companionship. She
was lonely.

"How is your sister doing?" Annabelle asked softly.

"She'll be having a test next week to see, so I've got my
fingers crossed."

"I'll say a prayer for her."

"Thank you, Reverend. I think she's finding the chemo
tough."

Annabelle nodded solemnly. Shona stood up and got to
work making the tea. Annabelle gazed at the paintings
around the room. They were mainly watercolors that
depicted the various familiar hills and locations of Upton
St. Mary. She had always loved Shona's work, and indeed,
had first become friends with her when commissioning a
small piece that now hung in her church office.

"Annabelle!" squealed Dougie from the doorway.

"Hello, you!" Annabelle replied as the boy walked
toward her.

"Dougie! Where are your manners? You're to call the
Reverend, 'Reverend'."

"It's fine," Annabelle said, tousling the young boy's hair
affectionately. "You've certainly been the center of attention today, haven't you Dougie?"

Dougie beamed proudly.

"I found a skeleton!"

"Dougie!" exclaimed Shona. "It was just a bone!"

"But I heard them *say* it was a skeleton!" Dougie asked,
utterly confident in his assertion.

"Those insensitive police," muttered Shona disapprovingly. "They've only got their minds on their work and never think of how it affects people."

Annabelle smiled sympathetically.

"It's nothing to be afraid of," she said, half to Shona and half to Dougie. "Whoever is buried there died a very long time ago."

Shona brought the tea and biscuits to the table.

"What makes you say that, Reverend?"

"Well, they've been digging like a bunch of hyperactive moles all evening," Annabelle said, craning her neck to look out the window at the bright glow emanating from the woods, "and it looks like they're still at it. Whatever is in the ground, it's firmly planted there."

"The murderer could have dug a hole and put him in there last week! I saw it in a movie!"

"Dougie!"

Annabelle chuckled.

"Possibly, but then you would have tripped over a fleshy arm – not a bone, Dougie."

Dougie made a disgusted face and shook his head in an exaggerated motion. "Eurgh!"

"I've lived here for fifteen years," Shona said, thoughtfully, "and I've never heard of anybody going missing in the woods."

Annabelle shrugged.

"Maybe they've been there even longer than that. Or maybe it was a poor homeless person who froze to death."

"Makes me shiver to think what could be lying in the ground. Just on your doorstep."

"Maybe it's the ghost!" Dougie shouted, his eyes wide with excitement.

"Hush now, Dougie," Shona scolded, "whatever it is, it's none of our business now."

"Wait a minute," Annabelle said, a curious expression on her face, "did you say *the* ghost, Dougie?"

Dougie nodded, afraid to speak in case it resulted in more admonishments.

"You mean, there's rumors of a ghost in those woods?"

Dougie nodded again, his lips visibly pressed together, as if they would be compelled to speak if he didn't suppress them. He looked at Aunt Shona, who shrugged her permission for him to talk to Annabelle.

"Miss Montgomery's sister! She went missing in the woods a long, long time ago. Everyone thinks she died. Jack said he saw her running through there one time wearing a white dress. She looked much younger than Miss Montgomery, because she was only young when she disappeared. Ryan said it's because she went to see a film with a boy, but Angelina says that's rubbish because girls go to see films with boys all the time. She even dared Ryan to go to see a film with her to see if—"

"Miss Montgomery, your teacher?" Shona asked, knowing that unless she interrupted, Dougie would spin a story without an ending, forever and ever, amen.

Dougie nodded, gulping down air to catch his breath, so fast was his speech. "The one who told me off for doing my homework about Professor Xenomorph instead of the book she gave us. I didn't even read the book. Frank's teacher said that so long as you read, it doesn't matter what it is. Reading is itself a—"

"Okay, Dougie," Shona said, placing a hand over his arm and drawing him close to calm him down, "don't go getting all excited again. You'll never get to sleep. Why don't you go brush your teeth? I'll be up to read you a story as soon as I finish my tea."

"Bye Reverend!" Dougie shouted quickly, as if in an

incredible rush, his energy eager to be channeled into something, but his mind racing too quickly to find whatever that something might be.

Shona chuckled softly at the sound of his feet thumping quickly up the stairs.

"That boy has a mind that goes places as quickly and as randomly as his feet."

"Perhaps," uttered Annabelle slowly, lost in her own thoughts, "but I doubt he was lying about those rumors."

"Reverend, surely you don't think there's any value to them. They're just idle ghost stories! The kind of thing that children make up all the time about their teachers."

Annabelle nodded her agreement, but her eyes were still fixed somewhere in the distance of her thoughts.

"I suppose. Though even a broken clock is right twice a day."

Annabelle and Shona sipped the last of their tea simultaneously, before the Reverend slapped her knees and stood up.

"Well, I should get going. I'll drop by soon to see how you're getting on – though I'm sure you won't be bothered any more by all of this. It's purely a police matter now."

"You're welcome here anytime Annabelle. It was nice to see someone who wasn't wearing a uniform today."

Annabelle chuckled as she made her way to the door. Before she opened it, she turned and clasped Shona's hands in hers.

"Send my best wishes to your sister."

Shona nodded respectfully.

Annabelle stepped outside and began the long walk across the dark, open field toward her beloved blue Mini, guided by the flashing police lights and bright glow of the woods, her mind rolling with thoughts that were as lively as the young boy she had just left who was right now tossing in his bed trying to get to sleep.

Though Annabelle felt weary and ready for a good night's rest by the time she pulled into the yard that separated the church of Upton St. Mary and the small white cottage she called home, her mind was spinning with possibilities and theories.

She turned off the engine and stepped out of her car, bristling a little as a cold gust blew through her cassock. When she looked up, she noticed the small figure of Philippa, the church secretary, braving the wind as she ran with almost comically tiny steps toward the Reverend.

"Philippa! It's rather late for you to still be here, isn't it?"

Philippa clutched her coat around her as she drew close. "Hello, Reverend. I'm very sorry, but I was rather hoping you would give me a lift home. I completely lost track of time."

Though Annabelle was tired herself, she could never leave her most loyal friend to face the cool night alone. Philippa didn't live too far away, and in fact, it was a rather pleasant walk in the summertime. In unpredictable weather and cold snaps that emerged at other times of the year, however, it felt twice as long.

"Hop in," Annabelle said, with a good-natured shake of her head.

"Thank you, Annabelle," Philippa said, as she got in and placed her hands primly on her lap.

Annabelle reversed the car and pulled back out onto the country road.

"This is terribly unlike you, Philippa. Whatever were you doing that you lost track of the time?"

"Just my usual duties."

"Hmm," replied Annabelle, unconvinced, "you must have checked the accounting ledgers four times in the past week alone. And if you sweep those steps any more you'll wear them down to a ramp!"

"I'm just being thorough, Reverend."

Annabelle shook her head as she eased the car around the corners of the village's buildings.

"Believe it or not, yours isn't even the strangest behavior I've witnessed today. I'm beginning to wonder if there's something in the air."

Philippa remained silent.

Annabelle parked the car outside Philippa's well-maintained front garden and broke the silence with the click of her handbrake. Philippa promptly undid her seatbelt.

"Before you go," Annabelle said, turning in her seat to face her mousey friend, "I want to ask you something."

"Yes, Reverend?"

Annabelle frowned, seeking the right words. She didn't want to go spreading police business around – especially to someone as prone to gossip as Philippa – but she felt that she had to know more. And there was no better person to ask.

"Have you ever heard any rumors regarding a ghost in Upton St. Mary?"

Philippa's face stretched itself into an expression of such shock that all her wrinkles disappeared and she looked a full five years younger. She clasped a hand to her chest and stared at Annabelle as if she had transformed into a werewolf before her very own eyes.

"I... What.... Why would you ask me such a thing, Reverend?!"

Annabelle squinted at her colleague's overly dramatic reaction.

"Are you alright, Philippa?"

"Yes!" Philippa affirmed, sharply. "I'm absolutely perfectly fine! I just have no idea why you would ask me about a ghost!"

Annabelle opened her mouth to question Philippa's strange tone before thinking better of it. Philippa was a wonderful friend, but she had a habit of harnessing on to strange notions that caused her to act weirdly at times.

"Forget I asked. It was just a rumor I heard."

"What rumor?" Philippa blurted, almost before the Reverend had finished her sentence.

"Ah... Well..." Annabelle stuttered, suddenly feeling that she was the one put on the spot.

"Now you're the one acting strangely!" Philippa said triumphantly. She leaned forward, taking the initiative. "What's going on, Annabelle?"

"Nothing! Just... Well..."

For a few moments the two women exchanged odd looks with the rapidity of a tennis match, their expressions flickering between suspicious, annoyed, defensive, and frightened.

"Oh, this is ridiculous!" exclaimed Annabelle finally, throwing her hands in the air.

Philippa turned away, seeming relieved that whatever danger she had perceived from the Vicar's line of questioning was gone.

"Well, I'll see you tomorrow then, Philippa," Annabelle said, adding a shake of her head to her tone of defeat.

"Bye, Reverend," Philippa responded in a monotone as she got out of the car and made her way to her front door.

Annabelle watched her fumble for her keys and go inside before turning the car around and heading back to the church.

Ordinarily, Philippa's bizarre behavior would have been cause for concern enough. Today, it was just another strange event to add to the others. Almost everyone she had spoken to was exhibiting peculiar reactions, and Annabelle could not bear the feeling that she was standing on the edge of not just one, but several mysteries.

As a child, her father, a London cabbie who adhered to the profession's stereotype by having an opinion on everything, had a saying for certain kinds of drivers: 'They take a pound to start, and a pound to stop.' Annabelle felt that the saying could easily be applied to Upton St. Mary. A good event in the small village seemed to spark a snowball of positive feeling and good fortune that spread to everyone within its vicinity. Unfortunately, it worked the other way around too. If the behavior of DI Nicholls, Philippa, and Constable Raven were anything to go by, soon the whole village would be enraptured by the dark intrigue and paranoid speculation that seemed to be swirling around her.

She drove her Mini expertly along the winding roads. It was an experience that she usually savored as one of life's most underappreciated and satisfying pleasures. To drive along these elegantly arranged country lanes guided solely by the headlights of her car was, to her, heavenly. Tonight, however, it was a time of solitude and quiet during which her mind ran rampant with growing worries and concerns over the events of the day.

Top of the list had to be the identity of the body that

young Dougie had discovered. Though she had become as much a staple of village life as the annual cake competition, Annabelle had only been in Upton St. Mary for a few years. Usually her closest friend would fill her in (a little too eagerly, and with a little more information than was strictly necessary) when she found her knowledge of Upton St. Mary's past, or its inhabitants, was lacking. But with Philippa acting in a manner that was so out of the ordinary, Annabelle would have to find another long-time resident and expert gossip to aid her in the investigation to find out who the body might be.

Of course, the question of whether Annabelle should even be getting involved with this police matter never occurred to her. She regarded the unveiling of the village's mysteries as part of her Godly duties. The maintaining of the villagers' peace of mind was a matter of course for the church vicar. That's how she saw it.

After all, it would by no means be the first time police work had overlapped with her churchly responsibilities and on those previous occasions her diligence, curiosity, and astute intuition had borne rather satisfying results. Already, she felt she had gained some insight that had not yet reached the admirable Inspector Nicholls: The ghost of Miss Montgomery's sister.

There's no way Dougie would have divulged playground hearsay to DI Nicholls. The Inspector was much too intimidating and abrupt for that. And even if he had, it's the sort of thing the detective would have dismissed out of hand even on his better days. Annabelle, however, was a strong believer that "out of the mouth of babes comes truth." A slightly distorted truth, perhaps, but a truth worth considering.

Just as she was engrossed in these deepest of thoughts,

something darted across the road.

"Crikey!" Annabelle cried out, slamming on the brakes.

The car jolted to a halt, flinging Annabelle forward, then thumping her back against the seat. When she looked up again the road was empty. She had seen foxes cross the road before, and on one occasion a lone sheep, but this had looked more like a pig.

Surely not, thought Annabelle. Pigs were fenced in. They rarely roamed. She shook off the incident, too tired to add another question to her growing pile, and continued homewards.

When she reached the church, she parked her car beside her cottage and got out without taking a moment to appreciate the picturesque night sky as she usually did when arriving home at this hour. She entered her house in a hurry. She wanted to have a shower and get to bed; tomorrow was going to be a long and busy day. Especially if her instinct that this was only just the beginning of a period of complexity and intrigue turned out to be correct.

Dr. Robert Brownson could not stop fidgeting as he drove his white Honda Civic down the M3 toward Upton St. Mary. He alternated restlessly between having the radio on and turning it off, finding that his thoughts wandered out of control when it was off, and that most of the music reminded him of... her. At some point as he left behind the dense roads of London, he settled upon a talk radio station and decided to focus on the road that unfurled under the light of his car's headlamps. It was a long drive, made longer by his anticipation of what, and who, awaited him.

Ordinarily, he would not have driven throughout the

night, but these were no ordinary circumstances. This was an opportunity that he felt compelled to grab with both hands, an opportunity that he had been waiting for for years, and one which he was most certainly not going to let pass through his fingers.

Dr. Brownson shuffled a little in his seat, finding that his most expensive suit had shrunk in the year since he had last worn it. He was successful, talented, and had established himself in the most privileged and distinguished circles of London's scientific community. However, there were few events in the calendar of a forensic anthropologist grand enough to demand his best clothes. This occasion was an exception.

The request had come through during the evening, much later than he typically received business calls. He had almost ignored it completely. The voice on the other end had been friendly but officious, a young police constable who requested his assistance on a case.

"Can't the local pathologist handle it?"

"She requested a forensic anthropologist. You, specifically."

At the mention of a female pathologist, Robert Brownson's thoughts were already in the past.

"Who requested me?" he asked, tentatively.

Upon hearing her name, Dr. Brownson was thrust sharply back into the past. A magical day at the Oxford Cambridge boat race. Punting down the River Cherwell. Passionate discussions about history and philosophy, where romance had blossomed across the overlap in their interests.

Robert Brownson had always been slightly shy, the kind of person who took time to reveal the full spectrum of his personality. He was humorous and good-natured, but he struggled to find opportunities where these positive qualities could flourish. At the time of his relationship with the raven-haired angel, he had felt blessed by her strong independence. Her incredible ambition and dedicated humility had given her, and indeed, those around her a sense of strength. He had felt emboldened. He could remember almost every conversation they had had, almost every item of clothing she had worn, and every which way she had styled her hair, like the notes to a song listened to many times over.

Unfortunately, the most vivid memory was that of her revelation. She would leave Oxford to take up a once-in-a-lifetime Ph.D. opportunity at a top university in America. There was nothing he could do or say. She was determined. He had been bereft.

Decades later, he was hearing her name again, associated with a case in a small village somewhere near the south coast of England. At times throughout the intervening years, he had teased and fortified himself with the notion that one day he would hear of her and descend to declare thirty years of pent-up feelings for the woman he had not stopped thinking about for the duration. But he knew it was not in his character. He would crumble before such a grand gesture.

Now though, years of good karma had been cashed in. He had been handed the greatest opportunity he would ever get – a coincidence so extraordinary it was enough to make a scientist believe in God – to reconnect with his one true love, the one that got away, his soulmate: Harper Jones.

CHAPTER THREE

ANNABELLE AWOKE FEELING breezy and light for about five seconds. After that, the concerns and questions that had troubled her during the previous day flooded her mind so vehemently that not even the dappled morning light could lift her spirits. She showered, dressed, and made her way into the kitchen, opening curtains as she passed through the house to let the morning sunshine infuse some of its uplifting energy into the rooms. As she was about to place some bread in the toaster, however, she heard a distant scratching sound coming from the church. She paused, listening closely. It stopped for a few moments, before starting up again with even more vigor.

"What on earth could that be at this time of morning?" she muttered to herself as she leaned across the sink to see out of the window.

Outside, wielding a broom as if it were a weapon was the small figure of Philippa, an expression of grim determination upon her face. Biscuit was watching from a tree branch and after a few moments, she leapt down and began eagerly chasing the broom that Philippa was sweeping briskly from side to side. Biscuit's "help" didn't seem to improve Philippa's mood any and she brushed the step even harder for a few moments before quickly prodding Biscuit, an action designed to deter the cat. An action that was successful.

"She brushed those steps yesterday!" Annabelle exclaimed to nobody in particular.

Philippa was by no means lazy, and indeed, seemed to take great satisfaction in undertaking the lion's share of the church's upkeep. It was just a little past eight on a Saturday morning, however, and combined with Philippa's lateness in leaving the church the day before, Annabelle began to grow deeply worried about her church secretary's behavior.

She rapped on the window loudly until Philippa, who was so engrossed in her task that it took her a while to notice, looked up. She locked eyes with the vicar and waved. Annabelle gestured for Philippa to join her in her cottage kitchen, and watched as the church secretary placed her broomstick aside almost reluctantly, before making her way over.

"Morning, Reverend," Philippa said quietly, as she stepped into the kitchen.

"How long have you been out there, Philippa?" Annabelle said, readying an extra cup for morning tea.

"Oh, not long," Philippa replied, "about an hour or so."

Annabelle decided to hide her surprise.

"Are you not sleeping well?"

"No, Reverend. I'm sleeping perfectly fine."

"Hmm," Annabelle concluded, unconvinced. "Toast?"

"Yes please, Reverend," Philippa answered politely. "I was in such a rush this morning that I didn't have any breakfast."

Annabelle turned her back to put some more bread in the toaster and to hide the look on her face. The mystery of what was troubling Philippa only seemed to grow more and more curious.

Once breakfast was ready, Annabelle placed the plates on the table and took a seat beside Philippa, who was eerily quiet for a woman who enjoyed passing judgment on all and sundry and rarely missed the opportunity to do so. They ate in silence for a while, to the music of crunched toast and cutlery clinking as they dug into scrambled eggs and bacon.

Annabelle mentally toyed with various questions that she could ask Philippa in order to probe further into what was bothering her but decided against it. Philippa knew Annabelle well enough to detect when she was fishing for information. Still, she was beginning to grow tired of feeling like there was much that she didn't know.

"I don't suppose you've heard any gossip coming from the village today, have you?" Annabelle asked, in as innocent and casual a manner as she could manage.

"No," Philippa said solemnly. "Though I'm to meet Barbara Simpson in a bit."

"Ah, Barbara! I've not seen her in a while."

"Vicars are rarely close with village pub owners," Philippa said, allowing herself the little witticism despite her quiet mood.

"Still, I'm long overdue on catching up with her," Annabelle said, warming to the idea.

"You're welcome to join us," Philippa said.

"And here she is," Annabelle exclaimed, looking out of the window as she jumped from her seat.

Sure enough, the buxom figure of Barbara Simpson, owner of the Dog And Duck, the most frequented pub in

Upton St. Mary, was tottering into the church driveway upon her high-heeled stilettos. Despite being barely five feet tall, Barbara Simpson was easy to recognize even at a distance, for the extravagant fake-fur coats she wore and her propensity for lurid, clashing colors. Though she was well into her fifties and undeniably one of the most astute and successful women in the village, Barbara possessed the taste in fashion of an adolescent schoolgirl. Her high-pitched, girlish voice seemed to reverberate for miles wherever she went while above her perpetually smiling face, heavily made-up in hues of pink (lips), red (cheeks), and blue (eyes), sat her proudest possession: her thick, pale-blonde hair, arranged into an elaborately sculpted beehive that she would caress and puff up frequently with her inch-long fingernails.

Annabelle opened her door and invited the woman inside.

"Thank you, Reverend! Ooh, it's been such a long time since I've been to church. I'm feeling all guilty!" she giggled, stepping into the kitchen and greeting Philippa.

"It's rather early for you, isn't it Barbara?" Annabelle said.

"Oh, I had to go to the market. Get the best veg for tonight's dinner menu before I was left with the scraps. Chef's off until lunchtime or he'd do it. I thought I'd have a chat with Philippa before going back to the pub."

"Would you like some tea?" Annabelle asked.

Barbara's larger-than-life face lit up as it did when she found something funny, which was rather often. "I always like it when I'm the one being offered a drink instead of the other way around. Especially when it's a vicar doing the asking!"

Annabelle smiled and got to work on the tea.

"How are you, my darling?" Barbara said to Philippa, placing an affectionate hand on her knee. "I've not seen you in days!"

"I've been a little busy at the church," said Philippa, smiling at her friend's concern.

"Well, you've missed out on all the juicy gossip! So much has been going on that even *I* can barely keep up with it!"

Annabelle placed Barbara's tea in front of her and sat down hopefully, ready to finally hear something that could give her a sense of what was happening.

"Thank you ever so much, Vicar. I know you don't drink, but if you ever fancy a good pot roast, it's on the house."

"Thank you, Barbara. You're always welcome to come to Sunday service yourself," Annabelle joked.

Barbara threw her head back and released her high-pitched giggle.

"You are a laugh, Vicar!"

"What's been going on?" Philippa asked uneasily, once the pub owner's laughter had died down.

"Well," Barbara began, leaning forward and taking on the low, astounded tone she usually used for dispensing gossip, "they found a body in the woods. A dead body. They've been running around all over the place to figure out what its doing there. They've even gone—"

Suddenly, Philippa stood up out of her seat, the squeak of the chair on the kitchen floor interrupting Barbara.

"Excuse me," Philippa said, her face pale, "I need to visit the little girls' room."

Annabelle and Barbara watched Philippa scurry out of the kitchen clutching a napkin to her face.

"Is there something wrong with Philippa?" Barbara

asked Annabelle, full of concern. "She looks like she's seen a ghost."

Annabelle shook her head regretfully.

"She's been acting strangely for a few days now. It's just one of the many mysteries that's cropped up lately."

"I hope she's alright," Barbara said, her brightly-painted lips pouting with worry.

"I don't know what the matter is. I would just avoid raising the subject of this body until she's feeling better."

"Right you are, Vicar," the blonde woman replied, nodding to confirm she understood.

"Actually," Annabelle began, leaning forward and lowering her voice, "there is something I would like to ask you. I had hoped Philippa would be able to help me, but as you can see, she's not very willing to discuss such things."

"Of course I'll help you. Ask away."

"It's about the body, actually. You've lived in Upton St. Mary for a long time, haven't you, Barbara?"

Barbara smiled. "Born and raised, Vicar! Though I always prefer telling people I've not been alive that long!"

Annabelle chuckled a little.

"Well, have you ever heard any rumors about Miss Montgomery the school teacher? Specifically her sister?"

Barbara's long, thick eyelashes splayed outward as she gasped her surprise. "You know what, I never thought of that! Yes, you're right, Vicar. That body could very well be her!"

"Who?" Annabelle said quickly, almost pleading for a name.

"Lucy. Louisa Montgomery's sister. I haven't thought about Lucy in years. I still see Louisa around sometimes though, carrying her huge carpet bag, as uptight as anything. She doesn't seem to have changed in – gosh –

twenty years, now? Lives just opposite Katie Flynn's tea shop – terrible fuss they had a while ago."

"Yes. But what about Lucy? Why did her sister disapp—"

Annabelle was so eager to blurt out her questions that she almost didn't notice Philippa's shuffling footsteps emerge from the bathroom. She stopped herself mid-sentence to smile at the small woman as she came back into the kitchen.

"Am I interrupting?" Philippa said quietly, almost hanging her head with embarrassment.

"Of course not!" Annabelle assured her, standing up from her seat. "I was just on my way out to perform some errands. I'll leave you two to yourselves."

"See you, Vicar."

"It was a pleasure catching up, Barbara. Hopefully I'll see you around."

"Likewise," Barbara said.

Philippa merely nodded, before sitting down and clasping her teacup with both hands in order to stop them from shaking.

Annabelle leaped into her Mini and started the engine. It roared into life eagerly, mirroring her mood that had been kick-started by the information she had just gleaned.

Barbara had not said much, indeed, she had been interrupted before fully embarking on her train of thought, but she had said enough. The teacher's name was Louisa Montgomery; her sister's name was Lucy. She lived opposite Katie Flynn's tea shop, a place that Annabelle knew well.

That was all Annabelle needed.

In all her time in Upton St. Mary, and of all the pieces of gossip she had come across, there was only one solution she knew would work when one wanted the truth and nothing but the truth: Go right to the source.

If there was any connection between that body in the woods and the alleged disappearance of Lucy Montgomery, she would find out from Louisa herself.

Even at this early hour, the village was bustling as it always was on Saturdays with the farmer's market at its center. Annabelle weaved her Mini through the rough, cobbled streets and turned the corner that led to Katie Flynn's tea shop.

The tea shop was situated on one of the most well-preserved, delightfully colorful, and sleepy – even by Upton St. Mary's standards – streets. What Annabelle found, however, as she drove her Mini carefully down its bumpy cobbles, was anything but calm.

"I saw you! That's not the way you hold a dog! If he wants to sniff the lamppost, you let him sniff the lamppost! Who do you think you are?" bellowed none other than DI Nicholls.

"I... I... I'm Terry Watson," stammered the frightened man who was cowering in the presence of the tall, imposing figure of the Inspector.

"I don't care what your name is! I don't care if you're the King of Egypt! When your dog wants to sniff something, you jolly well let him!"

Annabelle parked the car beside the two figures and jumped out of it.

"What's going on?" she said, walking up to the two men.

The Inspector turned to Annabelle and jabbed his finger toward Terry. "This man thinks it's okay to treat a dog as if it doesn't have feelings, as if it doesn't have instincts. He wants the dog to go against its very nature!"

"I do not!" Terry exclaimed, managing to muster enough courage to argue now that Annabelle was there.

"I bloody well saw you!" the Inspector roared. "What kind of man doesn't allow his dog to sniff a lamppost?! I've locked up hardened criminals more reasonable than you! This is animal cruelty! I've got half a mind to arrest you right now and stick you in a cell. Then you'll know what it's like to have somebody stopping you from doing what *you* want!"

"Stop it!" Annabelle shouted, firmly. "This is ludicrous. Terry loves his dog as well as if he were his own child. Why, Chester is one of the most well-behaved dogs in the county."

"Thank you, Annabelle."

"Are you taking his side?" Nicholls growled, his eyes wild.

"No!" Annabelle asserted. "Because there are no sides to take, Inspector. This is obviously a misunderstanding. Though I would expect better than berating a man on the street from an officer of the law!"

Terry shimmied slightly to the side as Annabelle and the Inspector locked gazes. With small steps, he shuffled away, and when he was certain that they hadn't noticed, he began walking briskly down the street, casting fearful glances behind him.

"Reverend," the Inspector began, some calm seeping into his voice, though he had a resolute expression on this face, "that was a police matter, one in which you had no business interfering."

Annabelle pursed her lips in frustration.

"I have every right to defend the respectability of people

living in my parish, Inspector. Especially when they are being subjected to the fury of a.... a... grump!"

The Inspector breathed heavily, blood dissipating from his cheeks as he slowly gathered his emotions.

"I have a deep respect for you, Reverend, but you can't tell me how to do my job."

Annabelle raised her chin.

"And how, Inspector, did your conversation with Louisa Montgomery go, exactly? You haven't been to see her already have you? You must have got her out of bed."

The Inspector's mouth opened in awe.

"How did you—"

"It's a fairly obvious connection to make, considering the body must have been in the woods for a many years and her sister disappeared two decades ago. You certainly didn't come here to partake in the wonderful delicacies available at Flynn's tea shop or you would be a lot less abrasive. In fact, I would even surmise that your conversation with Louisa proved rather fruitless, considering the temper you just subjected that poor dog-walker to."

Annabelle watched as the Inspector mouthed the beginning of several words, before giving up entirely and bounding off down the street in a huff.

"This case won't go anywhere if you insist on being so hot-headed," Annabelle muttered to herself, as she watched him go.

She returned to her Mini, locked it, and strolled down the street. When she reached Flynn's tea shop, she examined the small house that was set a little way back from the road, directly opposite. It was rather less elegant than most houses in Upton St. Mary, though no less comfortable. Its well-trimmed hedges, crisply starched curtains, and buffed windows hinted at a houseproud, hard-working owner.

Annabelle took another step toward it before catching sight of something in the corner of her eye.

There were cupcakes with strawberry icing, a treat she had not enjoyed for some time. Éclairs with soft cream spilling out of them. A cheesecake set to the side topped with raspberries and blueberries. These visions seemed to permeate and gain control over her mind as they sat on sumptuous display in the window of Katie Flynn's tea shop. Momentarily forgetting the matter in hand, Annabelle entered a deep, hypnotic state from which she emerged to find herself, remarkably, standing at the tea shop counter speaking to Katie Flynn herself just a few seconds later.

"Hello, Reverend. The usual éclair?"

"Um... I think I'll try that cupcake, if I may. And a pot of Earl Grey, please."

"Absolutely. Take a seat, Reverend. I'll bring it over."

"Thank you, Katie."

Of course, Annabelle was still brimming with a sense of purpose and determination, but there was no harm in a little treat, surely?

She had decided to give Louisa a respite from visitors. If the Inspector had just been to see her, Annabelle would almost certainly be unwelcome, especially considering the Inspector's irritable mood. So she took a seat in the tea shop window that allowed her a full view of Louisa's home.

The cake and tea were brought over, and Annabelle savored every mouthful of the spongy, sugary, frosted confection. She washed it down with one cup of tea, and was just considering a second, when the door to the teacher's home opened. Annabelle leaned forward, focusing on the prim figure that diligently locked her front door and walked out to the street.

With her salt-and-pepper hair tied in a chignon at the

nape of her neck, and in a tweed skirt and jacket, a crisp white shirt complementing the ensemble, Miss Montgomery certainly appeared the part of a strict, spinster schoolteacher. She looked like she brooked no nonsense with the eight-year-olds she taught, particularly those as rambunctious as Dougie Dewar. Her signature look was completed, sure enough, by the large carpet bag she carried, the handles of which were looped over her forearm – just as Barbara had described.

Though she wore her hair in a severe style and had on only light-make up, her delicately featured face, with her strong cheekbones, supple skin, and mesmerizingly deep-green eyes, hinted at a once-great beauty. Her lovely features were not uplifted by an expression of goodwill or even good-naturedness, however, such was her downcast look. She looked at the ground as she hurried off.

In between bites of strawberry cupcake, Annabelle had been pondering whether she should actually speak to Louisa. The Inspector would no doubt have left a bad impression, and the subject of her sister may be a painful subject for Louisa. Annabelle waggled her head from side to side as she considered the pros and cons.

Still trapped in her indecision, Annabelle threw the last of her cupcake into her mouth, absent-mindedly stepping away from her table, through the door of the tea shop, and into the street. Soon she was following Louisa, hoping that she would get some sign that it might be possible to approach the teacher and get a reasonable reception.

Guiltily, Annabelle felt a certain glamour and excitement as she followed the woman through the quiet back streets of Upton St. Mary. She imagined herself one of the detectives she often saw in movies or on TV, secretly tracking their target to the source of the grand intrigue, though it was a little difficult to maintain necessary elusive, shadow-like qualities, due to the large black cassock she wore and the constant greetings she received from passers-by.

Annabelle was so engrossed in her private game of "chase" that she almost didn't notice the direction in which Louisa was heading. After five minutes it became clear that Louisa was not, in fact, shopping for groceries as Annabelle had thought. After ten, it was also apparent that she wasn't heading anywhere within the village, as she took a rarely-used path that led toward allotments that were situated on the fringes of Upton St. Mary.

Annabelle suddenly found herself sidling along hedgerows and hopping behind trees in order to remain out of sight as her quarry traversed the open fields beyond the path. Her playful "trailing" of the target had taken on a very ominous turn indeed.

Eventually, Louisa turned in toward a section of the allotments, balancing delicately on the grass corridors that crisscrossed between the vegetable plots. Annabelle hopped through some nettles, mouthed her frustration, and crouched behind a tree as she rubbed her stinging hands. In her ludicrous position, she was clearly visible to anybody passing by on the paths, and she prayed that she would not be required to explain herself. She peered around the oak tree trunk and watched as Louisa strolled up to a particularly beaten-looking shed and placed her carpet bag down carefully on the ground. Louisa unlocked the multiple padlocks which held the shed door shut, and went inside.

Annabelle watched the door close behind the teacher, and shuffled her feet as she tried to find a comfortable position in the nettles. She looked around and, mercifully, saw no one. How she would explain what a vicar was doing hiding behind a tree, in the midst of a patch of nettles, in the middle of a field, she had no idea. She kept her fingers crossed that her solitary status wouldn't change as, judging by the closed shed door, she was going to have to wait.

After about half an hour, Annabelle gave up all pretense of stealth. The excitement and thrill of the chase had evaporated, leaving her feeling ridiculous and in pain. Her crouching position had given her an incredible cramp, and each time she shuffled around to make herself more comfortable, she gathered another nasty sting on her hands, which were now red and swollen.

She had been lucky to not be seen from the path, but every additional minute was test of her fortune, and she had had about enough of this "game." With no sign that Louisa was about to emerge from her shed anytime soon, Annabelle stood up, brushed down her cassock, and dolefully limped back along the path, soothing her hands by rubbing them gently.

The lingering taste of strawberry cupcake, and her deep and sincere belief that she had earned another one, compelled her to return to Flynn's tea shop. As she opened the door once again, its sugary aroma struck her closely followed by an idea. She wondered briefly if the two were connected. Sugar. Idea.

Shaking her head, Annabelle returned to the matter in hand. Who better to ask about the enigmatic Louisa Montgomery than Katie Flynn, who no doubt saw the teacher frequently from across the street? Annabelle was also reminded of a remark that Barbara had made about some sort of "fuss" between the two. It was a perfect excuse for another cupcake.

"Hello again, Reverend," smiled Katie, with a wink. "Have you come in for another bite to eat?"

Annabelle chuckled. "You know me too well, Katie."

Katie laughed as she placed a cupcake on a plate and began fixing Annabelle more tea.

"Actually, Katie," Annabelle said, "do you have a moment to talk? I have something I'd rather like to ask you."

Katie looked around the tea shop, taking in the quiet atmosphere, then spoke to her niece and assistant, a wonderfully pretty girl who always had her head tucked into a book. "Sally? Would you mind taking care of any customers while I speak with the Reverend?"

Sally shrugged and nodded, before bowing her head once more into her paperback. Katie rolled her eyes, then walked with Annabelle to her table by the window.

"So, what's on your mind, Reverend?"

"Well, I was rather hoping to pick your brain about your neighbor across the road," Annabelle said, nodding toward Louisa's home.

"Oh," Katie said, her lips pursing disapprovingly, "I can tell you plenty about *her,* but it wouldn't be very neighborly."

Annabelle frowned with curiosity.

"I heard you had some fuss?"

"'Some fuss,' indeed, Reverend. If she had had her way, this place wouldn't even exist."

"The tea shop?"

"The very same," Katie said, nodding toward the strawberry cupcake between them.

"Why so?"

Katie looked across the road wistfully.

"It was a long time ago, but you don't forget that kind of thing. You see, I grew up here – in this very tea shop. It used to be our family home. Louisa," Katie said, almost struggling to say the name without grimacing, "and her family lived over there in that tiny house that Louisa now lives in by herself. So we sort of grew up together."

"You were friends?"

"Sure, I suppose," Katie said, reluctantly, after a moment's thought.

"What happened?" Annabelle asked earnestly, on the edge of her seat.

"About ten years ago, I married Tom Flynn – you know him. Well, when it came to deciding where we would live, it was an easy choice. Tom's house over on the hill was ten times the size of ours! As I was the eldest, and Harry – my brother – was away working in London, I didn't want to leave our family home empty."

"So you decided to turn it into a tea shop."

"And I've never looked back."

"It's the best in Cornwall."

Katie chuckled. "Thank you, Reverend. Certain people were against the idea from the start, however."

"Why?"

Katie shook her head in confusion. "I still don't really know. She said it would be 'noisy,' that it would 'ruin the aesthetics of the street,' that the house had been a home for years, and it would be a tragedy to change it into a business. At first I thought it was just the typical grumbles and resistance to change you hear at any old town hall meeting, but when she began getting lawyers involved, I got very upset indeed. They threw out her claims, of course, but it left a very bitter taste in my mouth – especially when the shop was supposed to bring pleasure, and tourists, to the whole village. Personally I think she's been a teacher for too long. She thinks she can boss around adults just as easily as she does her pupils!"

"It is rather strange."

"She's never been the same since her sister disappeared – not that she was so wonderful then, of course."

"Do you think her objections to the shop were about clinging to the past? Albeit in an odd way?"

Katie shrugged.

"Frankly, Reverend, I think you'd need more Godly forgiveness than I'm capable of to give her the benefit of the doubt to that extent."

Annabelle sighed sadly.

"Can you tell me anything about her sister? About how she disappeared?"

"Ah, you're going very far back there, Reverend. I can't even remember what I had for breakfast!"

"Please try."

Katie looked up and squinted as she brought forth memories long forgotten.

"Well, the one thing I do remember is that Lucy was as sweet as Louisa was sour. She was always smiling, always laughing. Everybody loved her. None of that intensity or aloofness that Louisa has. No, Lucy was an utterly lovely girl. I'm sure that's why they never got on."

"They argued?"

"No, nothing like that. They just... weren't like sisters at all. They never did anything together. Partly because Louisa always thought she was better than anyone else. If there was a school dance, you could be sure that Louisa wouldn't show up, and just as sure that Lucy would be the life of the party. If it was a nice day, you were sure to find Lucy skipping down the street to meet her friends, while

Louisa was locked up in her room with nothing but her books. I mean, put it this way, Reverend, you know almost every person in this village, and yet here you are, having to ask me about Louisa Montgomery. What does that say about her as a person?"

"Hmm," Annabelle murmured, "I suppose you have a point."

"Oh! And she was so disapproving of Lucy having a boyfriend. You'd think she was her mother, rather than her older sister! The crazy thing was that Louisa herself had a boyfriend! If that's not the definition of hypocrisy then I don't know what is!"

"So she was protective of Lucy?"

"Bah!" Katie said, brushing the idea aside. "If you're looking for good intentions from Louisa Montgomery, you'll need to dig very deep. If you ask me, Louisa was jealous of Lucy. Lucy was younger, prettier, more popular, and had the entire world at her feet. Most people would be proud to call Lucy their sister. Louisa was simply proud."

Annabelle thought over what Katie was saying as she took a large bite of her cupcake and followed it up with some sips of piping hot tea. She placed the cup down gently and looked once more at the tea shop owner.

"How did Lucy disappear?"

Katie looked once again into the distance, her mind diving into the depths of her memories.

"It was about twenty years ago, now. I believe she had gone out with her boyfriend, and she just vanished. Never came home."

"Did they question the boyfriend?"

"I believe they did," Katie said, the slowness of her words and the troubled look in her eyes indicating that she was at the limits of what her memory could bring forth, "but they never arrested him. I think he had an alibi, or perhaps there was some confusion over exactly when it happened."

"It's all very curious."

"Oh," Katie said adamantly, "I remember the impact it had very well. The whole village was stunned. Lucy was a friend to everyone, her loss affected all of us. Some people were angry, some wouldn't let it go, and most of us were extremely sad. It was a very dark time."

"For Louisa, too?"

"Yeah," Katie said, "even for her. If she was prickly previously, she was positively reclusive after the incident. You'd get an occasional 'hello,' or a simple conversation out of her before her sister disappeared, but when she lost her sister, she gave up on other people completely."

"That's a terrible story," Annabelle said.

"Yes, it is," Katie agreed. "It takes a long time for such wounds to heal."

"For some people those kinds of wounds never fully do," Annabelle replied.

Katie nodded.

"Do you remember who Lucy's boyfriend was?"

Katie once again peered into the distance, lines of deep concentration forming around her eyes.

"You know, I really don't. My memory is fuzzy. I could tell you a dozen names, but I wouldn't be sure about any of them!" she laughed.

"That's alright," Annabelle said. "Twenty years is a long time. I doubt I could remember much of what I was doing twenty years ago."

"It's like I say, Reverend, you remember the things that change your life."

"That's very true, Katie."

"How come you're so interested in this, Reverend? Has Philippa been regaling you with stories from the past?"

Annabelle smiled. "No, Philippa's been rather introspective herself, lately. Actually, I'm surprised you haven't heard the news yourself, Katie. I'm under strict orders not to tell anyone."

"Oh, come now, Reverend! Surely I deserve something in return for my history lesson!"

Annabelle chuckled.

"You'll probably hear it soon anyway. This business with Louisa's sister is about to become the talk of the town once again."

Katie's face dropped.

"What do you mean?"

"They found a body in the woods last night."

"Lucy's?!"

Annabelle shrugged.

"From what you tell me, Katie, I don't see who else it could be."

CHAPTER FOUR

D R. BROWNSON'S FOOTSTEPS echoed ominously around the clean, hard walls of the hospital. There were few people around at this time of the morning, his only interactions being with the receptionist who indicated in which direction he would find the morgue and the cleaner who nodded a perfunctory greeting.

He walked slowly and steadily, his bearing almost regal. He felt like a man about to meet his fate, a prince about to take the crown, an athlete about to ascend the podium. He distracted himself from his jangling nerves by fidgeting with the bouquet of roses he carried delicately in his clammy palm, and brushing the sides of his grey-brown curls, occasionally checking his reflection in a well-polished window to make sure he hadn't brushed his hair too much. The large double doors loomed at the end of the corridor like the gates to heaven, and his heart raced ever more quickly as he made his way forward, step by step.

Robert Brownson was suddenly struck by a thought that seared through him with the power of a lightning bolt:

Would Harper Jones still remember him? He stopped in his tracks, his mouth open with shock. After a moment to gather his senses, he realized the stupidity of the thought – Harper Jones had been the one who asked for him! He smiled to himself, shook his head, and slowly began walking again.

After another few steps he froze once more. What would he say? It had been so long. He vividly remembered Harper's keen gaze, her brevity with words, and her ability to make others feel like they were in the spotlight. When they were younger, he had often struggled to say the right thing to her. Now that they had not spoken for so long, he had even less of an idea of what to say. What if she had not lost that focused, silent intensity, just as he had not lost his bumbling clumsiness when it came to conversation?

Brownson took out the white handkerchief he had spent over five minutes neatly folding into his pocket, adjusting it to be as precise and as neat as Harper herself, and wiped it across his brow. He was sweating and suddenly felt immensely claustrophobic in the hospital hallway. He caught sight of a water cooler some way down another corridor and hurried toward it. The glug of the water echoed against the walls as he filled paper cup after paper cup and downed them one after the other.

He breathed deeply, feeling both calmer and cooler.

For goodness sake, Robert! he thought to himself. *You're a man of over fifty! You can't be nervous at the prospect of meeting a colleague!*

After preparing himself with these words, however unconvinced of them he really was, he threw the paper cup into the nearby bin, picked up the bouquet once again, stiffened his back, and marched toward the doors marked 'morgue.'

As soon as he entered the room, however, whatever romantic scene Dr. Brownson had imagined previously disappeared entirely, as half a dozen people of various ages and sizes, all clothed in white coats, spun their heads and caught sight of him standing there with the bouquet in front of him like a knight preparing to joust.

Up until now, Brownson had imagined his meeting with Harper as intimate, the two of them greeting in a warm, friendly manner among the scientific paraphernalia they had once spent so much time with. In his daydreams, he had seen them leaning over some wonderful artifact, enthralled by a particular aspect of it as much as by each other's company, two dedicated scientists indulging their similarly potent passions for enlightened thinking.

Instead, the morgue was bustling with movement and the clinking of equipment – at least, until he walked in. The people in white coats were all moving around a table at the center of the room, the bones lying upon it anything but wonderful. Dirt, greenery, and pebbles were in the process of being cleaned from them, the messy debris providing a stark contrast to the sterile mortuary. The decomposed figure laid out looked almost terrifying and even at his distracted first glance, Dr. Brownson could tell that this skeleton had a rather sad story to tell.

"Ah..." he stammered, taken aback by the sheer number of people looking at him, as well as the clinical, deathly atmosphere that befell the room and the shattering of his fantasies. He glanced at the roses in his hand, looking at them as if they had been placed there by someone else, then tossed them aside onto a counter, causing instruments to clang to the floor. Everyone stared at him as the last vibrato tone of a fallen tong preceded complete and utter silence.

Just as Dr. Brownson was about to make his apologies

and scurry out of the hospital, into his car, and back to his home in London, the figure at the head of the table took off her glasses and smiled.

"Robert!"

It was Harper. As radiant as ever. Still impossibly beautiful and almost magically youthful. So startling was she that Brownson almost believed her to be somebody else. She looked a full two decades younger than her forty-eight years. The bright sparkle of her green eyes and wide lips which seemed to save all their light for rare, powerful smiles were unmistakable, however.

Dr. Brownson's earlier embarrassment disappeared along with his awareness of the rest of the room, as his eyes focused only upon Harper making her way toward him and taking his arm. Suddenly, he felt as if he were an audience in his own mind, unable to believe this was really happening, watching what unfolded as though it was happening to somebody else.

"Everyone," Harper called to the rest of the team, "this is Dr. Robert Brownson, the finest forensic anthropologist in England. Robert, this is a small team of people I've brought in to help. They're mostly medical students and assistants who will cater to your every whim. Whatever you wish for, they shall divine."

The team nodded respectfully, a few of them uttering courteous 'hellos,' though Dr. Brownson's eyes were fixed upon the transcendent figure next to him.

"Harper!" he managed to say, as she led him toward the table. "How are you? Why, you look as wonderf—"

"So as you can see, the bones have been underground long enough that roots have formed between them. I'm no botanist, but it seems to me that an estimate of..."

Brownson gazed into her face, her words growing ever

more incomprehensible and elusive to follow. Try as he might to concentrate upon what she was saying, the sound of her voice captivated him so intensely that he struggled to focus on the meaning of her words. He basked in the music and the rhythm of her exquisite voice, vowels pitched in the most heavenly keys possible, consonants so expertly and delicately uttered. He felt himself carried away on a soft pillow of sound he had almost forgotten.

"...though in my personal opinion the femur indicates an age of mid to late-teens, what do you think?"

Brownson's eyes were closed, but after a few moments he noticed that the beautiful sound of Harper's voice had disappeared, and he re-opened them.

"Robert?" Harper repeated, the anthropologist's silence catching the attention of several team members who shot surprised glances at Harper.

"Ah... Yes... Sorry."

Harper looked at Dr. Brownson with a furrow in her brow.

"Let me see," he said, buying himself time to gather his senses by peering at the bones in front of him.

Harper leaned down and spoke into his ear.

"Are you quite alright, Robert? Do you need some rest before we start? You've been driving all night."

"No, no, I shall be fine. Your smile has infused me with an energy no amount of sleep could replicate," he whispered.

Harper looked at Brownson and squinted suspiciously. The group that had by now all gathered around the body shuffled awkwardly before observing the anthropologist keenly as he resumed probing and poking absently at the skeleton.

"So what do you think, Dr. Brownson?" one of the assistants piped up.

"Do you remember," Dr. Brownson ignored his inquisitor, and began to speak again to Harper, his mind far too captivated by his thoughts to concentrate upon his work, "when we took a trip to Brighton Beach? We went in the water, but you were so concerned about your hair that you would only go up to your waist!"

Brownson laughed heartily, causing a few more members to cast confused expressions toward him.

"Um..." Harper said, clearing her throat. "Yes. I was just wondering, however, what age you would place the body based on the—"

"Of course, of course," Dr. Brownson said, turning his head once more to the collection of bones. He prodded a little more but when everyone had turned their attention once again to the skeleton on the table, Dr. Brownson leaned in toward Harper again, a warm smile upon his face.

"I must say," he whispered, as his hands continued to work a particularly tough particle of dirt away from one of the bones, "you don't look a day older than the last time I saw you. It's simply remarkable."

Harper smiled neatly, though there was a certain amount of tension around her jaw. She looked straight at him and indicated with her eyes for him to focus on the bones. "Thank you. That's nice of you to say. You look very well yourself, Robert."

Dr. Brownson smiled warmly and cast his eyes around the table at the assistants who returned his inexplicable grin politely. He continued to work on the bones, grasping at a nearby brush in order to get a better look at a cavity.

"Canst thou O cruel, say I love thee not, when I against

my self with thee partake?" he said.

"Ah... Dr. Brownson."

"Do I not think on thee when I forgot, am of my self, all-tyrant, for thy sake?"

"Doctor..."

"That was one of your favorite sonnets, do you remember?" Dr. Brownson said, with glee, all attempts at discretion now discarded. "I would read you a different one each time we parted. That particular one was when—"

Dr. Brownson felt firm fingers grip his forearm and pull him toward the morgue entrance. Harper wrenched the door open and yanked the doctor outside with an ease that suggested remarkable strength for such a slight woman.

He looked around him, as if stunned to find himself outside, before settling his eyes once again on Harper and smiling as if he realized her intentions.

"What is the matter with you? This is neither the time nor the place, Robert," said Harper, her voice firm and resolute.

"You're right," replied Dr. Brownson, standing upright. "I'm sorry. I just got carried away."

"I have a team in there, hadn't you noticed?" continued Harper. "They expected an experienced forensic anthropologist...not a Shakespeare-quoting, sonnet-serenading poet!"

Dr. Brownson nodded apologetically. "You're right. I'm being terribly unprofessional. It's just that it's been so long since I've seen you, and it's stirring so many pleasant memories!"

Harper sighed.

"Let's get back in there and do our work," Dr. Brownson said, wearing a pleased smile, "and as soon as we're done, I would be honored if you would join me for dinner, I mean, breakfast. We'll catch up – we've got decades to get through after all!"

Dr. Brownson chuckled and stepped toward the door, but a strong grip pulled him back once again. When his eyes met Harper's, his face dropped.

"Robert..."

"Don't look so shocked! I know it's been a long time, but just looking at you I can see you've not changed very much at all. As for me, well, I'm pretty much the same man you knew at Oxford! I daresay it'll be just as if you never left!"

"Robert... Are you implying what I think you're implying?"

Dr. Brownson smiled and nodded happily.

"Yes, Harper. Though it's been over twenty years, my feelings haven't changed one bit."

She looked up at him sorrowfully, her eyes full of pity. She raised her hand for Dr. Brownson to see the large emerald ring on her third finger.

"I'm married, Robert. I have been for many years now. I'm sorry if you thought this was anything more than a professional consultation."

Dr. Brownson opened his mouth but found himself empty of words. Once again he felt as if the hospital walls were constricting him, causing his brow to sweat and a slight feeling of nausea to well up inside of him. He gulped loudly, his mouth dry, and stammered.

"Ah...Well..."

"I'm sorry, this," she nodded at the morgue entrance, "was insensitive of me. I should have met with you first. Privately." Robert looked down at the floor.

"If you prefer," continued Harper, her voice exhibiting a gentleness she was unused to showing, "I can arrange for another forensic anthropologist. Dr. Livingstone lives only a few mi– "

"Ha," Dr. Brownson said, with unconvincing joviality, "Livingstone is a hack. He couldn't distinguish a homo sapien from a homophone."

They smiled at each other, though Harper couldn't help noticing the pained look in Dr. Brownson's eyes. He took a deep breath, shuffling his feet and smoothing his clothes briskly, feeling ever more lost under the gaze of the woman he loved.

"Married. Of course. Why wouldn't you be? Sorry. Got it wrong, obviously. You know me, imagination like a unicorn – fantastical! Never was good with people – give me some dusty, dry old bones any day!"

Harper smiled sweetly, hoping it would soothe Dr. Brownson's embarrassment and hurt feelings, but the beauty of it only made his pining more sorrowful. Somehow, he managed to force a little laugh which sounded shallow in the long echoing emptiness of the hospital hallway.

"Perhaps you should go home, Robert."

"No, no, it's okay," he said, after a few deep breaths. "There's only really one thing that will take my mind off this, and that's work. Lead the way, Dr. Jones."

Harper led Dr. Brownson back into the morgue. There were a few snickers and giggles, but Harper quickly stared those down. She stood beside the cranium on the table and was joined by Dr. Brownson.

"So what do you estimate for an age?"

"Fifteen, sixteen. Certainly fits the profile of a girl that age," Dr. Brownson said, briskly. "The bone remodeling on the hips hasn't deteriorated much. That, combined with the fully–grown tibia makes it a near certainty."

A few of the younger team members gathered around the table, still smiling at the doctor's earlier antics. Harper cast them a steely look to remind them that mockery would not be tolerated.

"This damage to the cranial cavity is very interesting."

"We thought so too," piped up a rather confident young male assistant. "But there was a tree root grown through it. Because of that, we thought the damage to the skull likely occurred after death, posthumously."

Dr. Brownson glanced quickly at the assistant.

"The root that went through the bottom of her skull?"

The assistant nodded, smiling.

"That's a rather long leap of logic. You assume a root that was weak enough to go around the jawline, was suddenly strong enough to burst through the cranium? I have to disagree with your conclusion there, young man. This cranium was crushed *before* the root began growing through it. The damage may have increased, but if you look at the skull in profile, you can clearly see how it has been altered by a blow."

The young man shared an abashed glance with his equally-young neighbor, his earlier silent mockery of Dr. Brownson quickly dissipating in the face of his humiliation.

"This is strange," Dr. Brownson said, as he probed inside the skull. Slowly, he pulled out a wrinkly object from its center: A shriveled apple.

"Wow!" came a voice from one of the assembled team members. "How did that get there?"

Dr. Brownson shook his head. "These entire remains present a box of mysteries. Look at these fractures along the arms and legs. They're small, but they were undoubtedly created during this person's lifetime. If you look closely," he said, leaning to inspect the bones and rub away some of the dirt, "you can even find evidence of healing. This kind of healing occurs in childhood."

"What does it mean?" the young man asked again, his cockiness giving way to genuine curiosity.

"This person was beaten throughout her lifetime. Since childhood, in fact. I'd even posit that the beatings increased in severity. She was a healthy person so they may not have been obvious, and they quickly healed, but they were severe nonetheless."

"That's horrendous!" came a voice from around the table again.

"Indeed," replied Dr. Brownson.

"And the apple?" asked the young man, respect for Dr. Brownson now having replaced his earlier ridicule.

Dr. Brownson shrugged. "It would have decomposed by now if it were placed inside the skull at the time of death so I think we can conclude it is a relatively recent addition to the crime scene. I imagine the body was found in a rather shallow grave, yes?"

Harper nodded.

"It's possible that the apple was put there by someone or merely discarded close by and happened to find its way into the skull cavity, perhaps carried there by an animal. A bizarre coincidence, if that is the case."

Lulled by the warm, inviting atmosphere of the tea shop, and pondering over the elaborate picture of the past that Katie Flynn had just painted for her, Annabelle had spent the past thirty minutes gazing out of the window, deep in thought. Deciding that she should give herself some respite from her reflections on disturbing village events, she picked up a local newspaper from the counter and decided to peruse the lighter, more entertaining sections.

She took a final bite of her cheesecake (which had appeared at her table after she had dispatched the last of her cupcake as if by magic, so little did she remember ordering it), and feeling rather full, she smiled as she read the story of a young boy from Upton St. Mary who had just returned from a trip to the North Pole. She looked up, hoping to find another tea shop customer with whom she could coo over the brave young man, when a stern, familiar figure across the street caught her eye. Louisa Montgomery.

Sure enough, Louisa must have attended to her shopping after that mysterious business in her allotment shed, for her carpet bag was so full that it weighed the teacher down and dramatically slowed her pace. Leeks, bread, and cucumbers were peering precariously over the bag's rim.

Annabelle hurriedly popped the last raspberry from her cheesecake into her mouth and bustled toward the counter to pay her bill. As soon as she was done, she opened the tea shop door, the bell above it tinkling as she did so. She walked quickly across the street, glad of fresh air and exercise with which to assuage her guilty feelings for being a "little piggy" as her mother used to say.

"Miss Montgomery!" cried Annabelle, cheerily.

At the sound of her name, Louisa spun around so quickly that the cucumber that had been trying to escape from her bag finally made it. It dropped to the ground, bounced once, and began to roll into the road. Louisa quickly leaned forward to pick up the errant vegetable, completely forgetting about the others that were on the edge of jumping ship, too. Three oranges, two apples, and a grimy-looking cabbage were soon rolling away in different directions as Louisa wrestled with her bag to stifle any more escapees.

"Oh gosh!" Annabelle exclaimed, as she quickly darted around the teacher, picking the food items up. "I'm sorry. I didn't mean to startle you."

"Hmph," grunted Miss Montgomery, her condescending gaze and the barely perceptible shake of her head saying everything her words were not. Annabelle was suddenly all too aware of what Katie had meant when she said that Louisa spoke to everybody as if they were children.

"There you go," Annabelle said, tucking the veggies back into Louisa's bag. Louisa snatched the remaining cucumber from Annabelle's hands and placed it in the bag herself.

"Thank you," she said, with great difficulty. "But I do not need your help. I do not intend to attend church anytime soon."

Annabelle, once she had recovered from Miss Montgomery's startlingly curt tone, said, "I do apologize. I was only trying to be helpful."

"If you wish to be helpful, then do not call my name so rudely when I am carrying my shopping."

Annabelle watched as Louisa continued to jostle the food, forcing it deeper into her bag insistently. She could see that Louisa was in no mood to talk so turned away and took a few steps down the street before changing her mind and circling back.

"I only wished to advise you, Miss Montgomery, that it would be a good idea to assist the police in their investigation into your sister's disappearance."

The close attention Miss Montgomery had been paying to securing the vegetables in her bag was suddenly replaced with a look of astonishment that she shot toward the Vicar. Annabelle held her gaze, waiting for Louisa to take the next step.

After looking up and down the road and swallowing, Louisa gestured for Annabelle to walk up the path to her house.

"Please come in, Reverend."

Annabelle duly obliged.

Louisa unlocked her door and stepped inside. She was shaking as Annabelle followed her. As soon as Annabelle had passed into the hallway, Louisa quickly shut the door and addressed her visitor.

"How do you know? The Inspector insisted that nobody knew about this."

"Actually, it seems like most people in the village are aware of the new developments in your sister's case – more so than me. As for the body found in the woods, I witnessed the scene myself last night."

"It can't be my sister," Louisa said, as if to herself.

Annabelle hung her head solemnly.

"The body was... It's been there for a long time."

"That doesn't mean anything."

"Maybe we should sit down and talk about this."

"What is there to talk about?!" Louisa cried, desperation suddenly sparking fiercely in her eyes. "My sister is gone! That's it! Talking won't bring her back!"

Louisa grabbed her bag in frustration and marched into her kitchen, where she angrily began unpacking her groceries. Annabelle turned to the door, then back to the kitchen, wondering what she should do. The teacher seemed entirely unable to discuss anything right now, let alone the matter of her sister's death, but Annabelle was certain that such an opportunity would not present itself again. Slowly, she inched forward into the kitchen, where she saw Miss Montgomery grabbing and stacking groceries with alarming fury.

She watched for a few moments, searching her mind for words that would both calm the angry woman and encourage her to reveal something pertinent. Sensing her presence, Louisa spun around to face Annabelle, a bunch of carrots in her hand, clutched as forcefully as a weapon.

"There is simply no use in digging up the past. What's done is done. I don't see why it's anybody's business but my own."

"I understand," Annabelle said sympathetically, stepping forward. "But there will be a police investigation. They will most likely reopen the case now they have new evidence."

"If they could have found out who did it, they would have found out back then!" Louisa said in a pleading voice. "This will achieve nothing!"

"But don't you want to know who did this?"

Louisa seemed to crumble, falling into a chair like a puppet whose strings had been cut.

"I don't care who did it," she said, mournfully, "I just don't want to deal with all the gossip again. The half-truths, the wild stories, the speculation. About my sister. About me. About Daniel."

"Daniel?" Annabelle said, quickly.

"Her boyfriend," Louisa said, softly, before adding, "at the time."

Annabelle mused over the name for a few seconds.

"Was he suspected of having something to do with her disappearance?"

Louisa closed her eyes and nodded slowly.

"What happened to him?"

Louisa – her eyes still closed – merely shrugged.

Taking note of Louisa's growing reluctance to talk about Daniel, Annabelle decided to change tack.

"You had a boyfriend at the time too, didn't you?"

Louisa looked at Annabelle, her eyes hardening. "I did."

"Wh... What happened?" Annabelle asked, as gently as she could, hoping that Louisa would not have another outburst.

Instead, Louisa snorted derisively.

"We got married. And then we got divorced."

"Why?" asked Annabelle again, feeling she were pushing her luck somewhat.

She watched Louisa stare into the distance, silent and contemplative. Just as Annabelle was sure that Louisa had not heard the question or simply would not answer it, she said:

"Because I didn't love him."

Annabelle felt like she was about to burst, she was so full of questions and curiosity. Louisa Montgomery had turned out to be a fascinating figure, both brusque and rude, yet vulnerable and hurt. Annabelle left her sitting alone, staring out of the window, no doubt burrowing deep into her past where her memories and reflections would only bring her pain.

Annabelle jumped into her car and drove away from the village center, turning over each word of Louisa's conversation in her mind as she searched for clues. Not that she needed to, because she had already received the biggest one yet – Daniel, Lucy's boyfriend.

Something about the way Louisa had spoken his name had resonated in Annabelle's mind. She had spoken it with the same warmth that she had spoken about her sister. Annabelle was in no doubt that Daniel was an integral part of this story. She had to find him.

Annabelle knew plenty of Daniels. Daniel was a popular name in the village and surrounding area, from Terry the dog-walker's quiet, well-spoken nephew, Daniel Robbins, to Daniel Holden, the village's only war veteran.

Of course, it was entirely possible, perhaps even likely, that Lucy's boyfriend had left Upton St. Mary after the macabre incident, but it was still worth investigating. People who grew up in the village tended to return frequently, its idyllic vistas and strong sense of community a rarity elsewhere in the world.

Annabelle was proud of her ability to commit the contacts in her address book to memory, and she was still mentally flicking through its pages when she parked the car in the churchyard. She hopped out of her car and walked to the door at the back of the church.

"...Daniel Jones, the pharmacist – but he moved here shortly before me. Then there's Daniella Watson – of course not. Daniel... Daniel.... Dani–"

"Eeeeek!" came a shriek, as Annabelle turned a corner in the passage to her office and bumped into something small and hard.

Philippa spun around, saw Annabelle, and screamed again. "Aaaaaah!"

"Philippa!" Annabelle shouted, her face twisting into a look of sheer horror and confusion. "What's wrong?!"

"Oh, Reverend," Philippa said, immediately calming down. She was clutching at her chest with one hand and rubbing her cheek with the other. "It's you."

"Of course, it's me!" Annabelle said, still filled with

astonishment at her church secretary's reaction. "Who else would it be?!"

Philippa shook her head and turned back to her work, anxiously sifting through prayer books. "Never mind."

Annabelle put her hands on her hips and frowned.

"That's enough, Philippa. This has gone far beyond ridiculous. I demand that you tell me what it is that's troubling you, this instant."

Philippa once again shook her head, quietly counting the prayer books out to herself.

"Philippa," Annabelle continued sternly, "if you do not tell me what is wrong, then I will regard it as the height of rudeness."

Philippa slowly counted out one more prayer book, then turned to face Annabelle with a look of deep reluctance.

"I'm sorry, Reverend. I would like to tell you, but it's not something that can be spoken of in a house of God – nor to a person of the cloth."

Annabelle's eyes widened.

"Don't be silly, Philippa. You're just making me even more determined to find out what it is you are hiding! What would make you say such a thing?"

"I'm sorry, Annabelle."

"Well, if you insist on not telling me, then I'll just have to guess."

"Please don't."

"Let's see now," hummed Annabelle, placing a finger upon her lips and looking up, "what could be so embarrassing that you wouldn't even say it to a priest..."

"I'd rather not–"

"I've got it. It's those scratch cards, isn't it? You've developed an addiction to them, and you're worried about how sinful it is."

"No!" Philippa said, appalled at the accusation. "I've not committed any sin! Well, none that I'm terribly ashamed of."

Annabelle smiled.

"Okay. So what is it, then?"

Philippa shifted her weight from one foot to the other, looking around her as if hoping for some escape route that would lead her away from the Reverend's line of inquiry. When she realized that she was well and truly trapped, she spoke reticently.

"I... I saw something."

Annabelle knit her brow.

"What?"

"That's all I'm going to say, Reverend. Please, don't ask me any more," Philippa begged, before turning back to the prayer books and beginning her count from the beginning.

Annabelle gave her friend one last sympathetic purse of the lips before resting her questions. She already had more than one mystery tugging at her capacities. She would have to be patient regarding Philippa's.

CHAPTER FIVE

AS IT APPEARED to be one of the last days of the year that the sun was going to be generous with its warmth, Annabelle sat with a mug of tea on the bench that overlooked the cemetery behind St. Mary's church. With a large ringed notebook on her knee, a cup of tea steaming beside her, and a pen she twirled and tapped against her lips, Annabelle intended to conceive the Sunday sermon she would have to perform tomorrow, as well as come up with some ideas for the autumnal events the church had in its calendar.

She gazed out beyond the thick, aged stones that comprised the wall that surrounded part of the churchyard and looked toward the rolling hills that extended far into the turquoise sky. She tried to keep her thoughts focused. Somewhere on the horizon, she noticed a figure rising slowly and purposefully up one of the largest hills, before perching on its crest and unloading what seemed like a square board from a bag. She squinted and peered keenly, hoping to discern what the person was doing, before another form toward the bottom of the hill caught her eye. It looked like it was a four-legged animal, rapidly moving across the fields with a clumsy gait and a confused, lost air about it.

The sound of crunching footsteps behind her pulled her attention away from the surprisingly busy scene on the hillside and she turned to look in their direction.

"I've brought you some biscuits, Reverend," Philippa said, holding out a plate of chocolate shortbread.

"Oh, these will hit the spot!" Annabelle said, glad of the interruption.

Philippa placed the plate beside Annabelle's tea, nodded formally, and turned back toward the church. From the corner of her eye, Annabelle noticed the church cat, Biscuit, silently making her way around the back of the bench. Annabelle pulled the plate of shortbread closer toward her to thwart the greedy tabby's thieving intent.

"Philippa! I had hoped you would keep me company. I have something I rather want to ask you."

Philippa turned around slowly, seeming to look for an excuse, and then reluctantly sat down.

"Reverend, I'd really rather not talk about—"

"Oh, tosh. I didn't mean that," Annabelle said, reassuringly.

Philippa seemed to relax and she turned her head inquisitively, inviting Annabelle to speak her mind.

"Do you happen to know any Daniels in the village?"

Philippa tilted her head away for just a moment to think, before turning back to Annabelle and saying, "To be perfectly honest, Reverend, I can think of quite a few."

Annabelle nodded. "I believe the one I am looking for is in his late-thirties. I'm not even sure he is even still *in* the village, but I know with some certainty that he was here roughly twenty years ago."

Philippa looked to the ground as she mentally sifted

through the ample list of people she knew. Annabelle watched her, patiently waiting for her reply.

"The only person I can think of that fits that description is Daniel Green, the butcher. Daniel Thompson is in his forties, but he only moved here a decade ago. Daniel Smalling has lived here all his life, all sixty years of it. There's Daniel Bennett, but he's only seven. No, Daniel Green is the only one I can think of who is in his late thirties and grew up here."

Annabelle bit into the end of her pen as she considered Philippa's words.

"I don't believe I've ever had the pleasure of Daniel Green's acquaintance."

"Oh, but you've most certainly had the pleasure of his meat, Reverend. Green's Butchers are renowned all over Upton St. Mary and beyond. His smoked cuts caused a sensation during last year's farmers' fair, don't you remember?"

"Hmm," Annabelle said, "I remember hearing something to that effect. Though as someone who'd munch her way through a chocolate log over a chicken leg, I can see why I'd never have met him."

"He slaughters the animals himself. It's the freshest meat you'll find in Cornwall," Philippa said, livening up at the chance of indulging in some gossip, however mundane, "and he's turned it into a very tidy business for himself. He's not bad looking either, and he's single!"

"I hope you're not implying what I think you are," Annabelle said, with a note of humor.

"Implying?" Philippa said, failing to hide her wry smirk. "I'm just saying he's one of Upton St. Mary's most eligible bachelors. He'll make a woman very happy one day – especially if she likes to eat well."

"Philippa!" Annabelle said with mock anger, before laughing good-naturedly. She considered whether she should probe Philippa as to the relationship Daniel had had with Lucy Montgomery, but she was afraid it would ignite another bout of paranoid nervousness and decided against it. It was nice to see her friend smile again and she didn't want to break her good mood. It had been rather a long time.

"Sorry, Reverend. Why do you ask?"

"I must speak with him about something."

"You can usually find him at his butcher's shop, he's often out the back."

"Right," Annabelle said, standing up and tucking her notepad and pen into her cassock, "I'll go find him right away." Then she noticed the plate Philippa had placed between them on the bench and sat down abruptly once again. "Right after I taste these shortbread biscuits," she added, biting into one almost before she had finished the sentence.

Philippa certainly wasn't overstating the point about it being a thriving business, thought Annabelle as she arrived outside Green's Butchers. Though the afternoon was already turning to evening and the shop itself was about to close, there was still a crowd of Saturday shoppers gathered around the counter. Orders were called out loudly to be heard over the din, and hands holding money were held aloft in order to be seen. Annabelle opened the door and found herself in a crowd five deep away.

Though she was taller than most of the people who were snapping up the meat at a voracious pace, she could see no way in which she could ask after Daniel. She tried pushing her way through the crowd gently and politely but quickly found herself shoved backward to her rightful spot in the queue.

"Is Daniel Green here?" Annabelle called, finding her voice drowned out in the loud, rapid slamming of cleaver on chopping board. "I said," she repeated, more loudly, "is Daniel Green here?"

Somehow, one of the assistants who was busily slicing rashers of smoked bacon seemed to hear her.

"Boss!" he called, toward a door at the back. "Boss! Someone here to see you!"

Annabelle turned toward the door and watched a tall, handsome man with a chiseled jawline and crystal-blue eyes emerge. Philippa certainly wasn't overstating the point about him either.

Daniel looked over the crowd and caught Annabelle's eye. She waved at him, and he gestured for her to join him at a space beside the counter.

"Hello," he said, in a pleasant, lilting Cornish burr. "How can I help you?"

"I'm Reverend Annabelle Dixon from St. Mary's church. I'd like to speak with you about something."

Annabelle thought she detected an ever-so-slight cloud of apprehension pass across Daniel's hypnotizingly blue eyes, before dismissing it as the usual mixture of emotion non-church-attendees felt when they first met her. It was a feeling that combined awkwardness at not attending church recently (or ever) with suspicion that she was about to persuade them otherwise in future.

"Um... Of course," Daniel said. "What is it about?"

"Actually, I was rather hoping we could talk somewhere quiet. It's rather important."

"I see," Daniel said, nodding cautiously, a cloud of doubt now blatant upon his face. "Well, I would say we could talk at the pub since it's nearby, but being a vicar I don't—"

"The pub is fine," Annabelle smiled. "Shall I wait for you there?"

Daniel looked surprised but nodded. "Sure. I'll see you there in a few minutes after I've finished up here."

Roughly ten minutes later, Annabelle was sitting at a table near the entrance to the King's Head, sipping gingerly from a half-pint of cider and trying to pace her nibbling of a packet of peanuts so that they lasted as long as possible. Though the King's Head was nowhere near as popular as the Dog And Duck, Barbara's pub, it did very well nonetheless. Especially on Saturdays, when the shoppers who flocked to the nearby market and shops such as Daniel's found it a calming pit stop.

The atmosphere was pleasant. The pub was half-full with families partaking of a hearty meal, regulars indulging in habitual conversations, the subjects of which seemed to comprise only three in number, and working men enjoying the freedom of their weekend. Annabelle gazed at the door absently, until it finally opened and Daniel's tall, athletic frame stepped inside.

"Daniel! Yoo-hoo!" Annabelle called.

Daniel turned his head, and once again, Annabelle felt as if the good-looking man were holding something back. He gestured a brief greeting, before getting the bartender's attention. The barman nodded an acknowledgement as Daniel took a seat opposite Annabelle and settled down.

"I never thought I'd be drinking with a priest in a pub when I got up this morning!" he joked, his laugh slightly guarded.

Annabelle laughed along with him. "I would say the same, but in the life of a church vicar, you learn to expect the unexpected!"

The barman placed Daniel's drink – a pint of dark ale – on the table in front of him and walked away. Daniel grabbed it in his large, strong palm and gulped almost half of it down in one fell swoop.

"Oh, my," Annabelle said. "We've not even said a toast yet."

Daniel laughed nervously, before wiping his lips on the back of his hand.

"Sorry," he stammered.

Annabelle noted the anxious expression of the large man. The working men of Upton St. Mary were a warm, laid-back, talkative bunch, so it was rather alarming to see such a successful tradesman so ill at ease, particularly when in his element. She sipped from her cider slowly, giving her mind time to consider Daniel's bizarre behavior.

Daniel watched her intently, waiting for her to make the first move, to reveal her hand.

"Business certainly seems to be good," Annabelle said.

"Yes," Daniel said, slowly, "it is."

In the silence that followed, the tension between the two grew ever thicker, until Daniel grabbed his pint glass again and finished off his drink in an impressive display. Almost immediately, he turned to the man behind the bar and raised his empty glass. In accordance with the ritual they had obviously practiced over and over, the bartender again nodded back nonchalantly.

"Sorry, Vicar. What exactly is this about?"

Annabelle spun the bag of peanuts around to offer some to the butcher, who refused, shaking his head.

"I wanted to ask you about your upbringing in Upton St. Mary."

"My *upbringing?*" Daniel exclaimed in a voice that sounded extremely relieved, while a look of utter surprise swept across his face.

"Specifically, your girlfriends."

"Ohhhhh!" Daniel smiled, leaning back and nodding. "Lucy? Right?"

"Yes," Annabelle said, taken aback by Daniel's newfound ease.

Daniel chuckled, and for the first time, his humor seemed genuine to Annabelle.

"Well, what do you want to know?"

"Tell me about you and Lucy."

"Okay," Daniel said, receiving his drink from the barman and taking a sip from it that was a lot less ferocious than before. "Let's see. I don't really remember where we met. Everybody knew everyone else back in those days. I asked her out at a dance, and she said yes. We met up the next day, at the church, in fact, and just talked for hours. That was that, really. After that day, we did pretty much everything together. Went to the cinema, took bike rides together. She'd come and watch me play football, I'd go and see her performances."

"Performances? She was an actress?"

Daniel laughed. "She was a little bit of everything! She wanted to be an actress, a dancer, a vet, and a nurse, if you can believe that!"

Annabelle smiled. "How long were you together?"

Daniel screwed his face up in thought. "Under a year, I

think. Not long when you say it like that, but when you're young, it feels like forever."

Annabelle nodded and popped some more peanuts into her mouth. Daniel followed suit, tilting his head back, opening his mouth and dropping them into it.

"Did you love her?" Annabelle asked, as carefully as she could.

Daniel screwed his face up once again, crunching through his peanuts as he searched for the words. His eyes turned pensive as he looked to the side.

"What does a kid know about love at that age?" he said, eventually.

Annabelle shrugged. "You do seem like you were very taken with her."

"I was," Daniel said, his face serious now. "She was a fantastic girl. But Louisa was the one that really took my breath away."

Annabelle almost fell off her chair at this revelation.

"Louisa Montgomery? Her sister? The teacher?"

Daniel nodded, his silence only adding to the conviction behind his words.

"You were in love with Louisa? Not Lucy?"

"Don't get me wrong, Lucy was wonderful. She was pretty, charming, easy to talk to. She was the second most attractive girl in the entire village."

"But Louisa was the first?"

"Louisa was the most beautiful girl I'd ever seen, even to this day," Daniel said, his palm slapping gently on the tabletop as if to emphasize his point. "Pretty girls are ten a penny, but Louisa had something more about her, a quality, a magnetism. She was like a queen. And smart, too. Almost scarily so. I know it's hard to believe looking at her now but she was the kind of girl who made you feel like you were in the presence of something magnificent."

Annabelle found herself stunned into silence at the sincerity and devotion that came through in Daniel's words.

"But..." Annabelle stammered, searching for some logic in this new perspective, "if you felt that way about Louisa and not Lucy, why did you date Lucy and not her sister?"

Daniel leaned back in his chair and opened his palms in a gesture of defeat. "Louisa had a boyfriend. She was taken. Gary Barnes, a boring bloke if you ask me. They were 'childhood sweethearts,' together since they were too young to really know what they were doing. They even got married eventually, but they divorced soon afterward."

"Why?"

"I don't know the details, but Gary worked for a car manufacturer and got offered a position in their American office. He wanted to go, and she didn't. Simple, really. Knowing Gary, though, it makes perfect sense. He was always the kind of person who put work before anything else."

"Hmm," Annabelle said, fishing around in the peanut packet with no luck. Daniel plucked it from the table and waved it in the direction of the bar. The man behind it nodded once more.

"Katie Flynn painted a very different picture of Louisa when I asked about her earlier."

"Bah," Daniel scoffed, "of course she would. She's had it in for her since that whole mess with the tea shop. Katie's always been one to hold a grudge. She's been like that since we were young."

A new packet of peanuts was placed on the table and Daniel opened it for Annabelle as she furrowed her brow in thought.

"Thank you," Annabelle said, plucking a few nuts from the proffered packet and munching on them absent-mindedly.

"Is there a particular reason you're asking about all of this, Reverend?"

Annabelle swallowed and washed the peanuts down with another sip from what little was left of her cider. "Just curiosity," she lied, acceding to the Inspector's wishes for once. "I only recently heard of Lucy's disappearance. It seemed rather odd to me."

"What was odd about it?"

"Well, that she disappeared without a trace. Excuse my directness, but it seemed like, as someone close to her, you would have known what had happened or even been under suspicion yourself."

Daniel laughed nervously. "I was! The police asked me so many questions that I thought I was going to get a grade at the end of it!"

Annabelle's refusal to acknowledge his joke urged Daniel to continue.

"I don't know what happened. I wish I did..."

"When did you last see her?"

"We had gone to the cinema to see a film. A chick flick. Her choice, of course. Afterward, she was in a good mood. We walked about the village and stopped at Benjamin's, a nice pie shop by the library that isn't there anymore. We talked and ate, then I walked her home. Louisa met us at the door, I kissed her goodbye, and that was that."

"When did you realize she was gone?"

"A few days later, we were supposed to meet on the edge of the village, across the woods from Shona Alexander's place. I waited at the bus stop for an hour because she was late. But see, she was always late. I'd get so worked up, but she was the kind of person who could make you forget how angry you were by saying something silly. This time though, I was so cheesed off that I was thinking about how I wouldn't let that happen this time. Eventually, I went home. I called her house, this was before mobile phones, and Louisa told me she was definitely out because she had seen her leave the house. That's when I realized something was up."

"Did anyone see you at the bus stop?"

"Not really. I mean, a few buses went past, but if I asked you who was waiting at a bus stop when you drove past, would you remember?"

"Did anyone else see her leave?"

"Her mother. Her father was dead at that point. Once Louisa told me they had seen her go out the door, I got a bit anxious, still angry, but a little bit worried. I went around the village asking everyone if they'd seen her. Nobody had. That night her mother called the police. The night after that, they were asking me about every conversation we'd ever had. It was like they thought I'd kidnapped her and hidden her somewhere!"

"What do you think happened?"

Daniel thought over the question a little, though it was clear he had an answer ready.

"I think she ran away, to tell you the truth. Like I said, she wanted to be an actress, a singer, have adventures, and see the world. My guess is that she just left, probably to make her fortune in London or some other big city."

"But without telling anyone? Without packing anything?"

Daniel shrugged. "Maybe she was fed up with village life, fed up of the same people. Maybe she wanted a clean break from everything. God knows I've wanted that myself sometimes. Lucy was a poet, an idealist. She probably thought it would be romantic to run away to London one day and see if she could make it with nothing in her pocket. The funny thing is, I'd bet that she could."

Annabelle found Daniel's casual manner in discussing Lucy's disappearance slightly concerning until she reminded herself that he had no idea about the body in the woods. For him, this was a long gone incident that was dead and buried. If he had been aware of the imminent news that the affair was to be revisited, he would almost certainly not have been so open about his dismissive feelings toward Lucy or his still rather strong ones for Louisa.

After sipping the last of her cider, Annabelle placed the glass down softly and looked once again at the attractive face of the man sitting across from her.

"Would you like another?" he asked.

"No, thank you, I should get going."

Daniel looked askance at the Reverend while a playful smile worked its way onto his face.

"Is that really all that you wanted to ask me about, Reverend?"

"Yes, though I may have more to ask you soon. Thank you for your time, Daniel."

Daniel chuckled. "My pleasure. It's always nice to share a pint with someone new."

Annabelle dropped the payment for her drink and peanuts in coins on the table and left Daniel to join some friends of his. As soon as she stepped outside, a cold snap of wind and the surprisingly dark street once again reminded her of the approaching season. She pulled her cassock in around her a little more tightly and began walking.

Annabelle decided not to drive home immediately. After her cider, she needed to wait before she could get safely back behind the wheel. She had an hour to kill so she decided to amble around the village and use the time to think about what she had learned from the surprisingly forthright butcher.

She now had an idea of the time and events that had surrounded Lucy's disappearance, though she was still grappling with wildly differing accounts. The enigmatic Louisa Montgomery was growing ever more difficult to discern. To Katie, she was an introverted shrew who lived in the shadow of her sister's charming personality and radiant popularity. To Daniel, she was a magnetic beauty who surpassed her sister in all aspects, and for whom he would have dismissed Lucy in an instant were Louisa not bound to a dullard since youth.

And still, despite the detailed, honest reports of these two childhood friends who had been present at the time of her disappearance, Annabelle could not ascertain a motive or reason for Lucy's murder, if indeed it was murder.

Feeling the corner of her notepad jut into her waist, Annabelle was reminded once again of her need to deliver the Sunday sermon. She decided to visit the local library. It was always a peaceful, inspiring place for such things, and there, she could focus her thoughts on something other than the mysteries that were causing her such consternation.

With the purpose of a destination in mind, she quickened her pace and took a rather discreet shortcut through a cobblestoned alleyway that always made her feel as if she had stepped back in time to the eighteenth century.

"You can't have her!" came a faint voice from the darkness at the end of the alley. "She's mine! She's always been mine! Who do you think you are to take her from me!?"

Something about the voice seemed familiar to Annabelle, but the anger and aggressiveness threw all of her

senses for a spin. Had she stumbled upon a physical altercation? Was somebody in danger? Annabelle flew into a stride
that carried her down the short length of the alleyway in
seconds, grimly determined to ensure that no harm would
come to anybody, her arms raised in preparation for whatever lurked in the shadows.

"She belongs with me! And I'll do everything in my
power to keep her!"

As Annabelle drew closer, the silhouette became recognizable. She slowed down as she reached within a few yards
of the wildly gesticulating, hurriedly pacing figure who was
screaming into his phone.

"Just you try and stop me! She's mine! She's always
been mine!"

It was the Inspector, and he was shouting so viciously
into his phone that Annabelle could see the spittle flying
from his gnarled mouth even in the darkness. She held back,
hoping the Inspector would not see her, but when he hung
up with an immense amount of frustration, he spun around
to walk away and was immediately confronted by the sight
of the embarrassed Vicar.

"Ah... Hello Inspector?"

"What do you want? Are you listening in on my conversations now as well?"

"Absolutely not! I was just on my way to the library."

"And you decided to stop and tell me how to do my job
again, did you?"

Annabelle's embarrassment was replaced by an assuredness that ran confidently through her in the face of the
Inspector's rudeness.

"You were shouting at the top of your lungs, Inspector.
You cannot expect privacy when you choose to rant and
rave in public so."

The Inspector breathed deeply, unable to find a retort amid the muddled thoughts of his anger.

"Now," continued Annabelle, taking this moment of confusion to assert herself, "I was simply passing when I heard you and if you'd care to calm down and talk reasonably with me, Inspector, I believe I may be able to provide some information that would be pertinent to your current case."

At this the Inspector straightened himself and looked at Annabelle directly.

"Go on."

Annabelle smiled at the Inspector's receptiveness.

"This is terribly exciting, isn't it?" she giggled. "Two people exchanging information in a dark alleyway. It's like a scene from one of those exotic spy films, or a romantic thriller..."

"Reverend..."

"We're almost making a habit of meeting in dark places, Inspector. If I didn't know bett—"

"Please, Reverend. I'm not in the mood. Just tell me what you've found out."

"Yes, of course," Annabelle said, clearing her throat. "Well, I've learned that Lucy's boyfriend at the time of her disappearance was Daniel Green, a local butcher."

"Excellent," the Inspector said sincerely, though his voice still bore the remnants of his earlier fury. "Then we have a suspect."

Annabelle balked at the Inspector's speedy conclusion.

"Oh no! I didn't mean to imply... I mean, perhaps. It's not implausible... But I was by no means saying..."

"What did he tell you?"

"Well, this is the interesting aspect, he told me he wasn't

particularly attached to Lucy at all. In fact, it was *Louisa* that his heart was truly set on."

Even in the darkness Annabelle could see the Inspector's expression settle firmly.

"You've just given me a suspect and a motive, Reverend. This 'butcher' prefers the sister to Lucy, so he offs Lucy and hopes it'll bring him closer to the girl he wants."

"Inspector! Surely you cannot reduce this to something so simple. I am certain there are more layers of complexity to this."

The Inspector sighed deeply, regretting his recent outburst. "You're right. I've just got a lot on my mind. It's a possibility though. We've confirmed the body is Lucy's. She died from a blow to the head, and it appears that she was being regularly beaten throughout her life."

Annabelle gasped. "Surely not!"

"Oh, it's for sure, all right. The forensic anthropologist confirmed it."

"That's dreadful!" Annabelle said.

"These things often are."

Annabelle cast her eyes down mournfully.

"There's something else," Annabelle said, raising her eyes to meet the Inspector's, "I followed Louisa today."

"Is that normal behavior for a Reverend?"

"Is shouting in the street normal for a detective?"

"I'm sorry. Continue."

"Well, she did something rather strange. She visited a shed, over on the allotments at the edge of the village. I waited for half an hour, and she didn't come back out."

The Inspector scratched his stubble as he thought over this.

"Isn't that what people usually do when they're at their allotments?"

"Not really... Perhaps. I found her behavior rather strange. She went there right after her meeting with you. She wasn't dressed for digging. Then she got her groceries. I have a peculiar feeling that there may be something worth investigating in that shed."

The Inspector digested Annabelle's words then shrugged.

"Maybe so, but to check it we'd need a search warrant. And to get a search warrant you need more than a 'peculiar feeling'."

Annabelle brushed off the Inspector's condescension and decided she was far too cold to stay a moment longer. She would much rather go home to a hot cup of tea and a cozy blanket than be outside in the chilly evening air with the crotchety Inspector.

"Well, if I find out anything else I feel is important, I'll let you know, Inspector."

"Hmph."

"Goodbye, Inspector."

Annabelle watched the Inspector march away, stamping his shoes onto the pavement, his shoulders hunched up defensively.

"Hmph, yourself," she muttered, "You're never going to win me over with an attitude like that, Inspector."

CHAPTER SIX

WHEN ANNABELLE ARRIVED back at the church, it was already dark, and the streets had emptied of families, couples, and animated Saturday afternoon shoppers, who had earlier filled the air with chatter. Now the only people who could be seen were the men making their way to the pubs for a few pints, perhaps a game of darts, or a conversation about the day's football results.

Annabelle was so lost among her thoughts that she almost didn't notice the white car that sat in the spot where she usually parked. Annabelle made out the shape of a man slumped over the wheel. She deftly eased her Mini beside the other vehicle and as the lights of her car flashed across him, the man spun around. Annabelle smoothly finished bringing her own car parallel to the other and locked eyes with the rather embarrassed-looking fellow inside it.

The man fidgeted with his keys before placing them in the ignition and starting his engine. He eased off his hand-brake, turned his lights on, and then checked his mirrors, only to find the approaching figure of the Reverend in them.

She rapped on his window with her knuckles and leaned down to get a good look at him. He was a decent-looking chap, with wiry curls of neatly cut, brown-grey hair. With his full lips and big, brown eyes that were set beneath thick eyebrows, he had the air of a friendly, undemanding neighbor about him. The kind of man who would never be a hero but always remember a birthday.

When he saw the cheerful and inviting (if somewhat fatigued) smile on the Reverend's face, his embarrassment seemed to disappear. He turned off the engine. Annabelle stepped away from the door, allowing him space to open it. With a deep sigh, he got out of the car.

"Hello!" Annabelle said, with a hint of curiosity in her voice.

"Hello," the man replied, bowing his head slightly.

"I'm Reverend Annabelle, I take it you've come to see me?" Annabelle said, offering her hand.

The man took it and held it limply for a few seconds before pulling away.

"I'm Dr. Robert Brownson. I... Well... I saw the church spire and just... Sorry..."

Annabelle looked back at the church as if to check it was still there. "Yes," she said. "It is rather noticeable, isn't it? No matter where you are in Upton St. Mary, you can see it."

"Yes," Dr. Brownson said. "I saw it from the hills this morning."

"That was you?" Annabelle remarked, pointing toward the hills beyond the cemetery. "I think I saw you make your way to the top of the hill."

Dr. Brownson nodded.

When it was clear he wasn't going to say anything

further, Annabelle said: "Would you like a cup of tea? My cottage is just behind you. I'd appreciate the company."

Dr. Brownson nodded gratefully and followed the Reverend as she led the way to her warm, cozy kitchen.

"So, Dr. Brownson, have you been waiting long?" Annabelle said, as she readied the cups and tea bags.

"Not really. Perhaps. I'm not too sure."

Annabelle frowned at her visitor's confusion. She had had rather an eventful day herself and felt that she had little energy left for yet another mysterious problem. But such is the life of a village priest.

With the teapot full and the cups laid out, Annabelle brought over the plate of shortbread Philippa had left out and took a seat opposite the quiet stranger. The gentle sound of the cat door caught Annabelle's attention before she could speak, and she noticed Biscuit entering the kitchen, her eyes focused on the table.

"Honestly," Annabelle said, "I believe that cat has the ability to detect a sugary treat from the other side of the village."

Dr. Brownson smiled awkwardly as the cat leaped onto his lap and settled herself into a comfortable position.

"May I ask what brings you to this corner of the king-dom, Dr. Brownson?"

"Please, call me Robert," he said, as he tentatively leaned forward over the cat, careful not to disturb her, and measured out half a teaspoon of sugar before dropping it into his cup with great care. "I am a forensic anthropologist. I was called here on business."

Annabelle felt her tiredness evaporate. "The body in the woods?" she blurted out eagerly, before remembering that she had promised the Inspector she would keep it a secret.

"Why yes," Robert said, surprised.

"That's strange," Annabelle said, pursing her lips. "We already have someone who does that kind of thing around here, Dr. Harper Jones."

Robert's expression flickered through a number of emotions before he sighed slowly and abjectly. "Harper is a pathologist."

"Ah yes, of course she is," Annabelle said, emphatically pretending she knew the difference.

They sipped their hot teas, each passing the time by taking a shortbread. Robert slowly stroked the cat in his lap, though Biscuit, seeing that no treats were about to be offered, promptly decided she had had quite enough of their company and leaped down to the floor. In silence, they watched her make her way to the living room where she would no doubt enjoy the luxury of choosing the perfect sleeping spot, the better to be refreshed for her nightly excursion around the village that was just a few hours away. After a minute's silence, Robert's shoulders slumped, and he resolutely placed his teacup down.

"Actually, Harper is the reason that…"

Annabelle waited for an end to the sentence, but the man across the table seemed incapable of concluding any of his thoughts, either in his head or out loud. Annabelle realized that something was troubling him, and that he would need some assistance in discussing it. She placed her own teacup down and leaned forward sympathetically.

"If there is anything troubling you, Robert, you're welcome to talk about it with me, whether it's spiritual or not."

As if realizing how close he was to spilling out his thoughts, Dr. Brownson immediately sat up rigid as a post, an innocuous smile forcefully stretched across his face.

"Ah! It's nothing! A silly notion that will be gone by tomorrow morning."

Annabelle glared at the doctor, unconvinced.

"Hmm. It often takes more than a 'silly notion' to draw people to the spire of the church. People tend only to notice it when they look to the sky for help, having found none elsewhere."

"Really, Reverend..."

"Okay," Annabelle said, shrugging lightly, "I remain unconvinced, however. And if you're unable to convince me that it's not worth talking about, I doubt you'll convince yourself, Robert."

Robert glanced only for a moment at Annabelle, but it was enough to see the sincerity and openness in the Reverend's eyes. He sighed once more and smiled.

"You're sharp, Reverend. I suppose talking couldn't hurt."

"Of course."

Robert nodded, staring at his teacup as he galvanized himself to say things that he had not told anyone.

"It's Harper Jones."

"What about her?" Annabelle said quickly, her tone full of worry.

"Oh, no... Nothing like that," assured Robert when he saw the fear in Annabelle's eyes. "It's just that... she's married."

Robert looked up, deep pain written across his face. Annabelle searched it for some clue as to what exactly the problem was and shook her head when she couldn't find one.

"I'm sorry, Robert. What's the problem?"

Robert sighed again. "I've never been very good at explaining these kinds of things."

"It's fine. Just take a deep breath, and start from the beginning."

Robert did as he was told before speaking again.

"We met just under thirty years ago. I was doing a Ph.D. in biological anthropology at the time. Harper was an undergraduate studying medicine. I remember I had visited the library in search of a specific book, and it wasn't on the shelves. I looked around, and there she was, angelic, yet magnificent. Her skin was almost luminescent, and the determined, penetrating manner in which she read her book was so striking. She had the very book I intended to read."

"Well, over the coming weeks, in the library, this happened again, and again, and again! Sometimes she would seek a certain book that I had already taken from the shelves and had begun to work from. Other times I would arrive at the library and find her using the very one I had come for. We'd exchange knowing nods and patiently wait for the other to finish. Sometimes we would talk, and each time we did we discovered we shared more than a few interests and ideas. It was no coincidence. It was fate!

"We discovered that we had a mutual love of history. We were both enamored with the idea of unlocking the mysteries of things that had once been alive. Our fields were different, but our passions were almost perfectly attuned. We soon began to help each other in our work, Harper's rationality and clarity of thought combining with my rather creative and intuitive approach. Two people with different personalities but the same goals. We were perfectly balanced. There was only one thing we could do..."

"What?" Annabelle interjected, wide-eyed.

Robert looked up with sorrow in his brown eyes.

"Fall in love."

The words hung in the air like the final note of a

symphony, resonating in Annabelle's mind. Dr. Brownson continued, "Of course, Harper caught the attention of most men on campus. She was an extraordinarily beautiful woman. She still is. But Harper has always been a formidable creature of intellect. For us, our love of history and love of ideas easily transformed into a love for each other. We were inseparable for the few years we were together. A more perfectly matched pair you couldn't find! We lived in our very own world of study and simple pleasures. We didn't even argue or disagree as normal couples do. Our only disagreements were academic, and we resolved them using rigorous research and the scientific method. That may sound staid to many, but to two people in love with knowledge, it was the ideal relationship."

"What happened?" Annabelle asked, eventually.

"To put it simply, Reverend, life happened. I have always been an academic at heart. I still am. I love the musty smell of university libraries. The hallowed halls of institutes dedicated to the sole pursuit of pure knowledge. To surround myself with others who are just as focused upon the furthering of science and wisdom as I am is blissful to me. I am, to put it bluntly, a stuffy professor, and always have been. Harper, on the other hand..."

"Likes to get her hands dirty," Annabelle added, helpfully.

"Precisely," nodded Robert, sadly. "She wanted to see the world. To put her knowledge to work in the wild, as it were. She felt that theory was worthless unless one could put it into practice. She was soon gone, regretfully, of course, but gone nonetheless. Her insight and intelligence brought her plenty of attention from other universities around the world and some very inviting prospects, if I say so myself. Eventually she received an offer that was too good to refuse. We stayed in touch for several years, but she was so busy, and I was somewhat... bitter, I'm ashamed to say. I longed for her to return. Indeed, I always expected that she would, but it never happened."

Robert took a bite from his biscuit and then a long sip of his tea, as if concluding his story. However, Annabelle found herself feeling that this was not the end of his tale.

"It's been over twenty years since you last saw her, you say?"

"Yes, twenty-five, in fact."

"And you've not met anyone else in all this time?"

"I know it sounds pathetic, Reverend. Nobody is more aware of that than me. I'm a university professor, however. My kind are not easy with women. There are not many opportunities for me to meet them, and even when I have, it has never worked out. The heart wants what it wants, as they say. After Harper, I found it difficult to compare another woman favorably. No woman could match her, and to delude either myself or them would have been unfair."

"I take it you've spoken to Harper?"

Robert nodded.

"I saw her today. As radiant as ever. I also learned that she was married. It's funny, but now that I know she's gone for good, I feel bereaved. Not just because I finally realize that I've lost her, but because I also feel that I've lost all those years I was waiting for her to return. "

Annabelle reached out her hand and placed it over the doctor's. He smiled appreciatively.

"I know it's stupid of me," Robert continued, "but I almost feel like I should fight for her. I know it's wrong, but to just walk away feels like throwing away nearly thirty years. Years in which not a day passed by when I didn't think about what she might be doing. It has been like walking around with a ghost; one who is there, and yet not there. Always in my peripheral vision, always at the edge of my thoughts."

"I can't say I understand what that is like," Annabelle said, "but there is no 'fight' to be had, Robert. If you don't let Harper go, then you'll never be happy."

"I know, Reverend. But I don't feel as if I'll ever be truly happy without her, either."

Annabelle looked at the pained man in front of her with a deep sense of pity.

"There is joy and happiness waiting for you in the world, Robert. As soon as you open your eyes to it."

"Thank you, Reverend. You know, I was actually supposed to return to London today, but I found myself feeling uplifted by the countryside here, however depressed I've also felt."

"That's good," Annabelle smiled. "Perhaps you've already begun to forge a new beginning for yourself."

"I'd like to think so, Reverend. Though I feel I'm struggling right now."

"These things take time, Robert."

Robert nodded, picked up his teacup and drank the last drops from it. He slowly pulled his hand away from under the Reverend's, returned her smile, and stood up.

"Well, I'm sincerely grateful, Reverend. I know this has been an inconvenience, especially at this late hou—"

"Oh, tosh!" Annabelle interrupted. "It was a pleasure to meet you, Robert. I sincerely hope you find the right path, and I also hope this is not the last time we'll talk to each other."

Robert threw on his coat and made his way to the door.

"I hope so too, Reverend," he gazed at the floor thoughtfully. "You know, I can sort of see why Harper moved to this area. It's beautiful, full of history, and if you're any indication, Reverend, the people are remarkably kind."

Annabelle giggled a little as Robert stepped through the door.

"With charm such as that, Professor, I am sure you won't be wanting of a woman for very long!"

Robert laughed as he waved at the Reverend and got in his car. Annabelle watched his car turn around in the yard and roll through the church gates before closing the door. She walked into the living room, and slumped onto the couch. It seemed that love was very much the theme of the day in Upton St. Mary, though unfortunately only the unrequited and rather destructive kind.

Annabelle had found herself too distracted to formulate the notes and thoughts she usually did when planning a sermon, but the unusual events that had transpired over the previous days along with the many stories she had heard inspired her to give an excellent sermon "off the cuff." In her gentle, humorous, and friendly manner, she delivered a thought-provoking talk about secrets, honesty, and the spiritual benefits of letting go. The quiet, attentive crowd nodded their heads in agreement and smiled their approval as she dispensed advice to her flock.

Annabelle's pleasure at the reception of her spontaneous sermon intensified as she bade goodbye to her congregation at the church doors. They poured praise and compliments on her, some even saying that it was the best they had ever heard. Annabelle accepted their good wishes politely, and when the last church-goer had expressed his gratitude and set off through the gates, she turned back inside with a large smile that seemed to begin from the depths of her heart.

After taking a few steps, however, the positive feelings that seemed to vibrate around her gave way to something more ominous and troubling. Philippa was standing in front of her, her skin once again pale and sickly, stress apparent in her face.

"Reverend..." she uttered reluctantly.

"Yes, Philippa? Is everything alright?"

"Your sermon was very good today, Reverend..."

"Why thank you, Philippa! I'm glad you liked it."

"...It has persuaded me... to think that... I should tell you what's been bothering me, however ashamed I am of it."

Annabelle quickly walked up to her troubled friend and gently brought her toward a pew.

"Of course you should tell me, Philippa. You've no need to feel ashamed when you're with me! After all, we're friends!"

"Thank you, Reverend."

Annabelle sat beside Philippa and patiently waited for her friend to begin.

"Take your time, Philippa."

"Well, it happened about a week ago now... Oh Reverend, I hope you don't think this is terribly un-Godly. I've never had anything like this happen to me before!"

"I won't judge. Just tell me what it is, and we can talk about it."

Philippa took in a deep breath.

"I saw a vision."

"A vision?"

"A terrible vision. Horrifying. I've spent the past week wondering what it might mean. Hoping that it wouldn't happen again."

"I'm sure it's nothing, Philippa. It was probably just a dream, or something just as innocent."

"Oh no, Reverend," Philippa said, looking up at Annabelle with her eyes wide, "this was so vivid. I would swear it was real."

"What was it exactly?"

"It happened during the night, perhaps two or three in the morning. I woke up in order to visit the bathroom. I've been drinking a terribly large amount of tea lately, as I always do when autumn is approaching. I tell you, I always know when the cold weather's about to hit by how many cups I find myself—"

"The vision, Philippa?"

"Oh yes, sorry, Reverend. I suppose my mind isn't keen on remembering it. I was on my way to the bathroom when I heard an awful screaming. Oh Annabelle, it was terrifying. It sounded like the screams of hell, almost animal in its pain. I went to my kitchen window and pulled aside the curtain and...."

Philippa shook her head and buried it in her hands, gasping.

"What was it? What did you see Philippa?"

"It looked like... like a ghost! Running across the field. It was all in white, lit up like the light of the moon."

"A ghost?"

"It was monstrous, Reverend. It was covered in blood, and was wielding some kind of weapon. My body froze, I couldn't move, I wasn't even able to scream. I just went cold all of a sudden, as the figure tore across the field."

"Did you see its face? Perhaps it was a real person?"

Philippa breathed deeply again.

"Its eyes were big and white, and there was a look of fearsome determination. I don't know how, but I could tell this monster was intent upon wreaking destruction. It had the eyes of something evil, something with murderous intent. The eyes, the blood, the shrieking.... I've never seen anything like it. I know it didn't come from my imagination. Even my nightmares aren't as horrible as that!"

Annabelle rubbed Philippa's back gently.

"Perhaps it was something else."

"What else could it be, Reverend? The next day you were even talking about a dead body in the woods!"

"Oh Philippa, I told you that body had been buried for years!"

"Yes, but... perhaps the spirit... or..."

"Come now, don't go letting your imagination run wild. I'm sure there's a perfectly reasonable explanation."

"Like what?"

Annabelle opened her mouth, hoping something logical and rational would pour forth, but she quickly closed it when she found herself out of ideas.

"I... don't know. But that doesn't mean there isn't an explanation."

"I sincerely hope you're right, Reverend," Philippa said, her eyes as pleading and as vulnerable as a child's, "but I'm deeply afraid you're not."

"Would you like a cup of tea?"

"No, thank you. I should get back to tidying the church."

"Indeed. I'll help you."

"No, Reverend. I'd prefer to do it myself. I... like to keep myself occupied. It helps me not to think about it."

Annabelle nodded supportively. "As you wish. If you need anything, just tell me. Try to be patient, I'm sure we'll get to the bottom of this."

"Thank you, Annabelle. I do appreciate it. I hope you don't think I'm going mad."

"Of course not! Why, I've even seen some sights myself lately that I haven't been able to explain."

Philippa grabbed the Reverend's arm tightly and glared at her.

"Such as what, Reverend?"

"Oh, I'm sure it's nothing. And I don't want to feed your already active imagination. I assure you that what I saw was both vivid and bizarre, and has an explanation. I just don't know what it is yet. But I will find out, don't you worry! "

Philippa stood up and began to collect the prayer books from the pews. Annabelle made her way home and considered putting on the kettle, before changing her mind, throwing on her coat, and heading back out to her Mini.

It seemed that Annabelle couldn't take more than a few steps without encountering strange behavior, peculiar incidents, and yet more mysteries. She was used to conundrums, and indeed, she rather enjoyed using her charm and wits to discover the truth behind seemingly odd events. However, she was beginning to feel that the sheer volume of questions she had been trying to answer for days was overwhelming.

First, there was the Inspector's behavior that had become increasingly concerning. He was waspish when she had encountered him in the woods after Dougie tripped over the bone, behavior that Constable Raven had told her had been a consistent theme for weeks. Following the incident with Terry's dog, Annabelle knew that the Inspector was not only growing increasingly erratic and temperamental, but also that he would be fairly ineffectual in getting to the bottom of the very case he was in Upton St. Mary to pursue. His shouted phone call in the alleyway still resonated in her mind. Was he involved in some kind of love triangle? As far as Annabelle knew, the Inspector had divorced years ago and had been single for a while now. However, the romantic overtones of his cryptic demands were unavoidable. As she frowned at the memory of the shouted phone call, Annabelle found herself feeling a little envious of whoever had managed to place such a stranglehold on the Inspector's affections but quickly swept the feeling away before it took too firm a hold.

Now there was Philippa's "vision." Though she was deeply religious, Annabelle could not entertain any notion of it being a spiritual one, knowing only too well that Philippa had an imagination that ran as wild and free as the wind. But her friend had obviously seen something that had initiated such horror in her mind, although even Annabelle's easy ability to jump to far-reaching conclusions failed her when she tried to explain it.

Finally, there was the increasingly complex matter of Lucy's death. The body in the woods had been confirmed as Louisa's sister, and the Inspector had revealed that she was murdered, but in her quest to discover a possible killer, or even a motive, she had been met only with contradictions and misunderstandings.

She could not shake the idea that Daniel Green's behavior at the beginning of their meeting was highly suspicious, and the way he had loosened up when talking about Louisa perturbed her. As the most plausible suspect, it was the opposite of what she had expected. Likewise, Louisa's mysterious and oddly-timed trip to a shed on the allotments had seemed very peculiar to Annabelle, though the Inspector was correct in saying that it indicated nothing very much of anything at all.

Most confusing had been the difference in the stories she had heard from Katie Flynn and Daniel Green. Katie's had no doubt been colored by her conflict with Louisa. It also wasn't clear that she was a reliable witness. Daniel's story had seemed almost too extraordinary to be believable. Had he constructed his story about having feelings for Louisa to suit some ulterior motive? If so, why?

Annabelle knew she had to get the story from an unbiased source. A person who had been around at the time, but who had not been involved. A person who was tuned in to all of Upton St. Mary's gossip, past and present. Someone who was guardian of the village's secrets, who saw people at their worst, but also at their best.

Annabelle parked her beloved Mini outside The Dog and Duck and stepped out of it. It was time she talked to Barbara Simpson, the pub landlady, once again.

"Reverend!" she called, as she watched Annabelle enter. "Have you come for that lunch I promised? Wouldn't be surprised if you'd worked up an appetite, I heard your sermon was a good one today."

Annabelle smiled as she stepped toward the bar, behind which Barbara was sporting a leopard-print blouse and hoop earrings so large they could have been frisbees. Her long eyelashes fluttered with glee, and she seemed to radiate a warm, inviting aura that encouraged the good-natured laughing of the Sunday drinkers as she chatted back and forth with them.

"Actually," Annabelle said, "I was rather hoping you would have time for a chat."

"Oh," Barbara said, as if greatly honored by the attention, "well, in that case, we should have a drink. What'll you have?"

Barbara was already fixing herself a white wine when Annabelle responded.

"Just an orange juice would be fine."

"Orange juice, it is. Let's go over here," Barbara said, as she sidled around the bar and carried the drinks to the booth in the corner.

"So what is it, Vicar?" Barbara said, after sipping heartily from her wine.

"Well it's—"

"Don't tell me, it's Lucy. That was her body in the woods, wasn't it?"

Annabelle considered the right response for a moment, but hesitation was all Barbara needed. She had a lifetime of experience reading faces.

"I knew it! Don't worry, Vicar, I won't tell anybody. Though there are a few people who've already made the connection. "

"Hmm, well I suppose it's a fairly obvious one."

Barbara shook her head sorrowfully.

"Such a sad story."

Annabelle leaned forward.

"What is the story, exactly? I've heard so many versions of the tale, but I still don't feel like I truly know what happened all those years ago between Lucy, Louisa, and Daniel."

"Ah yes," Barbara smiled, her blue eye shadow seeming to brighten as she recalled the memory. "The 'love triangle.' It went on for ages."

"What do you mean?"

"Well, you have to go back very far to get the full story,

Vicar. You see, they all grew up together. Louisa, Lucy, Daniel, and all the rest. They were all born within a few years of each other, and they were like a pack of wolves, I tell you! No, they were nice kids, really. Anyway, Louisa and Gary were both very quiet, intense kids. Both liked to read, both liked to be indoors. You could tell they would become a couple even before they knew it. Well, the thing was, Louisa grew up a real knockout. Oh, you should have seen her! Maybe one of the most beautiful girls I've ever seen in Upton St. Mary. She could have been a film star! Everybody said she was destined for great things. You know when you can just see it in someone? She was smart, too. She was still quiet, but she could have a laugh. Still loved being indoors, but you'd see her at a dance every once in a while usually surrounded by boys. Oh, the boys loved her, for sure."

"Including Daniel?"

"Especially Daniel! He ruled the roost! He was always a mischievous one, that Daniel. He was a bit older than her, but if any of the boys were going to have a chance, and in my opinion she was out of all their leagues, it was Daniel. The only problem was that she was still with Gary. He was a nice enough chap, don't get me wrong, but let's just say she made her choice before she even knew she had one."

"So Daniel began courting Lucy, instead?"

"Right. Lucy was a gorgeous girl too, but next to Louisa... Well, even Marilyn Monroe would have competition."

"Did Lucy and Louisa get along well?"

Barbara pursed her lips a little.

"Not really. It was a little strange, to be honest. Get either of them alone, and they were fine, but put them in the same room, and it was almost as if Lucy lost a little of her shine, and Louisa got a little more bossy. I think there was always a little jealousy between them. Lucy didn't like it that Louisa was prettier and bossed her around. Louisa didn't like it that Lucy was outgoing and loved by everyone for her personality and charm. I heard that they fought constantly behind closed doors."

"Hmm," Annabelle murmured. "That's certainly similar to what I heard."

"Oh, but that's not even half of it, Vicar," Barbara said eagerly, touching the Reverend's arm to add emphasis. "It gets much more complicated."

"How so?"

"Louisa fell in love with Daniel!"

"What?!"

Barbara nodded.

"She never said it, not to any of us, anyway, but it was obvious. You could tell by the way she looked at him, by the way she acted. You see, when Daniel began courting Lucy, he was suddenly always around Louisa too. Going to her house, asking Louisa where her sister was, having Louisa as their chaperone. Daniel was a handsome lad himself, and charming, too. It turns out all he needed was some time to work his magic. It was patently obvious that they both liked each other. Suddenly it wasn't just Gary who was Daniel's problem, it was Lucy too. Louisa started bossing her around even more, stopping her from going out with Daniel, asking her all these questions."

"There's one thing I just can't understand though, if all you're saying is true."

"No word of a lie, Vicar!"

"But in so many years, since Louisa's divorce and Daniel being single still, why have they never gotten together?"

Barbara shrugged.

"Beauty fades, Vicar, as does love. Plus, when Lucy disappeared, it affected everyone badly, especially their friends. They were never the same. No more regular Friday night dances, no more gatherings in the market square, no more parading through the streets like a marching band on its day off. Their group of friends broke up. Sure, they were still around, but they grew up the very night that Lucy disappeared."

"It's a tragic story."

"That it is, Vicar. Louisa got married to Gary as soon as she turned eighteen, went to university, and came back to teach. She barely spoke a word to anyone about anything, let alone about the past. Nobody even knew she was getting divorced until Gary came in one night with his bags packed saying he was going to America. Daniel got himself an apprenticeship, despite being a lazy so-and-so, and worked his socks off every day. Lucy had been like a free spirit in the town. When she disappeared, it was like she took all the childhoods of the village with her. Even I ended up taking a job at the florist's so that I'd have something to do during the summer. The dances and the company just weren't the same when she went. It was such a shame, Vicar."

"Thank you, Barbara," Annabelle said, gratefully, "I can't tell you how much of a help you've been."

"I don't know why you're asking about all of this, Vicar," Barbara said, downing the last of her wine, "and for once, I'd rather not know. Some things belong to the past and are better left to rest there."

CHAPTER SEVEN

ANNABELLE LEFT THE pub with her head spinning. So much so that she failed to notice the sight of Dr. Brownson carrying what looked like paint, an easel, and palette into the pub. He nodded warmly, but Annabelle decided not to stop and chat. She had far too much to think about, and a distraction was the last thing she needed.

Once again, her impression of what had gone on between Louisa, Daniel, and Lucy all those years ago had been completely turned around. Now she had a complex tale of fate, unrequited love, passion, and jealousy to chew over as she got inside her Mini.

Annabelle paused before starting her engine. Despite the huge amount of information she had gathered, there was still simply not enough for her to come to a conclusion. The more she learned, however, the more enigmatic Louisa became, and thus the more Annabelle wondered what Louisa kept in her allotment shed. It was, of course, entirely likely that there was nothing of any consequence in there, that Louisa had merely gone to the shed to gain some respite from the village she seemed to find so tiresome. Many a man would understand her sentiment entirely! But Annabelle felt that she had seen something in the manner of the teacher as she made her way toward the allotment. A strange atmosphere of grim determination and loss. A hurrying gait. Signs of a person who has an important thing to do or see.

She brought the key up to the ignition but hesitated once again.

The Inspector was right. There could be an entirely rational explanation. The shed could be filled with nothing but gardening tools and bags of seeds. Annabelle thought of herself as very much a rational person, but her instincts were inflamed with curiosity concerning the shed. Barbara's story had only made her more intrigued by the teacher and her erratic behavior, and Annabelle felt there had to be some side of her that she had not yet seen. Some secret that would not be revealed lightly.

She turned the key and fired up the engine with an air of purpose. The engine roared into life as if agreeing with her decision. She would find Inspector Nicholls, and they would discover the shed's secret, even if there weren't one.

As she puttered slowly toward the Upton St. Mary police station, she caught sight of Constable Jim Raven walking in the opposite direction. She gave a cheery beep to grab his attention and slid the car into a nearby parking spot.

"Hello, Reverend. Heard you had a successful sermon today," the officer said as she exited the car.

"Oh, thank you, though I doubt it will persuade you to attend in future."

Constable Raven laughed to hide his embarrassment.

"Well, I'm so busy... And I do like my Sundays..."

Annabelle waved away the Constable's weak excuses as she drew close.

"I'm looking for Inspector Nicholls. Is he in the station?"

Constable Raven sighed as if exhausted at the mere mention of the Inspector's name.

"Yes, he is, which is why I'm outside. He's getting worse, if anything."

"You mean his temper?"

The Constable nodded. "I still have no idea why."

"I think I might," Annabelle said.

Constable Raven's eyes almost doubled in size as he leaned forward.

"Well, tell me!" he pleaded.

Annabelle shrugged a little to indicate her lack of confidence in what she was about to say.

"I heard him shouting down his phone. About a woman, I think. I can't be sure."

"What did he say?" asked the Constable, with none of the methodical detachment one would expect from a police officer.

"'I want her back.' 'She's mine.' 'You can't take her from me.' Various things to that effect."

Raven folded his arms and looked to the side with a furrowed brow as he digested this information.

"That's rather strange. The Inspector spends all his time either sleeping or at work. He barely meets any women. Hmm, let me think. There's the female officers at

Truro, of course, but all of those are either taken or much too young... The girl in the canteen... but she's covered in tattoos and piercings. Not his thing at all. He practically recoils when she hands him a plate of her Chicken Alfredo. There's the office cleaning lady but she's sixty if she's a day... They're all the women I can think of. And Harper Jones, of course."

Suddenly it was Annabelle who leaned in with keen interest.

"Harper Jones?"

Constable Raven stared confusedly at the Reverend for a few moments before laughing off the idea.

"Give over! Harper Jones isn't that kind of woman. Plus she's married!"

"I wasn't insinuating anything!" declared Annabelle.

"Though Dr. Jones is a bit of a closed book. I mean, what do we know about her really? Have you ever met her husband?"

Annabelle found herself too deep in thought to speak, prompting the Constable to ask, "Reverend? You alright?"

"Oh, yes. I was just thinking. The Inspector wouldn't be the first man I'd met recently who was fighting for the attention of Dr. Jones. Perhaps there is something to it..."

Constable Raven chuckled away the thought.

"I think we're trying to explain the unexplainable, Reverend. Better not to know than to have the wrong idea. We'll just have to wait for it to pass, I suppose."

"Yes, I suppose."

"Well, see you around, Reverend."

"Bye, Constable."

Annabelle hurriedly made her way into the police station, and after exchanging pleasantries with the desk sergeant, she was shown into the office the Inspector had adopted as his own since the investigation in Upton St. Mary had begun.

True to recent form, the Inspector was slumped over, head in hands. She saw he was immersed in the examination of various documents that were frayed and brown from years of being stuffed in gloomy cabinets, no doubt cases that had been filed around the time of Lucy's disappearance.

She knocked gently on the door and waited for the Inspector to raise his head and notice her. It took one more knock, but eventually he huffed, looked at the Reverend, rolled his eyes, and then leaned back in his chair.

"What is it?" he asked curtly.

"I see you're still entrenched in your bad mood as firmly as you are in this case, Inspector."

Nicholls sighed deeply, and Annabelle took the Inspector's lack of words as an invitation to sit across the desk from him.

"Not for long," the Inspector growled as he tossed aside the document and pulled another from the tall pile beside him. "If I don't find anything substantial today, I'm going to close this case. I've got more important things to attend to back in Truro."

"You can't be serious!?" Annabelle burst. "This is a murder!"

"Nearly twenty years old. The trail is too cold at this point to make meaningful progress, let alone solve the case, close it, and secure a conviction."

"What on earth do you mean?"

Again, DI Nicholls sighed deeply, as if too tired to expend the effort of explaining himself.

"Look, Reverend. A young, pretty girl found dead in the woods is the kind of case that you'll find up and down the country, across the world, I daresay. It only takes one passing madman, the wrong kind of meeting with a lunatic in a quiet area. It's not nice, and it's not something you come across frequently out here among your tea shops and village fêtes, but it happens. There's nothing here. If there were, we'd have found it by now."

Annabelle knit her brow, gravely disappointed with the Inspector, and pushed aside the recent idea that he may not be as pure of heart as she had thought. She couldn't fully convince herself that the Inspector was indulging in such devilish behavior as chasing a married woman like Harper Jones. However, confronted with the brutal dismissiveness of his current thinking, she found herself wondering more and more.

"Before you drop this case, Inspector, I must make a strong request."

A raised eyebrow was Nicholls' only response.

"The allotment shed," Annabelle said, raising her hand to stop the Inspector speaking when he immediately began shaking his head. "I have found out rather a lot in the past couple of days regarding Lucy's life at the time of her disappearance, and I believe that whoever is responsible for this terrible deed may be closer than your 'random lunatic'."

"Okay, Reverend," the Inspector said after a moment's thought. "You have two minutes to persuade me."

Annabelle breathed deeply, placed her hands on the table, and began eagerly. She told the Inspector everything, from the unfulfilled desire Louisa and Daniel had had for one another, to the acrimonious relationship between Lucy and her sister. She even told him of the strange behavior Daniel had exhibited when she had spoken to him, and the rush with which Louisa had made her way to her allotment. Her story took far longer than two minutes, but the Inspector listened intently, possibly due to the fact he and his police team had uncovered very little of what Annabelle had managed to on her own. She spoke sincerely and passionately, putting all her charm and persuasiveness to work in order to get through the Inspector's tough shell.

"...if there is a secret yet to be discovered, a clue, then it has to lie with Louisa, and thus, the best chance we have of finding it is in that shed," Annabelle concluded, her eyes fixed upon the Inspector as she waited for his reaction.

He scratched his head for half a minute, sighed, and looked around his desk at the mess of paperwork he had sifted through, as he considered all of the Reverend's points.

"Okay," he muttered, eventually. "This case is a dead end anyway. But if there's nothing in the shed, Reverend, don't expect me to take your opinion seriously ever again. You're putting my trust in you on the line, here."

Annabelle nodded, her lips closed tightly for fear of changing the Inspector's mind once again.

Nicholls stood up, and walked to the door of his office.

"Where's Raven?" he shouted.

"He's just gone out," called Constable Colback, a slight tremor in his voice.

"The lazy so-and-so... You'll have to do the paperwork yourself then, Colback."

Colback mumbled for a few moments before managing to articulate himself more clearly.

"What paperwork's that, Chief?"

Nicholls emitted a sigh that was almost belligerent this time. "The search warrant on Louisa Montgomery's allotment! Do keep up, Colback!"

After increasingly exasperated calls from the Inspector, Colback had pulled in every favor with the Truro station he could to have the Inspector's search warrant ready in double-quick time. When it was ready, Detective Inspector Nicholls snatched it out of the young officer's hand with a glare and set off for his car. With Annabelle in the passenger's seat offering him directions to the allotment, the Inspector drove with the same quick temper and aggression that he had maintained since he arrived in the village. It was an experience that Annabelle, who prided herself on her exceptional driving skills and her respect for the speed limit, found deeply disturbing.

"Who examined the body, by the way?" Annabelle asked innocently after they'd arrived at their destination and she'd caught her breath.

"Harper," grunted the Inspector, "and some big shot from London."

Annabelle nodded.

"Harper's rather nice, isn't she?"

"She's a professional. Doesn't mess around. That's what I like," answered the Inspector, shooting her a glance.

"She's married, is she not?"

At this, the Inspector growled roughly. "Why would I care?" Then, under his breath, "Marriage is for fools. Pointless piece of paper that no one should pay any attention to."

Try as she might, Annabelle couldn't hide the concerned frown that emerged on her face. Suddenly all manner of dots connected up in her mind. Could the Inspector really be involved in a love triangle? With Harper and her husband!

They reached the allotments and got out of the car, the

Inspector slamming his door so hard that Annabelle shrieked a little at the sound. Carefully avoiding the nettles that had so pained her during her previous visit, she and the Inspector traipsed up the path that she had watched Louisa walk days earlier.

"It's just over here, Inspector."

"Hmph."

"Oh dear," Annabelle said, as she reached the shed door. "I completely forgot that the shed was locked when she—"

She turned around to address the Inspector just in time to see him retrieve a menacing-looking crowbar from his long coat and snap the locks apart as if they were made of flimsy plastic.

"Good thinking, Inspector."

"Police procedure, Reverend."

They exchanged a look to confirm their preparedness for whatever lay behind the shed door before DI Nicholls reached out and opened it carefully, peering into the gap as if something might leap out and attack him. When he had opened it enough to be sure nothing dangerous lay inside, he yanked the door open fully. Annabelle quickly followed him inside.

Nicholls cast his eyes over the sacks of soil, the dusty tools that lay haphazardly on the table, and the extensive range of other equipment piled up along the shed's walls. Dust motes floated in the slivers of light that pierced the gloom, the air filled with an aroma that could only be called "eau de gardening."

"Looks like we hit the jackpot," he muttered, in a tone unmistakably sarcastic.

"We certainly might have," Annabelle responded, as she brushed past the Inspector to the far end of the shed.

After pulling aside some brooms and a worn-looking stool, she looked over her shoulder at the Inspector.

"It's a cabinet?" he asked, frowning. "So what?"

Annabelle found the handles, and in a slow, steady gesture, pulled open the doors.

"Gosh!"

"Jesus Christ!"

Hanging in front of them, inside the cabinet among the dirty, old tools and gardening paraphernalia, was an elegant and striking wedding dress. The delicate white fabric seemed to glow in the murkiness and the intricate embroidery made everything in the shed seem even older and dirtier than it was.

They were both shocked to find this alien object in the most unlikely of places but the Inspector was the first one to come to his senses. He stepped toward the cabinet and pulled at a large suitcase which rested at its foot. After fiddling with the clasps he yanked it open.

"This is ever so strange," Annabelle muttered, as the Inspector foraged among clothes and toiletries that were obviously rather dated.

Something drew Annabelle's eye to the side of the cabinet. She carefully reached in to pull it out. It was a shoebox, but when she picked it up the weight seemed rather light for a pair of shoes. The Inspector stood beside her as she slowly lifted the lid. It was packed with yellowed tissue paper and she rustled around to pick out what was packed inside.

"Jewelry," muttered the Inspector.

"Wedding bands, and a necklace to be precise," replied Annabelle.

"Junk, to be even more precise," the Inspector retorted, "but incriminating junk, nonetheless."

Annabelle frowned as she dropped the solitaire diamond necklace back into the box.

"Inspector! Please don't allow your personal issues to cloud this!"

The Inspector looked back at Annabelle with almost angry disdain.

"My personal issues? What do you know of my personal issues!?"

"I know that they've become incredibly disruptive! As does anyone who has had the displeasure of being in your presence recently!"

The Inspector's hands went to his hips and he glowered at the Reverend.

"My personal issues are just that, Reverend – personal! Don't mistake me for a member of your flock, Vicar. I'm not looking for advice or guidance."

"Well, I should think not, Inspector," Annabelle said haughtily, taking a stance just as adamant. "You shouldn't need me to tell you that what you are doing is wrong!"

The Inspector's face seemed to redden even further.

"Wrong? How can... Who are... I am... I am not wrong! She belongs with me!"

"Harper is married, Inspector! She belongs with her husband!"

"What are y—"

"To think a grown man of your age, an Inspector in the police force, no less, would be chasing a married woman in such an impertinent, insolent manner is frankly shameful, Inspector!"

"Rever—"

"And it's no surprise to me, that regarding the circumstances of this case, you are struggling to see reason. You are acting quite disgracefully!"

"Are you quite finished, Reverend?"

Annabelle raised her chin and snorted dismissively.

"Let me put you clearly in the picture, Vicar. You have got the wrong end of the proverbial stick. I am not, as you so enthusiastically put it, 'chasing a married woman.' Least of all, Harper."

"The evidence—"

"The 'evidence'," interrupted the Inspector, crossly, "that you have gathered is clearly faulty, because the only 'female' I've been fighting over recently is a prize bitch."

Annabelle dropped the box of jewelry and gasped in horror. Her hand flew to her mouth.

"My Labrador by the name of 'Lulu,' to be precise. A former Crufts winner I took ownership of thirteen years ago and who has been my best friend ever since. My ex-wife is currently claiming that the dog belongs to her and has reopened our divorce settlement, despite it being two years old. She wants to gain custody of her."

Annabelle dropped her hand and began blushing so furiously that the Inspector wondered if her cheeks would explode. She looked at the ground and placed her hands on her hot face as if to cool it.

"I'm terribly sorry, Inspector. I heard you on the phone and I thought... I... I've made an utter and complete fool of myself."

"Hmph," the Inspector stared at her, his arms folded across his chest.

They stood there for a moment in the dark, the wedding dress hanging behind them, the jewelry at their feet, before the Inspector sighed dejectedly.

"It's okay. So long as you don't mention it outside this shed, I won't either. You're allowed a mistake after finding this," he said, gesturing to the uncommon haul they'd discovered in the shed.

Annabelle nodded shamefacedly, brushing her cheeks to soothe her embarrassment. She was mortified.

"What is this?!" came a shrieking voice from beyond the shed door.

Annabelle and the Inspector spun around to see the beige figure of Louisa, her carpet bag dropped to the ground, clutching her face in horror.

"We had reason to believe that you were hiding evidence, Miss Montgomery," said the Inspector, stepping toward her with the search warrant in hand. "Do you mind explaining what all this is?"

"This," Louisa spat, her voice filled with spiteful anger, "is Lucy's. I've been keeping it since she disappeared, and you have no right to go through it!"

She pushed past the Inspector into the shed and began rearranging the items within the suitcase. Annabelle glanced from Louisa, to the wedding dress, then back to the Inspector, who raised his eyebrows and gestured for the Reverend to join him outside, leaving the appalled teacher in peace.

When they had walked a few steps away, out of earshot, Annabelle clasped the Inspector's arm.

"What do you make of this, Inspector?"

"Well, Lucy was obviously ready for a wedding, and a quick one too, judging by the suitcase. Now, that leaves me with two lines of inquiry. Either she was planning to get married to Daniel or somebody else. Either way, he should have known something about it. The fact that he didn't mention anything about that to you is a pretty clear indicator that he's hiding something."

"Hiding what?"

"My guess is that he's the murderer," the Inspector said, marching off toward the car. Annabelle took one last look at the forlorn figure of Louisa, delicately rearranging the jewelry in the shoebox under the ominous gaze of that magnificent wedding dress, and turned around to run after him.

CHAPTER EIGHT

ONCE AGAIN, ANNABELLE clung to the passenger-side door handle and hummed her disapproval at the speed and level of aggression with which the Inspector drove. He was even more erratic than before as he zoomed through the narrow streets of Upton St. Mary toward the police station.

"Inspector, are you sure this isn't incredibly rash?" Annabelle managed to blurt out in between the sound of screeching tires.

"We'll give him a chance to explain himself," the Inspector replied, "but he's going to need a hell of a good story to get out of these knots."

Annabelle almost screamed as the Inspector brought the car to a stop inches away from Annabelle's Mini, so sure was she that he would drive straight into it. He leaped out and sprinted up the steps and through the entrance of the station.

"Raven! Colback! Get another car, we're going to arrest Daniel Green."

"The butcher, sir?" Raven asked, confusedly.

"Yes."

Raven and Colback exchanged brief looks before slapping on their hats and running outside.

Annabelle was standing on the pavement as the three officers jumped into their vehicles. Suddenly, sirens were blaring and flashing blue lights were blinding her. Before she could call out to one of the officers, the two cars – one containing Raven and Colback, the other the Inspector – had swarmed into the street and off into the distance. She hurried over to her Mini, miffed at the ease with which the police officers had left her behind and drove off to follow them.

Though she felt very much a part of this operation and was caught up in the noisy thrill and excitement of the racing police cars, Annabelle refused to break the speed limit. She quickly found herself left far behind. By the time she reached Daniel Green's butcher shop, he was already exiting it, accompanied by the constables on either side.

The Inspector followed closely behind. A small crowd of shoppers and Daniel's colleagues gathered at the door of the shop to observe the unexpected turn of events. Nobody, however, seemed more taken aback than Daniel, who had obviously been hard at work when the officers had found him. He was wearing his full butcher's garb, bloodied and messy, and was staring about him at the flashing sirens and officious constables as if struggling to make sense of it all.

Annabelle watched from behind the wheel as they put Daniel into the back of the Inspector's car and swerved briskly away again, back toward the police station. Bystanders quickly turned to one another to chatter and speculate on what it was all about as they watched the police cars race into the distance as quickly as they had arrived.

Seeing Daniel had given Annabelle an idea, though she wasn't quite sure what it was. Her instincts told her that there was something terribly wrong with the arrest. Without having the time she needed to formulate her thoughts, she spun the Mini around and once again began her pursuit of the police vehicles returning to the station.

As she drove along, again minding the speed limit, her thoughts raced much faster than her car. The sight of the butcher in his blood-spattered butcher's clothing was stirring some memory at the back of her mind, but what was it? She couldn't quite catch it.

She reached the police station and locked her car carefully before running inside. Just as she was about to rush past the desk through to the back where the interview rooms and offices were, Constable Colback stepped in front of her.

"I'm sorry, Reverend. The Inspector is about to interview someone, I'm afraid you'll have to—"

"Let her through, Colback!" came the Inspector's distinctive, irritated voice from the back. "Lord knows I'd rather have her with me in the interview room than you!"

Annabelle shot the Constable an apologetic look, but he was too embarrassed to catch her eye and simply slunk off to the side. She stepped toward the hallway that led off in the direction of the interview rooms, where the Inspector was waiting impatiently.

"He's waiting for us," the Inspector said, triumphantly, "all we have to do now is get the confession. Shouldn't be too hard considering how much we know."

"I'm not too sure that—"

"Come on, Reverend," the Inspector said, briskly, as he opened the door and gestured her inside.

"You!" Daniel said, as he saw the Vicar enter, followed by the Inspector.

Annabelle met his eyes and nodded a somewhat indecisive greeting. Daniel was sitting behind a table, his hands and clothes still bloody. At this close distance Annabelle could smell the freshly cut beef, pork and lamb emanating from him.

"What's... What's all this about?" Daniel pleaded, his eyes darting between the two visitors.

The Inspector glared silently at him as he pulled out a chair for Annabelle and then sat down himself. Daniel's eyes bore the look of being found out that the Inspector knew only too well, his tense body language demonstrating signs that he was hiding something. The Inspector was suddenly very sure he had made the right choice.

"This is about the truth, Daniel Green. The truth behind what happened that day in the woods between you and Lucy."

Daniel mouthed some words incomprehensibly, and his face turned from expression of fear into one of sheer incredulity.

"What?"

"Lucy's murder. Your ex-girlfriend."

"That was twenty years ago!"

"Justice doesn't come with an expiration date."

"This is crazy!"

"Why didn't you tell us that you were planning to marry Lucy?" the Inspector said, calmly.

Daniel shook his head in a gesture of utter befuddlement.

"Marriage? I was nineteen! I never intended to marry her!" Daniel looked down at his hands, still shaking his head at the absurdity.

"Well, she seemed to be very much of the impression somebody was about to marry her. She was about to turn sixteen. Had herself a nice little wedding dress and a suitcase already packed."

Daniel looked up at the Inspector.

"I don't understand."

"We just found them, over on the allotments. Her sister's been keeping them all this time."

"What... That... That doesn't make sense..."

The Inspector looked at Annabelle, but her face was fixed upon Daniel's in a look of pity. He waited for Daniel to add something meaningful to his confused mumblings, but the butcher only clasped his hands and glanced around him looking deeply perplexed.

"Okay. Let's say for a second that you weren't planning to marry Lucy. Who else could have been?"

Daniel shook his head once again, breathing deeply under the weight of the question's implications.

"It doesn't make sense."

"You said that already."

"No, Detective. I mean, it really doesn't. You see, Lucy wasn't the marrying type at all. She had so many things that she wanted to do. To be a singer, an actress. To travel the world. To meet new people. She never wanted to be tied down. She joked about marriage sometimes, but I think really she just thought it was very boring. She wanted to be young and free forever."

The Inspector sighed deeply.

"Maybe you didn't know her as well as you think you did."

Daniel hung his head.

"I don't know anything anymore. I don't know what to tell you, Detective."

Suddenly, the Inspector slammed his palm upon the table loudly.

"Enough! We've got all the evidence we need to put you away, Daniel Green! This act won't get you anything but a longer sentence! If you've got half as much brains in your head as you've got smeared over your apron there, then you'll talk!"

"But I don't know anything! I don't know how she died!"

The Inspector leaped from his seat and grabbed at Daniel's bloodied butcher's clothes from across the table, pulling the man's face up to his.

"You butchered her just like you butchered one of your animals! This time, though, it's me who will be eating you for breakfast!"

"Inspector!" shouted Annabelle, as she stood up and pulled his arms away from Daniel. "Please!"

The Inspector looked at her for a moment and then, like he were an uncooperative child, Annabelle gently but firmly ushered him out of the interview room, though he kept his stern glare fixed upon the frightened butcher all the way. She pushed the detective outside with a gentle shove and closed the door, leaving Daniel alone in the room behind them.

"This guy knows we don't have much to go on," said the Inspector, pacing up and down while rubbing his brow in frustration, "but he's hiding something. Of that I'm sure."

"Perhaps, Inspector, but you'll not get anywhere if you frighten him half to death!"

"I don't see how else we're ever going to put this case to bed."

Annabelle sighed as she watched the Inspector pace himself into a modicum of calmness. Suddenly a thought flashed across her mind like a bolt of lightning. She realized that the peculiarly familiar feeling she had had when seeing Daniel emerge from the butcher's shop mid-arrest could provide the answer to another question that had been plaguing her for a while. She clicked her fingers, and with a tone of sudden enthusiasm said:

"I have a strong suspicion that I know what our butcher may be hiding."

The Inspector stopped dead in his tracks and looked at Annabelle.

"But it may not actually help us in this case," she added.

"Right now I don't think anything will. But if it explains that man's behavior in any way, then it's worth a shot."

Annabelle nodded as she reopened the door to the interview room.

"Daniel," she said, calmly, as she sat opposite him. The Inspector decided to stand in the corner, hands in pockets, and subject Daniel to nothing but his focused glare. "Did you do anything.... um, peculiar, one night about a week ago?"

The change in Daniel's expression was impossible not to notice. His teeth clenched and his eyes fixed unblinkingly on the Reverend's face.

"I... Don't know... No. I didn't."

"You weren't outside? After midnight?"

"No... I..." he gulped, "What night was this? I'm sorry. I would have to check."

Annabelle looked over toward the Inspector, who was now wearing a look of intense anticipation, not unlike the one Biscuit wore when she was about to pounce.

"I think you may remember this. You were over by Hughes House, where Philippa lives. I believe you know her."

Daniel's eyes widened, and the shortness of his breath was visible in the rapid rising and falling of his chest.

"You were wearing your butcher's clothes," Annabelle continued, "and they were as bloodied and messy as they are now. Philippa saw you."

Daniel slumped over in defeat, before raising his eyes to greet Annabelle's.

"You know, don't you, Reverend?"

Annabelle remained silent.

Daniel shook his head, and with a deep intake of breath, began talking.

"It was an accident. A stupid one, but an accident nonetheless."

"What was?" came the Inspector's gruff tone from the corner of the room.

"I was slaughtering a couple of pigs over on Hughes' farm. I do it a couple of times a week on the quiet, see, and I've done it hundreds of times," Daniel said, as if excusing himself, "but that night I got a little... distracted."

"By what?"

Daniel shuffled in his seat, awkwardly.

"I'd had a few beers. Maybe a few too many," he said, before loudly exclaiming: "It was the night of the England game! We'd played so well! I mean, you'd be hard-pressed to find a man in the country who wasn't three sheets to the wind after that!"

Annabelle frowned and turned toward the Inspector, who was hiding his eyes under his hand. She turned back toward Daniel.

"So what happened?"

"I prepared everything as usual, and after doing one pig, I heard some loud squealing. Then I remembered that I'd left the pen open. I turned around and saw the other pig streaking away like a thoroughbred!"

"You chased after it?"

"Of course! I damn near ran a marathon trying to catch it, and it still got away when it went into the woods. I've searched and searched for days and nights but I've no idea where it is now."

"I have," Annabelle said, sighing deeply. "I had to swerve to avoid it just a few nights ago. I even saw it on the hills at the back of the church the other morning!"

If ever there was to be an explanation for Philippa's vision, this was undoubtedly one of the strangest, though Philippa would find a drunken butcher chasing a pig a lot less terrifying than a murderous ghost.

"Why is this important?" said the Inspector, stepping forward. "Are you telling me that the reason you're acting so suspiciously is because a bloody pig got the better of you!?"

"My business is my life, Detective," Daniel pleaded, "I could lose my slaughtering license. If this got out, the local gossip would destroy me. I've got competitors who've waited for years for such an opportunity. Meat is a cutthroat business."

Annabelle chuckled. The two men looked at her and frowned deeply, causing her to drop the grin quickly and replace it with a look of embarrassment.

"Reverend," the Inspector said, as he opened the door once again.

Annabelle stepped through it, and they stood closely in the hallway.

The Inspector said, "This has gone nowhere. Daniel's more concerned with stories about an errant pig than a possible murder charge. He's more innocent than I am, and without him as a suspect, we're at a dead end once again. I'm going to close this case and get back to Truro."

"No, wait!" Annabelle said, pressing a hand against his chest to stop him, before removing it with an awkward smile when she realized it was a gesture more intimate than the occasion, and indeed, the Inspector, demanded.

DI Nicholls sighed. "Give it up, Reverend. Sometimes you just have to admit defeat. We've searched the shed, questioned the butcher, and brought in an expert from London to assess the body. There's nothing more we can do. The secrets of that dress died with Lucy."

"Perhaps not, Inspector. Do you have a photo of Lucy?"

Nicholls shot Annabelle a quizzical look, before shrugging his shoulders and leading her to his office, where he sifted through the dozens of folders that had been scattered around his desk.

"I think... Somewhere here...Ah! Here it is," he said, as he handed a photocopy of a picture to the Reverend.

Though the picture was black and white, it was clear to see that Lucy had fair hair, which fell about her shoulders in curls, the epitome of a fairytale princess. She was standing next to a strapping young man, obviously Daniel, her arms around his waist, as he pulled a funny face at the camera.

"How old was she in this picture, Inspector?"

He pursed his lips. "Fifteen years, I should expect. That was taken within a year of her disappearance."

"Hmm," Annabelle muttered.

"Are you quite done, Reverend?"

Annabelle looked up from the photo.

"Not at all, Inspector. And neither are you."

The Inspector frowned his confusion. Annabelle stepped close to him so that he could see the photo.

"How tall is Daniel Green, would you say, Inspector?"

"About six foot on the button, I'd guess."

"And knowing that, how tall would you estimate Lucy to be in this photo?"

"Well, she barely comes to his shoulder. I'd say around five-three, give or take an inch."

"Precisely," Annabelle said, firmly.

The Inspector's confused frown remained.

"The wedding dress?" Annabelle reminded him, though his expression did not change. "There is no way that wedding dress would fit a woman of five foot three, Inspector."

"Are you sure about that?"

"I'm a vicar, Inspector. I've seen more ill-fitting wedding dresses than I'd care to, and I can tell you with certainty that that dress was certainly not meant for Lucy."

"But then..." the Inspector said, trailing off his sentence as he finally realized what Annabelle was insinuating.

"Yes, Inspector. The dress was not Lucy's. It was Louisa's."

"Are you sure?" the Inspector asked, disbelievingly.

"Almost certain, Inspector. I thought it peculiar at the time that Louisa would tend to her sister's wedding dress. Plus the dress itself..."

"Yes?" the Inspector urged, now enraptured by Annabelle's revelation.

"Well, I can't say for sure, but a dress such as that tends not to retain its shape very well unless it's worn occasionally. Especially when it's hanging in a dank cupboard on an allotment. A dress of that elaborate nature would only appear in such pristine condition if it was worn now and again."

The Inspector scratched his chin, shaking his head at the bizarre nature of it all.

"You've lost me, now. I'm beginning to feel like this case will go on forever."

Annabelle sighed, sympathetic to the Inspector's troubled look.

"Either way, it seems like the only thing we can do now is to talk to Louisa. At least to ask why she felt the need to lie to us."

CHAPTER NINE

ONCE DANIEL HAD been released, Annabelle and the Inspector solemnly made their way toward Louisa Montgomery's home. The sun had set, and Upton St. Mary was very definitely experiencing the crisp coolness of emerging autumn.

Whether it was the suspicion that they had perhaps reached a dead end with little to show for it but an embarrassing story of a drunk butcher chasing a pig or the awkwardness they felt over their recent altercation and the revealing of the Inspector's canine troubles, Annabelle and the Inspector drove in silence. DI Nicholls even stayed under the speed limit as he brought them to the brink of what felt like their last chance to understand the truth behind the murder of Lucy Montgomery. Annabelle watched the village that she loved pass by in the passenger-side window of the police car, reflecting upon all the joys, loves, mysteries, and tragedies that occurred beneath its seemingly placid and picturesque surface. She turned back to look at the Inspector and noted the pained expression with which he stared out of the windshield at the road. He didn't seem to notice her. For the first time, Annabelle seemed to recognize the deep concern that had imprinted itself on his face over the past week.

"I'm sure you'll get your dog back, Inspector," she said softly.

The Inspector furrowed his brow for a split-second, before looking at Annabelle and relaxing his face. The worried grimace and cold eyes disappeared like clouds in spring for the first time since he had arrived in Upton St. Mary. He smiled meekly, before turning his attention back to the road.

"Thanks, Reverend. I hope so."

A few minutes later, the detective brought the car to a stop outside Louisa's home. Across the road, Katie Flynn was walking away, having just closed her tea shop for the day. The streets were empty, most people having gone home to squeeze a little more relaxation out of the weekend before the work week began once more.

Annabelle peered at Louisa's house, searching for a light or an open window.

"I do hope she's at home."

"Let's find out," the Inspector replied, exiting the car.

They made their way up the path to her door, exchanging glances all the way. Annabelle rang the doorbell. After a minute of waiting, the Inspector sighed impatiently and rang it again, long and loud. The response, this time, was almost immediate.

"Who is it?" Louisa asked from the other side of the door, her exasperation and irritation evident in even those few, brief words.

"It's Detective Inspector Nicholls and the Reverend Annabelle Dixon. We'd like to speak with you, Miss Montgomery."

"Haven't you two bothered me enough today?" came the increasingly frustrated reply.

"We'd just like to ask you some questions, Louisa," the Inspector said firmly.

"I've said about as much as I'm going to say to you. Now if you don't mind, please leave my property."

The Inspector looked at Annabelle with increasing annoyance.

"We know the dress isn't Lucy's!" called Annabelle suddenly.

The Inspector cast another disapproving look toward Annabelle. He had not wanted them to reveal their hand this early. Seconds later, however, his vexation disappeared, as the door opened ever so slightly to reveal a sliver of Miss Montgomery's face.

"What do you mean?"

Seeing the opportunity, the Inspector decided to take the lead once again.

"The dress that you said was Lucy's; we know that it isn't. And we also know that it's most likely yours."

Though only a little of Louisa's face was visible behind the door frame, her raised eyebrow and concerned expression was clear. She opened the door a little more, cast her eyes around the street outside, and then gestured for the two to hurry in, as if they were the ones who had been dilly-dallying all this time.

They stopped in the hallway as Louisa closed the door and turned to them.

"Well, to the living room! Do you expect me to stand around in my own hallway chatting?"

They duly obliged, settling in to the floral-patterned couch that sat in the middle of a sparsely decorated room. Aside from an old, bulky TV and some elegant glass vases holding dahlias and other seasonal flowers, there was not much to Louisa's house. It was tidy, restrained, full of hard surfaces, and slightly cold, much like Louisa herself, thought Annabelle.

"I hope you do not expect me to provide tea or other comforts for this rudest of intrusions," Louisa said, sitting down carefully on the comfy chair beside the couch. "I would like to make this as short as possible."

"If you would like to make it brief, Miss Montgomery, then I suggest you stop being so—"

Annabelle placed her hand on the Inspector's arm to stop his anger getting the better of him, before addressing Louisa herself.

"Louisa, you told us that the wedding dress in your allotment shed was Lucy's, when that's patently not true. It does seem to be yours. It is your size and appears to have been worn occasionally over the years. Only you could have done that."

"And what of it? I don't see how or why my private property is of concern to your... investigation or whatever you call this harassment campaign you're indulging in."

"It seems rather strange that you would lie."

"Strange?" Louisa said, her voice turning sarcastic and venomous with ease. "Who are you to decide what's 'strange?' Do you make a habit of invading the property of others and passing such impertinent judgments? Personally, I find it rather 'strange' that a leader of the church and a police officer should be conducting themselves in a fashion more befitting the neighborhood gossips. What do you make of that, Reverend?"

"Now look here—" said the Inspector roughly, before Annabelle held him back by placing her hand once again upon his arm.

"It's just that the wedding dress being kept in such a way casts certain doubts upon—"

"In case you have forgotten," interrupted Louisa, "or merely failed to intrude upon that part of my past, I have been married before, Reverend. That is why I have a wedding dress."

The Inspector and Annabelle exchanged one last look. Though he still wore his mask of skepticism, Annabelle could see the defeat in the Inspector's eyes. He leaned in toward her and whispered in Annabelle's ear.

"That's it, Reverend. We don't have anything else on her. We may as well leave now."

"But why would she lie about it being Lucy's in the first place?" Annabelle whispered back.

"The fact remains we have no evidence." The Inspector pulled away, shrugging as he did so.

Annabelle pursed her lips, deep in thought. She had come too far and discovered too much to give up now.

"Is there anything else?" Louisa asked, haughtily, though the question was intoned more like an order.

"There is one thing," Annabelle said, tentatively but with an air of knowing. "You told me you didn't love your husband, Gary. If that was the case, then why would you be so sentimental about your wedding to him? Why would you keep your dress and even wear it occasionally?"

Louisa raised an eyebrow, her face full of stern reproach.

"A wedding is a momentous occasion in anybody's life, regardless of the emotional entanglements therein."

"And yet I see no other signs. I don't see a wedding band still affixed to your finger. Indeed, you don't seem to have any photos of the wedding situated in your house, either."

Louisa's eyes narrowed into tightly wound beams of black light, so intense that Annabelle felt them almost physically piercing her.

"I prefer to keep my sentimentality private, Reverend. What exactly are you suggesting?"

Annabelle galvanized herself against Louisa's formidable and intimidating presence as she prepared to risk everything in pursuit of the truth. She had taken a few gambles already today, and while her instincts regarding the shed had proved fruitful, her assumptions about the Inspector's phone call had been ludicrously wrong. She prayed quickly that what she was about to say would be one of her better judgment calls.

"I believe that dress has never been near a wedding. It was intended to be worn in a wedding that never happened."

"Bah!" Louisa snorted, dismissively. "What utter nonsense! Keep a wedding dress without using it? Why on earth would I do such a thing!? As I said before, Reverend, I was very much married, albeit briefly. That was my wedding dress from my marriage to Gary Barnes."

"Maybe, but there is a very important fact that leads me to believe that that wedding dress wasn't retained in order to remember your marriage to Gary, if indeed it was the same wedding dress you married him in, but for another purpose entirely."

"And what would that be, might I ask?"

"Why would you pack a suitcase of clothes and preserve them just as lovingly as the dress itself, especially for all this time?"

Louisa's eyes narrowed once again, only this time there was a weakness in them, a chink in the armor that Annabelle detected and that spurred her on.

"A suitcase full of clothes," Annabelle continued, her words gathering force as she blustered through them, "makes a strange souvenir from a wedding which has already occurred, but for a wedding that never happened, a wedding for a love that never died, a love that you still, to this day, bear some small hope will be requited, it is oddly appropriate!" She ended with a flourish.

Now it was the Inspector's turn to put a hand on Annabelle's arm. She turned to look at him, expecting him to calm her down, but instead he gave a mild nod for her to continue.

Louisa blurted angrily, "This is ludicrous, Reverend. Almost as ludicrous as the tales you spin in your pulpit. I, however, am not obliged to sit and listen to you 'preach.' I have classes to prepare for, and I believe I have entertained the two of you quite enough tonight. If you don't mind—"

"Answer the question, Miss Montgomery," DI Nicholls said, his voice calm yet strong. "This is not a casual conversation nor idle chit-chat for the benefit of ourselves. This involves a high-profile murder case, one of the most serious cold cases that currently exists in the county of Cornwall."

Louisa said nothing but stared hard at him, her arms folded in defiance.

"Look, Miss Montgomery," the Inspector's voice grew colder, "I've given you the benefit of the doubt. Especially considering that we're talking about your sister, and that you were one of the last people to see her alive. I believed you when you lied to me about whose wedding dress it was, and I've given you a lot of leeway, as you asked, during my questioning. The time has come, however, for you to be upfront with me, with us, now. If you insist on making this difficult, I can quite easily take you to the station and charge you with the obstruction of justice, but I sincerely hope that we can talk about this in a civil, adult manner."

Louisa raised her chin, her jaw clenched so tightly that sharp dimples appeared in her cheeks. She pouted before clearing her throat regally and speaking.

"Very well. If you wish to make this an official matter, I understand I must oblige. Please, then, ask me what it is you wish me to help with, and I shall do my best."

"Thank you," the Inspector said.

Annabelle and the Inspector looked at each other for support in the tense atmosphere of Louisa's living room. They hadn't expected to face such a difficult challenge when they first decided to visit her, but the struggle they were having getting information out of Louisa merely made them feel that there was some truth to be had that was just out of their grasp.

"Did you have feelings for Daniel Green?" the Inspector asked.

Louisa raised her eyebrows and smiled wryly.

"Is this what your investigation is predicated upon, Detective? Teenage hormones?"

"Answer the question, Miss Montgomery."

"I may have had some brief feelings, at some point in time, yes."

"Were you jealous then, of your sister Lucy's relationship with him?"

"Are you implying that I—"

"Stick to the question, please."

Louisa raised her chin once more.

"No. I was not."

"But you were constantly pestering her about the fact that she was seeing him, were you not?" Annabelle added.

"'Pestering'? No. I was her older sister. It was my duty

to ensure that she remained safe and on the right track. Gallivanting about town with cocky boys such as... him... was not suitable for a girl her age."

"So you fought with Lucy a lot?" Annabelle asked.

Louisa's eyes narrowed in on the Reverend, once again spearing her with their sharp beam.

"Sibling disagreements are an unfortunate inevitability, Reverend. I take it you are an only child?"

"Did these fights ever get physical?" asked the Inspector, distracting Louisa from Annabelle.

"Absolutely not."

"Your sister's body showed signs of multiple healed fractures. The pathologist said she'd experienced some pretty bad beatings growing up. You don't know anything about that?"

Louisa paused uncharacteristically before answering this question.

"I..." she shook her head. "No. I don't know anything about that."

The Inspector looked toward Annabelle with another shrug of defeat. They had pretty much gone through everything they had, and Louisa had still retained her tough shell, deflecting everything.

"That's a lot of side-stepping that you're doing, Miss Montgomery," the Inspector sighed.

"Are you implying something, Detective?"

The question hung in the air for a few seconds, fermenting the tension that had reached almost boiling point between the three of them. Suddenly, Annabelle got to her feet, her face flustered and red.

"You know jolly well what we're implying, Louisa!" she shouted, all her good grace and gentleness eroded in the face of the teacher's evasiveness. "You killed your sister!"

Louisa gasped. "This is preposterous!" she exclaimed, her voice full of indignation and surprise.

"Reverend," warned the Inspector.

"No!" cried Annabelle, shrugging the Inspector off as he tried to pull her back to her seat. "This has gone on long enough!" She turned to the seated teacher, who gazed up at her, quietly fuming behind her stony expression. "You fought with Lucy constantly. You were jealous of her popularity, just as she was jealous of your looks. The fights got so bad that they frequently became physical."

"Ridiculous!" Louisa spurted adamantly, but the quiver in her voice was unmistakable.

"But you also became jealous of her relationship with Daniel. You bullied and berated her, hoping that you could force them apart."

Louisa shook her head madly, wincing at the words that Annabelle spoke as if they were weapons tearing her apart.

"You were so madly in love with him, so intent upon a future with him, that you even prepared for the moment that you would have him to yourself. You bought a wedding dress, and packed a suitcase."

"Stop it. Stop..."

"But you just waited and waited. The chance you were looking for never came, and with each day you grew increasingly despairing, tortured not just by your unfulfilled love, but by the fact that your despised sister was the one enjoying the company of Daniel and not you. Until one day, you snapped."

"Enough... Please..."

"What was it? Did she find the wedding dress? Did you simply run out of patience? Did you realize how easy it would be to just—?"

"She knew I loved him!" Louisa screamed suddenly,

interrupting Annabelle so harshly that the Reverend fell back onto her seat upon the couch while the Inspector's jaw dropped almost entirely to the floor.

Louisa trembled in the heavy silence which followed her outburst. She pressed her fingers daintily to the bridge of her nose and pinched it as she struggled to suppress the sobs of her emotions.

"She knew... That's why she was with him... To spite me..." Louisa's sobs grew, her body almost convulsing as she struggled to keep down the twenty-year-old secret, the decades of lies, and repressed feelings.

Annabelle pulled out a packet of tissues from her pocket and handed one to Louisa.

"You will never know...never know what it's like...to bear such a secret...for so long...." Louisa uttered, in between the gasping sobs of her crying. She raised her eyes to meet Annabelle's, but this time the small intense beads of dark light were soft and wet with tears and pain. Her pursed lips trembled maniacally, and the tightly controlled expression on her face softened into the round openness of a broken woman.

"Lucy was popular, but that didn't stop her from detesting me. She always wanted to get the better of me. She'd never had a boyfriend for more than a month before Daniel, but when she realized how much I loved him, she decided to torture me, to keep him for herself, have him hanging around, doting on her every whim. All so that she could rub in my face that the man I loved was hers, and there was nothing I could do about it. Yes. We fought, of course we did. If they'd found my body in the ground, I'm sure they'd discover just as many bruised and broken bones."

Annabelle cast a sorrowful look at the Inspector, but his

eyes were intense and focused, waiting for the crucial moment that Louisa would say what he needed to hear.

"The dress, the wedding bands, the jewelry," Louisa continued, as she swayed from side to side, sobbing and dabbing at her red, wet cheeks, "I gathered them myself in readiness. The suitcase of clothes I packed myself. It's stupid, but I've always been one for preparation. I always thought that if I had a plan, had some money, had everything ready, then the final piece would just fall into place. The way I saw it, the way Daniel looked at me, the way he spoke to me back then, I was sure that one day, he would turn up on my doorstep and declare his undying love for me, the kind of love I had for him. In my dreams, Daniel and I would live blissfully and happily ever after."

Annabelle shook her head sorrowfully. "But why, in all this time, did you never simply tell Daniel about your feelings toward him? Particularly if they were so strong?"

"I may be passionate, Reverend. I may be proud. But I have always lacked confidence. My mother always told me that I was born out of time. I have never felt it was ladylike for a woman to announce her intentions. It is enough for her merely to entice. Besides," she said, blinking away tears, "rejection would have crushed me overwhelmingly. I daren't risk it. No, he had to come to me."

"What happened, Louisa?" asked Annabelle gently, as she offered another tissue.

Louisa breathed deeply, her face twisted into a look of sadness so deep that Annabelle felt pained just to observe it. With the greatest of struggles, Louisa sat up, tightened her throat, swallowed her sobs, and began talking, her voice taking on a cold, detached monotone.

"We argued, as was typical for us. I told her I didn't want her out too long, she told me she would do as she pleased. It escalated, again, as was usual, and she told me precisely what she intended."

"Which was?"

"To keep Daniel and to stop us from ever getting together."

"That must have made you angry."

Louisa glared at the Inspector through her tears and hurt.

"It wasn't the only thing she said. She called me pathetic for pining after her boyfriend. She ridiculed me. She told me that even were she to leave Daniel, he would never be with a wretch like me for more than a week. And then she left."

The Inspector leaned forward.

"And then?"

"I was so mad. I could barely think. The gall of that girl! To keep us apart simply for her petulant enjoyment! The anger... All the pain... It possessed me. I lost my sense of composure, of rationality. All I could think about was how much I hated her, and how much happiness awaited me if she would only... disappear."

"You followed her?"

Louisa nodded, absently staring at the floor with eyes that were wide and wild.

"I grabbed the first thing I saw – a rolling pin from the kitchen – and then I just ran. Out into the woods. I wasn't even looking for her. I just needed to run. To rid myself of all the anger and passion that flowed through my veins. I ran in the knowledge that there was almost no chance we would bump into each other in those vast woods because, you see, I didn't really want to hurt her. But after a few minutes, I saw her. Walking, so pleased with herself. Smiling, even though nobody was there to see it. She caught sight of me and laughed. She told me once again about how pathetic I was, sprinting through the forest with a stupid rolling pin. She said I was too meek and afraid to do anything. That I was a 'talker' not a 'doer.' Just seeing the smugness in her face, hearing the mockery in her laughter, the ease with which she demeaned me, I lost control. Anger took over once again and...."

Louisa slumped over as she broke down into sobs. This time Annabelle stepped out of her chair and knelt beside the woman, a fresh tissue in her hand. She rubbed her back gently, as more pain was released from the deep well of sorrow that had been residing inside of Louisa Montgomery.

"I hit her. The rolling pin was heavy, and it didn't take much to knock her out, but again and again I hit her until the mockery and the shame was no more. Until the derision in her eyes was gone. Then, I buried her. It was as if I exited my body and watched myself from somewhere above the treetops, clawing and scratching at the dirt until I'd made a hole big enough to bury her inside.

"I didn't do a good job; it was a shallow grave. I lived in perpetual fear that somebody would stumble upon it. Over the years, I would sometimes make my way there in the darkness of the night, to see if she had been discovered. I would talk to her, sometimes. Full of rage, full of regret, full of despair.

"Last month, it was her birthday. I went to 'visit' her, and for the first time I saw that the soil had dried up to the point that her skull was visible. I hurriedly covered it but dropped the apple I had brought. I knew then my secret would be discovered soon. Somebody would find her eventually. I often felt that the fact that nobody had, for all these years, had been the worst punishment of all. To be confined with a secret for so long..."

"Tell us what happened after you buried her, Louisa," Annabelle gently prompted her as Louisa's words trailed off and she stared out the window, lost in thoughts as deep as the forest in which she had killed her sister.

"I don't even remember anymore. What I can remember feels like something I witnessed, not something I did. I ran back to the house, and when Daniel called to ask where Lucy was, I told him I had no idea. However strange it sounds, I actually believed it. It was the truth. It took me weeks, months even, to realize that what I had done was real and not simply something I had dreamed." Louisa looked up at the Inspector, then at Annabelle. "Has that never happened to you?"

Annabelle looked back at the Inspector, whose face was neutral, but whose eyes seemed wet with compassion.

"Strangely enough, Miss Montgomery, it has. Though the consequences were nowhere near as severe as yours."

Louisa gazed at the Inspector for a few moments, as if finding some respite in her engulfing misery through his words, before the shudders and the sobs overwhelmed her body once again and she began to cry uncontrollably.

"After the original investigation turned up nothing, we all returned to our lives. I got married and went to university. But Gary noticed that something had changed and we divorced," she muttered, in between sobs. "I told people that he had left for America because of his work. In truth, it was because I was unbearable to him. I kept him at a distance even after the marriage. Oh, I was my regular self on the outside, but inside I was dying. I had committed fratricide! I killed my own sister! I was deplorable, deviant. I've hurt almost everybody that was close to me..."

The Inspector stood up and watched Annabelle gently console the teacher as she released years of pain and anguish. He stepped into the hallway and pulled out his radio.

"Raven?" he said quietly into the receiver. "Louisa Montgomery's house... Opposite Flynn's tea shop... We're to arrest her... Yes, turns out she is."

He clicked off the receiver and cast one more look at the despairing woman. Annabelle stood up and joined him.

"Is she going to be alright?" he asked.

Annabelle shrugged pityingly.

"I don't suppose one can ever be alright after committing an act like that."

The Inspector's face settled into a forlorn sadness.

"It's strange. A case like this, a pretty young girl murdered in the woods, it usually gives a sense of satisfaction when you solve it. A clear sense of right and wrong, black and white, good and evil. This though, this is a mess."

They watched Louisa silently for a few minutes. Raven arrived and entered the house eagerly.

"She's in there, Constable," the Inspector ordered, some formality and direction returning to his manner. As Raven stepped past him, however, he put a hand on his shoulder to stop him. "Take it easy. Be gentle with her."

Raven nodded. He carefully led Louisa out of her home into the waiting police car. Annabelle and the Inspector followed. They watched the vehicle make its way back to the police station.

"You seem rather reflective, Inspector," Annabelle said, looking up at his furrowed brow.

"Well, when you hear a story like that, it's difficult not to be. It makes you think about your own life."

Annabelle sighed.

"It's a simple matter of letting go, Inspector. Whether it's a lover, a family member, an idea, or – dare I say it – a dog."

Nicholls looked at Annabelle, his eyes as innocent as a child's.

"And what if there is nothing to replace what you let go?"

"That's just it, Inspector," Annabelle replied, "you'll never know what can replace it if you don't give it a chance."

Inspector Nicholls smiled slightly and nodded his head. He shoved his hands into his pockets and took a step toward the car.

"Would you like me to drop you off home, Reverend?"

"No, thank you." Annabelle looked about her at the nighttime street. "I'd like to pay someone a visit. All this talk has reminded me of a promise I made."

Nicholls nodded, exchanged one more smile with Annabelle, and walked to his car.

EPILOGUE

AUTUMN SWEPT OVER the village of Upton St. Mary in waves of brown. Leaves lay on soil darkened by the increasingly regular rainfall. Where before, the villagers had puttered along the sunny streets slowly, their heads raised in case the opportunity to stop and exchange news presented itself, now they clutched their coats tightly around their bodies and hurried to their destinations.

The faces of the children were no longer red and sweaty from days of physical activity in the hot sun but were sleepy and pale with the return of the new school year and classroom work. The sound of chatter from mothers outside the school gates and raucous banter between men on their way to the pub had been replaced by the sound of wind through dry tree branches and the rustle of crunchy leaves underfoot. Picnics of sandwiches, cake, and fruit had given way to hearty meals of soup, meat, and roasted vegetables. Yes, autumn and the approaching winter prevailed and ordered the lives of the good people of Upton St. Mary as it had for centuries.

"Oh, Reverend," cooed Philippa as she stood beside Annabelle who was leaning over the stove, "I do wish you'd go easier on the pepper."

"A soup with a good kick is just the remedy for this weather."

Philippa shook her head and darted to the other side of the kitchen to cut some bread. She squeezed the loaf, testing it.

"Did you buy this bread today, Reverend? It's lost much of its freshness."

"I did, Philippa," sighed Annabelle, before turning to face her, gesturing with the pepper shaker. "And I dare say that I rather preferred it when you were too frightened by outside "events" to offer me your running commentary on my cooking. I am not a total beginner in the kitchen, you know."

"Oh, don't say that, Reverend. You'll never know how stressful it was. I didn't sleep for a week!"

"Well, if you don't concentrate on your own duties and instead focus on mine, I might just consider hiring Daniel to give you another scare."

"Oh, Reverend, I feel such a fool," Philippa said, as she tossed the bread into a basket and tidied up the crumbs.

Annabelle chuckled as she brought the soup to the table.

"Don't worry, Philippa. You're right, I can't imagine what it must have been like. I don't know what I would have done if I'd seen him at that hour of the night, all bloodied and determined."

"You'd probably have run out and bonked him on the head with a saucepan, Reverend," chuckled Philippa.

Annabelle laughed and mimicked herself bashing someone over the head clumsily when the doorbell rang.

"They're here!" Philippa said.

"Go let them in. I'll set the food out."

Annabelle hurriedly placed the bowls of boiled peas, roasted carrots, potatoes, and parsnips out on the table. Seconds later, Dr. Brownson, Shona Alexander, and her nephew, little Dougie, entered the room, followed by Philippa.

"Hello!" Annabelle smiled, happily.

"Hello, Reverend," Shona said, embracing Annabelle with a warmth that she had rarely seen in the woman.

"How are you?" Robert added, smiling his appreciation politely.

"I'm fine, thank you, Robert. Oh," Annabelle said, noticing young Dougie holding Robert's hand beside him. "And how are you, young man?"

"Hungry!" exclaimed the boy.

Annabelle laughed. "Well you'd better get yourself a place at the table then, hadn't you?"

"We've brought you a present, Reverend," Shona said, exchanging an affectionate look with Dr. Brownson.

"Oh yes?"

Shona lifted the large bag that she was carrying, and with Robert's help, pulled out a canvas. She presented it to Annabelle, who took it slowly and studied it with a big grin on her face. Philippa stepped beside her to get a look.

"It's lovely!" Annabelle gushed.

"It's the church from the hills!" Philippa added, just as stunned by the wonderfully thoughtful gift.

Shona smiled, slightly embarrassed, but pleased with the reception.

"We just wanted to say thank you... for introducing us." Shona turned to smile at Dr. Brownson.

Annabelle looked from Shona to Robert and back again.

"I thought you weren't painting these days, Shona."

"I've started up again," she said, once again looking at Robert, "now that I have someone to paint alongside. But this isn't actually one of mine, Reverend."

"Oh?"

"It's mine," Robert beamed, happily. "Though I did benefit from the advice of an expert," he added, placing an arm around Shona's shoulders.

Annabelle and Philippa looked at the painting, appreciating its detailed strokes and the radiant colors. It showed the church towering magnificently in front of the intricate rows of houses and properties that made up the village, with Cornwall's impressive hills rolling off into the distance.

"Wait a minute," Philippa said, pointing out a spot on the painting. "There are two figures there…"

Annabelle peered closely at the painting. "I believe you're right, Philippa. In fact, isn't that…"

"You and me!" Philippa smiled. "Oh! And even Biscuit is there! Just behind the bench!"

They looked at Robert, who shrugged awkwardly.

"I saw you both there, when I began painting this. At the time I didn't know who you were, but I thought you made a nice addition to the painting."

Annabelle smiled and took one last appreciative look at the canvas.

"Well, you've certainly earned your meal!" Philippa joked.

"I'll just go and put this somewhere safe. Take a seat and help yourselves," Annabelle said as she pottered off, still smiling at the painting. She returned promptly and was about to speak when a shrill sound burst through the restful atmosphere. Everybody turned toward the source – little Dougie. He had his fingers in his mouth.

"Dougie!" Shona exclaimed. "What on earth are you doing?"

Her answer came in the form of the church tabby, Biscuit, as she sprinted into the kitchen from some corner of the cottage, head raised and ears pointed. Dougie whistled twice again in quick succession, at which Biscuit spun around and did a quick circuit of the kitchen table, to the amazement of everybody there.

"Well, I never!" Annabelle uttered in sheer astonishment. "I can barely get that cat up from the couch!"

"I'm training her to be a sheepcat!" Dougie said, beaming with pride. Biscuit sidled up to him, and he promptly stroked her between the ears, causing her to close her eyes with pleasure.

"Wonders never cease," Philippa said, smiling.

"In Upton St. Mary, at least," added Annabelle. "Come on, let's eat. I'm absolutely ravenous."

The diners took their seats, and enticed by the rich smell of soup and the succulent taste of the meat, were soon busily involved in eating away the chill of the weather outside. Young Dougie turned out to have a hearty appetite and ate just as much as the adults, while Shona and Robert exchanged glances and smiles throughout the meal.

"So Robert," Philippa said, as she sat back from the table having just about eaten her fill, "will you be staying in Upton St. Mary?"

Robert finished sipping his wine and placed the glass carefully in front of him.

"I have some things I need to attend to in London, of course." He looked at Shona. "But once that's done, I imagine there's nothing to stop me living here permanently and certainly plenty of reasons compelling me to."

"How wonderful!" Annabelle added, before noticing

the smile on Dougie's face. "And it seems that you've already made a friend here, as well."

Dougie's cheeks went red, but his smile was difficult to hide. He turned to Annabelle.

"Aunt Shona says you have bees."

Annabelle glanced at Shona. "I do, but you won't see many of them at this time of year."

Dougie's face fell, his hopes dashed.

"Still," Robert said, "I imagine we could see where they're kept. You might even learn a thing or two!" He turned to Shona, then Annabelle, "Would that be alright?"

Shona and Annabelle nodded their permission, and Robert stood up with almost as much excitement as Dougie.

"Come on, young fella, let's go. But get your coat on, you don't want to get a cold now," Robert tousled the boy's hair all the way into the hallway.

The three women smiled as they watched them leave, a warm feeling of friendship pervading the room.

"I take it you two have been getting on rather well?"

"Yes," Shona said, somewhat self-consciously. "I must admit, Reverend, when you invited us for tea together, I winced. Blind dates are excruciating."

"I simply wanted to introduce both of you as lovers of painting."

"Oh, come now, Reverend," Philippa said, her smile full of humor. "You knew perfectly well what you were doing!"

They laughed. Philippa placed one of Annabelle's favorite desserts, an apricot tart she had baked, on the table and turned to Shona.

"He's terribly good with children, too, it seems," she added, her smile still full of humor.

Shona looked down at her lap.

"Stop it, Philippa!" laughed Annabelle. "You're embarrassing the poor woman!"

"No, it's fine," Shona said, regaining her composure. "It is actually one of the reasons I've grown so fond of Robert. Speaking of Dougie, it seems that he may be returning to Scotland, soon."

Annabelle gasped for a moment as she absorbed the full meaning of what Shona was saying.

"You mean your sister's getting better?"

Shona nodded slightly, a smile upon her face. "It's not certain – these things never are – but she's certainly making an improvement. She's up and about. If it carries on this way, she'll be well enough to have him back in a month or so."

"Why that's simply wonderful news!" Annabelle exclaimed.

Just then, Robert and Dougie burst into the kitchen again, Dougie having been filled with excitement and energy at the sight of the beehive.

"I saw where they live!" he squealed eagerly, as he ran around the table.

"How did it look?" Shona asked him.

"Scary. Bees are dangerous!"

"They certainly can be, if you don't respect them," Shona replied.

"Do you like scary stories?" Annabelle asked, playfully.

"Gosh, yes!" Dougie replied, his eyes lighting up.

"Would you like to hear one?"

"Yes, please!"

"Come over here, then," Annabelle said, "and I'll tell of a true story that happened to a friend of mine. It's a terrible tale of a mysterious ghost that roams the fields. One night, she woke up and heard a shrieking sound..."

Suddenly, Philippa's face dropped.

"Reverend Annabelle!"

REVERENTIAL RECIPES

CONTINUE ON TO CHECK OUT THE RECIPES FOR GOODIES FEATURED IN THIS BOOK...

ECCLESIASTICAL CHOCOLATE ÉCLAIRS

For the choux pastry:
½ cup water
2 oz. (½ stick) unsalted butter
Pinch of salt
⅓ cup flour
2 eggs, beaten

For the chocolate icing:
2 oz. dark chocolate, broken into pieces
Pat of butter
2 tablespoons water
¾ cup powdered sugar, sifted

For the filling:
½ cup fresh cream whipped with 1 tablespoon of sugar

Preheat the oven to 400°F. To prepare the pastry, put the water, butter and salt in a saucepan and heat gently until the fat has melted. Bring to the boil and, when bubbling vigorously, remove the pan from the heat. Quickly beat in the flour all at once.

Continue beating until the mixture draws away from the sides of the pan and forms a ball: do not overbeat or the mixture will become fatty. Leave to cool slightly. Beat in the eggs gradually until the pastry is smooth and glossy.

Put the mixture into a piping bag fitted with a ½ inch plain nozzle. Pipe onto greased baking sheets, either in finger shapes approximately 3 inches long for éclairs or in rounds approximately 2 inches in diameter for profiteroles. Allow room between each shape for expansion during cooking.

Bake just above the center of the oven for 15 or 20 minutes or until the pastry is well-risen and crisp. Remove from the oven and make a slit along the sides of the éclairs, or in the base of the profiteroles. Leave to cool on a wire rack.

To prepare the chocolate icing, put the chocolate pieces, butter, and one tablespoon of water in a heatproof bowl over a pan of hot water and heat gently until melted. Remove from the heat and gradually beat in the powdered sugar until the icing is thick and smooth. If the icing is too thick, add water a few drops at a time until the required consistency is reached.

Fill the pastry with the sweetened cream, then frost the tops of the éclairs with the chocolate icing. (If making profiteroles, pile onto a serving dish or in individual serving bowls and pour over hot chocolate sauce.)

Makes approximately 8.

DIVINE CHOCOLATE DIPPED SHORTBREAD

1⅓ cups flour
2 teaspoons baking powder
½ teaspoon salt
¼ cup sugar
5 oz. (1¼ stick) unsalted butter
4 oz. chocolate, broken into pieces

Preheat the oven to 325°F. Sift the flour, baking powder, and salt into a mixing bowl and stir in the sugar. Add the butter, in one piece, and gradually rub into the dry ingredients. Knead until well mixed but do not allow the dough to become sticky.

Roll out the dough evenly on a floured board, then cut into approximately 2-inch rounds with a fluted pastry cutter. Place the shortbread on a lined baking sheet, leaving room between each to allow for spreading during cooking. Prick the shortbread with a fork and chill in the refrigerator for a further 15 minutes.

Bake for 14 minutes or until pale-golden in color. If the

shortbread becomes too brown during the cooking time, cover with foil. Remove from the oven, leave to cool slightly, then transfer to a wire rack to cool completely.

Melt the chocolate in a small heatproof bowl over a pan of hot water. Dip the edge of the shortbread into the chocolate and roll your wrist to coat the shortbread with the chocolate in a "half moon" shape. Place on wax paper and chill.

Makes approximately 8.

RAPTUROUS RASPBERRY CHEESECAKE

8 oz. graham crackers
4 oz. (1 stick) unsalted butter, melted
1 lb cream cheese
2 oz. sugar
2 egg yolks
8 oz. fresh raspberries
¼ pint heavy whipping cream
1 sachet gelatin
4 tablespoons water
Sugar to finish

Put the graham crackers between two sheets of wax paper or in a zippered plastic bag and crush finely with a rolling pin. Put in a mixing bowl. Pour in the melted butter and stir to combine. Using a metal spoon, press into the base of an 8-inch loose-bottomed cake tin. Chill in the refrigerator for 30 minutes or until quite firm.

Meanwhile, make the filling. Put the cream cheese, sugar, egg yolks and three-quarters of the raspberries in a bowl and beat together. Whip the cream until it holds its shape, then fold into the cream cheese mixture. Set aside.

Sprinkle the gelatin over the water in a small heatproof bowl and leave until spongy, then place the bowl in a pan of hot water and stir over low heat until the gelatin has dissolved. Remove the bowl from the pan and leave to cool slightly. Stir into the cheese mixture. Pour into the prepared base and chill in the refrigerator for 4 hours or overnight, until set.

Take the cheesecake carefully out of the tin (the base may be left on if difficult to move) and place on a serving platter. Top with the reserved raspberries, sprinkle with sugar and serve.

Serves 8 to 10.

ANNABELLE'S FAVORITE APRICOT TART

For the French flan pastry:
1 cup flour
Pinch of salt
4oz. (1 stick) unsalted butter
2 egg yolks
2 tablespoons sugar

For the filling:
2 lbs. fresh apricots, halved and stoned
½ cup sugar
1 vanilla pod
or
2 15 oz. cans of apricots in syrup or juice
½ teaspoon vanilla extract

For the glaze:
1 tablespoon arrowroot
1 tablespoon sieved apricot jelly

Preheat the oven to 375°F. Sift the flour and salt into a bowl. Make a well in the center, then put in the butter in pieces, the egg yolks and sugar. With your fingertips, draw the flour into the center and work all the ingredients together until a soft dough is formed. Form into a smooth ball and wrap in aluminum foil or wax paper. Chill in the refrigerator for 30 minutes.

Press the chilled dough into an 8 inch flan ring placed on a baking sheet. Prick the base with a fork. Chill in the refrigerator for a further 15 minutes.

Cover the dough with crumpled parchment paper and three-quarters fill with rice or baking beans. Bake in the oven for 15 minutes, then remove the rice or beans and parchment paper and bake for a further 5 minutes. Take from the oven and remove the flan ring. Leave to cool.

Put fresh apricots in a saucepan. Just cover with water, add the sugar and vanilla pod, if using, and heat very slowly until the sugar dissolves, stirring gently with a wooden spoon. Simmer for 15 to 20 minutes or until the apricots are soft and tender. Leave to cool in the juices, then lift them out with a slotted spoon, reserving the juice. Discard the vanilla pod. If using canned apricot halves, drain well and reserve the juice. Mix with the vanilla essence. Arrange the apricot halves in the flan case.

To prepare the apricot glaze, put the reserved juice (there should be ½ pint so make up to this amount with water if necessary) in a small pan and heat through. Dissolve the arrowroot in a little water, then stir into the juice with the apricot jelly. Bring to the boil and simmer until thick. Cool slightly, then pour over the apricots. Cool completely before serving.

Serves 8.

SAINTLY STRAWBERRY CUPCAKES

For the cupcakes:
1 ½ cups flour
1 teaspoon baking powder
Pinch of salt
4 tablespoons whole milk
1 teaspoon vanilla extract
6 tablespoons of strawberry purée (blend fresh or frozen
strawberries in food processor)
4oz. (1 stick) softened unsalted butter
1 cup sugar
2 eggs

For the frosting:
¼ cup soft butter
3 ½ cups thawed frozen or fresh strawberries
3 ½ cups powdered sugar
½ teaspoon vanilla extract

Preheat the oven to 350°F. Line cupcake tins with paper
liners. Sift flour, baking powder, and salt together. Set aside.

In a small bowl, whisk together the milk, vanilla, and strawberry purée. Cream the butter with an electric mixer and add the sugar. Beat until light and fluffy.

Add the eggs and mix slowly until combined. Add half the flour mixture and mix briefly. Scrape down the bowl and add the milk mixture, mixing just until combined. Scrape down the bowl and add the remaining flour mixture. Mix carefully and then divide the batter evenly among the cupcake liners. Bake the cupcakes until a toothpick inserted into the center comes out clean, about 20 to 25 minutes. Cool in the pans for about 5 minutes then transfer to a wire rack to let them cool completely.

To prepare the frosting, purée then simmer strawberries until reduced by half. Beat the butter, sugar, and vanilla extract with an electric mixer. Add the strawberry purée a teaspoon at a time until the frosting is smooth and easy to spread. Pipe each cupcake with frosting and top with a strawberry slice.

Makes approximately 14.

All ingredients are available from your local store or online retailer.

You can find links to the ingredients used in these recipes at http://cozymysteries.com/body-in-the-woods-recipes

A Reverend Annabelle Dixon Mystery

GRAVE IN
THE GARAGE
Alison Golden
Jamie Vougeot

GRAVE IN THE GARAGE

BOOK FOUR

Cover Illustration: Rosalie Yachi Clarita

Published by Mesa Verde Publishing
P.O. Box 1002
San Carlos, CA 94070

Edited by
Marjorie Kramer

CHAPTER ONE

THE USUAL SENSE of peace and tranquility that beset Annabelle whenever she walked around St. Mary's centuries-old graveyard was not present today. She stepped slowly between the decrepit and leaning stones, her feet heavier than normal as they crunched against the dry leaves and patches of sodden, forlorn grass that even a cow would turn its nose up at. She shivered and pulled her black cassock tighter around her, not yet accustomed to the winter's particularly sharp and sudden chilliness.

Her time as Vicar at St. Mary's Church had been a consistent, daily process of rejuvenation; spiritually, socially, and not least, architecturally. She had taken every care to ensure that the church was a wonderful and pleasing tribute to the Lord, from the luxurious velvet of the kneeling cushions to the inch-perfect preservation of its roof tiles. The leafy shrubs and flowering plants that ran all around the church had been carefully maintained and groomed into a flourishing yet orderly arrangement, a delightful array of colored blossoms in summer and a thick display of sculpted, earthy tones in winter. She had even varnished the mahogany pews and tenderly polished the stained glass windows herself.

The graveyard, however, had remained an untouched thorn in her side. All its residents were a few generations dead, their descendants having long since moved away or been neglectful in the upkeep of their deceased relatives' crumbling memories. Annabelle had ignored the cemetery during her persistent improvements and renovations to the church, partly because she was loathe to disrupt the time-worn dignity of the area, partly because she had always favored life and vitality over the solemnity of death. But now that the graveyard had taken on a wild, unrestrained, and almost ghoulish appearance, she could no longer delay addressing its deterioration.

The gravestones were mostly covered in moss and trailing plants. Some of them so much so that even the names and dates carefully engraved on them once upon a time had become obscured. What must have formerly been a flat, manicured plot of land was now a bumpy mass of mud and weeds. Even the solid, sturdy, iron railings that fenced half the graveyard perimeter were rusted and weather-beaten all out of shape.

The dark, brooding place had long since become a fearful place for children and a source of their horror stories. Now many grieving families preferred to lay the remains of their loved ones in the more attractive and well-maintained plots of a neighboring new town cemetery. There had not been a burial in the church grounds for over a year.

Such a state of affairs was unacceptable to Annabelle. After both a church and town meeting, which nobody seemed to care a fraction about as much as Annabelle, the

Reverend put her plan for revitalizing the graveyard to a vote. With a new sense of purpose and the villagers' somewhat tepid approval, Annabelle was filled with enthusiasm and optimism as she prepared for yet another refreshing and invigorating project of improvement.

Until she saw the costs.

Fixing a graveyard was a task far too detailed and delicate for mere elbow grease, some hearty volunteers, and a few shovels. Annabelle would need the deftest green thumb to bring its wretched soil back to a state of well-nourished uniformity and the experience of a true craftsman to restore stones in such a bad state.

She pulled a notepad and pencil out from beneath her cassock and intensely studied the figures once more, the wind tossing her hair against her brow as vigorously as her thoughts rushed about her mind.

"If staring at the price made things cheaper," came the warm, lively voice from behind her, "then I'd have a house on the south coast of Spain already. Tea, Vicar?"

Annabelle spun around to see the always comforting sight of her friend and church bookkeeper, Philippa, carefully treading between the stones, a mug of steaming tea in her hand.

"Oh yes, that's just what I need." Annabelle put her notepad away and took the mug.

"You'll catch your death of cold if you keep coming out here, Vicar. Why, you're not even wearing your coat!"

Annabelle sipped slowly from the mug and gazed out into the cemetery before musing, almost to herself, "We shall need another fundraiser."

"Reverend!" Philippa gasped as she hugged herself tightly against the wind. "We've already had *three* in the past month! The bake sale, the children's talent show, and the raffle. That raffle prize was one of the best I've ever seen! *A custom-made coat from Mrs. Shoreditch?!* I've never seen such immaculate tailoring. I bought a dozen tickets myself!"

"Then why are we still so short?" Annabelle replied with a tone of exasperation that Philippa knew not to take personally. "We raised more money when we held a flower sale for the path to be re-graveled! I just don't understand it."

Philippa sighed and placed a hand on the tall Vicar's shoulder. Annabelle turned, her face a mixture of confusion and desperation.

"Are people tired of the church, Philippa?" Annabelle asked her friend, as if pleading for an answer. "Have they run out of sympathy for its causes? Maybe it's the graveyard. Perhaps it's too macabre for most of them to care about. Do they believe the childish tales of ghosts and goblins?"

As the Vicar gazed at her, Philippa opened her mouth as if to say something, before quickly closing it and putting a finger over her lips.

"What?" Annabelle said, picking up on Philippa's hesitation. "What is it?"

With an unconvincing sigh of reluctance, Philippa spoke quietly, as if someone nearby might hear.

"Now Vicar, you know I hate nothing more than gossip and rumor-mongering. If I have one sin, it's that I'm harshly judgmental of those who engage in it..."

"Go on," Annabelle urged, stemming the impulse to roll her eyes. Philippa's skills in ferreting out village tittle-tattle were legendary.

Philippa sighed once again. She looked around her carefully, her gesture adding weight to her words.

"This is probably just idle speculation, of the kind dull

types use to sound more intriguing, and bored types use to fill the time—"

"Come on, Philippa! At this rate, by the time you tell me, I really will catch a cold!"

"Well," Philippa said, unaffected by Annabelle's impatience, "I've heard it muttered in certain circles that a number of families are having financial difficulties."

Annabelle sipped her tea and frowned.

"Doesn't every family have financial difficulties at this time of year? So soon after taking expensive summer holidays, when the heating bills start coming in, and Christmas is just around the corner?"

"Perhaps, Reverend," Philippa said, her tone still conspiratorial and low, "but there's an added element here. You see, a lot of the women are complaining that their husbands are being stingy with money, hiding it. And they're saying the men are spending more and more time away from home."

Annabelle took another sip and frowned once more.

"But is that really anything new, Philippa? The soccer season is in full swing, and it's too cold to do anything but go to the pub in the evening."

This time it was Philippa who frowned, annoyed that her privileged, secretive insights had been dismissed.

"Perhaps, Reverend," she said, in a tightly-controlled tone, "but I just thought you'd like to know what your parishioners were saying."

"I'm sorry, Philippa. You're right. Maybe there is something to it. But financial difficulties or not, the result is the same." Annabelle turned back to face the gravestones. "Without help, this cemetery will remain a sorry state of affairs. If it snows again this year, I daren't think how much worse it could get."

"I'm sorry, Reverend. I'm sure we'll get it fixed," Philippa said, placing her hand once more on the Vicar's arm.

"Thank you for being so positive," Annabelle said, placing a hand over her friend's. "You know, I've taken to coming out here and praying. Even though it's cold and rather ugly, I've always felt like saying my prayers in places that needed them most." Annabelle smiled self-deprecatingly. "I know it's terribly superstitious and silly for a Reverend, but I even find myself looking for a sign. Some sort of signal from the Lord that'll help guide me."

Just then, the air was filled with a low, powerful, rumbling sound. It rolled through the air like a wave before dissipating.

Philippa and Annabelle clutched at each other in shock.

"What was that?!" Philippa squealed.

"I don't know!"

"Did you hear it?"

"Of course, I heard it! I wouldn't be grabbing you if I hadn't!"

Once again, the low hum sounded out again, louder and more melodic this time. The two women turned to face each other, their eyes wide and mouths open with awe.

Then Annabelle sighed and chuckled, as more notes were added, and the throbbing sound turned into a moving, atmospheric melody; the distinctive sound of the church organ.

"It's only Jeremy!" Annabelle said, as Philippa let go of her arm and slowly returned to a state of calm.

"So it is," Philippa said, smiling. "He scared me half to death! It's rather early for him, though, isn't it? He doesn't usually start practicing until ten, and it's only eight."

Annabelle handed her empty cup back to Philippa before straightening her clerical robe.

"I'll see what he's up to. You'd better go feed those pups before they start digging up this graveyard for bones."

"Of course, Vicar," Philippa said, turning away and leading Annabelle out of the graveyard.

"Did Janet give you any word on whether the shelter will be able to house them soon?"

"Not yet, Vicar," Philippa replied, "I shall have a word with her today though, I imagine."

"No rush," Annabelle smiled, "I rather like having them around. Dogs are such happy creatures. I rather think of them as a blessing, turning up out of the blue like that."

"Considering the state of them when they were found, huddled around their mother in the freezing cold, whining like human babies, I rather think they're the ones who feel blessed right now."

They smiled at each other as they went their separate ways; Philippa to the cottage and its two wet-nosed house guests, and Annabelle to the church and its diligent, early-rising organ master.

"Jeremy!" Annabelle called, over the cascade of notes. "Jeremy! Yoo-hoo!"

It was only when Annabelle was close enough to Jeremy to wave energetically in his field of vision that he stopped playing, so deeply was he engrossed in his music. He noticed her with a start and pulled his hands away from the keyboard abruptly.

"Oh! Sorry, Vicar. I didn't see you there," he said, in his soft voice.

Jeremy Cunningham was an extremely tall, slim man, his rather pasty face topped with neatly-thatched blond hair. Despite his pale complexion, his blue eyes, and his thin, pink lips that all betrayed his youthfulness, his penchant for thickly-knitted sweaters and sharply-creased trousers indicated a taste that was much older than his twenty-eight years.

"Don't apologize," Annabelle said, "it's rather lovely, if a little macabre at this time of the morning."

"It was Brahm's Requiem. One of my favorites. I tend to play slower pieces in the morning, to warm up my hands," he said, holding his fingers up and wiggling them with a polite smile.

"Indeed," Annabelle replied, marveling at what she saw in front of her. "I must say, I continue to be amazed by the size of your hands, Jeremy. I've never seen such long and elegant fingers! They are quite extraordinary."

Jeremy nodded gracefully. "My old pastor in Bristol said that 'the Lord provides the very gifts we require in order to worship Him.'"

Annabelle smiled. Jeremy was one of the most devout members of her flock as well as one of the most recent additions. He had moved to Upton St. Mary six months ago and made Annabelle's acquaintance very quickly, presenting himself at the first opportunity in order to offer his services. She quickly found a use for him as the church organist. Jeremy immediately set to work cleaning and repairing the vintage organ. It was a complex contraption, with pipes that reached up one side of the stained glass window on the church's north wall, but Jeremy was up to the job.

Until the dexterous young man arrived in the village, the organ had stood dormant since the death of the previous church organist in 1989. Few of the members of

Annabelle's parish even knew the pipes were there until they blasted into life one Sunday morning on Jeremy's command. It caused quite a stir. Postmistress Mrs. Turner nearly fainted, and Mr. Briggs, the local baker, thought he was having another heart attack. They both had to be attended to by paramedic Joe Cox while Annabelle worriedly hovered close by, mentally making note to raise the idea of a defibrillator at the next parish council meeting.

Since then, Jeremy had taken it upon himself to keep the pipes sparkling clean. They often shimmered in the early morning glow that poured forth through the church's colorful windows. Ever the assiduous and attentive caretaker, Jeremy also kept the keys dusted, the pedals oiled, and the wood that encased it all, well-polished.

His accompaniments to the hymns and other musical arrangements were an instant success, adding yet another quality to Annabelle's already popular services. The villagers quickly found themselves drawn to the shy, quiet, young man with nimble fingers who blossomed when conversation turned to the Bible. Some of the more excitable ladies of the village had even taken it upon themselves to find the bachelor a nice young woman to meet.

For now, though, Jeremy was staying with his grandmother, a pleasant woman in her nineties who lived alone in the village. Her health had recently taken a turn for the worse, and the support of her neighbors was no longer enough to ensure her well-being. Jeremy had left his position as a music teacher in Bristol to care for her during what many felt would be her last stretch on this earth.

"It's rather early even for you, isn't it?" Annabelle inquired.

"I do apologize, Vicar. I would have looked for you, but I

saw the door to the church was open and thought it best not to disturb you if I could – though I obviously did!"

"Oh no, not at all!" Annabelle chuckled. "You just startled us. We were standing in the cemetery when you began. Not the sort of place you suddenly want to hear a requiem! I thought the dead were about to rise up!"

Jeremy's face remained solidly blank.

"Nobody but the Lord is capable of such a thing, Vicar, as you well know," he said, in a clipped monotone.

Annabelle's chuckle was quickly replaced with a solemn, serious look. If there had been one deficit in their otherwise easy relationship, it was Jeremy's distinct lack of humor – particularly regarding matters of faith.

"Of course," Annabelle said, in her most sanctimonious of voices. "Well... Carry on."

Jeremy nodded and turned back to the church organ as Annabelle spun on her heel and walked briskly away, her cheeks flushed with red.

Annabelle's discomfiture was quickly dispelled, however, when she stepped out of the church doors and caught sight of Philippa coming from the cottage with two bounding puppies at her heels. Their faces with their large black noses and big brown eyes were framed by pairs of floppy ears that flapped constantly in the bouncy manner of pups. Both tan in color, the female of the two was distinguished by a white streak that ran from the tip of her long snout to the top of her head. The moment they heard Annabelle's feet on the gravel, they quickly ran to greet her.

"*Hello!*" Annabelle cooed cheerily, crouching down to scrub their ears. They yipped and panted their approval. She looked up at Philippa. "Are you taking them to Janet?"

"Yes," Philippa said, taking the opportunity to attach their leashes while Annabelle distracted them with her petting. "For a check-up and a chat. Are you *sure* you want me to give them to the shelter?"

Annabelle pursed her lips regretfully as she continued to stroke the soft fur of the floppy-eared strays.

"Oh, I don't know, Philippa. It's a terribly big responsibility. We would have to buy all sorts of things for them, and what about the flowers? Once they get bigger, they might trample all over the garden!"

"Hmm, they haven't done it yet. They've actually been rather well-behaved for a couple of puppies."

"They certainly have," Annabelle said, giving them one more playful chuck behind the ears before standing up. "But dogs are like people – they have the capacity to do the most unexpected things."

Philippa smiled. "But you do say that it is our duty to help our fellow man when he is in need. I'm sure that applies to dogs too."

"We've already got Biscuit."

"Oh! That cat is never around anyway! Plus she's already taken a shine to the pups. You should have seen them all sleeping together this morning."

"You seem awfully fond of them. Why don't you adopt them?"

"I would, Reverend, but I spend so much time at the church that they might as well live here all the time." She looked down at the two puppies who were standing to attention, their tails wagging, and their big brown eyes fixed upon Annabelle. "Plus they seem to have made their own preference rather clear."

"We'll see," said Annabelle, nodding a farewell and heading to the cottage.

It was still early when Annabelle got into her Mini Cooper and shut the door with the same satisfaction as the day she had first driven it. She settled herself snugly into the seat, drew her seatbelt across her chest, and turned the keys in the ignition. The motor chugged into life, and Annabelle felt a sense of girlish delight emanate from her fingers upon the wheel. As long as she could drive her little Mini wherever she liked, she would be happy; a simple, but endless, pleasure.

The car had always been more than a mere mode of transport for the Reverend. As she spent most of her days either in church or around others, her time in the car was a much appreciated opportunity to enjoy the idyllic landscapes that surrounded Upton St. Mary in solitary contemplation. The fervent beauty of the small, Cornish village and the local countryside had been one of the most compelling reasons to leave her inaugural clerical position in her hometown of London.

The deeply satisfying sensation of being cocooned in the Mini's small yet cozy interior while the exquisite English landscape sped by her window was never greater than during winter. The cold weather made it difficult to take the kind of striding jaunts across endless fields and sunspeckled woods she enjoyed so much in the summertime. However, with the Mini's tiny heater on full blast and its puppy-esque enthusiasm for the open road, she never felt confined.

In fact, Annabelle spent many happy hours in her car. She had built up a warm affection for the automobile that she lovingly kept pristine. In her more whimsical moods, she could even fancy that it spoke to her. It was almost as though the thrum of its engine indicated its contentment like the purr of a cat, while the gentle squeak of its seat as she sat on it was like a greeting from an old friend. Even the bumps and wheezes of its wheels as it navigated obstacles in the road sounded like the grunts and groans of an old man hurdling an obstacle.

The musical tics and idiosyncrasies of her Mini were like a song she knew intimately, which is why she found herself increasingly bothered by the weak sound of the engine as she made her way to the hamlet at Folly's Bottom. She had intended to discuss the failing attempts to raise funds for the cemetery renovations with a parish council member there, but she had barely reached the halfway point of the five-mile trip when the Mini Cooper's trials grew noticeably worse.

"What on earth is the matter with you?" She pressed the accelerator harder and found the Mini struggling to respond with its typical ready increase in speed.

For the next half-mile, the Mini's engine weakly hummed at an almost inaudible level, occasionally sputtering back into life again with a snap, only to trail off once more. Eventually, Annabelle's fear became a reality – the car stopped entirely.

Annabelle turned the key back and forth a few times in an attempt to get the car started, but the Mini only offered a limp whine in response. Breathing deeply, Annabelle refused to get angry. Instead, she lifted her gaze to the ceiling of the car and silently demanded an explanation from God.

Tightening her coat around her, she stepped out into the chilly wind and closed the door. For a brief moment, she considered checking beneath the hood for the cause of the car's problems, but she quickly realized that would be of little use. Annabelle's passion for driving did not extend to a mechanical aptitude, and she didn't want to make anything worse. She looked in both directions up and down the road, and with one final huff and frown, she began marching her way back toward Upton St. Mary and the local car workshop and gas station, owned by Mildred Smith and rather unimaginatively named Mildred's Garage.

A short way into her trek, Annabelle decided to take a shortcut and avoid the need to walk along a large curve in the road that went around a farmhouse. She took a small, rough path, fenced on both sides by the fields and surrounding hills. For a few minutes, Annabelle was rather pleased and allowed herself to feel proud of her knowledge of the extensive web of footpaths, lanes, and fields that radiated from, through, and around the vicinity of Upton St. Mary.

Her sense of triumph proved brief, however, when soon into her walk she found the entire way ahead obstructed by a densely packed herd of cows, moving slowly along toward their milking shed.

"Excuse me!" Annabelle politely asked, as she tottered and nudged them to find a gap. "Vicar coming through!"

She quickly realized the animals were – rather rudely, in her opinion – in no mood to let her pass, their stoic faces uninterested in her pleas and their large bodies incapable of moving at a greater speed anyway. Annabelle gazed beyond the large mass of white, brown, and black to find farmer Leo Tremethick at their head.

"Leo! Over here! Leo!" she called, waving her arms frantically like a woman drowning at sea.

The overall-clad figure in the distance briefly turned and removed his flat cap to wave back at the Reverend. Annabelle smiled widely, thinking that the farmer would surely do something to allow her to pass, but instead he merely smiled back, gestured at the cows and shrugged his shoulders apologetically. The meaning was clear; there was nothing he could do. He shouted something that Annabelle couldn't quite make out over the sound of cows mooing and hooves clopping, then turned back to trudge on in front of them.

"I know that you cows are God's creatures," Annabelle exclaimed, as she narrowly avoided yet another cowpat, "But I really must say, you're showing very little respect for the authority of the church!"

For a full twelve minutes, Annabelle inched forward through the muddy, cowpat-filled path behind the herd, pulled along only by the prospect of treating herself to a nice slice of cake at the end of it. When the cows finally turned off into their milking shed, she hurried forward into the junction where the path rejoined the road.

As she made her way to the garage, which was situated on the outskirts of the village alongside one of its largest family pubs, Annabelle found herself with plenty of time to notice her surroundings, including the occasional car that sped by. One of them struck her in particular, a black, sporty Mercedes Benz with dark tinted windows. It was the kind of car one would usually encounter outside a nightclub in a bustling city, so it stood out starkly in this part of the world. The villagers of Upton St. Mary, and indeed, the wealthier families who lived in the mansions and estates surrounding the village, had rather conservative tastes in cars. SUVs, the odd BMW, possibly a classic British sports car or luxury sedan were the most expensive vehicles that you were likely to find on the roads through and around Upton St. Mary. Most people drove pickup trucks, small hatchbacks, or minivans. The very notion of blacked-out windows seemed preposterous. Annabelle wondered just who could possibly be driving such a car, or even more intriguingly, why they would feel the need to hide themselves away as they did.

Her ruminations were quickly broken, however, when a small van pulled up beside her. She recognized it immediately and walked up to the passenger side window.

"Alfred Roper!" Annabelle called as greeting. "How are you? Off to a job?"

"Aye, Vicar. Busy weekend."

Alfred had become well-known for his wonderful gardening and landscaping skills during the thirty-odd years he had been tending to the grounds of larger houses in the area. He was almost sixty, yet the fresh air and physical nature of his work gave him a fit, powerful bearing. His brown eyes and grizzled beard were rarely accompanied by anything but a pleasant smile, and Annabelle always enjoyed his company.

"But not too busy that I can't give you a lift," he continued with a wink. "Hop in."

Annabelle clapped her hands with glee and eagerly got inside the earthy-smelling van, its comforting warmth making her realize how cold she had been previously.

"Oh, thank you so much, Alfred. My car—"

"Broke down on the road to Folly's Bottom? Aye, I just passed it," Alfred said in his gruff voice.

"Yes," Annabelle laughed. "If you could just drop me off—"

"At Mildred's Garage? Of course, Vicar."

Annabelle smiled and settled into the seat.

"Well, I owe you a cup of tea for this at the very least, Alfred. Do drop by the church if you find the time."

"Oh, it's nothing, Vicar, I always offer anyway. In fact, you're the fourth person I've picked up from the roadside this week."

Annabelle turned her head to Alfred with a look of disbelief.

"Really?" she said.

"Aye." He chuckled slightly as he noticed her reaction. "If you ask me, it's all these new *technologies* they keep sticking in the cars. So many dongles and apps and mp3s and i-whatsits – something's bound to go wrong! I don't even trust automatic transmissions, myself," he said, patting his gearstick affectionately.

"But Alfred, my car is a Mini! It might have go-faster stripes, but it's hardly tricked out with all the latest doo-dads, for heaven's sake!"

Alfred shrugged slowly before turning his chin up musing. "Probably the spark plugs then. Yeah. That'll be it."

He pulled the van over to the curb in front of Mildred's Garage and nodded his head politely as Annabelle effusively offered her gratitude and the promise of a cup of tea once more. She waved as he sped off to his next job and walked over to the short, wide building that housed Mildred's workshop.

Mildred's Garage had seen better days. Its paint was peeling, and both of the large metal shutters that fronted the workshop were rusting, but the reputation of the business was spotless. Since inheriting it from her father, Eric, nearly thirty-five years earlier, Mildred had overseen most of the villagers' very first cars, their upgrades to family vehicles, and for the more successful community members, their luxury vehicles and sports cars. In many respects, Annabelle often thought, Mildred was much like a vicar herself, witnessing and supporting people through the gravest and grandest milestones of their lives.

Though the world had changed and most vehicles were now computers on wheels, Mildred's was still a comforting first port of call for many when a knocking noise started up, a tire ran flat, or a simple oil change was needed. In many respects, much of the garage's popularity was down to its old-fashioned values. People knew they would get a job well done at Mildred's for a fair price – and more often than not, plenty of courtesy and a cup of tea thrown in. She or her assistants would even pump gas for customers while they sat in the comfort of their cars, a luxury long since abandoned just about everywhere else in England.

Despite being sixty-two, Mildred was enthusiastic, gnarly, and as strong as an ox – though only half the size. Annabelle marched up the front lot, in between the vintage cars (restoration projects Mildred enjoyed in her spare time), scanning for a glimpse of her frizzy red hair.

"Mildred!" she called, as she drew closer to the garage. "Mildred! It's Annabelle!"

One of the bay doors was open, a small hatchback neatly parked inside. Annabelle noticed the peculiar silence that seemed to permeate the garage. She visited regularly, at least once a week to fuel up, and got regular check-ups throughout the year, but she had never seen it as quiet as this. It often seemed that Mildred spent every waking hour at the garage, hammering or clanking away at some problem or dealing with the phone calls that seemed to interrupt her work every few minutes. On the rare occasions that she was away, one of her assistants would be there: Ted, a grizzled man in his forties who always wore the pained, despondent expression of a man recovering from a hangover, or Aziz, the teenage apprentice who would, to the chagrin of his colleagues, blare hip hop music from a device on his workbench as he tinkered with the cars.

Annabelle stepped into the garage, around the hatchback, and alongside the cluttered workbench.

"Ted! Aziz! Anyone?!"

She knew Mildred well enough to know that neither she nor her assistants would leave the garage unattended. Not without a notice of some kind, unless something was severely amiss. She strode back into the center of the garage, spinning around as she scanned its walls and the two bays.

Apart from the hatchback, there was no other vehicle inside, and with the garage's open plan, there were few nooks and crannies to investigate. Annabelle paced anxiously, keenly studying everything around her for something out of the ordinary.

Just as she was about to go outside and walk around the garage in search of clues, she crouched suddenly and looked beneath the small car in the middle of the workshop floor. It was dark, the lights of the inspection pit beneath the car were off. She strained to remember what such pits looked like. At the far end, toward the back, Annabelle thought she noticed something sticking out. A tool of some kind. She stood up, walked around, and crouched once more to see what it was and whether it could illuminate the mystery of the empty garage.

"Oh dear God!" Annabelle suddenly squealed, pulling back and covering her mouth.

It was no tool.

It was nothing mechanical of any kind.

It was a hand.

ANNABELLE FORCED HERSELF to crouch down again and look more intently under the car. She could see the hand reaching out from the pit, almost imploringly. After squinting and shuffling to gain a better perspective, Annabelle was in no doubt that the hand's rough texture and slim, taut muscles could only belong to one person – Mildred.

"Mildred!" Annabelle called desperately. "Mildred, are you alright?"

The hand remained still. Annabelle stood up and looked around nervously to consider her options. She could seek out the keys to the car and try to move it, but there was no guarantee she would find them, and she would waste precious, possibly crucial time trying. She could call for help, but when she patted herself down in search of her phone, she stamped her foot when she realized she had left it on the dashboard of her Mini.

Looking toward the office, she considered using the garage phone to call for help, before reconsidering. Something troubling had obviously happened here, and that phone might prove an important clue. She had seen enough drama in her career as a priest to know how important it was to leave a scene intact.

There was only one option, Annabelle thought, as she launched herself away from the garage using remarkably long, powerful strides. The pub across the road. *I'll get help there – maybe it won't be too late.*

Upton St. Mary boasted three pubs, the Dog and Duck, the King's Head, and the Silver Swan. It might seem to outsiders to be a tad excessive for a small village to have three drinking establishments, but it is by no means unusual in England. Annabelle had been inside them all on one occasion or another. The Silver Swan was a rather different pub from the other two. Whereas the Dog and Duck and the King's Head had catered to the working men of Upton St. Mary for generations, the air above their mahogany tables ever-crowded with the forceful rhythm of male conversation, the Silver Swan was a decidedly more laid-back establishment.

It had been owned and managed by the same family for three generations. With its famously hearty meals, leather chairs, and large fireplace, no patron left without feeling as if they had been a welcome visitor in somebody's home rather than a mere consumer of the excellent local beer. While patrons of the Dog and Duck or Kings Head could play a game of darts or pool and drink the stoutest of local ales, the Silver Swan had the great advantage of a large outside seating area, allowing drinkers to enjoy a magnificent view of the rolling hills that surrounded Upton St. Mary. This alone had made it a beacon for all the outdoor adventurers who enjoyed the miles of gorgeous countryside.

Every Saturday and Sunday, the pub would be filled with members of the local cycling club both before and after their scenic rural rides. Until they were banned, Wednesdays and Fridays saw outdoor explorers of a starkly different kind when the pub hosted the local pipe-smoking club that convened to puff away at the vast outdoor benches while comparing tobaccos. Every day, hikers would plan their routes so that they found themselves at the pub at lunchtime in order to enjoy the hearty fare on offer and rest their weary feet. Yes, it was a place that did brisk business, indeed.

Inevitably, the weekends were always busiest for The Silver Swan. Families came together to enjoy its cheap and filling cuisine and its welcoming atmosphere. Even at this early hour, as Annabelle burst through its large doors panting and looking wildly about, half the tables were filled with families from all around chattering through their breakfasts.

Annabelle made a beeline for the bar, already preparing the most efficient way to explain the situation to the bartender. She didn't want to waste any time. She stopped suddenly, catching sight of someone familiar in the corner of her eye. The tall, imposing – and somewhat dashing, she had to admit – figure of Inspector Mike Nicholls sat alone at a table. The exact man she would have hoped to bump into at this very particular moment.

Changing direction, she weaved through the tables toward his booth, where he was engrossed in the study of a large map. She slapped her palms on the table. He looked up with the kind of seasoned composure you would expect from an officer of the law who had dealt with agitated members of the public many times before.

"Inspector! What are you doing here?"

"Hello Reverend," he replied, visibly perplexed by Annabelle's somewhat aggressive introduction. "I'm glad I bumped into you. You wouldn't happen to know where I could find a James Paynton around here by any—"

"Never mind that," Annabelle interrupted breathlessly. "Something very serious has happened to Mildred!"

"Mildred?"

"The mechanic who owns the garage across the road."

The Inspector raised an eyebrow. "What's happened?"

"It would be easier to show you, Inspector. Though you'd better call an ambulance."

The Inspector was more accustomed to giving orders rather than taking them, particularly from officious vicars. However, the look of shock on Annabelle's face, as well as the begrudging trust he had developed in her during their partnership solving two recent crimes, made him scrunch up the map and follow her hastily out of the pub.

As they jogged the short distance that separated the pub from the garage, the Inspector ordered an ambulance and some police backup from the local constabulary for good measure. They reached the garage, and Annabelle led him to the cause of her concern. The two of them bent down as she pointed out what was unmistakably Mildred's hand – unmoved from where she had first spied it.

"We'd better move the car," Nicholls said, standing up.

"The keys may be in the office," Annabelle said, leading the way to the cramped corner of the garage. She felt more confident now that she was in the presence of a policeman.

They stood in the doorway of the tiny office, rapidly scanning the mass of paperwork and files that filled the desk and shelves.

"These must be the keys," the Inspector said finally, pointing to a set marked with a Ford emblem hanging on the wall next to Annabelle. She spun around and picked them off the hook. "Why don't you go move the car?"

Annabelle nodded self-importantly and quickly darted toward the vehicle, followed by the now-thoughtful Inspector. She got in, started the ignition and reversed the car out of the garage, revealing the pit and its contents to the Inspector, who stood over it. When she got out, the Inspector was crouching again, scrutinizing the pits contents. He held a palm out toward Annabelle.

"You may not want to see this, Reverend," he cautioned.

The warning only made Annabelle more curious, and she quickly moved to the Inspector's side.

"Oh!" she said, her voice fluttering with shock.

It was Mildred, and there was no doubt about it, she was dead.

Her body was leaning face first against the side of the pit, one arm extended upward, the hand they had seen positioned in mid-air, as though waving. Her other arm was by her side. The back of her ever-wild, frizzy red hair was matted with blood. Her overalls bore the stains of numerous types of fluid, but there was no mistaking the dark-red patch of wetness that trailed down from her skull and onto her collar.

The Inspector sighed, stood up, and walked away from the pit.

"Where are you going?" Annabelle said, her voice quivering in fear and grief.

"To call off the ambulance," the Inspector replied, pulling his phone from his coat pocket. "We need a pathologist."

In less than an hour, the once-silent garage became a hotbed of activity. Over a dozen officers were combing the entire area for evidence, the crackle and blare of their radios filling the air. Over the determined, hurried tones of the officers, the commanding voice of the pathologist, Harper Jones, could easily be recognized as she directed her crew in the tricky task of extracting the body from its most unlikely of graves.

Annabelle clutched herself tightly as she stood in front of the wide open doorway that led inside the garage, her shivering only partly due to the cold. She had, of course, seen a lot of death in her line of work, yet rarely as the result of murder. She had always shared a strong bond with Mildred. As a woman who had served the community of Upton St. Mary for decades, Annabelle had developed a tremendous amount of respect and admiration for her. As a recipient of the longtime garage owner's work and generosity, Annabelle had often thought that if she was half as good at her job as Mildred, she would be very proud indeed.

Mildred had been a pillar of the community, a friend to everyone who passed through her garage, and a role model for all who saw her perform her duties. Annabelle knew for certain that the deep sense of shock she was now feeling was only the beginning of a wave that was sure to affect the entire village of Upton St. Mary and beyond.

"Are you okay, Reverend?" the Inspector said, before Annabelle felt his broad, comforting hand on her shoulder.

She turned around to face him and forced a weak smile.

"I should be used to this," she said, "considering what I do."

"Nobody gets used to losing people," the Inspector said in a low voice. "I take it you knew her well?"

"Quite well. As did most of the villagers."

Nicholls turned to gaze at the activity inside the garage for a moment before turning back to Annabelle. He sighed deeply.

"Reverend, you know I'll have to ask you a few questions."

"Of course."

"But if you're still in shock, I can give you some time to compose yourself. Leave it until evening, perhaps. I shouldn't really, it's against procedure, but... Well... it's you. If I can't bend a few rules for you then I may as well be a constable."

Annabelle smiled at the Inspector's clumsy effort at humor.

"Thank you very much, Inspector. But I assure you, I'm fine. If anything, the sadness of this makes me even more willing to do anything I can in order to help."

Returning her smile warmly, Nicholls nodded. He reached into his pocket to fish out his notebook.

"When did you find Mildred?"

"Minutes before I met you, Inspector. My car had broken down on the road to Folly's Bottom. I walked for a while until Alfred Roper came along and gave me a lift. As soon as I entered the garage I noticed how... *quiet* everything was. I called out, to see if Mildred or her assistants were here, but there was no response. I was about to leave when it occurred to me to look under the car. That's when I saw the... hand."

Her voice broke on the last word.

"It's okay, Reverend," he said soothingly, before pulling out a pack of tissues from his pocket. He offered one to Annabelle, who took it and blew her nose loudly.

"Thank you, Inspector," she said, a little more composed.

"You said something about 'assistants?'"

"Yes. Ted and Aziz."

"Can you tell me anything about them?"

"Let's see... Ted Lovesey. He's in his forties. He's worked here since I arrived in Upton St. Mary three years ago. He's a rather pleasant man, if a little... *indulgent*."

"What do you mean by that?" Nicholls asked curtly.

"Well, he smokes heavily. Drinks heavily. Has a rather keen eye for the ladies, and tends to lose his money as quickly as he earns it. But other than that, he's a wonderful member of our community."

Nicholls eyed Annabelle with confusion.

"Any idea where he is now?"

"Oh, still recovering from his Friday night, I shouldn't wonder. He lives alone on Violet Lane."

Nicholls scribbled on his notepad for a few seconds before looking back at Annabelle.

"And this... Aziz?"

Annabelle pondered for a moment before answering. "Aziz Malik is his full name. Actually, he should have been here today. He's a teenager, and he works here at the weekends and some evenings when he's not at school."

"Okay. Can you tell me a little about Mildred?" the Inspector asked, before adding sympathetically, "if you can."

Annabelle appreciated the Inspector's kindness and

nodded her acquiescence. "She was the nicest person you could possibly imagine. She lived nearby, though she spent almost all of her time at the garage. She never really spoke about family or her relationships, though I gather she was never married and had no siblings. The only relative she had that I heard of was her father, and he passed away over thirty years ago."

"So you can't think of any reason why someone would do this to her? Possible grudges? Maybe a high repair bill? A poor job?"

"Absolutely not!" Annabelle said, horrified at the thought. "She was loved by everyone! Her prices were very fair – if not overly so! And as for her workmanship, Mildred could turn a rustbucket into a rocket quicker than you could say thank you!"

The Inspector tapped his pencil to his lips as he mused over Annabelle's description of Mildred.

"Perhaps she was too good."

"What do you mean?"

"Well, if I owned a garage, and I had to compete with somebody who was spoken of with the kind of enthusiasm that you use when talking about Mildred, I'd feel pretty resentful."

Annabelle frowned. "But... There *is* no competition. Mildred's Garage is the only one in Upton St. Mary."

Nicholls snorted a knowing laugh.

"There's *always* competition, Reverend. Even when it seems otherwise."

"Who?"

"Well, you say your car has broken down. It seems unlikely you'll be able to use the service of this garage – so who will you go to now?"

Annabelle's eyes widened a little.

"Crawford Motors. In Crenoweth, around ten miles away. It's run by Ian Crawford. But I'm sure he's not behi—"

"Why not? How well do you know him?"

Annabelle stuttered a little as she sought out the right words, somehow feeling like she was indicting someone perniciously.

"Well... Not very well. I've only used his garage a few times..."

Inspector Nicholls indicated that he had heard everything he needed to know by scribbling into his notebook.

"I know you prefer to see the good in people, Reverend, but it's my job to see the bad. And this guy sounds like a possible suspect in my eyes," Nicholls said in a grave tone, as he finished writing.

"Inspector. Reverend." A cool and calm voice interrupted them.

Annabelle and the Inspector immediately turned in the direction of the brisk, confident voice. Harper Jones was walking toward them in her typically clipped fashion. She had been the local pathologist for more than a few years now, yet her gritty determination and relentless focus on her work showed little sign of abating. With her immaculate raven-black hair and sharp features, her striking looks garnered her much attention wherever she went, but only those who knew the extent of her professional talent truly saw how remarkable she was. The Inspector most of all.

"What have you got for me, Harper?" he said, knowing that the pathologist enjoyed wasting no time on courtesies.

"Blunt force to the back of the head. My early assessment is that there were multiple strikes. Quick. Rapid. The weapon must have been long enough to swing hard, and heavy enough to strike deep. The garage and the pit are full of such objects. Could have been any of them. It'll be difficult to ascertain the exact weapon used. There's a lot of blood, along with plenty of other fluids. Gasoline, oil, lubricants. It's a mess. My guys are taking the body away now, as well as the tools. We'll study them and hopefully find which one was the murder weapon. After that, I'll pass it on to your people for fingerprinting."

The Inspector looked at Annabelle, hoping she wouldn't be affected by the pathologist's detached recounting of the gruesome details. He needn't have worried. It seemed as if Annabelle's focus on the facts was almost as intense as Harper's.

"She was killed *inside* the pit?" Annabelle asked quickly.

Harper looked at Annabelle and nodded.

"But, the car..." Annabelle mused to herself.

"She was definitely murdered in the pit," Harper interrupted. "There would be blood everywhere if she was killed outside of it."

"Was she already inside the pit when she was attacked or could she have been dragged into the pit, and then killed?" Annabelle asked.

"Either is a possibility," Harper said, her blunt tone softening as she considered it, "we should check the floor for signs of dragged boots."

"Good idea. Can anyone get in and out of that pit when there's a car over it?" the Inspector asked.

"Mildred could," Annabelle replied. "She was rather slight. Even if the car was small like my Mini, she could climb down quite easily."

"What about Ted? Or the teenager?"

"Certainly not Ted. His paunch wouldn't allow it. Aziz

probably could," Annabelle said, before suddenly feeling that she was incriminating someone again.

"Hmm," the Inspector said, tapping his pencil against his pad. "That leaves us with two options. Either somebody small – possibly Aziz – slid into the pit while Mildred was working and killed her, or somebody threw her in there, killed her, then parked the car over her."

"And put the keys back on the rack of the office wall," Annabelle said, her voice softening at the thought of such cold-blooded behavior. "Maybe we should check them for fingerprints?"

Harper fixed her eyes on Annabelle. "Cars and their keys are some of the worst things to get fingerprints from. Too many people handle them. You did, remember. I've checked the car briefly for traces of blood, the keys too, but I've not found anything. It might be worth looking further, but much of the blood flow happened after she was dead, and whoever did this was very careful."

"Cauldwell!" Nicholls spoke sharply to a nearby officer.

"Yes, Inspector?" the eager young man responded, appearing quickly by his side.

"It's a long shot, but I want to know who that hatchback belongs to and what it was in the garage for." He tore a sheet from his pad and handed it to the Constable. "Last thing, Aziz Malik and Ted Lovesey. Find them and bring them in for questioning."

"Yes, sir!"

The young officer left, and Nicholls turned toward Harper.

"Thanks, Harper. Keep me posted."

She nodded curtly before returning quickly to the scene, leaving Annabelle and the Inspector standing outside on the garage forecourt together. They looked at each other rather awkwardly for a few moments until Annabelle broke the silence.

"I must say, today has been full of strange occurrences."

"Indeed," replied the Inspector.

"It's one thing after another."

"What do you mean?"

"Oh, it's nothing, really."

"Tell me, it could be important," the Inspector insisted, his curiosity quickly turning professional.

"Where do I start!? I mean, it's nothing next to the fact that one of my dearest community members and a well-respected businesswoman in the village has just been murdered in cold blood."

"Still, it's important to be observant."

"The devil is in the details, I believe you mean," Annabelle said, wryly, smiling in spite of herself.

Nicholls chuckled warmly. "I wouldn't want to offend you."

"Tosh!" Annabelle exclaimed good naturedly. "I've far too much to worry about already to be offended by such trivialities."

"May I offer you a lift somewhere?" he asked, gracefully, "You can tell me about these 'strange occurrences' on the way."

Annabelle smiled, shyly this time, and nodded so deeply she almost curtseyed.

"Back to my car would be most helpful, Inspector."

"Of course, Reverend."

They began making their way across the road toward the Silver Swan.

"So, about these 'strange' things..." he began.

"Ah, yes. Well, my Mini breaking down for one thing. Not that it's strange in itself, but it was the *way* that it happened. If I had to guess, and I can only guess because I know nothing worth knowing about cars, it was as if something wore out."

"These things happen."

"I know. But Mildred really was very good at spotting problems. And I had brought my car in only last week."

"What for?"

"Oh, just to fuel it up."

"Well she couldn't have diagnosed any problem from that. Not unless she checked the engine as well."

"I know," admitted Annabelle with a note of sorrow. "But then there was a car I noticed earlier. It was very odd, much flashier than anything you typically see driven around here – even by the wealthier estate owners."

"Hmm."

"It even had blacked-out windows. Imagine that!"

"Could have been a limo. Somebody important heading to the city."

Annabelle shook her head. "No. Unless it was owned by one of the very few families in Folly's Bottom, and I can certainly say it wasn't, it wouldn't have been going that way. There are much quicker routes to take."

"Are you thinking it could have something to do with what happened at the garage? Should I ask my boys to check for tracks?"

As they walked, Annabelle looked at the Inspector with a mischievous smile.

"Inspector, are you asking for my advice regarding your police work?"

Nicholls laughed breezily. "You tend to offer it regardless."

Annabelle grinned and turned her gaze to look ahead again. "No. I don't think so. It was going so fast that it would have overshot the garage, and it wasn't long afterward that I got the ride from Alfred. There was no time to..." She trailed off, looking forlorn.

"As I said then, it was probably a villager's more successful relative from the city," the Inspector said quickly, keen to return to safer conversational ground.

"Perhaps," Annabelle rallied, unconvinced. "But then there was the rumor I heard this morning."

"Oh?" the Inspector said, his interest still piqued.

"Some nonsense about the men of Upton St. Mary disappearing all night and spending lots of money."

"Ah," Nicholls smiled, his interest satisfied, "well that's only natural for this time of year. The football season's started, those tickets aren't cheap. And it's too cold to do anything but go to the pub."

Annabelle laughed quietly, almost to herself.

"What?" the Inspector asked, confused. "Something I said?"

"No," Annabelle sighed, "that was my conclusion exactly."

They reached the Inspector's car, and Annabelle walked over to the passenger side. The Inspector opened his door, but before he could get in, Annabelle spoke to him over the roof of his car.

"There was one more thing," she said.

The Inspector looked at her. "What?"

"Something you said to me just before we left the Silver Swan. You told me you were looking for James Paynton."

Nicholls laughed nervously, as if caught out.

"That's one mystery you can almost certainly solve for me."

"Yes," Annabelle smiled, "but it raises yet another one:

Why are you visiting a pedigree dog breeder in Upton St. Mary?"

Nicholls stretched out his arm and checked his watch.

"If you're not in a rush to retrieve your car, maybe you can accompany me, and I'll tell you on the way. I was supposed to meet him half an hour ago."

CHAPTER THREE

"IS THIS NOT a strange time to be running errands, Inspector? You've only just discovered a dead body," Annabelle asked, as she settled herself into the passenger seat of the Inspector's car. "Shouldn't you be investigating, um, something?"

"If I had to take a break, now is the best time. The boys are out looking for Mildred's mechanics, and Harper needs to conduct the post mortem and get back to me with her results. I can't do much more right now."

"I see," Annabelle nodded.

"Anyway, thank you for helping, Reverend," the Inspector said as he put the car into gear and urged it out into the road. "Today is going to be very busy, what with all this trouble. Any time saved is much appreciated."

"Please, think nothing of it, Inspector," Annabelle smiled, before noticing the small screen perched in the middle of the Inspector's dashboard. She pointed at it quickly and looked at him with bewilderment. "But you've got a GPS? Won't that get you to Paynton's place?"

"That thing?" Nicholls said. "Never use it. Can't stand them. Give me a proper map any day."

Annabelle chuckled and leaned toward him. "Something of a technophobe, are we? An old-fashioned man? These GPSs are really rather simple to use, you know, once you learn the ins and outs."

"Oh, I know how to use it alright," the Inspector responded dismissively.

"Then why do you prefer a map?" Annabelle inquired. "A GPS is so much easier and faster. And safer. You can't exactly open a map every few minutes while driving. Especially along these lanes. You need to keep your eye on the road."

Nicholls sighed deeply, as if his reasons were a long and deeply held burden.

"I don't like the GPS for exactly those reasons. It's easier and faster."

Annabelle furrowed her brow, wondering if she had misheard the Inspector. "I'm not sure I follow."

"Reverend, my job depends on me having tightly-honed instincts. I need a sharp mind, keen eyes, and quick wits. But it's very difficult to maintain those when you have a hunk of plastic and a microchip doing most of your thinking for you."

"Ah," Annabelle said, nodding her head. "I understand. Turn left here, by the way. James lives about a mile up this road."

The Inspector followed her direction, then said, "What will you do about your car?"

"I shall call a tow truck. It should be alright. I steered it off the road when the engine stopped."

"Well, I'll happily drive you there once I'm done with my appointment."

"Thank you," Annabelle said, pausing briefly before adding, "I must say I'm incredibly curious as to why you're visiting a dog breeder."

"Ah," the Inspector said, remembering his promise to reveal all to the Reverend, "Well, my ex-wife got Lulu. My dog."

"Surely not!" Annabelle exclaimed. "You adored that dog!"

"I did," Nicholls sighed. "But so did my wife. Not as much as me, but enough. It was the only aspect of the divorce that we fought over."

"I'm sorry, Inspector."

Nicholls breathed deeply. "It was inevitable. I'm a detective. It's a difficult job, and the hours can get very long. I had a neighbor who fed her when I was stuck at work, and a few regular dog walkers, but... It wasn't enough. Not for the judge at least. "

Annabelle paused for a few moments as the Inspector's voice trailed off. There was not much she could say, and she knew that with men such as the Inspector, listening was often more appreciated than offering advice. After a few moments, the vast property belonging to James Paynton came into view, and Annabelle took the opportunity to distract the Inspector from his thoughts.

"Here we are," she said, pointing at the buildings.

Beyond the immaculately maintained wooden fencing surrounding its large, verdant-green front lawns, the modern, two-story, L-shaped farmhouse stood proudly at the end of the long driveway. As the Inspector drove up, he took notice of how well-off the inhabitants were. The house itself was lush with decoration. Well-maintained, over-flowing hanging baskets and window boxes were arranged around an exquisitely made front door and solid window frames. To one side of the house, a large conservatory was attached, perfectly placed to receive just the right amount of light, even on the most overcast days. To the other were three paddocks that contained five horses that looked, to the Inspector's untrained eye, like thoroughbreds, their coats gleaming as they quietly grazed. Two Range Rovers with personalized number plates and a luxury convertible were parked next to a bank of stables to the rear. To the back of the farmhouse were two brick-built barns, and no fewer than four pens of varying sizes. It was apparent, even from a distance, that an extraordinary amount of money was swashing about here and that even the most casual observer was to know it.

The Inspector pulled up and parked between a classic Jaguar and a boat trailer. He turned the car engine off and looked around.

"Are you sure this is the place?"

"Of course, Inspector."

Nicholls whistled softly. "The dog business certainly pays better than the police force."

"Well, James's dogs are sought after by people from all over Britain – perhaps the world. They do very well in dog shows. His Basset Hounds are particularly popular."

"So I've heard."

"I take it you're here in search of a new dog?"

"That's the plan," he said, opening the door.

"Inspector! Wait!" Annabelle said, clutching his arm to stop him getting out of the car. He turned around and looked down at her hand in surprise. "I've just realized! Oh yes! It's almost too perfect!"

"What is?" Nicholls said bemused.

"A few weeks ago, after morning tea, Philippa and I were inspecting the grounds of the church when we stumbled upon a stray and her pups amid the under-growth beside the cemetery. We immediately called Janet – she runs the local dog shelter – and asked for her help. Unfortunately, due to a mishap between a Doberman and a pit bull, she couldn't take all the pups, so Philippa and I decided to take care of two of them until she's ready."

The Inspector's face remained blank, as if he was expecting more. "Well, that's a nice story. I hope things resolve themselves soon."

"But don't you *see*, Inspector? The timing is simply perfect! It's almost as if it were planned by the Lord himself!"

With growing exasperation the Inspector closed his car door again and turned his attention fully to Annabelle. "What are you trying to say, Reverend?"

"Why, you should adopt the pups!"

"Oh, boy," Nicholls said, looking upward and sighing. "One minute somebody's taking the only dog I have away from me, the next I'm getting offered more dogs than I can handle."

"They're simply delightful little creatures, Inspector. Impossible not to love."

"What are they? Labs? German Shepherds?"

"Well... They're, um, mixed."

"Mongrels."

"Yes, but they're extremely well-behaved. Energetic and full of beans, but they haven't destroyed anything important yet."

Nicholls raised a suspicious eyebrow.

"Nothing but an old cushion I never liked anyway," Annabelle said, getting flustered beneath his intense gaze, "a few items of clothing, maybe, but I had too many. Regardless, it's all just part of their charm. You really must see them, Inspector."

"Look, Reverend, ordinarily I'd jump at the chance to help you out and take one of them off your hands—"

"It's not for my sake, Inspector!" Annabelle exclaimed, her blush of embarrassment turning into one of exasperation. "It's for *theirs!* These dogs need a home! The dog shelter is wonderful, but they deserve an owner who will love and respect them!"

"Don't these dogs need a home, too?" the Inspector asked, gesturing toward the farmhouse.

Annabelle snorted haughtily. "These are pedigree dogs. They are bred to order. People pay hundreds of pounds for the privilege of giving them a home!"

Nicholls softened his gaze and breathed deeply for a few moments, allowing the silence to take the edge away from the terse conversation.

"Reverend. My job is very demanding," he said, in a soft, persuading voice. "I need a dog that is disciplined, healthy, well-adjusted. I simply wouldn't be able to handle taking in a stray."

"Hmph," Annabelle grumbled, folding her arms and looking out of the side window. "You know, I once read a rather apt saying: 'People who love dogs, love them all. People who love themselves will pick an expensive one.'"

Nicholls couldn't recall having heard that particular saying before and looked at Annabelle quizzically. He opened his mouth to say something but found himself at a loss for words. Instead, he shook his head gruffly and stepped out of the car. Annabelle pursed her lips then quickly did the same.

James Paynton was already emerging from behind the farmhouse. He was a short man, with a bald pate and a broad, round nose. His puffy cheeks revealed deep dimples whenever he smiled, which he did frequently.

"Hello there!" he called, as they marched toward him. "Inspector Nicholls, I presume."

The two men shook hands firmly, then James directed his smile at Annabelle.

"Reverend, it's nice to see you. I wasn't expecting you, too."

"We bumped into each other on the way," Nicholls explained.

"I helped him find your, um, farm." Annabelle added.

"Sorry I'm so late," Nicholls said, grimly.

"It's alright," James smiled. "I understand your job is unpredictable."

Nicholls glanced at Annabelle. "It certainly is."

"Good," James said, clapping his hands together. "Shall we?"

"Lead the way," the Inspector replied, as they proceeded to walk toward one of the barns.

"So, as I told you over the phone," James began, the Inspector walking beside him, Annabelle remaining a half-step behind in order to absorb the rather pleasing surroundings, "I breed three types here: Bernese Mountain Dogs, Border Collies, and Basset Hounds – though as I said to you over the phone, the hounds are exclusively for hunters. I have a waiting list for those so if that's what you're looking for you're out of luck, I'm afraid."

The barn was a long rectangle that seemed to radiate warmth. They walked through the open entrance, the gravel of James's driveway giving way to the feeling of soft grass and hay underfoot.

"The dogs have access to an indoor and outdoor area. They tend to wander in and out depending on the weather, their temperament, and their inclination. I usually allow the dogs the run of the field, while the puppies are kept in a smaller pen. If it's raining, they are kept inside, separated by breed, of course, though I do let them intermingle every once in a while; it keeps them stimulated. I've kept them all in the pens today so you can take a good look at them. I'd just about given you up so it's lucky you arrived just now, I was about to let them all out."

Against the two length-wise interior walls of the barn were fenced areas. On one side, there were two gigantic yet composed dogs lying lazily on the ground. They raised their eyelids upon seeing their visitors, their thick, shaggy fur hanging off their bodies like luxurious blankets. Around them a half-dozen smaller versions scampered and rolled. James walked up to a gate and unlatched it.

"These are the Bernese Mountain Dogs," he said, holding the gate open for the Inspector and Annabelle to step through.

The puppies gazed at the intruders doubtfully for a moment before one adventurous pup crawled over to Annabelle and flopped over to better receive the vigorous tummy tickling that Annabelle immediately gave him.

"Oh, they're simply gorgeous!" Annabelle squealed.

Seeing their sibling receive such attention, the rest of the puppies ran toward the visitors. The Inspector bent down and playfully rolled his hand around the puppies thick coats.

"These pups are knocking on three months, now," James said, observing the scene with his fists on his hips, "so they're ready to be rehomed. To tell you the truth, these are my favorites. Very intelligent, very *sympathetic* dogs."

The Inspector stood up and backed away toward James,

watching as one of the adult dogs lumbered over to Annabelle.

"Oh! Aren't you a friendly fellow!" she said, still crouching as she was greeted by the dog's tongue licking her neck. The dog panted and shook a little. Annabelle felt a warm, light shower douse her face.

"Are they strong dogs?" the Inspector asked, as the big canine pressed evermore affectionately against the Reverend. She put a hand out to steady herself.

"Strong as an ox, though you wouldn't know it, what with how gentle they are."

"Hmm," the Inspector said, as he watched Annabelle push the dog away and stand upright, noticing that the dog's height was level with her hip. "Rather big, aren't they?"

"Oh, absolutely," James replied. "Big in all sense of the word. Big brains. Big hearts. Big coat of fur. Why? Is that a problem?"

"Well, my place isn't small, but it's no farmhouse either," Nicholls said, looking around him.

"I understand," James said, snapping his fingers and turning quickly, "come with me. I'll show you the Border Collies."

The Inspector obliged, following James's swift gait out of the barn. Later he told Annabelle he had no idea that the adult Bernese had leaped up and placed its paws on her shoulders.

"Now this is more like it!" the Inspector said as he leaned over the fence and caught sight of the excited, playful collies.

"I trust you're familiar with this breed?" James said, unlatching the gate and stepping through.

"Indeed I am," Nicholls said, immediately crouching to play and roll the pups. "Come here, you!"

"Well, there are seven puppies here, two haven't been reserved yet. This one over here with his ears in the air, and that one by your left foot."

"Ah, this one?" the Inspector said, immediately ruffling the ears of the one next to him. "Oh, this one looks a right little scamp – *aren't you?*"

"I'm happy to let you have one, but these were only born eight weeks ago. They'll need to stay here for a while longer. I don't let my pups go until the tenth or preferably twelfth-week mark."

Nicholls stood up.

"That sounds reasonable to me."

"Great," James said, as they left the pen and he closed the gate behind him. They walked slowly out of the barn into the cool air once again.

"So what should I do? Come back in a few weeks?"

"Well, usually I'd ask for a deposit and then let you know when I feel the pup is ready to go, but seeing as it's you, Inspector, I don't think there will be any need for that. I'll give you a call when he's ready, and if you're still interested, he's yours."

Nicholls smiled gratefully. "I can't really ask for a better deal than that, can I? Thank you, James."

"No problem," the dog breeder beamed. "Hey, where is the Reverend?"

The two men scanned their surroundings quickly before their gaze settled upon the first barn. With impeccable timing, Annabelle staggered out of the open entrance, squinting in the daylight. She was hazily brushing at the large amount of grass that now clung to her clothes. Her disordered hair seemed to have been shambolically thrown in every direction, itself having gathered numerous strands of hay and straw, presumably from the barn floor.

"Are you okay, Reverend?" James called as they walked toward each other.

"Oh yes! Fine!" Annabelle said, breathlessly. She wiped her face. "Rather playful chap, that dog."

"He must have taken a shine to you, Reverend!" James smiled. "He's a very good judge of character."

Annabelle smiled awkwardly. "He's terribly heavy, too," she said, pressing her shoulder.

Nicholls could not hold back any longer, suddenly bursting into a deep belly laugh.

"Reverend," he said, "perhaps I should be adopting you, rather than a dog!"

Annabelle was still smoothing herself down and combing out the debris from her hair when the Inspector pulled up behind her Mini Cooper on the roadside where she had left it. He pulled on the handbrake with a rapid-fire click and turned to face her in the passenger seat.

"Are you sure you wouldn't like me to wait with you for the tow truck?"

"Absolutely not, Inspector," replied Annabelle. "You've got a murder investigation to conduct, and you've already wasted an hour visiting a dog breeder!"

"Hmph," snorted the Inspector. "I have faith in my constables to follow procedure. When it's time for initiative, that's when I'm most useful. Besides, I've got a funny feeling about this case."

"A 'hunch,' as they say in the movies?"

"Something like that."

"What is it?"

The Inspector sighed, then looked at Annabelle. When

he had first met her, this would have been the moment at which he would have told her that this was police business and that she had no reason to get involved. Looking at her now, however, and knowing her genuine compassion and dedication to every member of her community, he realized that she had become a valuable companion whenever his work brought him to Upton St. Mary. Her abundant care for and astute knowledge of people was an appreciated asset. Her lack of conceit and gentle humor was a refreshing change from the kinds of people – criminals and officious colleagues – that he was used to back in Truro. It occurred to him that these visits to Upton St. Mary, and specifically the time he spent in Annabelle's company, had become a welcome respite for him. A place in which he felt welcomed, relaxed, and a little more human.

"I think Mildred's death is part of something bigger," he said slowly.

"How so?"

"As I say, it's just speculation on my part, but do you remember what you told me earlier? About today turning into a strange day? About the car with blacked-out windows, the breakdown, the rumors?"

"Of course."

"Well I had my own 'strange' encounter today. Earlier, while I was in the pub preparing to meet James, there were two men, well-known criminals. I would recognize them anywhere, and I'm sure they recognized me. They operate mostly in Falmouth, and I have no idea what they would be doing in Upton St. Mary."

"Murderers?"

"No," Nicholls said, shaking his head, "but they *are* versatile. Drugs, prostitution, stolen goods; anything they can make a little money from."

"Oh dear," Annabelle murmured at the thought of such criminality in heavenly Upton St. Mary.

"Don't worry about it, Reverend," the Inspector said with a change of tone. "They've probably just met some women here or angered someone who's higher up than them on the ladder of thuggery, and they've come here to hide out."

"Well, if you think so..." Annabelle nodded, unconvinced, before getting out of the car. "Thank you for everything, Inspector."

"My pleasure, Reverend," Nicholls smiled.

Ian Crawford, owner of Crawford Motors, was a smug and arrogant man. He was muscular and broad-shouldered, and he walked with the swagger of an overly aggressive alpha male. His strong jawline seemed to be the result of constantly clenched teeth, and his eyes were perpetually fixed into a menacing stare, even when he was joking. No one ever laughed at his jokes, but it didn't stop him making them.

As she thanked the driver and stepped out of the tow truck, Annabelle remembered something she had heard about Crawford's dubious past as a purveyor of stolen cars and told herself to look a little more deeply into it when she had the chance. Despite this, however, she had visited Crawford Motors multiple times before, and though she found the owner's personality somewhat abrasive, she had no complaints about his mechanical abilities.

Once her Mini Cooper was unhooked from the tow truck and sitting in the lot, Annabelle began walking into the large, four-bay garage.

"Hello, Ms. Dixon," said the unmistakably slow, slithery voice of Ian Crawford. He pushed himself out from beneath a nearby car and grinned, unashamed of his remarkably crooked, yellow teeth.

Annabelle opened her mouth in order to correct his addressing of her as "Ms." before remembering that she did so every single time she visited him to no avail. She stopped herself. It was entirely likely he did it on purpose.

Ian stood up and crossed himself.

Annabelle smiled calmly at the joke. It took much, much more to faze her. She said nothing. In the battle between vengeful response and reserved decorum, she thought, the latter always wins.

"Hello Ian," she said, with the same warmth she used to greet children. "I'm here to get my car fixed."

"Of course. Just like everyone else in Upton St. Mary."

"What do you mean?"

Crawford grinned again before pointing at the cars at the other end of the lot.

"Greg Fauster's Punto. Danielle Welbeck's Audi. Harry Loftus' Honda. And now your Mini. All of you just came in this morning. First time I've seen any of you in a long time. What's going on?"

"Something bad has happened to Mildred."

"Oh?" Crawford said, smiling broadly.

"She's dead."

His grin dropped, and he gulped deeply.

"Huh. Interesting."

"The police are investigating."

Crawford squinted slightly as if looking for some further meaning.

"Investigating? Why?"

Whether it was the guilt of having given his name to the

Inspector, the irritation at Crawford's obnoxious behavior, or an attempt to gauge his reaction, Annabelle found herself saying the next few words with less forethought than she usually employed.

"It would appear she was murdered. They think it could be a competitor," she said, impulsively.

Crawford revealed his ugly smile slowly this time, as if relishing it more than the previous ones.

"Me? Ha! Now isn't that something! Well, I hope the coppers do come by here and ask me a few questions, actually."

Annabelle frowned apprehensively. "Why would you want that?"

Crawford's laugh was abrupt and throaty.

"I'd soon set them straight!"

"What do you mean?"

Crawford stuck a tongue in his cheek with a sense of mischief, before nodding behind Annabelle at her Mini.

"What's wrong with your car?" he said, as he stepped over to it.

"It broke down while I was driving. But back to—"

"The engine just stopped working suddenly?"

"Yes. What do you mean abo—"

"And before that, the accelerator kept trailing off? Coming and going?"

"Yes, it was."

Crawford nodded as he opened the fuel tank flap and unscrewed the cap.

"And the last place you got fuel was at Mildred's, I'm guessing," he said, though it clearly wasn't a question that he expected an answer to.

Annabelle watched with a furrowed brow as Crawford

leaned his head toward the open fuel tank and sniffed deeply.

"Yep," he said, nodding to himself. "Hey Gary! Come over here. We've got another one."

From inside the garage, a husky teenager with an acne riven face sloped toward his boss, who pointed at the open gas tank.

"What you reckon?" Crawford asked.

The teenager, much the same as Crawford had done, leaned in and sniffed deeply.

"Yeah. No doubt about it."

"What's going on?" Annabelle asked, her curiosity at its peak.

Crawford nodded the teenager away, replaced the cap, and walked back to Annabelle.

"Sugar water. It's been mixed in with the fuel. Just like every other car that the old bat fueled up in the past couple of weeks."

The shock of this heinous idea was enough to stop Annabelle from noticing the insult directed at Mildred.

"Why would she do that?"

Crawford shrugged emphatically. "No idea. Maybe she went senile. Working on cars at her age shouldn't be allowed, anyway. Maybe she was trying to squeeze a little more profit out of the gas or to keep people coming in for repairs. The real question is why anyone would get their gas from the last garage in England to pull it straight out of a barrel. Stupid, if you ask me."

"I can't believe it," Annabelle said, her head spinning with the implications of this discovery.

Crawford laughed again, before turning his head and spitting. "It was probably somebody who found out what she was doing that did the old bird in. Judging by how many people are turning up here, it could have been any one of her customers or even a whole bunch of them."

Annabelle stared intensely at her car, her mind desperately scrabbling to remember anything notable about the last time she had fueled the Mini up. She had been to Mildred's so many times, it was difficult to remember any one incidence specifically, let alone anything that seemed out of place.

"Can you fix it?" she asked. "My car?"

"Yeah. Just need to flush everything out and put something in there that actually burns."

"Thank you," Annabelle said. "Please call me when it's done."

Crawford nodded.

Just before she made it out of the garage forecourt, Annabelle turned back to Crawford, who was pulling out a stick of gum from a packet and shoving it into his mouth greedily.

"One more thing."

Crawford turned his ear to the Reverend.

"Have you noticed any cars with tinted windows around here? Those blacked-out ones you can't see through from the outside?"

Crawford smiled one last crooked grin.

"Ms. Dixon, it's better not to ask questions about cars like that."

CHAPTER FOUR

FTER TAKING A taxi back to St. Mary's, Annabelle marched up the path to her cottage with a head full of knotted thoughts and irritating, confusing questions. Only the sight of Biscuit, perched upon the low cobbled wall gazing at the two puppies chasing and tumbling over each other broke her contemplations.

"Biscuit! How are you enjoying your new companions?"

The cat responded by lazily getting up and walking in the opposite direction. The pups, however, leaped toward her at the sound of her voice, their wet tongues hanging and their tails wagging. She laughed as she crouched in front of them and rubbed their sides as they clambered over her in their attempts to lick her face.

As she enjoyed the unbridled attention of the dogs, her mind immediately went to the Inspector. If only he could experience their scrappy enthusiasm first hand! She was sure that if he caught a glimpse of them, there would be no way he'd be able to resist their shining eyes and panting smiles.

"What are you pups yapping about — Oh! It's you, Reverend," Philippa said, emerging from the cottage.

"Yes," Annabelle said, reluctantly pulling herself away from the dogs in order to walk inside, "I see Janet still doesn't have space for these rascals yet."

"No," Philippa said, following Annabelle and the puppies back inside, "and you seem rather pleased about it."

Annabelle smiled warmly as she took off her coat and hung it on the rack, enjoying the last sting of the chill as the warmth of the cottage seeped into her bones. She walked into the kitchen and immediately felt her nostrils fill with the heavenly scent of Philippa's cooking.

"Oh, that smells wonderful! Whatever are you concocting, Philippa?"

"Nothing but a shepherd's pie, Reverend, although I am experimenting with some new flavors. I enjoyed making that curry last week!"

"You should be careful, Philippa. If your cooking continues to get any more experimental, people around here will start thinking you a witch!"

Philippa laughed and waved the joke away as she knelt in front of the oven.

"I'm sure there are many who do already, Reverend," she murmured.

Annabelle sat at the table, kicked off her shoes, and stretched out her toes, allowing herself a deep, exhausted groan now that she was back home. She smiled as she watched the pups amble slowly over to the corner of the kitchen and curl themselves up against the radiator. Philippa joined her at the opposite end of the table, where she had previously laid out a crossword puzzle and a mug of tea.

"I suppose you've already heard about what happened

today," Annabelle said, grimly, "seeing as you've not asked me why I'm back so late."

Philippa pursed her lips and frowned sadly. "It's terrible. I never knew Mildred that well, not being a driver myself, but I hadn't heard a bad word said about her in all my days living in Upton St. Mary."

"I know," Annabelle replied, wistfully. "This entire day seems like a surreal nightmare. I'm glad it's finally over."

"It's not over yet," Philippa said, her voice knowing and wily.

Annabelle turned a suspicious gaze toward her friend. "Are you implying that it can get worse?"

"No," Philippa said, a glint in her eye. "I'm saying it can still get better."

Annabelle watched a smile form on Philippa's lips.

"You're up to something, aren't you!" she said. "What is it?"

Philippa paused and smiled with a sense of drama.

"I've invited Inspector Nicholls to join us for supper," she said, finally.

"What? Why?" Annabelle said, knowing her friend far too well to believe there was no reason, and dreading to hear what it was.

Philippa sat upright haughtily and spoke with the manner of a judge casting a verdict.

"It's about time you and the good Inspector grew more acquainted," she said, before adding, "on a more *personal* level."

"Philippa!" Annabelle cried, almost leaping onto the table. "We *are* acquainted!"

"You know very well what I mean, Reverend. You're an upstanding, much-respected member of this community, but you can't do everything alone. It would be good for you to have someone you can depend on intimately, someone trustworthy, loyal, determined, and good. Someone just like the Inspector."

Annabelle shook her head in disbelief, opening her mouth to give voice to the deep sense of disquiet she was feeling, but finding that words failed her.

"Philippa," Annabelle said, struggling to calm herself down, "the Inspector is in the middle of a very serious murder investigation. He doesn't have time to play match-making games!"

"Well, the midst of an investigation is the only time the Inspector is in Upton St. Mary long enough to play them!" Philippa said, indignantly.

Annabelle softened slightly, though her face wore a deep frown.

"How did you manage to convince the Inspector to visit us for dinner, anyway?"

Philippa shrugged. "Oh, that was easy. I simply told him I had important information regarding the investigation."

"Philippa!" Annabelle squealed once again, her jaw dropping almost to the table. "How could you?! That's... That's... awfully unlike you! You can't lie to the Inspector like that!"

"It's no lie, Reverend."

"What do you mean?"

"I know—" Just then, the doorbell rang, causing Annabelle to jump. "That must be him now! Why don't you let him in, Reverend? I'll set the table."

Annabelle frowned once more at her church secretary's attempts to play cupid, but she made her way to the door, pausing briefly to straighten her hair in the hallway mirror.

"Inspector!" Annabelle said warmly as she opened the door to him.

"Hello, Reverend," he replied, somewhat shyly.

"Thank you for coming." She gestured him inside.

Annabelle followed the Inspector into the kitchen, which Philippa had managed to transform in the seconds it had taken the Reverend to go to the front door. No longer was the cozy kitchen lit-up by the bright fluorescent ceiling light. Instead, three candles sat in the middle of the table casting a warm, flickering glow on the wood-grained surroundings. The table had been set with red napkins alongside a bottle of red wine that Annabelle hadn't even known was in her possession. She silently suspected it was the bottle previously destined for Sunday's Holy Communion and purloined by Philippa from the church office. Most alarmingly of all, there were just two plates on the table, placed across from one another.

Annabelle shot a wide-eyed look at Philippa, who stood by the table with her hands clasped behind her like a maître d' at a fancy restaurant.

"Take a seat, Inspector," Philippa said, enunciating every syllable.

"Thank you," he said, sitting in the chair she had pulled out for him. "Won't you be joining us?"

"Oh... ah... no..." Philippa said, suddenly flustered. "My... um... I just received a call from... ah... my niece's brother..."

"Your nephew, then," Annabelle corrected pointedly, unwilling to let Philippa's floundering attempts to fib pass by unnoticed.

"Yes... he... um... needs me..."

"I see," the Inspector said, growing evidently uneasy at the bizarre situation in which he found himself. "You mentioned that you knew something about the case?"

"Ah yes," Philippa said, as she picked the Inspector's

plate from in front of him and took it to the counter, "it's about Ted Lovesey. The mechanic at Mildred's."

"You know where he is?" the Inspector asked. "We haven't been able to locate him."

"Not exactly," Philippa said, placing the plate of steaming hot shepherd's pie in front of him.

"This looks very tasty," the Inspector said.

"Oh, our Reverend is quite the cook," Philippa said, winking at Annabelle as she took her seat, and receiving a look of horror in return.

"You were saying?" urged the Inspector.

"Yes. Well. Every Friday, without fail, Ted spends the entire night at the Dog and Duck," Philippa said, placing Annabelle's plate in front of her, then quickly making her way to the coatrack, "except last night he wasn't there."

"Do you have any idea where he went?"

"I'm afraid not, Inspector," Philippa said as she roughly shrugged on her thick coat, "but I can assure you, if Ted isn't in the Dog and Duck on a Friday night, something is very wrong." Philippa was now talking very quickly. One might think that she wanted to get out of the cottage as quick as she could.

"I've had men looking for him all day. Nobody's seen him since Friday afternoon," the Inspector muttered.

"Well, I hope you find him soon," Philippa said breathlessly, jamming her woolly hat on her head as she walked swiftly to the door. "Cheerio!"

Before Annabelle could even think about calling Philippa back, the sound of the front door slamming echoed through the passage. She turned to the Inspector, wondering if he was feeling as vulnerable as she was on the other side of the flickering candles. She poured them each a glass of wine.

They glanced at each other awkwardly for a few more moments, flashing embarrassed smiles across the silence. With every moment that passed, the atmosphere seemed to grow more uncomfortable.

"Did you make any progress today?" Annabelle finally asked.

"No, not much. As well as Ted, the teenager, Aziz Malik, is still missing, and a check on the car that was parked over the top of the pit we found Mildred in, turned up nothing."

They exchanged a few more flushed smiles before turning their attention to the food.

"This really does look delicious," the Inspector said quickly. "I had no idea you could cook."

"Um, yes," Annabelle stuttered, unable to add anything more complex to the conversation. Immediately, she was mortified by her inability to refute the whopper Philippa had propagated about her cooking.

In her confusion, Annabelle grabbed the wine bottle and offered the Inspector more of its contents, even though his glass was full. He shook his head. Annabelle nodded in acknowledgment, feeling foolish, and put the wine down as they once more settled back down into silence.

After a few more seconds of what seemed to be turning into a game of patience, the Inspector picked up his fork.

"Well, let's dig in, shall we?"

"Er," Annabelle said. The Inspector looked up. "Well, Philippa can be rather insistent at times. You know, I would understand perfectly if you didn't have the time to stay. You must have an awful lot of work to do."

"No, it's fine. I haven't eaten since breakfast. The last thing I had was a pint of bitter at the Silver Swan, and I didn't even finish that." He looked down appreciatively at his plate. "Besides, I doubt I could find a better meal anywhere."

Annabelle smiled warmly, glad that he wanted to stay and that at least some of the awkwardness had finally dissipated. They began eating, the clink of fork against plate adding some much-needed sound to the silence.

Suddenly the Inspector jumped in his seat, his eyes fixed upon Annabelle in a look of surprise. "Reverend!"

"Yes?"

"I... Didn't think... That you were that kind of..." He mumbled, utterly confused.

"Yes?"

"Um... never mind," he said, anxiously turning back to his plate.

Annabelle shrugged and resumed eating.

"So will you be staying in Upton St. Mary for a few days?" Annabelle asked as she blew on her piping-hot mixture of ground beef and potato.

"Yes," Nicholls replied, doing the same, "I'm staying with Constable Raven's mother. She has a room available, so I'll be there at least until Monday."

"That's good to know. I'll be sure to— Oh!"

Annabelle jerked backward so suddenly her knee hit the table, causing all the plates to rattle and shift.

"What is it?" the Inspector asked quickly.

"Oh my!" Annabelle said, going a deep shade of red, again.

"Reverend?"

"That's very forward of you, I must say!" she said, stroking her cheek demurely.

"What is?"

Annabelle bowed her head and smiled slightly at her pie. "Nothing. It's perfectly fine."

The Inspector watched her for a moment, frowning a little before shaking his head and resuming his meal. They continued to eat heartily, humming with appreciation at their meal.

"By the way," Nicholls said suddenly, after swallowing another hefty mouthful, "where are those puppies you mentioned? Did they find space for them at the shelter?"

"Oh no, they're right here." She turned to the corner that the puppies had made their regular sleeping spot and was surprised to find neither of them there. "Hmm. That's strange. I wonder where they are."

She leaned back in her chair to check the living room, and spun her head around to scan the kitchen. On a whim, she lifted the tablecloth.

"There you are!" The puppies ran out from beneath the table and placed their paws on her lap.

Annabelle and the Inspector smiled at each other for a full three seconds before breaking out into hysterical laughter.

"I thought that you were—"

"I thought that you were too, but—"

"But it was the puppies!"

"Those rascals nearly gave me a heart attack!"

They continued to laugh for a full minute, enjoying the release of tension that had built up between them. The pups, sensitive to the atmosphere, seemed to laugh along with them, wagging their tails excitedly. The female puppy leaped up onto the Inspector's lap, and a moment later, the other pup pounced upon Annabelle's.

"I do believe these puppies are angling for some pie," Annabelle giggled.

"Would you mind if—"

"Oh no. There's plenty more."

With childlike glee, the Inspector took some of the meat in his palm and grinned widely as the puppy licked it from his hand within seconds.

"You know, Inspector, I don't think I've ever seen you quite so happy."

"I'm much like a dog myself in many respects," he said, taking another handful of beef and offering it to his eager companion. "Excitement and unbridled happiness are infectious. It rubs off on me when it comes around. It's just that I don't see a lot of it in my line of work."

Annabelle sat back and stroked the puppy in her lap as she enjoyed the sight of the Inspector feeding the one in his own.

"You certainly wouldn't be short of fun and excitement with that one," she said.

Nicholls glanced at her reflectively. "I don't know..."

"Why don't you take care of her for the next few days, while you're in Upton St. Mary? Constable Raven's mother already has a dog, so she would have no objections, I'm sure."

Nicholls laughed as the dog licked his empty palm.

"I'm supposed to be conducting a murder investigation, Reverend. Not pet-sitting!"

"She might even help you! She'd make a terribly good sniffer dog. Why, just the other day she found a pair of gardening gloves that I could have sworn I'd thrown away."

"Hmm," the Inspector mused as he allowed the pup to nuzzle his neck, "are you sure Mrs. Raven wouldn't mind?"

"I'm absolutely positive."

Nicholls scrubbed the dog's ears and smiled into its big, soppy eyes. "I suppose it couldn't hurt to have a four-legged companion watching my back."

"Wonderful!" Annabelle said, finally satisfied. "That's settled then."

The next morning, no matter how much she attempted to focus herself upon the Sunday service, Annabelle could not remove the peculiarities surrounding Mildred's murder from her mind. It seemed to her like a complex, macabre jigsaw. She felt she already possessed half the pieces but was missing the other half. Even as she spoke to her congregation of the importance of remembrance, her mind was elsewhere looking for threads and themes connecting all the strange occurrences from the day before.

After the service, Annabelle stood at the doors of her church, smiling and making small talk with her parishioners as they poured out of its large arched entrance to the sound of Jeremy's organ-playing. Even though she shook hands warmly and engaged her congregation with as much personality and humor as she always employed, her mind continued to swirl with the intricacies of the case. When the last of them left, she instinctively thought of taking her Mini Cooper for a spin around the village lanes in order to clear her thoughts, before realizing with a sense of longing that her car was still at Ian Crawford's garage. Her disappointment was immediately followed by thoughts about the perplexing question of the village's fuel problems.

She walked back into the church and thoughtfully made her way to the office where Philippa was waiting for her. Her church secretary always helped her hang her vestments after Holy Communion.

"You're very quiet today, Vicar. Are you alright? How

was your evening with the Inspector?" Philippa sounded concerned.

"Hmm? Oh, it was fine. Yes, really. Fine."

Philippa looked at Annabelle carefully. "Just fine? Nothing more?" There was no reply. Philippa let out a deep sigh as she slipped a coat hanger inside Annabelle's white alb.

Annabelle's words came out in a rush. "Oh, Philippa, I'm perplexed. What is going on? Ted's absence from the Dog and Duck is extraordinary. It almost certainly puts him at the top of the Inspector's list of suspects!"

"He is a bit of a rum 'un, that Ted, Vicar. I'll give you that. Are you so sure of his innocence? We are all capable of strange deeds when we don't follow the word of the Lord. And he certainly doesn't do that!"

"Yes, I know. He's frequently drunk, driven more by worldly desires than is good for him, but I just can't believe it. There's no logic to it. No money was stolen, no obvious benefit to be gained from Mildred's murder. What could have been behind her killing?" Annabelle racked her brain, but the motive proved to be as elusive as the culprit.

"Ted's disappeared, Vicar. You have to face it. It seems a clear act of guilt."

"More is going on, Philippa. There's been tampering of the fuel pumped at Mildred's." Philippa stared at Annabelle, stunned at this news. "Ian Crawford thinks that Mildred did it herself for monetary gain of some sort, but why would she do that?"

"Do you think Mildred was in trouble, perhaps? Financially, I mean. Perhaps eking out the fuel helped her make ends meet? Small savings can make a big difference. That's why I turn off *all* the lights in church."

Philippa looked pointedly at Annabelle. The church

lights were a bone of contention between them. Annabelle liked to keep a few on at all times, even when the church wasn't being used. Philippa thought it a sinful waste of money.

"I doubt it. Mildred's Garage always had plenty of work on. Her prices were cheap enough that no one would have objected if she needed to raise them. The financial benefits of stretching the fuel or even fixing the cars that broke down as a result simply wouldn't have been worth it. Perhaps someone devised the scheme to jeopardize Mildred's reputation?

Philippa looked at the Vicar for a long moment. Annabelle, seeing her skepticism, appealed to her, "But what about the men disappearing from home for long periods of time? Perhaps there's a connection there?"

"Now, now, Vicar. I'm sure there's a simple explanation for that. Why don't I go and make you a nice cup of tea?"

"Thank you, Philippa, but I must get on. Sundays can be such busy days. Oh," Annabelle paused and half turned to Philippa, "I don't suppose you've heard if they've found Aziz yet? The Inspector told me last night that he was still missing, too."

"No, nothing, Vicar, sorry."

"The Inspector went to see his parents, you know. He had a difficult time, poor man. Their English isn't the best." Annabelle looked at the floor, as if it were a map on which she'd find buried treasure in the form of answers to her questions, "But they are such lovely people! Surely Aziz couldn't be involved?"

"He's certainly a good boy from all accounts. Mrs. Whitbread says he always helps her with her groceries and won't accept anything but thanks in return." Philippa was now carefully laying Annabelle's stole in a drawer.

Annabelle started to pace the small office.

"According to the Inspector, his parents told him that Aziz spends much of his time out of the house, studying at the library, riding his bike, and socializing with friends."

"Sounds like a typical teenage boy to me," Philippa murmured as she closed the drawer.

"And he often spends weekends sleeping over at the houses of his schoolmates after particularly grueling study sessions. But he hasn't been seen since teatime on Friday. His parents told the Inspector that they didn't know what he had been doing or where he was."

"What about his phone? He must have a phone. All the young ones do these days."

"Not answering it. The Inspector thinks it is all rather suspicious, but I think there must be a simple explanation. It just doesn't feel right to me. Oh, Philippa, it is so vexing!"

Annabelle's thoughts continued to whirl around in her brain like screaming banshees. When she started to feel dizzy and saw spots before her eyes, she realized she needed to calm herself down. She went outside and stood on the church steps. She breathed in the cold, damp air for a few moments, feeling refreshed by its invigorating crispness.

Shortly, Annabelle turned back to the church and walked toward the pulpit, calmer but still deep in thought. Jeremy was at his organ, sifting through sheets of music.

"Hello Jeremy," Annabelle said, reassured by his stable, reliable presence.

"Oh, hello Vicar," Jeremy replied, putting his music down and turning to Annabelle, giving her the full respect he always afforded her. "You led a remarkable service today. Thank you."

"I'm glad you thought so, Jeremy. Although honestly, my thoughts have been terribly clouded all morning."

"What's bothering you, Vicar? If I may be bold enough to ask," he added.

"It would be quicker to tell you what *isn't* bothering me," Annabelle said with a glum laugh. "Frankly, I had enough to concern me before all of this dreadful business with Mildred: the cemetery renovation project, my car breaking down, and what we're going to do with those puppies."

Jeremy shifted in his seat and gave Annabelle a sympathetic look. "What can seem like problems are often blessings in disguise, Vicar."

"Yes, that's true," Annabelle said wistfully.

"I'm sorry, Reverend Dixon," Jeremy said suddenly, hanging his head in shame. "You are the last person I should be offering guidance to. Please excuse me. I was being presumptuous."

Annabelle laughed softly. "Don't be so bashful, Jeremy. Your advice is welcome and much-appreciated. And spot on. I'm sure that once these travails are put to rest, we'll all emerge from them stronger and wiser."

Jeremy's grin was wide and boyish, like that of a boy scout receiving a badge.

"Thank you, Vicar. You are most sensible."

Annabelle chuckled at this rather archaic compliment.

"Oh," Jeremy continued, "I almost forgot. I do have some good news for you."

"Yes?"

"Your car – a Mini, I believe? It's been repaired. Ian Crawford told me that you can pick it up today, if you like."

"Ah! That's wonderful," Annabelle said, clapping her hands. "At least I won't have to ride a bike in this weather. A bad case of the sniffles would *really* not be a blessing at this point!"

"Of course, Vicar."

"So you visited Crenoweth?" Annabelle asked.

"No. I saw Mr. Crawford here, in Upton St. Mary, last night."

Annabelle scratched her head and pursed her lips.

"Really? Strange..."

"What is, Vicar?"

"I don't believe Ian Crawford is the sort of chap for whom there is anything of interest in Upton St. Mary. In fact, I've never seen him here in all my time serving at the church. I'm surprised, Jeremy, that you and he are acquainted. I wouldn't have thought you two have much in common."

"Oh, I'm terribly sorry, Vicar," Jeremy said, his long fingers fidgeting in his lap, "I do hope I haven't given you any further cause for concern."

"Don't be silly, Jeremy," Annabelle said. She was about to start ruminating again but quickly stopped herself. "I pretty much reached my full capacity for worrying long ago!" she replied, brightly.

Annabelle was glad that the cab ride she was taking to Crenoweth would be her last – at least for the foreseeable future. She had never enjoyed the experience of being a passenger very much and would often find herself pressing phantom pedals when sitting next to the driver. At her worst, she would silently judge the driver's heaviness on the brakes, their inability to maintain smooth acceleration, their inexpert steering skills, and clunky gear changes. She knew backseat driving wasn't her most positive of traits.

In between silently critiquing the cab driver's handling

of his taxi, Annabelle thought about what she would ask Ian
Crawford once she reached his garage. The mechanic came
across as shifty and devious at the best of times and seemed
to revel in his ability to arouse suspicion and distrust in
others. While Annabelle refused to indulge his provocative
manner, she could not dismiss the deeply bothersome idea
that Ian had visited Upton St. Mary recently. It was most
unlike him. Annabelle knew for a fact that, when occasionally called out to the village by some unfortunate car owner
who needed his services, Ian sent one of his many
mechanics rather than go himself. So why had he come to
the village the night following the day of the Mildred's
murder? She would ask him a few questions.

Her prepared inquisition was for naught, however.
Crawford was not to be found at the garage. Instead, the
same rotund teenager who had sniffed out the cause of her
Mini's problem emerged from the office to present her with
the keys and a bill for the repair. When asked about his
boss's whereabouts, the teenager merely shrugged and
offered a mumbled reply.

"He don't work Sundays."

Dissatisfied and with a sense of anticlimax, Annabelle
paid her bill. As she walked to her Mini, however, her
excitement at getting behind the wheel once again hit her
with a rush, and she got in with anticipation and relish. She
turned the key in the ignition and smiled broadly when the
Mini responded with a loud purr like an old pet seeing its
master for the first time after an absence. She took her time
settling back into the well-worn seat, savoring the feel of the
wheel's leather covering. She released the handbrake with a
sense of ceremony, and seconds later, she was off, her smile
stretching wide across her face.

As the leafless trees and curling roads began to zip by in

their familiar pattern and Annabelle had settled back into the pleasing rhythm of changing gears as she rounded blind corners and revved away from junctions, her mind turned once more to the events of the past twenty-four hours. This time, boosted by being once again behind the wheel of her car, her thoughts seemed sharper. They were more focused, as if regaining control over her own car had given her back control over her own mind. She began to see a pattern.

Both Ted and Aziz had disappeared at roughly the same time and remained missing. Ian Crawford, a man ill-suited to the slowness and provincial nature of village life, and a couple of criminals, known to the Inspector, had turned up in the village with little reason. The village's men were out of the house more than usual and keeping money from their wives, a rumor that seemed at least a little more meaningful than the usual rattle-tattle that entertained the bored house-wives of Upton St. Mary. Adding to this, her sighting of the car with blacked-out windows and the sheer outlandishness of Ted's absence from the pub on a Friday night, Annabelle became convinced that something was seriously afoot regarding the men of Upton St. Mary.

As with anything concerning men in the village, there was one place she was sure to find something of an answer: the Dog and Duck.

Annabelle parked her car along the cobbled street that hosted the inviting old-fashioned pub. She got out of her Mini and walked toward it but not before stopping to cast one last smile at her sorely missed but now reclaimed vehicle. Inside, the pub was already experiencing the heightened chatter and elbow-to-elbow business of the Sunday lunch crowd. Annabelle slid through the drinkers in a haze of greetings, seeing many of them for the second time that day, a glass of red wine in their hand. No doubt, she thought wryly, they were continuing their celebration of the Blood of Christ, the bar presumably substituting for the Communion table on this occasion.

When Annabelle reached the bar, the short but unmissable, busty, blond-beehived bartender that she was hoping to see was already there.

"Reverend!"

"Hello Barbara," Annabelle said to the bubbly pub landlady.

"It's always a lovely surprise to see you here," Barbara said in her high, musical voice. "Would you like something to eat?"

Annabelle cast a quick glance at the pub's filled booths.

"I doubt I could find a seat even if I did! No, thank you."

"Something to drink? Orange juice?"

"Thank you, but no. I just wanted to drop by and ask you something quickly."

"Oh, of course, Reverend," Barbara said, leaning forward over the bar to hear better.

"Actually, it's somewhat private."

"Ah! Come on through to the back then," Barbara said, moving to the corner of the bar and lifting the hatch.

Annabelle stepped through, then followed Barbara's platinum-blond hair into the back of the pub. There a small passage with stairs led up to Barbara's apartment above and another door lead into the storage room.

"So what's the matter, Reverend?" Barbara asked, her long eyelashes fluttering with concern.

"Well, it's probably nothing, and I'm sorry to take up your time when you're as busy as this but—"

"Oh, forget it, Reverend," Barbara laughed, nodding at the crowded pub. "These men can wait for their drinks. They don't know how to pace their drinking, most of them! You're doing them a favor!"

Annabelle chuckled ruefully.

"Do you happen to know Ian Crawford?"

"The mechanic down in Crenoweth? Of course. My sister lives there."

"Was he in here last night, by any chance?"

"Ian? No. In fact, the only time I can remember seeing him here was when we had that darts competition a few years ago. Oh! He kicked up a hell of a fuss about the entry fee when he lost! I've half a mind not to let him in again!"

"Hmm," Annabelle said, contemplatively. "Have you noticed any new people visiting the pub? Men who rarely come here? Oh, I know I'm not being very clear about this but—"

"Let me stop you there, Reverend. I know what this is about."

"You *do?*"

"Yes," Barbara said, putting her long, brightly-colored nail to her lips and frowning pensively. "It's about those rumors isn't it? The men running off and not going home all night."

"Yes! You know something about it?"

Barbara nodded ominously. "I can't tell you much, Reverend. But I can tell you one thing for sure. They're not spending all that time in my pub. Don't be fooled by that lunch crowd out there. Come evening, this place will be virtually empty, and it has been like that every night this week."

CHAPTER FIVE

TRY AS HE might to remain as officious as possible and to act with as much professional distance as his role demanded, the Inspector could not stop smiling like a young boy in a sweet shop whenever he looked at his furry companion. After his meal with Annabelle, he had spent much of the night playing with the puppy in his rented room at Mrs. Raven's and already felt that they had developed a rapport. By two in the morning, he had taught the dog to sit on her hind legs when he raised his palm. Pleasantly surprised at both the pup's intelligence and his own mentoring capabilities, Nicholls realized he was already impossibly infatuated with the dog.

"Damn that Vicar woman!" he muttered, smiling as he gave the mutt another playful scrub behind the ears. "She *knew* I'd never be able to give you back!"

Having quickly and almost completely overcome his initial resistance to adopting a rescue, the Inspector settled into bed and allowed the puppy to make her own on top of the quilt down by his feet.

Now, on this clear, cool Sunday morning, the Inspector

was up brighter and earlier than the puppy. She looked at him curiously through groggy, lidded eyes as he readied himself for the day. Though Nicholls had been careful to make sure his work wasn't impacted by his doggie diversions, he still felt that he had wasted far too much time already. It had been less than twenty-four hours since the discovery of Mildred's body, but he normally would have expected at least some progress in that time. So far, he had only added more questions to the many that surrounded Mildred's death, and it was time to find answers to them.

After retrieving some giblets and bones for the pup from Mrs. Raven's fridge and wrapping them in newspaper, he made his way to the village police station in the light of dawn. The dog followed eagerly on his heels, a noticeable bounce in her steps, especially as she smelled something fresh and raw coming from the bag he was carrying. Nicholls wondered for a moment as he walked along what Annabelle was doing at that very moment and surmised that she was probably preparing for her Sunday morning service. He had no difficulty imagining her standing up in the pulpit, charming a crowd of villagers with her smile, and discussing matters of the soul in her engaging yet humble manner.

"I really should check the church out for myself, one of these days," he mused as he pushed open the doors of the police station and held them for the pup to pass through. "Not today, though. Today I've got my own matters to attend to."

Nicholls greeted the night-shift officer, ignoring her inquisitive look when she noticed he had company. He made his way to the small side room he typically appropriated as his office when visiting the village. After carefully setting the dog's food in the corner alongside a bowl of water, he watched for a few moments as the pup tucked eagerly into her meal. He then went to sit behind his desk to take his own breakfast: a cup of poisonously strong tea and all the reports the officers had made regarding the case so far.

"It's looking pretty empty," he muttered, talking presumably to the dog who was the only other living, breathing creature in the room. "I'm not seeing any connections."

He still had Harper's initial report on the murder weapon and time of death to guide him, but even her always-astute evaluations could not help him if he had nothing with which to connect them.

"No apparent motive. No clues unknowingly left at the scene. Seems like premeditated murder to me. Cold-blooded, don't you think?" he said, raising his eyes to the puppy. She looked over from her doggie feast and held his gaze with the same intelligence and curiosity that she always seemed to regard him. Her ears lifted, and she cocked her head.

Nicholls laughed and turned back to his papers. The key had to lie with Ted or Aziz. He still had some hope that Aziz would turn up, but Ted's disappearance troubled him, especially after hearing Philippa's assertion that he never usually missed his Friday night drinking sessions.

Rather than focusing on all the possible avenues and reasons for Ted's disappearance, however, the Inspector found himself recollecting his meal with Annabelle. He sat back in his chair, tea mug in hand and a slight smile on his face as he reminisced the previous evening, utterly distracted from the important matter that lay on his desk.

"She's really quite a remarkable woman, when you think about it," he said as the puppy having finished her meal, padded toward him in a slow, satisfied manner, and curled up beside his chair. "To be a vicar in a village such as this and to still have such good street smarts. She's really rather astute, you know, a fine set of instincts – if a little overzealous at times." He paused for a moment, before starting to chat to the dog once more. "It's rather interesting to talk to her, you know. I spend so much time dealing with the very worst aspects of people that I rarely think of their better qualities. The Vicar is pretty clever in bringing the good side out in those around her, wouldn't you agree?" Nicholls looked down at the puppy beside him, who lazily raised an eyebrow in acknowledgement. "Yes, they don't make them like the Reverend very often, that's for sure," he said with a sigh. "To be honest, the first time I met her, I thought that she was rather bumbli—"

"Yes, Inspector?" came a light voice from the door. The Inspector jumped suddenly, noticing the friendly face of Constable McAllister in the doorframe. "Did you call for me?"

"Oh yes," the Inspector began, quickly sitting upright and guiltily sifting through his papers. "Yes, I did. Come in and sit down a moment, would you, McAllister?"

Police Constable Jenny McAllister was a relatively new recruit to the Upton St. Mary police force. She was a young officer, sympathetic and bubbly, possessed of a deep respect for her superiors. Despite still learning the ropes, she had displayed an enormous talent for dealing with people. Confronted with her big, blue eyes and her genuine smile, others found themselves softening, opening up, and often forgetful of whatever bother had brought them into contact with a police officer in the first place.

Jenny McAllister also had another skill that set her apart from her peers. She had an uncanny flair for organization. No one was faster, more thorough, and more meticulous in completing the paperwork that accompanied many of the duties of a police officer than Jenny. Soon, she had flipped the tables on her more senior colleagues, and her fellow constables found themselves deferring to her whenever confused about best practices, correct procedure, and the greatest efficiencies. As a new, and therefore lowly, police officer, she had been given plenty of night-shifts, a hectic and unpredictable duty in many places, but a predictably quiet one in Upton St. Mary, and she had taken them on with good grace and a cheerful smile.

Jenny had soon made the management of the small police station her own. If something were to happen, nobody could co-ordinate a response better than Jenny. She had an almost telepathic ability to know where the other officers in Upton St. Mary were patrolling, and who would be most suited to respond at any particular moment. This, along with her impeccable trustworthiness, meant that she was frequently allowed to watch the police station on her own.

She smiled as she took the seat opposite the Inspector's desk and sat down cheerfully.

"How can I help you, Inspector?" she said.

"You grew up in Upton St. Mary, didn't you?" he said, clutching some papers and pushing all thoughts of Annabelle and her wonderfulness aside.

"I did indeed."

"Do you know Ted Lovesey at all?"

McAllister shrugged her small shoulders. "I suppose. He spends most of his time at the pub."

"I know," the Inspector grumbled. "Do you know if he has a car?"

"Oh, no," McAllister said, with certainty. "He drinks far

too much for that. I suppose that's sort of funny – a mechanic who barely drives."

"Hmm," the Inspector said, nodding. "How does he get to work then?"

McAllister put a finger to her lips and frowned as she searched the vast database that was her mind.

"Well, I've seen Greg Bradley pick him up a few times, so perhaps Greg gives him a lift to work? The fire station isn't too far from Mildred's. Greg's a firefighter, so he's always on call, and he sleeps when he can. They're an odd couple, but they live almost next to each other. Greg doesn't drink at all. He doesn't even eat meat." McAllister stopped suddenly, blushing slightly. "Just a guess, sir. About the lifts, I mean. He might even walk. It's not far. Nothing's far in Upton St. Mary."

Nicholls raised an impressed eyebrow at the young woman across the desk. He dropped the papers on the table and sat back.

"You've just achieved more in a couple of minutes than I have all morning. Keep that sort of thing up and you'll be sitting where I am sooner than you think."

McAllister's blush transformed into a beam of delight at the compliment.

"Thank you, Inspector!"

"Have we sent anyone to question this...Greg Bradley?"

"No, we haven't," she said, turning formal again. "I can do that, but we've only got two other officers on duty right now. Constable Raven is guarding the crime scene at Mildred's, and Constable Harris is investigating reports of an illegally parked mobile library on Crowley Street."

"Send Harris to question him when he's done," Inspector Nicholls said, rising from his chair. "I'll go tell

Raven to come back here. There's not much else we're going to get out of that garage."

Nicholls walked over to the coat rack and put on his trenchcoat. To the puppy's great excitement, he picked up the dog leash and attached it to her collar. McAllister stood up with him and moved to the door, but not before the Inspector could utter one more compliment in her direction.

"I meant what I said, McAllister. You've got a spark I've not seen in a while – not in a police officer, at least."

Still satisfied from her earlier meal, the small, brown puppy remained alert but calm as she sat on the front passenger seat of the Inspector's car. She appeared to be quietly taking in everything going on around her. The Inspector mulled over what a suitable name might be for her as he drove through the morning light of an Upton St. Mary Sunday.

Constable Raven spotted the Inspector's car from his guard post in the garage office and ambled out to greet him.

"Morning, Raven," the Inspector said.

"Morning, Inspector," the Constable replied, before glancing bemusedly at his furry companion. "Is that your dog, sir?"

"It might be," Nicholls replied.

Knowing that even this brief reply was more explanation than the Inspector usually gave in response to questions he regarded as personal, Constable Raven set aside his curiosity for the time being.

Nicholls stepped under the crime scene tape and walked slowly toward the open garage bay, looking casually around as if he might stumble across something he had previously missed. Raven followed half a step behind.

"So did you notice anything overnight, Raven?"

"No, sir. Didn't hear or see a thing. Not even a mouse squeak."

"Hmm. Well, you should lock up and get yourself back to the station then," Nicholls said, pulling the puppy gently toward him. "I think we've got everything we're going to get from this place. Leave the tape up, and check in on it from time to time."

"Yes, sir," Raven said, though his eyes were fixed upon the puppy still. "Er... Inspector?"

"Yes?"

"Forgive me if I'm speaking out of turn, but it looks like your friend here is interested in something," The constable nodded at the dog.

Nicholls looked down at the pup he had absent-mindedly been tugging closer to him and saw that she had her wet nose to the ground, sniffing enthusiastically.

"Oh yes," the Inspector remarked. "So she is." He suddenly felt as proud as the father of a newborn. He bent down to put his hand under the puppy's chin. He looked into her eyes. "What is it, girl?"

Nicholls loosened his grip on the leash as the puppy jerked her head away, keen to get on with uncovering the source of her interest. The two men followed as the puppy diligently led them in a zig-zag pattern around the outside of the garage. After drawing them to five large barrels stacked up against the rear of the building, the puppy began repeatedly pointing her nose toward the containers before recoiling with a rapid shake of her head.

"What are these?" the Inspector asked his Constable.

"They're fuel barrels," Raven replied, his eyes keenly

watching the puppy. He grimaced. "The ones that were tampered with. I checked them myself. They come from a fuel depot all the way in Newquay. I've asked one of the officers there to check them out."

After sniffing around the barrels a little longer, the puppy drew the men away. She quickly trotted toward a corner where a high, sturdy fence separated the garage from its neighbor. There, the ground was piled high with old car parts and boxes. Within a few minutes and after many changes of direction and dead ends, the puppy quickly focused on a small, red fuel can that sat at the edge of the pile.

"What do you think it is, Inspector?"

"Let's find out," Nicholls replied as he took out his handkerchief and threaded it through the fuel can's handle. He sniffed slowly at the open spout. "Smells like some kind of soft drink."

He offered it for Raven's olfactory inspection, and the Constable quickly pulled away in disgust.

"Ugh! That's not like any soft drink I've ever had! It's so sweet, it's nauseating!"

Nicholls nodded reflectively.

"Sugar water," he said. "You can call off your friends in Newquay – our fuel tamperer did his dirty work right here."

"So it must have been one of the assistant mechanics!" Raven said, triumphantly.

"Not necessarily," Nicholls replied, immediately deflating his officer's rather premature celebration. He looked at the fence that circled the garage. "Somebody could have climbed over that with a little effort."

"I suppose you're right," Raven sighed.

Nicholls handed him the fuel can, which the Constable

took carefully by the handkerchief still passed through its handle.

"Get this checked for prints, Raven. Maybe that will tell us which one of us is right."

"Of course, Inspector," Raven said, interrupted by the crackle of his radio. Nicholls watched carefully as the Constable answered the call.

"Raven here."

"Constable Raven, is the Inspector with you?"

It was McAllister.

"I'm here," growled the Inspector, leaning in to be heard over the radio.

"You might want to come to the station as soon as you can, Inspector," McAllister said, her voice hazy over the radio network. "We've found Ted Lovesey."

Minutes later, both Inspector Nicholls' and Constable Raven's cars screeched to a halt outside the Upton St. Mary police station with a sense of urgency that the village rarely saw, especially on a Sunday. The Inspector leaped out in such a hurry that he completely forgot about his furry companion lying with her chin on her paws in the passenger seat. She had to employ her quick reflexes to jump out before the Inspector slammed the door shut and trapped her in. Both the puppy and the Constable followed the Inspector as he burst through the doors of the small station, a full six feet of determination and energy.

"He's in the interview room," Constable McAllister said upon seeing the Inspector and standing up quickly from behind her desk. There was no doubting the Inspector's agitation.

"Where was he when you found him?" Nicholls asked, stopping in front of her.

"At Greg Bradley's house, sir."

"Was Greg there?"

"No. Greg's currently working a shift. Constable Harris spoke to him, however. Apparently, he was as surprised as anyone when Ted didn't ask him for a lift home from the pub late Friday night like he does every weekend."

Nicholls raised an eyebrow. "So what happened? Why wasn't Ted at his own home?"

Constable McAllister shrugged apologetically. "Greg seems just as confused as we are. He said that yesterday afternoon Ted turned up on his doorstep and asked if he could stay a while. He looked pretty shaken up, Greg said, so he didn't ask any questions, and they just sat around watching TV together. Last night, Greg had to work a long shift, and since then, it doesn't look like Ted has left Greg's house."

Nicholls frowned at the peculiar circumstances. "Well, maybe Mr. Bradley doesn't like to ask questions, but I certainly do," he said, as he made his way to the interview room. He stopped after a few steps and nodded at his puppy. "McAllister, make sure the dog's entertained. This could take a while."

"Of course, sir."

Inspector Nicholls placed his hand on the doorknob to the interview room, took a deep breath, and went in.

Everything the Inspector had heard about the drifting, drunken mechanic had informed his mental picture of him. Lacking in self-control, bad with money, and with seemingly no stability in his life apart from his job as a mechanic, Ted Lovesey, Nicholls had inevitably concluded, was more of a criminal type than a typical Upton St. Mary villager.

Just the sort of person the Inspector was deeply familiar with.

And yet, seeing him now, sitting behind the simple table of the interview room, his big round eyes more like those of a frightened kitten than a ferocious killer, the Inspector found his expectations deeply challenged. Ted's round, puffy face was childlike, and his hair sat lank and thin upon his head as if mirroring his defeated, submissive body language.

The Inspector closed the door behind him slowly and stepped toward the desk.

"Are you Ted Lovesey?"

The man nodded slowly, his hands clasped between his thighs, his shoulders hunched over as if bracing himself for an attack.

Nicholls sat down opposite him and leaned back. Ted's eyes glanced back and forth from the floor to the Inspector, unable to meet his glare for longer than a second.

"I didn't know," he said suddenly, in a soft and quiet voice.

"What didn't you know?" the Inspector asked sharply.

"About Mildred. Jenny just told me now—"

"Constable McAllister to you, man."

"Sorry. Constable McAllister. It's just that I've known Jenny – Constable McAllister – since I arrived here, so I've always called her Je—"

"What didn't you know about Mildred?" the Inspector interrupted, wanting to keep the anxious man's thoughts on track.

"That she died!" Ted said, his lips quivering. His eyes were glassy with moisture as the words hung in the air. "I don't believe it! Who could have done that?"

Nicholls frowned and shifted in his seat. This was not what he had been expecting.

"That's what I'm working to find out," he said, sternly. "Let's start from the beginning: Where were you on Friday night?"

Ted gasped and looked directly at the floor, his clasped hands increasingly fidgety. Nicholls waited a whole minute for an answer, until he realized one wasn't about to be forthcoming.

"Well?" the Inspector urged heavily.

Ted shook his head, a strained expression on his face.

"I can't say," he mumbled into his lap.

Nicholls leaned forward.

"And why is that?"

"I just can't. I'm sorry."

Nicholls frowned again.

"Okay. Tell me why didn't you go home yesterday? Why did you go to Greg Bradley's house?"

Now Ted was wild-eyed.

"I can't! Please. I'm sorry... I can't tell you."

"What's going on, Ted? Are you afraid of something? Someone?"

Ted raised his eyes from the floor to meet Nicholls' glare, the sheer terror emanating from them plain to see.

"Okay," Nicholls said, shifting his tone. "Let's try something else. What do you know about the fuel tampering going on at Mildred's Garage?"

Ted stopped fidgeting for the first time since the Inspector had entered the room.

"Fuel tampering?"

Nicholls sighed. "Is that something else that you 'can't' talk about?"

"Honestly, I don't know anything about it."

"The sugar water mixed into the fuel that was coming from *your* garage.

"But that's ridiculous!" Ted said, animatedly. "I mean, for a start, sugar water in the fuel tank doesn't stall a car. It's an urban myth."

"What?"

Ted's nervousness seemed to dissipate as he put his hands on the table and leaned forward to explain.

"Well, the whole 'sugar' thing is just unnecessary. Just simple, plain water is enough to ruin the petrol in a car."

Nicholls leaned back and scrutinized the suspect with a tiny smirk on his face.

"So you're saying you're far too smart to be involved in this fuel tampering scheme, and that if you had been responsible, you'd have just used water. Is that supposed to convince me you didn't do it?"

"No. I'm just trying to understand what you're talking about. I'm sorry if I offended you," Ted said, returning to his hunched-over nervousness.

Nicholls tapped his finger impatiently on the table as he looked at the man opposite him. He had pinned much of the investigation on this moment. Questioning Ted – and Aziz – had been his top priorities. But while it was clear Ted was hiding something, it was even clearer that Ted was not ready to talk about it. Frightened, anxious, and seemingly unaware of what exactly had happened to Mildred, Ted had given him no answers. Nothing, in fact, but more questions. The Inspector found himself frustrated, but he wouldn't let his impatience obstruct his effectiveness.

He stood up from his chair, surprising Ted in the process, and briskly walked out of the interview room.

Constables McAllister, Harris, and Raven were seated at their desks, chattering away and laughing as they played with the puppy between them. When they heard the Inspector shut the door of the interview room, they stopped immediately and each spun in their chairs expectantly, their faces open and inquisitive like baby birds watching the return of a parent. Even the dog turned her head to pant in the Inspector's direction.

"What did he say, Inspector?"

"Do you think it was him, sir?"

"Shall we get a cell ready?"

Nicholls looked at each of them, then thrust his hands in his pockets and sighed deeply. His shoulders dropped.

"He didn't say anything. We just went around in circles a few times. He's scared, badly shaken-up. I'm sure he knows something."

"But you don't think he did it?" Raven asked.

Nicholls looked back at the door of the interview room with a puzzled expression.

"I don't know. But if I didn't know any better, I'd say he was a victim, rather than a perpetrator."

Annabelle pulled her car into a tiny parking spot in front of the Inspector's vehicle with such a swoop that several passersby brought their hands to their mouths in the expectation that she was about to hit something. When instead she parked cleanly and braked smartly, their gasps were replaced by smiles, accompanied by a new respect for her driving skills. It wasn't every day you saw a Vicar handle a car like that.

Annabelle's bustling, black-clad figure emerged from the Mini and quickly made her way up the steps.

"Is it true?" Annabelle said, the moment she caught

sight of Constable Raven behind the reception desk. "Have you found Ted?"

"Yes," said Raven with a confused look. "But how did you—"

"Oh, everyone in the pub is talking about it," Annabelle said, slightly out of breath. "Timmy Trelawny saw him get into a police car outside Greg Bradley's house."

"What were you doing in the pub, Reverend?" McAllister piped up from her desk beyond the reception.

"Ah," said Annabelle, "just having a post-church chat with my flock. They were keen to continue Holy Communion. You know, wine," she held up an imaginary glass, "and bread." She nodded and chortled, snorting slightly.

"What's all this?" Inspector Nicholls said, emerging from his side office at the flurry of excitement.

"Inspector!" called Annabelle, marching past the reception desk to meet him. "I heard you found Ted Lovesey finally."

"Yes?" the Inspector replied, dubiously.

"I was wondering if I could speak to him. You see, I've been thinking about the case rather a lot, and I think that—"

"Reverend," the Inspector said, assertively. "He's being held for interrogation!"

"I do hope not, Inspector!" Annabelle cried. "He isn't a terrorist! And I think I know *just* what to ask him if we want to get to the bottom of—"

"Reverend," the Inspector repeated. "This is a police matter. You can't just come barging in and demand to interview our suspects! There's procedure to follow. We're trying to solve a murder here. Look, I respect your interest and investment in this, and you've provided us with some valuable information so far, but right now the best thing for you to do is to leave us to conduct this investigation in a professional and methodical manner."

"But Inspector!" Annabelle cried, gazing at him incredulously. "I'm trying to help!"

"I'm sorry, Reverend, but you shouldn't be here, and you certainly shouldn't be asking to speak to someone who is helping us with our inquiries."

"Actually, Inspector," said Raven, looking up from the puppy that was perched on his lap, "perhaps the Reverend can help us."

Nicholls glared at the Constable.

"Yes," added McAllister, "if Ted is holding something back, he'd be far more likely to talk to the Reverend than any of us."

"You said it yourself, Inspector. He's scared," Constable Harris continued, "but he knows something. Maybe revealing it to us is too dangerous for him."

Nicholls gritted his teeth and scowled. Annabelle smiled apologetically.

"Well, I guess I'm outvoted. I'll give you five minutes, Reverend, but I'm going in with you."

"Of course!" Annabelle said.

Nicholls turned on his heel and walked briskly over to the interview room, opening the door for the Vicar with a combative look on his face. Annabelle stepped inside the room.

"Oh, hello Reverend," Ted said, his tone a mixture of surprise and amiability.

"Hello Ted. How are you?" Annabelle took a seat opposite him. The Inspector closed the door, crossed his arms, and glowered at them from the corner of the room. As much as he wouldn't care to admit it, he saw the change in Ted's body language immediately.

"I don't know," Ted said, with a sigh. "I can't tell if I'm coming or going."

"Yes, I understand," Annabelle said, with a sympathetic smile. "It's been a rather busy weekend."

"I can't believe what's happened to Mildred," Ted said, shaking his head. "It's just... I... I don't understand."

"None of us do, Ted. That's why we have to help the police, so that the person who did this gets their comeuppance. I mean, who knows if they'll try to do it again!"

Ted's eyes widened.

"You think they might kill someone else?"

Annabelle directed a worried look at him.

"If they can murder somebody as beloved as Mildred, then nobody is safe."

"Oh my God!"

Annabelle glanced back at the Inspector, who remained stony-faced.

"Ted, you're an intelligent man," Annabelle began. "You know how bad this looks. You don't go to the pub on a Friday evening for the first time in years, Mildred is murdered sometime early the following morning, and then you turn up at Greg Bradley's house without going home. Now I don't believe you had anything to do with her murder, but I'm afraid I might be the only one."

"I didn't do anything wrong!" Ted pleaded, reaching his hands out over the table as if clutching at hope. "I can't tell you where I went, though. I just can't! Please trust me!"

"You don't have to tell anyone anything, Ted. But if you don't tell the Inspector where you were, then he really has no option other than to assume you had something to do with the murder. There's very little evidence to the contrary."

Ted buried his face in his hands and sobbed uncontrollably.

"How about this," Annabelle continued in a gentle voice, "I tell you what I think might be going on, and you don't have to say a word."

Ted pulled his face up to look at Annabelle, then at Nicholls, then back again. With a confused expression, he shrugged mildly and wiped his tears.

"Okay," he said, slowly.

Annabelle smiled, then cleared her throat.

"I believe there is illegal activity occurring on a regular basis in Upton St. Mary. Activity entertaining enough to entice many of the men who live here, yet illicit enough for them to keep it a secret."

Ted raised his chin and narrowed his eyes. His mouth was open slightly. Whether it was in awe of what she was saying or anxiety at what she was about to say, she couldn't tell. Either way, Annabelle had certainly struck a chord. She turned briefly and exchanged a look with the Inspector, who had dropped his fixed glare at the prospect of a revelation.

"Now I also believe," Annabelle said, "that this activity involves and is perhaps controlled by criminal elements from outside the village. A criminal element dangerous and organized enough to make a man keep the activity a secret even when faced with a murder charge."

Ted's eyes widened even further, the whites revealing his deepest fears.

"The only thing that I'm struggling with, Ted, is just *what* this illegal activity is."

Ted was breathing heavily now, but he managed a nervous semi-chuckle.

"There are only so many vices, Vicar."

Annabelle grinned.

"Indeed, and they haven't changed much since the Bible was written," she said. "One learns just how diverse a man's sins can be from the good book."

Ted opened his mouth as if to speak, before shutting it and shaking his head again. He covered his eyes with his hand and sighed deeply.

"Let's see," Annabelle persisted, "it wouldn't be drink. You're quite adequately catered-to in that department. It's not women, either. Many of these men have wives, and it's unlikely that even the most dubious of men in Upton St. Mary would be that adventurous. Drugs, perhaps? I can't believe that, myself. That doesn't leave many options."

"Say it, Vicar," Ted challenged, as if unable to endure the torture of suspense any longer.

Annabelle looked back at the Inspector one more time. He nodded his agreement, and she turned to the forlorn figure on the opposite side of the table. Ted looked beaten-up and exhausted.

"It's gambling, isn't it Ted? The only thing accessible and entertaining enough to tempt the men of Upton St. Mary. The only thing you would find more exciting than a typical Friday night getting drunk at the Dog and Duck or watching England lose again on the big screen."

Ted shook and sighed and fidgeted and winced for a long time before finally sitting upright. He looked directly into the Reverend's eyes and nodded gently.

Annabelle stood up.

"Don't worry, Ted. You didn't tell us anything." She turned to the Inspector. "Did he?"

Nicholls bit his lip, glanced between the two of them, and then shook his head just as gently as Ted.

"But what about Mildred's murder, Reverend? Do you think it has anything to with—"

"I don't know, Ted. I don't know," Annabelle looked Ted directly in the eyes. "But I promise you, I'm going to find out."

The Inspector closed the interview room door once again and gently took Annabelle by the arm. He ushered her into his office, to the puzzlement of both his constables and the puppy, before shutting the door firmly behind him.

"Reverend! What was *that?*"

"Whatever do you mean, Inspector?"

Nicholls rubbed his brow hard and paced around the room.

"I'm trying to solve a murder case!" he said, with exasperation. "And hopefully in the process, figure out who is tampering with people's fuel. Now I have a *gambling ring* to investigate? Where did you get that idea? From all those strange occurrences you were telling me about? Mysterious cars, disappearing men?"

"From a lot of thought and attention to the facts," Annabelle said, defiantly putting her hands on her hips. "And Ted has just confirmed it!"

"Ah yes," Nicholls said, exasperation turning to sarcasm. "The man who is the prime suspect in a murder investigation just confirmed that he was taking part in a far less serious crime at the time of the murder. What a surprise! If you suspected that he had built a rocket ship to Mars and visited it during the time of the murder, he'd probably have confirmed that, too!"

Annabelle scowled. "Inspector, I am gravely disappointed in your reaction!"

"How is any of this supposed to help me, Reverend?" the Inspector said. "I'm a *detective*. It's my job to answer questions, tie up loose ends, and close cases; not create more of them with wild speculations and gigantic leaps of logic!"

"I'm a woman of the cloth, Inspector" Annabelle said, lowering her voice as she put her hand on the doorknob, readying herself to leave, "and it's my job to understand that in a community such as Upton St. Mary, everything is connected – even when it may appear otherwise. I sincerely hope you understand this simple fact sooner rather than later. Goodbye, Inspector."

"REVEREND, WAIT!" THE Inspector ran out of the station just as Annabelle was opening the door to her Mini.

He leaped down the steps with an energy that matched the puppy that followed him and brought himself to a stop in front of Annabelle where he hung his head.

"Reverend," he began, "I apologize. I should not have said those things. It was disrespectful of me."

Annabelle raised her chin as she considered this.

"I was only trying to help, Inspector."

"I know. But even you must admit, Reverend, that's a pretty giant leap you took there. A *gambling ring?* You'd never mentioned anything of the kind to me before."

"That's because I had not considered anything of the kind before," Annabelle said, coolly. "It was only this morning that I realized how it all fit together."

"But why would you surmise such a thing from mere hearsay about men disappearing for hours and the sighting of a car with tinted windows? It seems a rather flimsy basis."

Annabelle placed her hands on her hips and pursed her

lips at the Inspector's refusal to believe in her theory, however polite he now was about it.

"I did not surmise it because of those things, Inspector. I came to the conclusion because I happen to know Ted and the people of this village very well. It may not seem as rational to you as counting facts and sticking them together logically, but an understanding of *people* is often a far better path to the truth."

She sighed deeply, her hand still on the car door. She shut it softly, and bent over to scratch behind the puppy's ears briefly before looking back at Nicholls.

"If you must know, Inspector," Annabelle continued, her tone a little softer now, "I had been thinking of such things long before this terrible business with Mildred occurred. In recent months the church has been struggling to raise funds, a rather remarkable fact considering the generosity of the village during even the toughest of times in the past. Of course, these things can happen. However, when I questioned Barbara, she's the landlady at the Dog and Duck, if you remember, she seemed even more convinced than I was that something was afoot. Ted wasn't the only person who seemed too preoccupied to visit her pub. In fact, he was one of the last regulars she had until even he didn't turn up last Friday night."

Nicholls frowned and looked away.

"You don't believe me," Annabelle said, noticing the skeptical look he was attempting to hide.

"Look at it from my perspective, Reverend," he said. "A Vicar trying to understand why she can't raise funds, a pub landlady trying to explain why her pub suddenly seems so unpopular, and a prime suspect seeking an alibi and an excuse for his strange behavior. Of course a story to explain away those problems all at once would be appealing – but a *gambling ring*? In Upton St. Mary? It's just implausible! There must be a million other ways to explain it."

"Such as?"

Nicholls' barely flinched.

"Honestly?" he said, placing a hand gently on the car's roof, as if placing it upon Annabelle's shoulder. "One thing you learn pretty quickly as a detective is that the most boring, unexciting, and ultimately disappointing supposition is frequently the most accurate one."

"And what is that?"

"I think Ted's our man and that he's a good liar. I think people aren't drinking at the Dog and Duck because of the cold weather or because one of the other pubs in the village has become more popular. And as for your church..." Nicholls paused, looking down at his feet before braving to look Annabelle in the eye again, "I'm afraid it's just a sign of the times, Reverend. People aren't interested. Or not interested *enough* to part with money for your project. Face it."

They gazed at each other for a few moments, the contrast of their arguments seeming to play out in the heady tension.

"Look," the Inspector said, trying to bridge the gap between them. "Let's just assume that you're right. None of this is bringing us any closer to the *real* mystery: Who killed Mildred, and why?"

Annabelle raised an amused eyebrow.

"'Us?' Inspector?"

Nicholls laughed.

"I'm sorry. But can you blame me for thinking of you as a fellow investigator?"

"Not at all," Annabelle smiled. "I'm flattered."

"You're certainly correct about one thing, Reverend," the Inspector said with all seriousness. "You know the villagers far better than I do, and you're much more effective at getting information out of them. That's why I'd like to ask you to come along with me now."

"Oh? Where to?"

"Aziz's parents," Nicholls said, determined now. "I want to see if he's come home yet, and if not, where the hell he's got to."

The Malik's were Pakistani immigrants who owned and lived above a shop that was a relatively short walk from the police station. As they ambled along the cobbled streets of Upton St. Mary in the Sunday quietude, their coats protecting them against the bracing, chilly wind, a happy puppy between them on a leash held by the Inspector, Annabelle could not shake the feeling that this felt more like a loving couple's Sunday afternoon stroll than two people seeking somebody with respect to a murder investigation. The Inspector seemed aware of this too, his face a little bashful as he walked by her side.

"How are you finding the puppy, Inspector?" Annabelle asked as she watched the dog bounce along for a few steps ahead of them, stop for a few seconds to wait, then bounce on happily again.

"Oh. She's pleasant enough company," he said. "She certainly eats a lot. And she does like to go off and sniff in any direction when she catches a scent," he added, this time tugging the puppy forward as she allowed herself to be beguiled by the wheel of a parked van.

"Well she's just a pup, Inspector. I'm sure she'll mature quickly alongside you."

"Now, now, Reverend, I'm fond of her, I won't deny

that, but I've yet to make up my mind as to whether I'll adopt her."

"Very well," smiled Annabelle, a knowing glint in her eye.

The Maliks' shop was situated on the corner of one of Upton St. Mary's most central junctions, among an array of other shops that saw a steady stream of shoppers from dawn until dusk on most days. Unlike the other shops, however, Malik's was open on a Sunday, and it was very much the first stop for the vast majority of villagers seeking their morning paper, a bottle of milk, or even a specialist tobacco that Mr. Malik would kindly order on request in his typically accommodating manner.

Next to the shop was a small driveway for deliveries, with a rear exit and a shuttered garage for the Maliks' mini-van. Annabelle noticed that there was a new, smaller car in the driveway as they walked past, one she had not seen before.

The Inspector attached the puppy's leash to a lamp post outside the shop and told her to "Sit." She obeyed immediately. He and the Vicar then stepped inside the small, yet neatly arranged and organized shop and walked up to the counter at the far end. Mr. Malik saw them approach. He stiffened as he always did in the presence of authority.

"Good afternoon sirs! And madams!" he said, in his heavily accented voice.

"Hello, Mr. Malik," Annabelle beamed.

"Have you heard from your son, yet?" Inspector Nicholls inquired directly, brooking no small talk and remembering vividly the difficulties they had had in their previous interview.

The shopkeeper shrugged and spread his hands widely.

"Aziz not here. Always busy. School. Study. Exercise with bike. Visit with friends. Work with cars. I told you."

"Aren't you worried?" Annabelle asked, speaking simply, so the shopkeeper could catch every word and understand. "Aziz has not been seen for two days!"

Mr. Malik beamed a wide smile and laughed gently.

"Aziz is good boy! When he finish with everything, then he come, eat, go out again."

"But it's dangerous. There's been a murder, Mr. Malik. Aziz should be home now!"

Mr. Malik wagged his finger furiously.

"No, no, no, no! Aziz not dangerous. Never. Very soft boy. Kind."

"No, you don't understand," Annabelle said, her tone growing ever-so-slightly frustrated. "It's dangerous *for* Aziz."

"No," the bearded shopkeeper repeated adamantly. "Seventeen years, no trouble. Teachers say perfect student. Go to Oxford. Very good to parents. Aziz not trouble, dangerous, nothing."

Annabelle exchanged a defeated look with the Inspector, who opened his mouth to speak, frustration clear on his face. Annabelle, sensing that his involvement in the exchange wasn't going to move the situation forward, quickly pressed a hand to his elbow. In the event, all the Inspector emitted was a deep sigh.

"We'll be back, Mr. Malik," he said.

"Thank you," Annabelle added.

"Anytime!" the shopkeeper called heartily.

They walked back outside, reclaimed the puppy, and took a few steps down the street before stopping. The Inspector shook his head angrily.

"Do you see what I'm dealing with, Reverend? I've

called for a translator to come from Truro, but they won't be here until tomorrow at the earliest. By then it could be too late."

Annabelle gazed around the street as if an answer might drive by at any moment. When she turned back to the Inspector, she noticed movement in the driveway beside Mr. Malik's corner shop. She watched intently as a tall, slim, and strikingly beautiful young woman slowly eased herself out of the shop's rear entrance, and closed the door silently behind her. Nicholls turned to look at who had caught Annabelle's eye.

"Officer!" the girl whispered, as she stepped quickly over to them. "Officer!"

She looked to be in her late-teens or early-twenties. She had a pair of intelligent hazel eyes set in a smooth, light-brown face. Her hair fell thick and lustrous about her shoulders. It swayed dramatically in the breeze. "My name is Samira Malik. I'm Aziz's sister."

Annabelle squinted at her for barely a second. "I know you."

"Yes," the girl smiled. "And I remember you, too. I met you at the village craft fair this summer. It's nice to see you again, Reverend Dixon."

They shook hands and smiled at each other, before a cloud of doubt entered Annabelle's thoughts.

"But I've not seen you since then... Where have you been?"

Samira nodded. "I'm at Brighton University. I'm only here for the weekend, though I didn't know all *this* would happen."

"All *this*?" the Inspector asked, keenly.

Samira scanned the street carefully before backing up into the driveway slowly. She beckoned the two inquisitors to her. Annabelle and Nicholls exchanged another brief glance before obliging. Once they were huddled into the tight space between the car and the wall, Samira leaned forward and spoke quietly, as if conspiring with them.

"Aziz *is* missing!" she said.

"What?!" Annabelle cried loudly, before covering her mouth. "What?" she repeated, much more quietly.

"Aziz should have come home already, and my father knows that. He's desperate to find him, even more than you."

"So let's go and speak to him," Nicholls insisted gruffly. "Surely you can communicate with him. Tell him that we're looking for Aziz, that he might be in danger, and anything he tells us will—"

"No," Samira interrupted, shaking her head gravely. "That wouldn't work. I heard you talking. My father is only pretending not to understand. You see, my dad thinks that Aziz has found a girlfriend. It's his biggest fear. Ever since Aziz was ten years old, my father has worried that Aziz would find some girl who would influence him badly and that he would run away with her. He's not telling you this because he is ashamed. Of all the plans my father has for Aziz, marrying a nice Pakistani girl is the most important to him."

"Well, isn't it possible?" the Inspector said, as he tugged the puppy back to stop it from exploring. "Could Aziz have run off with a girl?"

Samira shook her head firmly.

"No. Aziz already gets plenty of attention from girls. His mind is purely on his studies and doing things the right way – in that sense he's like my father."

"Seems unlikely to me," the Inspector said, bending down to scratch the puppy's ears and stop her gentle whining. "A teenage boy who isn't interested in girls? That's all I thought about when I was his age."

Annabelle frowned at the Inspector, but he was too preoccupied with the dog to notice.

"If he did run off, I would be the first to know," Samira said. "We tell each other everything. That's why I'm so worried—"

Samira turned her head sharply as she heard her father's voice call out from inside the shop. Upon hearing that he was merely having a simple exchange with a customer, but still unsettled by the sound of his voice, she stepped further back into the shadow of the shuttered garage. She kept her voice low as she leaned over once again to speak.

"I've not heard anything from Aziz since Friday morning."

"The day before yesterday."

"Yes. Not a call or a text. Nothing. And I've been sending him messages all weekend. He knew I was visiting. We're very close. There's no way he's alright and hasn't thought to message me back or come to see me. No way."

They were all quiet for a moment, as they reflected on what this might mean. Suddenly, their thoughts were interrupted by the sound of clattering metal as the puppy leaped toward the garage shutters, clawing at it roughly with her front paws.

"Hey!" called the Inspector, pulling the pup back. The puppy strained at her leash with every ounce of her strength, whining and barking.

Annabelle kneeled down and tried to placate her, but she remained intent on the metal garage doors, her front paws scrabbling at the air in her desperation.

The rear door to the shop opened suddenly, and Samira's eyes seemed to double in size. Her father came out screaming angrily, before his rage was replaced by confusion at the sight that greeted him.

"What's going on here?" he said, his eyes flicking rapidly between the three figures and a singular, small, yet loud and agitated puppy.

After the elder Malik exchanged some quick, tense words with Samira in their native language, the Inspector broke in.

"What have you got in here?" he said, holding the leash with both hands to stop the puppy from throwing herself against the doors again.

"Nothing!" Mr. Malik cried with a big shrug. "Delivery tonight. I not open since Friday!"

"Well, open it now!" the Inspector ordered in a voice he typically used for his officers. Annabelle winced.

Mr. Malik looked hard at the Inspector but quickly took a ring of keys from his pocket and made toward the padlock of the metal shutter. He went to unlock it, but when he got close, he found it hanging. Frowning, Malik set the lock aside, and lifted the wide shutter with the help of his knee.

It flew upwards with a heavy clank. The "thunk" as it rolled back echoed in a split-second of silence. As the echo reverberated, they briefly anticipated what they might find before the scene exploded in a blur of cries, shouts, and frenzied activity.

First, the puppy lunged once more toward the garage interior. The Inspector was taken by surprise and the leash flew out of his hands. The dog bounded down the side of the minivan parked inside toward the back of the garage, quickly followed by Samira, who immediately started to scream loudly. Then, with his hands on his head and a series of cries in Urdu, Mr. Malik did the same.

Annabelle and the Inspector followed only a step behind, but by the time they reached the source of everyone's panic, the scene at the back of the garage was frantic. Laments in foreign tongues, the puppy's furious barking, and Samira's long cries of horror and despair cut through the wintery, cold air.

There, in the corner at the back of the garage, was Aziz. And he was not in good shape. He had been badly beaten.

He was curled in a fetal position. Black, crusted blood stained half his face. He was clutching his right forearm to his body and his chin was tucked in defensively. His eyes were closed. His clothes were ripped and covered in dark stains. Blue bruises were visible on his legs and torso.

After stretching out to touch her brother but pulling back before she could hurt him further, Samira could not bear to look any more. He was shivering in the cold, hard corner of the garage. She stood up and turned away, her usually pretty face smeared with the ugliness of utter desolation. Annabelle opened her arms and the young woman fell into them, clutching the Vicar tightly as she allowed herself to sob and wail her agony.

"I've called an ambulance," Nicholls shouted.

"We'll meet you at the hospital," Annabelle shouted back, as she cajoled the sobbing girl away from the scene, the puppy trailing in her wake.

Nicholls rode with Mr. Malik and Aziz in the ambulance. Annabelle, meanwhile, drove Samira and the puppy in hot pursuit of the emergency vehicle, glancing over nervously and talking persistently to soothe the traumatized and now dumbstruck girl.

Upon reaching the hospital, Nicholls pulled Mr. Malik aside before he entered the building, knowing full well that the dazed and shocked father was too shaken to communicate in anything other than his native tongue and would only get in the way of the emergency medical team.

Annabelle took charge, following the medics as they pulled Aziz out of the vehicle and brought him quickly to the emergency room. With her arm around Samira's shoulders, she waited for ten minutes while the doctors looked Aziz over, and then she listened closely to their initial assessment. Eventually, Mr. Malik joined them, and Annabelle left them alone so that Samira could communicate the doctor's words to her father.

The Vicar rejoined the Inspector outside, where he had taken the puppy from Annabelle's car and was kneeling down to feed her some treats he had saved in his coat pocket.

"What did the doctors say?" Nicholls asked, standing up as Annabelle walked toward him with a face still gravely troubled.

She sighed deeply and shook her head at the brutality of it all.

"He's going to be alright, but it will take time. He's not only been beaten, but he's in shock now. It doesn't look like he's done anything apart from lie in the corner of the garage since yesterday."

"When will he be able to talk?"

"The doctor said he'll need at least twenty-four hours before he can talk to anyone," Annabelle said, sadly. "I don't understand. Why was he just lying there? His family was next door. Why would he suffer like that instead of going home?"

Nicholls stared into the distance.

"It's not so strange. Stupid, yes. But not uncommon. I see it a lot with young lads, tough ones especially. When they get beaten up like that, their first reaction is rarely to get help or tell someone. Their pride tends to hurt twice as much as their injuries. They worry more about what their peers will think when they find out, or in Aziz's case, his family."

"Surely not!"

"You'd be surprised, Reverend. Aziz's father seems to worship the boy for being spotless, a hard worker, and never in any trouble. Aziz doesn't even fool around with girls because his father doesn't want him to. The kid's probably deeply ashamed that this happened."

"It's such nonsense," Annabelle said, though she understood the Inspector was right. "I'll never understand men and their 'manly pride!'"

Nicholls gave the Vicar a rueful smile before turning back to her car.

"Do you mind giving me a lift back to the station, Reverend?"

"Of course not," Annabelle said, and began getting in the driver's side as the Inspector urged the puppy into the back.

"You know," Nicholls said, as they eased themselves into their seats, the Inspector's head grazing the roof of the small car, "I think patience is the only tool, pardon the pun, I have left to throw at this case."

Annabelle smiled sadly.

"I understand, Inspector. But it was only yesterday that the murder happened. You're not giving yourself much time."

"True," the Inspector sighed, looking into the back seat to check on his dog as they drove along. "Still, this is one of those cases where progress doesn't just seem slow, it seems to be going backward."

"Surely it's not that bad," Annabelle said, as she deftly shifted gear.

"I'm afraid it is," the Inspector sighed. "I mean no disrespect by this, Reverend, as I greatly admire your faith in people, but I believe it's a faith that is sometimes afforded to those who don't deserve it."

"What do you mean, Inspector?" Annabelle said, pouting slightly.

"Well, I trusted your judgment when you told me that you didn't believe Mildred's only competitor, Ian Crawford, had been tampering with the fuel, but I can think of nobody else who would have reason to do so. You're the one who believes in Ted Lovesey's innocence, and yet our only other suspect has just turned up in no state to talk and is more likely to be a victim than a murderer. In short, I'm saying that I think your openness and generosity regarding people is naïve."

"Inspector!" Annabelle exclaimed, extending her neck with surprise at his rudeness.

"Now calm down, Reverend," Nicholls continued in his commanding voice. "I'm not trying to insult you, I'm telling you this for your own good. These are not your typical parishioners we're dealing with. These are very dangerous people. Criminals, murderers, psychopaths. And they're frequently as good at lying as they are at committing misdeeds. A little bit of skepticism and distance wouldn't do you any harm, Reverend."

Annabelle gripped the wheel tightly and focused on parking the car, angered by the Inspector's criticism once again but unable to call upon sufficient evidence to dismiss it entirely.

"What will you do with Ted?" she asked, pulling at the handbrake with more force than was necessary.

Nicholls shrugged.

"I'll release him for now. We've got his prints, but we don't have the evidence to detain him further. Besides, if we get a match on the fuel can or the murder weapon, I doubt we'll have trouble finding him again. He doesn't seem like the smartest tool in the box."

"I shall come in with you," Annabelle announced defiantly, unclipping her seatbelt. "I'm sure Ted would appreciate a lift after this ordeal."

They entered the police station together, the dog once more cheerfully padding along between them, though there was no mistaking them for a happy couple this time.

As soon as Inspector Nicholls entered the reception area, Constable McAllister bounced up from her chair and made a beeline for him. Constables Harris and Raven watched her from behind their desks.

"Inspector!" she said.

"What is it, McAllister?"

"Well, there's good news and bad news," she said, casting her eyes toward Annabelle without moving her head. "Two bits of bad news, perhaps?"

"Go on," Nicholls urged.

"The bad news is that there were no prints on the fuel can. Either they were washed away, or the person who used it didn't leave any."

"Damnit. What's the good news?"

"Harper will give us the results of her tests on the murder weapon shortly," she added uncertainly, obviously fearful of what the Inspector might say about this delay. "It is taking longer than she thought."

As it turned out, the Inspector didn't say anything. He

looked from the young constable to Annabelle, then back again.

"I really hope Harper comes through for us. We need a breakthrough."

Despite their earlier disagreement, Annabelle found herself placing a sympathetic hand on the Inspector's arm at the sight of his downcast face.

"We may not agree on some things, Inspector, but I have a feeling we are closer to finding the person who did this than we think."

"Are you ever less than utterly optimistic, Reverend?"

"Golly gosh, Inspector. I hope not."

CHAPTER SEVEN

ANNABELLE'S THOUGHTS WERE so turbulent and confused that she muttered to herself as she drove, completely forgetting that Ted was sitting beside her in the passenger seat. Already uneasy from spending over two hours in the interview room, Ted glanced at the Reverend nervously and decided against saying anything.

When it became clear, however, that the Vicar was heading toward the church, and not, in fact, his own home, he found himself with no choice but to speak up.

"Um... Vicar?"

"Oh!" Annabelle exclaimed, swiveling her head, startled to find Ted beside her. "Yes?"

"I think you missed the turn. My house is down that way."

"Oh!" Annabelle repeated. "Sorry."

She looked out of the side window and wondered when the next opportunity to make a U-turn would be. Then she re-considered.

"Actually, would you like to come by my cottage and

have a cup of tea, Ted? I could give you a lift home later. I'm sure we could both do with some company considering what has happened."

Ted took a moment to think about the offer. He lived alone, had little money, and now that Mildred was dead, he had no job. He had nothing to do but sit at home or go down to the pub where he was likely to spend what little money he did have on drink.

"That sounds alright, actually. Thanks, Vicar."

Annabelle smiled warmly as she eased the car into the church driveway. Her cottage looked warm and inviting on this cold winter's evening.

A moment later, they went inside and made their way to the kitchen.

"Hello Reverend," Philippa said, her back to them as she pulled a tray out of the oven. She turned around and opened her eyes wide. "Oh, hello Ted."

"Hi, Philippa," he said meekly.

"Would you put the kettle on, Philippa? I need a cup of tea and a slice of cake even more desperately than usual."

Philippa obliged as the Reverend and the mechanic sat at the kitchen table.

"How are you feeling, Ted?" Annabelle said, as she foraged in her pockets.

Ted sighed sadly.

"Stunned. I haven't had a moment to think, let alone feel anything. One minute I'm being dragged out of Greg's house, the next I hear about Mildred, then I'm being treated like I'm the one who killed her! It's not like I was having the best weekend as it was, what with—"

Ted stopped himself abruptly, and looked over at Philippa. Annabelle understood perfectly. Ted had struggled to tell *her* about the gambling ring. He wasn't about to start spilling the beans with another person around, especially when that person was the village gossip extraordinaire.

Annabelle stood up and walked over to her church secretary.

"I'll make the tea, Philippa. You go sit down."

Annabelle poured a little water into the teapot and let it warm as she set the tray with cups, sugar, teaspoons, and milk. After she'd added the tea leaves and filled the pot with boiling water, she turned back to the table. She set the teapot and tray down before walking over to open a large square biscuit tin that sat on the counter.

"What's this?" Annabelle asked Philippa.

"What? Oh, Mrs. Clunes left those for you. She'd made too many and thought you might like a few."

"Well, she was right!" Annabelle exclaimed, as she looked over the half dozen madelines that sat daintily in the tin. Annabelle placed the coconut-covered pink spongy confections onto a plate and went to sit back down with the others.

"Oh!" Philippa exclaimed suddenly, before standing up. "I'll go get Jeremy. The poor boy's been weeding the cemetery all afternoon. I'm sure he'd love a cup of tea too."

"Good idea," Annabelle said, through a mouthful of cake.

Annabelle watched Philippa leave, then looked back at Ted. He smiled awkwardly as he took a slow sip of his tea, seeming to take some courage from the hot brew.

"Thanks, Vicar," he said, softly.

"Oh, tosh!" Annabelle smiled, gently placing her cup down. "I know you didn't do it, Ted. You've got nothing to worry about. You've no need to act so apologetic."

"Well, I'm not entirely innocent," he said.

Annabelle raised an eyebrow.

"The gambling," he added, in a whisper.

"Oh. Yes."

"Look, Vicar. Please don't tell anyone about that. If it got out that I'd—"

"Of course I won't, Ted. But you really should tell someone about it. Or at the very least get yourself away from such things. No good can come of it."

Ted put his cup down heavily, as if lacking even the energy to hold it.

"I know, Vicar."

He gazed at the table for a few moments.

"What exactly *is* this gambling ring?" Annabelle asked, hoping to interrupt his morose mood.

Ted looked up with frightened eyes. "If I tell you, you can't tell no one, right? Doctor-patient confidentiality, or... or like a confession? Something like that?"

Annabelle chuckled lightly.

"Well, I'm not quite a doctor, and confession is for Catholics. But I can promise you that I'm a woman of my word, and I won't say anything to anyone."

Ted's shoulders settled, and he breathed deeply. He began to tell his tale.

"It began as an innocent poker night. Just a few of the men getting together for the fun of it. They didn't even play for money to begin with. It was just a way for some of the men to relax. Upton St. Mary's a small place, so any chance to do something new or go somewhere different is welcome."

"Where did you play?"

"Various places. Someone's barn one week, an empty school the next. Whoever joined in would offer a place to play. That was part of the fun, I think: the whispers of where it would be, trying to find out, but keeping it all a secret. Only certain people were invited to join the ring. It was quite an honor. It was like a secret gentlemen's club."

"Sounds like a boy's club to me," Annabelle said, rolling her eyes.

"Not for long," Ted answered, ominously. "At first it was just a few of the guys, the ones with the... er... most 'difficult' wives... It was their chance to get away for a bit. I was never a regular. I only went a few times, and only once on a Friday, but the rest of us kept it a secret because we knew how much those men appreciated the chance to just disappear for a few hours. It was exciting. But then things changed."

"What?"

"I don't really know how it happened, exactly, but outsiders started coming. Men, dangerous men, from other places. It was perfect for them. Hidden locations, a system for inviting people. In the bigger cities, the police are always watching them and know all of the places where these kinds of things are held. But no copper would think to look for a high-rolling gambling ring in Upton St. Mary. It was perfect because it was so unlikely."

Annabelle sat back and shook her head at the sheer lunacy of it all.

"But why did the Upton St. Mary men continue to play? Weren't the outside men a little out of their league?"

"They had to!" Ted said as emphatically as if he were defending himself. "For one thing, the local boys knew the area. They were the ones providing the locations. Without them spreading the word and arranging it all, the outsiders wouldn't have been able to play. And these men, they just... well, they didn't *do* anything exactly, they just *felt* evil. A look. Or a walk, you know?

And who knew what these... *criminals* would do if someone stopped turning up to the tables? These men were not nice people, Vicar. I'm not saying nobody was enticed by winning big. These guys brought a lot of money to the table, but the vast majority of men who were taking part in the end did so out of fear, not greed, in my opinion."

"And what was the reason in your case, Ted?" Annabelle asked, gently.

Ted smiled weakly.

"You can probably guess, Vicar. I might have been afraid of those men, but I'm even more afraid of not having any money. I'm a forty-six-year-old mechanic who lives by himself and spends all his money on booze. The opportunity to win the kinds of amounts that were being thrown around at those games – and they were pretty big, let me tell you – was just too much for me to resist."

"You sound quite self-aware, though."

"Two hours locked up in a police station will do that to you," Ted said. Annabelle smirked sympathetically. "The only thing that keeps me going is the dream of hitting it big somehow, and with this gambling... I don't know. I suppose I thought I was due a bit of luck."

"But you lost everything, didn't you, Ted?"

"How did you know?"

"You didn't go home. You went to Greg's on Saturday morning. Were you scared? Do you owe those men money, now?"

Ted took his tea with shaky hands, lifted it to his lips, and gulped ferociously.

"We're back!" came Philippa's sing-songy voice from the front door, just before she slammed it shut. "Took forever to find him! I thought the ground had finally caved in and swallowed him up! But he was just behind that big tombstone at the back."

She stepped into the kitchen followed by Jeremy, who gently pulled off a pair of large, rough gardening gloves.

"Oh, Jeremy, you shouldn't be weeding. What about those lovely musician's hands of yours!" Annabelle laughed.

Jeremy smiled, mildly. "It's quite alright, Reverend."

"Ted," Annabelle said, "this is Jeremy. Our church organist."

"Pleased to meet you," Jeremy said, offering his long fingers.

Ted took his hand and shook it with a sudden look of curiosity on his face.

"Likewise... Have we met before?"

Jeremy's smile straightened into a thin line.

"I don't think so," Jeremy said.

Ted replied, "I could swear I've seen you recently."

"Ted is one of the mechanic's over at Mildred's," Philippa chipped in helpfully.

"Ah," Jeremy said suddenly, "I brought my car in for servicing a while back. That must be it."

"Yeah," Ted replied, unsure. "Maybe."

"Anyway," Philippa said, flapping the introductions away and pulling out a seat at the table, "sit yourself down and have a cup of tea, Jeremy. You must be freezing."

"Actually," Jeremy said, his eyes darting between the three of them, "I really should get going. I don't feel too well. My grandmother will be waiting."

"Oh poppycock!" Annabelle said. "I'm sure you can spare a few minutes for a cup of tea!"

Jeremy was already halfway to the door when he called back.

"I'll see you tomorrow, Vicar. Bye, Philippa."

"Jeremy!" Philippa called hopelessly before she heard the front door close. She turned to Annabelle with a bemused look.

"He's certainly a strange one, isn't he?" Annabelle said.

"But lovably so," Philippa smiled as she sat down at the table once again.

They chattered on for a few more minutes as they finished their teas. Graciously, Annabelle tried to steer the talk away from the bizarre and macabre events of the weekend, but Ted's morose state cast a dark cloud over the conversation.

Once he was done with his tea, Annabelle offered to drive Ted home. He accepted gratefully. It was a short trip, and one that the mechanic could easily have walked, yet Annabelle understood his reasons for wishing to spend a few more minutes in her company. Anything to stave off the desolate, fearful loneliness that awaited him at home.

"Do you have any plans now, Ted?" Annabelle said, as she revved her car around a corner. "Perhaps it would be nice to get away for a little while. Do you have any family outside the village?"

She kept her eyes on the road, but when Ted failed to respond she glanced over and noticed him looking down at the floor.

"Ted?"

"Yes?" he said, startled.

Annabelle frowned at him.

"Is everything alright?"

Ted opened his mouth, closed it again, gazed forward, then back to his lap. He was indecisive, she'd give him that.

"Ted..." Annabelle repeated, insistently. She could see something was very much on his mind, and that he was wrestling over whether to reveal it.

"I... I shouldn't really say this," Ted began, slowly, "but I suppose I owe you."

He paused for a long time. Annabelle parked the car easily in front of his house, stopped the engine and turned to him.

"I promise I won't tell anyone, if that's what you want."

Ted smiled shyly. "I know you won't. I don't even know if this is important. But I just thought you might want to know. You seem quite close..."

"Close? What are you talking about, Ted?"

"That man back at your cottage."

Annabelle took a second to think. "Jeremy?"

"Yes. I know exactly where I've seen him before. And I'm fairly certain he remembers where he's seen me, judging by the way he left in such a hurry."

"Surely not," Annabelle said, as the realization dawned on her. "You must be mistaken. Jeremy would never engage in those gambling games!"

Ted snorted and shook his head.

"He's pretty recognizable. Not the kind of man you can really mistake. He was a regular, I never went to a game where he *wasn't* there."

Annabelle sat back in the driver's seat, as if pinned to it.

"I don't believe it..."

"I told you. The ring is much bigger than it looks."

Annabelle turned to Ted defiantly. "He must have been one of those men trapped in the ring, as you said. Perhaps he went once, out of curiosity, and kept going because of fear."

Ted shook his head again.

"No. It wasn't that," Ted said, regretfully. "That's why I wanted to tell you. That guy – Jeremy – he was one of the biggest gamblers at the games. Loved it, he did. But he's in trouble, now. I owe them a lot, that's why I'm afraid to go home," Ted said, glancing sadly at his front door, "but *him*, he owes them even more."

Annabelle put her hands on the wheel and clenched it tightly, as if steadying herself against a hurricane.

"Be careful, Reverend," Ted said, finally. He opened the door and got out. Before shutting it, he leaned at the window to add, "And thank you again."

Annabelle felt a pang of sadness as Ted returned to his unlit, empty home, the street seeming even darker than usual for this time of night. She made a silent promise to check up on him first thing the next morning, and sped off, still digesting the utterly fantastical idea that Jeremy was a gambler.

Upon returning to the church and parking her car, Annabelle heard the loud, throbbing notes of the church organ. The churchyard was lit only by the two lamp posts that stood at its gate, the gentle glow of the church's stained-glass windows, and the warm orange light that emerged from behind the curtains of her cottage. She locked the car and looked over to her home, where Philippa was closing the door behind her, still fiddling with her coat buttons.

"Are you going home, Philippa?" Annabelle asked as they met on the short path to the cottage.

"Yes," Philippa answered, reaching around the back of her neck to find the end of her scarf. "The puppy's just fallen asleep, so I'm taking my chance while I can! He tends to follow me otherwise, and I have a terrible time getting him back in the house!"

Annabelle smiled and helped Philippa find the end of her scarf, bringing it around the front so that she could tie it.

"That's because you're just as attached to him as he is to you."

Philippa chuckled.

"Who wouldn't be? And how is the other little one? Has the Inspector fallen for her charms yet?"

"I believe so," Annabelle said. "She's terribly inquisitive. The perfect companion for a detective."

The two women turned toward the church as a loud swell of chords began.

"I see Jeremy's at it again. That boy has such dedication." Philippa shook her head in amazement.

"Indeed," Annabelle murmured."

"Well, I'll be off then, Vicar."

"Good night, Philippa."

Annabelle pottered over to her cottage and went inside. The moment she shut the door behind her, she felt a wave of exhaustion come over her. She had been buzzing around on her feet all day, performing the service in the morning, enduring the ordeal of discovering Aziz, and piecing together the story of the gambling ring. The emotional toll had been even greater. Although Mildred's murder had occurred only a day ago, it felt like a lifetime since she last experienced an innocent thought about something trivial. She had dedicated almost every ounce of her energy to discovering the truth, and as she stepped into her kitchen, she realized her reserves were in short supply.

She went straight for the box of meringues that Philippa had baked for her. Her church secretary usually made her something sweet on Sunday's, a sort of post-service treat. It was essential for Annabelle to always have a supply of sweet goods on hand. She needed an emergency stash to give her fortitude during those times she desperately needed it. This was one of those times.

It was only now, in the dying embers of the day, however, that Annabelle had both the time and freedom to indulge her passion. The very sight of the meringues perked her up no end, sandwiched as they were with thick, whipped, fresh Cornish cream, quite possibly from the milk of one of those cows belonging to Leo Tremethick that had held her up the day before. She took a plate, settled some of the meringues upon it, and made her way to the living room couch. She flopped down and smiled at the sweet-smelling treats. As if by magic, Biscuit appeared around the door.

"Hello, Biscuit. To what do I owe this pleasure?"

Annabelle scoffed one of the meringues in seconds, then slowed down to savor the taste of the second more fully. A few deliberate chews into the third and she found her sweet tooth finally satisfied. Biscuit, who had been circling her ankles, deftly jumped on to the arm of her chair and went to sniff the meringue plate, no doubt planning to finish off what Annabelle had left behind. Annabelle quickly whisked the plate out of her reach and gathered her up, placating her with vigorous strokes that the ginger tabby tolerated resignedly and with dignity.

In her sugary haze, Annabelle's thoughts slowly turned to the conundrums that had bothered her since showing up at Mildred's workshop and finding her body.

"I need to go to bed, Biscuit. Time for me to rest my weary head. Whittling and worrying away won't help anyone." She started to rise from her chair before immediately falling back into it. "But this news about Jeremy being a gambler is shocking! What would his grandmother say? I'm sure she would be horrified."

Biscuit indicated her disinterest in Jeremy's money and Nana problems by yawning and wriggling out of Annabelle's arms. Instead, the cat settled on the cushion beside her owner as a few short, sharp, stabbing, high notes drew Annabelle's attention to the window.

"There he is again. Playing as though nothing has happened. What do you think goes through his mind, eh, Biscuit?"

She could hear Jeremy playing the organ only faintly on most occasions, but this time the silence of her empty cottage, the lateness of the hour, and the sharpness of her thoughts served to make the sound pierce the air loudly. Annabelle felt she had a front row seat at a performance as he proceeded into a fast, manic, complex Bach concerto.

Annabelle felt a shiver run down her spine. The combination of the darkly powerful music, the blackness of the night, and her many unanswered questions were bothering her deeply.

"*Jeremy?*" she said to herself, finding the name almost too implausible to even set upon her lips.

Annabelle stared fixedly out of the window into a scene that now seemed entirely frightening. The tall, twisted, leafless branches of the churchyard trees cast imposing, stark outlines against the night sky. A round moon hid behind black clouds, as if afraid itself. Leaves swirled in the church courtyard.

To the strains of Bach's genius, Annabelle's thoughts raced so far ahead that she could barely catch them. She shook her head, continuing to talk to Biscuit as she ran her hands one after another from the baby-soft fur between the ginger tabby's ears to her tail in an attempt to calm her nerves.

"It's one thing for Ted to be involved, Biscuit. It seems perfectly natural for a man with such an addictive personality. It's even reasonable to think that many of the men in the village would indulge themselves in a spot of gambling now and again. Upton St. Mary is a wonderful, interesting, and accommodating place, but it does lack an element of danger and excitement. A clandestine game of cards would seem rather appealing to many men, I imagine.

"But Jeremy is different. He is not like many men. He is pure and good. He tells me so."

Annabelle rubbed the underside of Biscuit's chin. Now, not even Biscuit could hide her pleasure. The cat stretched her neck upward and closed her eyes in ecstasy.

"So what else might he be hiding?"

Annabelle began recalling all of the conversations she could between herself and Jeremy, searching them mentally for clues and indications about his secret life as a gambler. Nowhere, not even in his regularly odd or awkward behavior could she find any evidence of his subterfuge – and this worried her more than anything.

Still watching the church through the kitchen window, she noticed Jeremy's car. It was an old Toyota that he always parked snugly in the shadow of the trees.

"You know, Biscuit, I wonder if Jeremy was telling the truth when he gave me the message about my car and said that he'd met Ian Crawford in the village. While I have a hard time believing it of Jeremy, and far be it for me to cast aspersions, of course, he that is without sin and all that, I have no such struggle when it comes to Ian Crawford. Perhaps they are fellow gamblers!"

Annabelle went to her desk phone and began scanning her bulging phonebook for a number, before furiously dialing.

"Hello?" came a subdued and tremulous voice on the other end.

"Ted! It's Reverend Annabelle."

"Oh. I'm alright, Reverend," he said, his voice loosening into a gentle chuckle. "You don't have to check up on me every five minutes, though the thought is much appreciated."

"Oh, that's not why I'm calling," she said. "But I'm glad you're okay. Actually I wanted to ask you something... About what we talked about earlier."

"Yes?" Ted said, his voice tightening again.

"When you were here, Jeremy said that he'd brought his car in for servicing. Was that true? Or were you just covering up for each other?"

There was a slight pause.

"Oh," Ted exclaimed suddenly, as he remembered. "Yeah, he actually did bring it by. A nineties Toyota Corolla."

"Yes. That's it."

"I didn't work on it though, Mildred did. She and his grandmother go way back, or something like that. So I can't tell you what was wrong with it. Sorry."

"That's all I wanted to know, thanks, Ted."

"Anytime," he replied, as they both hung up.

Annabelle returned to the window, the sound of the music seeming to swell even louder now.

Something was very wrong with all of this, she thought. She could see how these things were easily explainable coincidences – Jeremy's visit to Mildred, his bumping into Ian Crawford, his appearance at the gambling games – but Annabelle's instincts were fired-up now, and they were telling her that there was something going on. Jeremy had been very much a blind spot for her, as church organist, a close friend, and valued member of her parish. He had reason to be excused of suspicion, but the moment she focused on him, her doubts surfaced.

"Come now, Annabelle," she told herself as she turned away from the window, "you're just getting paranoid and impatient. A good night's rest is what you need."

Just as she was about to walk upstairs, the phone startled her by ringing loudly. She jumped, then laughed away her surprise as she placed a palm over the quickened beat of her heart. Still smiling, she picked up the receiver.

"Hello?"

"Hello Reverend."

"Inspector! How are you?"

"Confused but persistent, as always, Reverend."

"Is there something I can help you with?"

"There always is," Nicholls sighed. "We just heard from Harper. Her report on the murder weapon. A wrench. No clear fingerprints, but she did suggest that the hand that wielded it to strike Mildred was unusually large. The thing is, they don't tend to ask for hand sizes in any public records. I was wondering if you could help me."

Annabelle laughed. "I suppose we should start measuring hands then! We could start with the musicians. Our church organist has—" she stopped suddenly, her smile turning into an expression that was a mixture of terror, confusion, and shock.

"Reverend?" the Inspector asked, after moments of silence.

"Yes," Annabelle replied slowly.

"You were saying something?"

Annabelle's mouth suddenly felt impossibly dry, and she realized that her heart was racing. She held her breath unconsciously and raised her eyes over to the church. Usually, she had plenty of time to think things through, and she enjoyed reaching decisions carefully and deliberately. At this moment, however, she realized that she had mere seconds to decide whether to reveal what she knew to the Inspector, incriminating a man she would not have suspected of even the smallest crime just minutes ago.

"Reverend?" the Inspector repeated, quicker this time. "Is everything alright?" he inquired anxiously.

"Inspector," she said, focusing upon the matter at hand, "would you mind dropping by so that we could go over something?"

"Now?" he replied. "I could come by after I've gone through some reports. Say about half an hour? Unless it's urgent?"

"No, it's not," Annabelle replied, narrowing her eyes in the direction of the church once more. "I can use that time to check things over myself, in fact."

CHAPTER EIGHT

JEREMY WAS STILL playing furiously when Annabelle stepped out of her cottage. The powerful, vibrating notes of the organ intermingled with the wind that whistled through the empty branches and rustled the dry leaves on the ground, creating a wall of bone-shudderingly eerie sounds.

The temperature had dropped, and the night sky had reached a shade of deep, velvety black. Her beloved church had never seemed so ominous and imposing to her as it did now. The elegant gothic structure reached up into the darkness, its stained glass windows glowing with shadowy, opaque light. Suddenly, she understood why the children of the village had concocted stories about the cemetery at night.

"Come now, Annabelle," she told herself. "There's nothing to worry about. It's just Jeremy, and it's just a particularly dark and chilly night."

It was with a sense of purpose only slightly stronger than the fear she was feeling that she walked toward the church. The sounds of her tentative feet upon the gravel were barely audible above the increasing volume of the church organ. She reached the big double doors and pushed through them into the church.

Once again, Annabelle was struck by just how different the church seemed at night. As usual, the low-wattage bulbs situated on the pillars around the pews as well as on the walls gave off a dim, flickering, yellow light. They allowed plenty of shadows to play around the church's nooks, corners, and crannies. Perhaps it was the music, she thought, so somber, dark, and dramatic. The sounds vibrated around the high walls of the centuries-old church, the hard, cold stone refusing to absorb the tones, the air pulsating slightly in her ears. Her stomach turned over. She felt like she was in a scene from an old black and white horror movie. She shivered as she made her way up the aisle.

Annabelle steeled herself as she approached the hunched figure of Jeremy, sitting with his back to her at the keys of the vast organ at the front of the church.

"Jeremy!" she called. Her voice shook. "Jeremy!"

The tall, young man continued to play, engrossed completely in the almost superhuman dexterity of his long fingers. Annabelle drew herself to within ten paces of the steps that led up to the altar, and slowed to a stop.

"Jeremy!" she called once again, but there was still no response. She breathed deeply and walked closer until she was within a few feet of him, close enough to see the stitches in the pattern of his dark-blue cardigan.

"Jere—"

With a dissonant clang of a minor chord, the organist stopped playing suddenly and spun around. Annabelle jumped back, one hand to her chest, the other out in front of her.

"Oh!" cried Jeremy, allowing himself to relax. "You startled me, Vicar!"

Annabelle smiled and took a moment to breathe out deeply.

"And you startled me!"

"I apologize," Jeremy said, bowing his head. "I was completely absorbed in my playing."

"Yes. I could tell."

"Am I bothering you? Is that what you came to tell me?" he said, checking his watch. "I suppose it is rather late."

"Actually," Annabelle began, stepping closer. She felt calmer now. The music had stopped and Jeremy's easy manner was relaxing her a little. "I wanted to speak with you about something else. Something rather serious."

Jeremy raised an eyebrow curiously, and shifted around on his stool to face the Reverend fully.

Annabelle clasped her hands together tightly, and gazed down at them as she considered how to begin. She had promised Ted that she would not mention what he had told her about Jeremy's gambling. She needed to be tactful, and if her deepest suspicions were correct, careful.

"How is your grandmother faring?"

"Quite well, Vicar. Of course, she doesn't get out much these days, but the villagers are very good to visit her. She is not short of company."

"How did she take the news of Mildred's death? I understand they were close."

Jeremy's smile remained on his face, his eyes dark in the gloom. "They'd known each other a long time, but my grandmother hadn't seen her for a while. Mildred was not one of her regular visitors. Too busy with her business, I expect."

Annabelle smiled back.

"Did you happen to know Mildred yourself?"

Jeremy smiled easily. "A little. My car breaks down rather a lot. It's old. I should get a new one."

Annabelle nodded respectfully. "Perhaps Ian Crawford would sell you one. He deals in used cars."

Jeremy stared at Annabelle, saying nothing.

"Do you happen to know anything about a gambling ring? One that some of the men in Upton St. Mary have become involved in? Maybe Ian Crawford, too?"

Jeremy shook his head and frowned.

"Vicar! I am surprised you see fit to question me about such things!" He paused for a second. "Did that mechanic say anything to you when he was at your cottage earlier?"

"Ted? No. Why would you think that?"

Jeremy was flustered for a moment before settling down.

"If he did, then I would assume you have enough sense to take them as the ramblings of a drunk; one who has done plenty to distance himself from the church, and almost nothing to support it."

The way Jeremy spoke bothered her terribly. He was typically one of the more obtuse people in her congregation, but this seemed a little overly-defensive even for him.

Annabelle frowned and looked up at the large crucifix mounted tall and proud on the altar table. She gazed at the figure of Jesus on the cross, thinking furiously. *What would you do now if you were me, boy-o?*

"How do you know Ted is a drunk? I thought you barely knew him?"

"I don't. Why are you asking so many questions?" Jeremy said, his smile suddenly disappearing and his tone shifting an octave lower, as full and as powerful as a bass note. "I feel you are casting judgment upon me for some reason."

"No," Annabelle said, appealingly. "I'm investigating a very serious matter in the parish. I need to be exact about every detail."

Jeremy's thin lips pursed themselves tightly. He placed his hands carefully on his knees, as if meditating. Annabelle glanced at his long, extended fingers as he sat on his organ stool and wondered if such soft, delicate hands could have wielded the wrench that killed Mildred so brutally. She shook the thought away quickly.

"Vicar," Jeremy said, deliberately, "if there is something you wish to tell me, please do so. You are a woman of the cloth, after all. You have nothing to be afraid of."

Annabelle noticed something in Jeremy's eyes that she had never before seen. A hardness that seemed almost impenetrable. She had never grown fully comfortable with the young man's awkward, reserved, and somewhat anti-social manner, but she hadn't felt intimidated or frightened by him until now. She stiffened her back, gathering her composure for a confrontation she anticipated would be deeply unsettling, and spoke.

"Jeremy, I believe there is something you are not telling me. Something extremely important. In the short time you've been in Upton St. Mary, I've grown very fond of you, respectful of you, and in some ways, admiring of you, so it makes me deeply uncomfortable to talk to you in this way. But I'm certain that you are somehow involved in the disturbing events that have been occurring in the village, and I want you to tell me in what manner."

A wry smile played on Jeremy's lips. In the dim glow of the church light, and after her plea for an explanation, Annabelle found his amusement rather distressing.

"I have the greatest of respect for you too, Vicar," said Jeremy, slowly, "as I do all those who dedicate their lives to the church. But I am surprised at the dogged determination with which you seek to know everything. Only He above may know all things, and it is churlish and indolent of us to attempt His greatness. Was not Adam's aimless pursuit of knowledge man's first sin?"

Annabelle screwed her face up in defiance. She was accustomed to Jeremy's often annoying deference to scripture, but this time he seemed to be wholly avoiding her questions.

"Jeremy, you know very well that I am happy to engage in philosophical discussions with you at almost any time. We have had many productive, informative conversations. But right now I beg you to stick to the subject. Don't you understand how serious this matter is?"

"What are you talking about, Reverend?"

She could no longer beat about the bush. She had to speak plainly.

"We're talking about a person's death, Jeremy! A murder!"

Jeremy stood up. A half-foot taller than Annabelle, he cast an intimidating shadow over her. She took a small step back but kept a steely expression on her face.

"A death, indeed," Jeremy said, leaning over her. "And what is death but our day of judgment. The one we must all face. Death is sad, frightening, and to be avoided. But only by sinners. For the rest of us, for you and for me, Vicar, death is a glorious event."

He took a step toward her. Annabelle took two steps back. This was not her humble, reserved church organist anymore. There was a fire behind Jeremy's eyes. His lips were curled with menace, and his usually-hunched shoulders seemed broad and strong as he walked toward the Vicar, danger and purpose emanating from his being.

"What are you doing, Jeremy!?" she cried. "You're scaring me!"

"I know, Vicar," he said, as he continued slowly toward her. "And that fact disappoints me greatly. A true follower of the Lord is never afraid. I've had my doubts about you for a long time. I've fought against them, but I'm finally coming to accept them as the truth."

"What do you mean?!" Annabelle cried, as she stepped back into the aisle, keeping a healthy ten feet of distance between them. "Jeremy! Stop!"

Unexpectedly, Jeremy obliged, his wry smile turning into a broad grin as he stood up at the front of the church, even taller and scarier than before.

Annabelle took the opportunity to gaze at him, still incredulous that this was the same man who asked so politely for a biscuit with his tea, the same man whose only goal, she had thought, was to play the best accompaniments to the psalms that he could.

"Tell me the truth, Jeremy," she said, too frightened for niceties and indirectness anymore, "did you kill Mildred?"

After a few moments of stony-faced staring, Jeremy shook his head slowly. "No, I did not, Vicar." Annabelle let out the deep breath she had been holding in for seconds.

"God did."

Jeremy looked upwards with a beatific smile as if he could see the heavens himself.

"What?!" Annabelle sputtered with astonishment.

Jeremy slowly closed his eyes. He seemed rapt and blissful. He lowered his head then opened his eyes once more and looked at her.

"Did you know that Mildred was proud? Proud enough

to pass judgment upon me? I know that I was a sinner, Vicar. Gambling is the resort of the scoundrel, the lowest of the low. I shall never forget the shame of indulging in such a pastime. But I repented, Vicar. I prayed for strength from morning until night. I dedicated every ounce of myself, body and soul, to the Lord. I did everything I could to purge myself of that dreadful sin."

"So you *were* part of the gambling ring." Annabelle said, the words tumbling from her lips.

"I was. But I am a sinner no more."

"And Mildred found out?"

"My carelessness," Jeremy said, shifting his eyes to the door behind Annabelle, as if talking to himself. "She found my gambling book in my car." He turned back to Annabelle, his face now twisted with anger and bitterness. "My sin was great, but it did not harm anyone, Vicar. Mildred threatened to tell my grandmother. Can someone as reverent as you even comprehend such evil? To turn my poor, sickly Nana's last days black with worry and concern that her only grandchild, the source of everything good and pure in her life, had committed such sin? Isn't that blackmail?"

This time Annabelle stepped forward, her own face snarled with anger and resentment.

"You killed Mildred because she found out about your *gambling?!*" she cried loudly.

Jeremy was unfazed. "As I told you before, Vicar," he said calmly, "I did not kill her. I am merely an instrument of God's will. I gave myself to Him long ago, and He has used me for many purposes since. Mildred's fate was in her own hands. Do not condemn the Lord for His just and Holy plans."

He looked to the side and slowly picked up a tall, brass

candlestick holder, one of two that stood either side of the pulpit.

"Jeremy..." Annabelle warned, holding her hand up. "Whatever you're thinking about doing, don't. Please."

With a quick flick Jeremy threw the candlestick holder into his other hand and smacked it into his palm like it was a baseball bat. He raised his eyes to the Reverend, his broad grin now a focused smirk once again and made toward her.

"The Lord tried to warn Mildred," he said. "He cast an affliction on her business first, but she was too corrupt, too twisted by her own ego to see His truth."

He was walking forward quickly now, quicker than Annabelle could retreat.

"Jeremy! Stop! Don't do this!"

"I am conveyor of the Lord's light!" Jeremy screamed in a voice Annabelle had never heard before. "I have given myself to Him entirely!"

Annabelle turned toward the door, only a few feet away. She scuttled a few steps in fear, before tripping over her cassock. She fell to her knees. She spun around quickly and saw Jeremy above her, tall and direct, wielding the candlestick holder above his head with both hands, ready to strike. She had contemplated death many times, wondering what her last moments would be like, but she had never accounted for a death that would come so swiftly, so quickly, without even a moment in which to say a prayer.

She cried out and shut her eyes tightly. There was a rush of air.

Thuds, grunts, and bizarre, animalistic snarling echoed around the church interior. Annabelle braced herself for an almighty bang and kept her eyes closed until she could stand it no longer. When the realization dawned upon her that she wasn't about to be released from this Earth, she tentatively opened her eyes.

Jeremy still stood in his menacing pose. He still clutched the candlestick holder combatively. He still had a murderous look on his face. But he had been prevented from striking Annabelle. For at the other end of the heavy, ornate candlestick, holding on for dear life, his face contorted with effort, was one Detective Inspector Michael Nicholls.

Jeremy and the Inspector were glaring over the top of the weapon, both intent on defeating the other in this murderous tug-of-war. Completing the picture, and as a counter to this sharply male-on-male aggression, the puppy was at Jeremy's heels. She was yapping, jumping, and nipping, eager to take a piece out his leg but not yet having quite the teeth to do so.

"Inspector!" Annabelle cried, her heart jumping.

As if spurred on by the sound of her voice, the Inspector seemed to double in strength. He gripped the candlestick holder evermore firmly and thrust it toward Jeremy, the end of it hitting him in the chest with a dull thump. Jeremy fell backward onto the floor of the church, and the Inspector tore the makeshift weapon out of his hands. The puppy quickly seized her opportunity to contribute to Annabelle's rescue and eagerly leaped upon Jeremy's chest, terrorizing him as he scrambled on his back like an overturned beetle.

But the heroic pair weren't finished. Tossing the candlestick roughly to one side, Nicholls forcefully lunged toward Jeremy, turned him over, and roughly snapped on a pair of handcuffs. The puppy snarled and nipped at his long, elegant fingers.

Jeremy struggled against his bonds, growling, furious at his capture, but his efforts were futile. He was caught.

Nicholls left the puppy to taunt Jeremy as she repeatedly pounced on his prone body while yipping in his ear. Quickly, he made his way to Annabelle, offering her his large, broad hand. She took it gratefully, and her savior pulled her up, steadying her as she came to a stand.

"Oh!" Annabelle said, throwing her arms around the Inspector as soon as she was on her feet. "I thought I was finished! You saved me! Thank you, Inspector!"

Nicholls allowed himself a small smile as Annabelle hugged him tightly, though he contrived to make it vanish as soon as she pulled back to look at him.

"Are you alright, Reverend?" he asked, carefully studying her face.

Annabelle smiled at him with huge relief. "Thanks to my knight in shining armor," she said, before looking over to the snapping puppy, "and his fellow crusader."

The Inspector took a deep breath, "What on earth happened?"

Annabelle looked up at the Inspector. Shaken and short of breath, she found in his stern expression a source of comfort.

"I believe you just stopped the murderer from striking again."

Nicholls looked at Jeremy, still squirming as the puppy jabbed her nose at him.

"Really? *Him?*" he gasped, his chest rising and falling rapidly as he recovered from his exertion.

"Inspector, you look more shaken than I am!"

"Of course, I'm shaken!" Nicholls cried, raising a hand to his stubble and rubbing it vigorously. "A second later and... Well, who knows what would have happened!" He clasped Annabelle's arms. "Promise me you won't put yourself in such a dangerous situation ever again, Reverend!"

Annabelle smiled awkwardly.

"I must say, Inspector. That's a rather strange reaction from a police detective!"

Nicholls released Annabelle and slowly smiled, chuckling some of his nerves away.

"It's not, Reverend. It's the reaction of someone who's grown rather fond of you, despite your habit of pushing him to his very limits!"

Annabelle smiled broadly this time.

"Perhaps it is *because* of that habit that he's grown fond of me."

"Perhaps, Reverend," Nicholls laughed. "Perhaps."

Two hours later, Annabelle sat in the Inspector's office, recounting her perspective of the events for the third time to Constable Raven. They both stopped and turned their heads as the Inspector walked into the office behind his excited puppy.

"Unless your church organist was about to bake the biggest cake Upton St. Mary has ever seen, it's a pretty sure thing that he was the one behind the fuel tampering," the Inspector said as he walked over to his chair behind the desk. "Thanks to my wet-nosed friend over there," he said, nodding at the puppy who was now tucking into her scraps in the corner of the room, "we found forty pounds of sugar and two unused fuel cans in his grandmother's house."

"*Your* wet-nosed friend?" Annabelle said.

Nicholls settled into his chair, shrugging his shoulders.

"Raven, we found something in the home that may prove useful with regards to this..." he glanced quickly at Annabelle, "gambling ring. Some directions – they seem to be in a sort of code – scribbled on the back of a beer mat."

The Inspector pulled out a plastic bag from his pocket. He leaned across his desk to hand it to the constable, but it was Annabelle who plucked it from the Inspector's fingers. She gazed at the scrappy, stained card for a few moments before handing it over to Constable Raven.

"They are directions to a pill box, that's an above-ground concrete bunker. They built many of them during the war as a line of defense in the event of an invasion. Soldiers could launch attacks from them, grenades and such. There's a large one on the outskirts of the woods beside Shona Alexander's house," Annabelle said confidently. "In the middle of the woods, there's a four-fingered tree that's a popular meeting spot for teenagers. If you walk in the direction of the shadows – assuming the gambling took place in the evening – you'll be heading east and will come across the pill box after a few minutes' walk."

"She's right, sir. On this occasion, they must have done their gambling inside the bunker. I'll take this and put it with the other evidence." Raven looked at the Inspector, who nodded as the man left the office.

Nicholls turned his eyes to the puppy for a few moments, deep in thought, before shaking his head incredulously.

"I still don't understand it," he said. "A young man. A church organist. So good that he quits his job and moves halfway across England to tend to his sick grandmother. It's not a profile I see very often in killers."

"That was precisely why he did it," Annabelle said, mournfully. "Jeremy had talent, youth, and the love of the whole community, but his only real passion, the thing he had based his entire identity upon, was his 'goodness.' It is rather ironic, in a sense, that he did the most awful thing imaginable in order to retain the appearance of being completely beyond reproach, completely 'pure.' The Bible is full of stories in which the consequences of one, small sin leads to the committing of many greater ones."

"My case reports are filled with many of the same stories," quipped the Inspector, darkly.

"Almost all acts of violence are committed following a humiliation of some kind," Annabelle continued, "Among young men in particular. It's the only way many of them feel they can redress the balance and cancel out the shame."

Nicholls eyed the Vicar, a humorous look in his eyes.

"Are you considering a career in criminal psychology, Reverend?"

Annabelle chuckled.

"It's certainly a fascinating subject."

"Well," Nicholls said, shuffling in his seat, "I'd much prefer studying it than engaging with it, to be honest. The real-life examples are a lot messier than the theories in text-books, that's for sure. When we dragged him in here, Jeremy told me everything like he was telling a bedtime story! No remorse, no sense of guilt or shame! Do you know, he waited outside the garage in the early morning on Saturday? He beat up Aziz before he got into work, wearing a balaclava so Aziz couldn't identify him. And of course, no one would suspect the 'pure and righteous' Jeremy right off the bat. He called Mildred to distract her and crept up behind her while they spoke on the phone. She couldn't even have looked him in the eye before he threw her in the pit, killed her, drove the car back over her and put the keys back on the rack! I'd have to go back years to remember a case where somebody murdered someone so clinically. It's... pretty distressing."

"Jeremy thought he was acting out God's will. He's obviously deeply troubled. His poor grandmother."

"And he was right under your nose the whole time," Nicholls said, a gently admonishing tone creeping into his voice. "You didn't realize he was a psychopath in all the time he spent at the church?"

Annabelle pursed her lips. "Upton St. Mary is full of people with quirks and foibles. I always thought of him as slightly odd, of course, but..." She paused. "I suppose the idea was a little too close to home for me."

"You found it hard to believe someone so devout could be so dangerous?" the Inspector asked.

Annabelle nodded. "Yes. Faith is a wonderful thing. It's difficult to witness it being used to justify such terrible deeds."

"He somehow thought tampering with the fuel would convince Mildred that God was punishing her for threatening to expose him. He thought it would stop her. I'm not sure it's even faith at that point. Sounds more like madness."

Annabelle shook her head, still unable to fully believe what she now knew to be the truth.

"It's so difficult to imagine that this was going on in Jeremy's life and I didn't know anything about it. Just the idea of him *gambling* is hard to imagine, but to then blackmail Mildred into keeping it a secret by trying to ruin her business... And then to *kill* her when that didn't work... You know, he must have come straight over to the church after murdering her. He sat there and played as if it were a typical Saturday. I even spoke to him! I would never have guessed he had just committed cold-blooded murder from our conversation."

"And assault," Nicholls added sorrowfully. "Don't forget about Aziz."

"Could he really be the one who attacked Aziz too?"

"He said he did, and I've all but confirmed it. We found Aziz's phone a little way down from the garage, he must have been holding it when he was attacked. There's a path that runs around the back of the garage leading to a small gap in the fence. Jeremy must have used it when he was diluting the fuel. The thing is, Aziz also seemed to have used it when walking to work. It makes a good shortcut if you're on foot, but only to the garage. Jeremy must have come upon him there. He probably attacked Aziz before he could see him. He couldn't have a fit, young lad come between him and what he had planned for Mildred."

"Oh my, it's so awful."

"When Aziz recovers, we'll talk to him and confirm it, though it's pretty much a foregone conclusion."

Annabelle sighed and placed her hands on the armrests of her chair in order to push herself out of it. She caught sight of the puppy, snoozing in the corner, exhausted after her day's efforts.

"I suppose that's everything then, Inspector. I should get home. I'm desperately in need of a good night's sleep, although how I'll ever relax enough to drift off, I don't know."

Annabelle stood up and walked to the door. She placed her hand on the doorknob and opened it.

"There was one more thing," the Inspector said, before Annabelle could step outside his office. She turned around to look at him. "I'd prefer it if you called me Mike. It's not like you have any respect for my authority anyway," he added, grinning.

After laughing gently, Annabelle said, "In that case, I'd like you to call me Annabelle." The Inspector nodded graciously. "I've always respected your humanity, Inspect— I mean, Mike. Perhaps this will help us relate on more equal terms."

Nicholls had an appreciative glint in his eye as he smiled at Annabelle.

"Perhaps, Annabelle. Perhaps."

EPILOGUE

DESPITE THE COLD, wind-whipped rain and only the barest glimmer of light peeking through the grey clouds, almost half the village dropped by the church of Upton St. Mary the following Sunday. When Annabelle had taken on her role as Reverend in the Cornish countryside, she had introduced the celebration of the Winter Solstice to her parishioners. Solstice was an opportunity for all the villagers, no matter what their faith, to show their generosity and gratitude by donating food items and other offerings to needy families just in time for Christmas. As a village full of cooks, bakers, and gardeners, Upton St. Mary was particularly well disposed toward anything culinary, and even more so when it involved sharing food with others.

Annabelle stood at the entrance to the church, offering her thanks as members of the community arrived. She watched as the villagers walked up the aisle to hand over their donations to Philippa and Mrs. Applebury. The two women usually decorated the church with large, abundant floral displays but now put their skills to work showing off the villagers' kindness with flourish and flair. The giant table placed at the front of the church was piled high with fruit, vegetables, pies, hams, poultry, joints of meat, cans, loaves of homemade bread, cakes, wine, and Christmas crackers. Spirits were high, and the villagers seemed as generous with their smiles and laughter as they were with their edibles as they milled around to talk and enjoy the convivial atmosphere of the church.

"A far better turnout than last year," Philippa said, as Annabelle walked up, "and it wasn't even raining then!"

Annabelle chuckled and exchanged a nod with a young child who walked up to proudly place a can of beans on top of the trembling table. The Vicar pulled a bonbon from the open bag in her pocket, a precautionary measure she had taken, knowing herself well enough to realize the sight and smell of so many baked treats would have her mouth watering.

"Well, I think this," she said as she looked around her, "has heightened everyone's mood." Annabelle rolled the soft sweet in her mouth for a few seconds before swallowing. "There hasn't been much cause for celebration in the village for a while now."

"Hmm," Philippa said, scanning the room before saying gravely, "That still might be the case. It's all well and good providing for the poor, and the Lord knows we have a few more needy families in the village this year." Philippa had been shocked and appalled at the news of the gambling ring. "But we're still nowhere near our goal of renovating the cemetery."

Annabelle turned to her beloved bookkeeper and smiled. "I'm sure we'll find a way, Philippa. We always do."

Philippa shrugged. The two women turned to look at the food table as they basked in the pleasant hum, chatter, and good humor that resonated within the church's great walls.

"Is that... Ted?" Philippa said, as a heavily-coated figure carrying multiple bags in each hand hustled his way through the doors.

"I believe it is," Annabelle replied, watching him bump his way through the crowd toward them.

"Hello, Vicar," Ted said, cheerfully. He placed his bags down in front of the table and began taking from them various cans and boxes. He placed his contributions on the table as Philippa hastily slotted them artfully into the display.

"Hello Ted," Annabelle said with confusion as he continued to pull from the seemingly bottomless bags. "Would you like some help?"

"Oh, no," Ted smiled, performing the task as though it were a complex mechanical maneuver requiring intense diligence and precision. "I've got it."

"Where on earth did you get all that?" Philippa asked abruptly.

Ted looked up at the church secretary and smiled shyly.

"I'm no cook," he said, in between exertions. "And I don't grow anything. But that doesn't mean I shouldn't help."

"But I thought you were broke!" Philippa exclaimed.

Ted laughed and placed a few more items on the table before realizing that there was no more space. He pushed his remaining bags underneath with his foot. "Actually," he said, "things are looking up for me."

"Oh?"

"Yes," he smiled. "I suppose you haven't heard. Apparently Mildred left the garage to me in her will. I'm the new owner!"

"That's wonderful, Ted!" Annabelle exclaimed, clasping her hands together.

"How are you going to manage that?" Philippa said, not appearing quite so joyful. "You can't run a garage when you're hitting the sauce every night!"

"Philippa!" scolded Annabelle.

Ted laughed again. "No, she's right, Vicar. Owning a garage is a lot more responsibility than simply turning up and doing what the boss tells me. That's why I'm staying sober. No more pubs. No more gambling," he said, winking at Annabelle.

"I'm so happy to hear that!"

Ted nodded shyly. "Well, I always said I just needed a lucky break. It doesn't get much luckier than suddenly being given your own business." He looked sadly at the giant cross at the head of the church. "Mildred's still taking care of me, even now that she's gone. I owe her."

"I think she would be very proud of you," Philippa said, her reproachful tone softening. "She obviously thought you could do it. She wouldn't have left the garage to you if she didn't."

"I won't be alone, of course," Ted added, "Aziz will still work with me, and he's a real talent, so it should make getting to grips with it a lot easier. That reminds me," he turned to Annabelle, "Aziz wanted me to thank you for helping him. He was going to come along, but he's got a lot of schoolwork to catch up on."

"I understand," Annabelle said. "How is he?"

"He's good. Recovering. He's a tough lad, more bothered about his studies than what happened."

"I'm glad to hear it," Annabelle said. "Take care, Ted."

"You too, Vicar," Ted said, turning away. "See you when your car breaks down!"

Annabelle laughed and watched Ted make his way out of the doors, only to be stopped and drawn into a conversation with someone.

"How about that?" Annabelle said.

"I don't care for surprises, myself," Philippa replied, "but there are some people for whom a shock does the world of good."

Annabelle looked at Philippa, acknowledging the wisdom of her words.

"I do believe you're right, Philippa."

Annabelle stood for a few more minutes, thanking the villagers who were still streaming into the church with their offerings as Philippa returned to helping Mrs. Applebury arrange the overflowing pile that had now exceeded the table's capacity and was spreading along the floor, the front pews, and all around the base of the pulpit.

Mr. Malik and his daughter Samira even dropped by to donate some fine tobacco and a plate of Mrs. Malik's Florentine slices.

"How are you, Samira?"

"Very well, Reverend. I want to thank you for what you did for us, for Aziz."

"Hush, it was nothing. I'm glad to hear that he's doing well. What are your plans now?"

"I'm going to stay in the village until the new year, but then I'll be off back to uni to my studies. I'm looking forward to it."

"I hope you'll enjoy your last few weeks with us. We'll miss you when you're gone."

The two women exchanged a hug, and Annabelle reciprocated Mr. Malik's slight bow with a hesitant and much deeper one of her own. She watched them walk proudly back down the aisle and out into the rain.

As she did so, her eye was caught by an old man who was making his way into the church. He had a distinctive bow-legged gait. She knew him to be a rather isolated man who lived by himself in a secluded, decrepit farmhouse a little outside the village. Not much was known about him other than he enjoyed collecting war memorabilia and that each Saturday he went to the pub to consume exactly two pints of bitter and a bag of peanuts in his favorite spot.

It was not only the surprise of his visit that got Annabelle's attention (she had never seen him in church before), but it was also what he was carrying. Rather than the plastic bags and cardboard boxes that the other villagers had used to carry their donations inside, the elderly man's hand was tightly clenched around the thin handle of a flat, metal box, something more appropriate for tools than food.

Annabelle watched patiently as he ambled with incredible slowness toward her. After a rather long time in which to consider the possibilities of his visit, he stood in front of her and raised his bald, liver-spotted head to look at Annabelle with his small, brown eyes.

"Hello."

"Hello, Mr. Austin. It's rather nice to see you in church."

Mr. Austin nodded slowly, as if the words took some time to reach him, then he spoke again.

"Can we talk somewhere private? Er... Father?"

Annabelle chuckled. "'Reverend,' is just fine, Mr. Austin. And of course, follow me."

She led the short man slowly off to the side, where the church office, kitchen, and storage spaces were located. After opening the door to the office for him and closing it behind her, Annabelle joined the old man as he stood beside the desk on which he had placed his peculiar storage container.

"So what did you want to speak to me about, Mr. Austin?"

"I'd like to make a donation to the church."

"Oh! That's marvelous! Thank you very much. We are always grateful for such kindnesses."

Once again, there was a pause of a few seconds before Mr. Austin nodded. He turned to the metal box, flipped the latch, and opened it.

"Golly gumdrops!" Annabelle cried loudly, placing her palms to her cheeks. She stared from the money that filled the entire interior of the toolbox to Mr. Austin and back again.

"It's yours," Mr. Austin said calmly. "But I would like my box back."

"How much is in there?" was all that Annabelle could muster.

"A little over fifteen thousand pounds, I should say."

"Golly," Annabelle repeated, this time in a whisper of amazement. "Mr. Austin, where exactly did all this money come from?"

The old man rarely grinned, but his eyes did sparkle as he looked up at the Reverend.

"Do you know anything about the card games that have been going on recently?"

Annabelle sighed. "I am rather more acquainted with those events than you would believe, Mr. Austin."

"Well," he said, gesturing at the money, "I'm a good card player."

Annabelle gawped with astonishment at the man before her. His sleepy appearance and innocent eyes seemed the very last place one would find the wits and shrewdness of a card maestro.

"Do you mean to say that you won this money from those crook-ridden card games?"

Once again Mr. Austin took a moment to answer, but when he did, his voice had a mischievous quality to it and his words seemed borne of a man who had seen a lot and thought even more throughout his decades on this earth.

"Card games are a simple matter of probability, Reverend. When you play with crooks, the probability is that someone is cheating. As I told you, I'm a good card player," Mr. Austin said, reaching into the pocket of his brown slacks and pulling out a bag of half-eaten bonbons, "but I'm even better at cheating."

It took a few seconds before Annabelle realized it, and when she did, her jaw dropped. Those were her bonbons! She searched her cassock for them but found her pockets empty. Mr. Austin held the packet out to her and winked. She took it slowly, stunned and speechless.

"How did you do that?" Annabelle said, once she had gathered enough composure to form her words again.

"Despite appearances," he began, "I am not from England. I was born in a far more unpleasant place. During the war I had to make my way across Europe any way I knew how, and I picked up a lot of skills along the road. Cards was one of them."

"Oh my!" Annabelle exclaimed. "That's quite a story!"

"It is no story," Mr. Austin said, seriously. "It is my life. Which is why I usually prefer not to reveal such things."

"Of course," Annabelle said, quickly matching the old man's seriousness, "but I'm afraid I can't accept this money, Mr. Austin. This money belongs to the men of Upton St. Mary. You should give it back."

"I already have," Mr. Austin replied. "This is what's left."

"You mean this is the money you took from the other men? The ones from outside the village?"

"Precisely."

Annabelle breathed deeply, struggling to keep up with this extraordinary turn of events.

"This money should go to the police," Annabelle said.

"No, it should not, Reverend," Mr. Austin replied adamantly. "This is my money, and it should go where I intend it. Now look, Reverend, I have heard about your difficulties in raising funds for the cemetery, and at my stage of life, this is troubling. I'll be needing it myself soon. Upton St. Mary has been my home for many years. It is a place that has allowed me to live out my life in peace and solitude, just as I wished it. I am deeply indebted and grateful to this corner of the world, and it is my last wish that I be buried here. Now, if you feel better about it, consider this payment in advance for my eternal resting place, plus funeral expenses."

"But Mr. Austin—"

"I am an old man, Reverend. Old enough to be stubborn. Old enough to be taken on authority. Take this money, and fix the cemetery. If, when my time comes, it is unable to accommodate me, then I shall regard it as a promise broken."

"Mr.—"

"Goodbye, Reverend."

Though Mr. Austin's words were quick and strong, the pace with which he turned and left was anything but. Were Annabelle not so taken aback by the events that had just unfolded, she might have stopped him, but instead she simply watched him amble out of the office in his uniquely awkward manner.

Once he was gone, Annabelle secured the money away in the safe and took a few moments to gather herself before rejoining the others out in the church. She emerged from the office beaming, and when she caught sight of the Inspector placing his gifts onto the gigantic pile, her smile grew even wider.

"Annabelle!" he called, relishing the informality.

"Hello, Mike," Annabelle replied, emphasizing his name with good humor. "I didn't expect you to still be in the village."

"Well," he said, leaning down to pet the puppy at his heel, "I was just clearing some things up before I take Molly here back to Truro."

"Molly! I like that name. Hello there, Molly!" Annabelle said, kneeling beside the Inspector to scratch the dog's head.

Nicholls laughed as Molly licked Annabelle's hand. They stood up together.

"So," Annabelle began, "the gambling ring. You've broken it up? Is it all over?"

"The gambling? Absolutely. We caught them at it, and it didn't take much for these criminals to spill the dirt on each other. 'No honor among thieves,' and all that. As for the men in the village, we decided to let them go. Their wives will judge and punish them much more effectively than the police ever could. I'm pretty sure none of them will go anywhere near so much as a betting shop ever again."

Annabelle smiled at the Inspector's good judgment.

"I am going to check into that Crawford character, though. I'd like to see what exactly he gets up to in that business of his. A gambling ring..." he mused, shaking his head. "Here in Upton St. Mary... I still can't believe it."

"I hate to say I told you so, but I was right."

"Yes, yes," the Inspector said. "You've got to admit, though, at the time it sounded ludicrous! A gambling ring! In Upton St. Mary?" he repeated, "Sometimes, Annabelle, you seem a little too ahead of us all when it comes to certain matters. If I didn't know better, I'd have suspected you were part of it. Or maybe you have a direct line to an all-knowing higher authority!" he added, chuckling.

Annabelle laughed heartily. "If that were true, I would be somewhere a lot sunnier and warmer than here!" she said, nodding at the pouring rain through the open doors of the church.

Nicholls turned to watch the downpour, then looked back to the Reverend with a small smile. "No, you wouldn't," he said. "I doubt the crown jewels could tempt you away from this village."

Annabelle blushed a little as she gazed over the departing villagers who were finally gathering up enough willpower to brave the rain and make their way home.

"There are more valuable things than riches, that's for sure," she said, looking up at the Inspector. "And the puppy? You're keeping her?"

The Inspector's eyes softened when he looked down at his small, brown faithful friend.

"Suppose I'll have to. Doesn't look like she wants to go anywhere, and I have to admit, she was pretty useful. I'll call James Paynton in the morning. Tell him I don't need one of his dogs after all."

Annabelle beamed with delight.

The Inspector looked back at her, his eyes still soft, both

of them seeming to consider the other in a different light and with a new perspective.

"I hope it doesn't take a murder to bring you back to Upton St. Mary again, Mike," said Annabelle, holding out her hand. Nicholls took it softly.

"Is that an invitation?"

Annabelle laughed lightly.

"If you need one."

"Then I suppose we'll be seeing each other very soon."

"I look forward to it. Goodbye, Mike."

"Until next time, Annabelle."

REVERENTIAL RECIPES

CONTINUE ON TO CHECK OUT THE RECIPES FOR GOODIES FEATURED IN THIS BOOK...

MIRACULOUS ENGLISH MADELINES

For the madelines:
1 stick butter, softened
½ cup sugar
2 eggs, beaten
½ cup flour
1 ½ teaspoons baking powder
¼ teaspoon salt
1 tablespoon warm water

To finish:
2-4 tablespoons red fruit jelly
4 tablespoons shredded coconut
6 candied cherries, halved

Preheat the oven to 350°F/180°C. Grease 6-8 dariole molds with butter and dust with flour.

Cream together the butter and sugar in a mixing bowl until light and fluffy, using an electric or rotary beater or wooden spoon. Beat in the eggs.

Sieve the flour with the baking powder and salt. Stir in 1 tablespoon of flour into the butter mixture until well mixed. Gradually fold in the remaining flour. Add enough water to give the mixture a soft, dropping consistency.

Divide the mixture equally between dariole molds. Bake for 15 to 20 minutes or until well-risen and golden.

Turn the madelines carefully out of the molds, upside down, and leave to cool. Trim the bases if they do not stand up well. When cool, brush with the sieved jelly, then roll in the coconut. Stand upright on a serving plate and decorate the top of each with a halved candied cherry.

Makes 6 to 8.

VENERABLE VICTORIA SANDWICH

For the sponge cake:
1 cup sugar
1 ½ sticks butter
3 eggs, beaten
1 ½ cups flour
2 ¼ teaspoons baking powder
¼ + ⅛ teaspoons salt
2 tablespoons warm water
Strawberry jelly for spreading

For the glacé icing:
1 ¼ cups powdered sugar
1-2 tablespoons warm water
Walnut halves for decoration

Preheat the oven to 375°F/190°C. Grease two 7-inch sandwich tins and dust with flour.

Cream together the sugar and butter in a mixing bowl until light and fluffy, using an electric beater or wooden spoon. Gradually beat in the eggs.

Sift the flour, baking powder, and salt. Stir 1 tablespoon of flour into the butter mixture until well mixed. Gradually fold in the remaining flour. Add enough water to give the mixture a soft, dropping consistency. Pour into sandwich tins.

Bake just above the center of the oven for about 20 minutes or until well-risen and golden, and the cakes have shrunk away from the sides of the baking tins.

Turn out onto a wire rack and leave to cool. Spread the jelly evenly over one cake and place the remaining cake on top.

To prepare the icing, sift the icing sugar into a mixing bowl. Gradually mix in the water until a smooth paste is formed. It should coat the back of the spoon. Quickly beat out any lumps. Spread over the cake before the icing is set, and decorate around the edge with your decoration.

Serves 8 – 10.

MARVELOUS MERINGUES

2 egg whites
½ cup fine sugar
A little fine sugar for dredging
1 cup of whipping cream, whisked to stiffness

Preheat the oven to 225°F/120°C. Put the egg whites in a large mixing bowl and beat until stiff with a balloon whisk, rotary, or electric beater. Fold in 1 tablespoon of the sugar, then beat again until smooth and satiny. It should stand in peaks. Fold in the remaining sugar with a large metal spoon.

Put the meringue mixture into an icing bag fitted with a ½-inch plain pipe. Pipe into small rounds on parchment paper placed on a baking sheet. Dredge with a little sugar.

Bake in the oven for 1 to 2 hours or until the meringues are crisp and firm to the touch. If the meringues begin to turn brown, open the oven door slightly.

Remove from the oven, and leave to cool on a wire rack. Peel off the paper when the meringues are completely cold, and sandwich together with the whipped cream just before serving.

Makes approximately 6.
Notes:

Meringues are easy to make if a few basic rules are followed. Make sure all your equipment is grease-free. Use 2 ounces of fine sugar for every egg white. Refrigerate the egg whites for 24 hours before using. Do not overbeat once the sugar is added. Bake at a very low temperature.

FLAMING FLORENTINE SLICES

12 oz. of semi-sweet baking chocolate, broken into pieces,
or chips
½ stick of butter
½ cup brown sugar
1 egg, beaten
2 oz. of mixed dried fruit
1 cup finely shredded coconut
2 oz. of candied cherries, quartered

Preheat the oven to 300°F/150°C. Put the chocolate pieces
in a heatproof bowl, and stand it over a pan of hot water
until melted, stirring occasionally. Spoon the chocolate into
a greased 8-inch square cake tin or silicone baking pan.
Spread out over the bottom and leave to set.

Meanwhile, cream together the butter and sugar until
the mixture is light and fluffy. Beat in the egg thoroughly.
Mix together the remaining ingredients and add to the
creamed mixture. Spoon into the tin and spread over the set
chocolate.

Bake in the center of the oven for 40 to 45 minutes, or

until golden-brown. Remove from the oven and leave for 5 minutes, then carefully mark into squares with a sharp knife. The mixture will be quite sticky at this stage.

Leave until cold, then loosen with a palette knife and lift carefully from the tin. Cut into squares.

Makes 12 to 16.

All ingredients are available from your local store or online retailer.

You can find links to the ingredients used in these recipes at http://cozymysteries.com/grave-in-the-garage-recipes/

FREE PREQUELS

FIND OUT WHERE THEY GOT STARTED...

To get two free books, updates about new releases, exclusive promotions, and other insider information, sign up for the Cozy Mysteries Insider mailing list at:

http://cozymysteries.com/annabelle

REVEREND ANNABELLE DIXON WILL RETURN...

WOULD YOU LIKE to find out what happens next for Annabelle? Check out the subsequent book in this fun, cozy mystery series, *Horror in the Highlands*. You can find an excerpt on the following pages.

HORROR IN THE HIGHLANDS

CHAPTER ONE

Friday

A SHORT, SHARP jolt woke Annabelle up, followed immediately by the queasy sensation of being gently rocked on her back. She found herself grasping wildly for something to steady herself, but succeeded only in banging her hand against the solid, cloth-covered wall next to which she lay. After opening her eyes, she went stiff with surprise, struck by the realization that this was not, indeed, her cozy bed in her cozy cottage in her cozy adopted parish of Upton St. Mary.

Her confusion only lasted a few moments, before the gentle chug of railway tracks and the sparse, old-fashioned decoration of the sleeper cabin reminded her of where she was.

Suddenly feeling entirely awake, Annabelle threw aside her sheet and leaped out of the narrow cabin bed, quickly turning to the window. She furiously rubbed at the light mist that covered the glass and gazed through it intently.

Her breath stopped, her eyes widened, and her heart began to sing as soon as she saw what lay on the other side of the inch-thick glass. The beautiful Scottish Highlands!

Annabelle was on the Caledonian sleeper train on her way from London to Inverness. She discovered the source of the rocky motions of her carriage when she saw that the train was winding itself along the crest of a riverbank, affording her an almost overwhelming view of the land that was unfurling ahead of her.

"Oh my!" gasped Annabelle, as magnificent, dark-green hills tumbled elegantly among the thick mists of the spring morning. Faint traces of winter snow graced their highest points. Silver-clear water glistened as it made its way over the craggy rocks that lay nestled on the riverbed. Even the gray clouds above, dense and heavy, that threatened to burst forth at any moment, somehow seemed joyous to her. It had been over a year since she last visited Scotland, and though she remembered well enough how impressed she always was by the Highland landscape, memories alone could not capture such magnificence.

She had grown rather accustomed to the quiet, natural beauty of her parish in Upton St. Mary. It was delicate and garden-like. Down there, spring was a time of blossoming color and light breezes that made the budding, sprouting, emerging flora dance cheerfully. Here, however, there was no light breeze. Thistles and nettles stood defiantly, sturdy and proud against the strong winds and heavy rains. One need only look at their surroundings to see why the Scots had a reputation for being a tough bunch. Demonstrations of courage and fortitude were all around them.

While Annabelle was basking in the glorious scenery, she said a quiet, humble prayer, and set about getting dressed. She still had rather a long way to go; yet another train journey, and two ferries to catch before she reached her journey's end.

Once ready, she picked up her heavy sports bag and made her way to the lounge car where she quickly secured herself a cup of hot tea and a comfortable seat from which to contemplate the view some more. It was an intimate carriage, and there were already a few early-risers enjoying their breakfasts. Annabelle glanced around and was greeted with quiet smiles and deferential nods, attracting instinctive respect despite wearing her regular clothes instead of her customary cassock or her black and white clerical collar.

It struck her that only a very particular type of traveler still took the train. A garishly-colored plane could take one most of the way in a tenth of the time for the same price. A leisurely drive while enjoying frequent pit stops and the company of friends or family, even unswerving solitude, was another alternative. As she sat at her table, it seemed to Annabelle that only those with a very contemplative, appreciative, and patient disposition would choose the train as their preferred mode of transport. It was this type of group that Annabelle was happiest to place herself among.

She sipped from her teacup and reached down into her sports bag for the oatcakes Philippa had prepared for her. As she pulled the foil-wrapped package out of her bag, she could almost hear the voice of her church secretary fussing.

"I don't care if they do serve food on the train! It'll be far too expensive and five days old anyway!"

Annabelle smiled as she nibbled delicately before furtively pushing an entire oatcake into her mouth and munching away. She brushed the crumbs from her fingers and sipped the last of her tea. Reaching once more into her bag, Annabelle pulled out the gifts she had procured for the two people who were the reason for this long journey; the two people she loved most in the world, her older brother, Roger, and his daughter, Bonnie.

The first gift was a hand-knitted scarf in red and white. These were the colors of Arsenal football club, her brother's singular passion during the time they had grown up together in the East of London. The scarf had been knitted by Mrs. Chamberlain, who lived just around the corner from St. Mary's Church, and who seemed to Annabelle to possess hands imbued with the dexterity of a concert pianist and the flight of a hummingbird. A computer analyst who worked from home, Roger still kept himself abreast of every fixture and transfer dealing that his beloved team were involved in. Annabelle knew the gift would be appreciated, especially on the blustery moors of Blodraigh, the outer Scottish island where he and Bonnie lived.

Roger was a single dad, a widower. His daughter was seven years old. Annabelle had visited her niece almost every spring since the death of her mother when Bonnie was a baby. Now, as Annabelle watched the young girl grow ever more confident, energetic, and tall, the trips had become one of the highlights of the year for both of them. Annabelle adored her niece, finding in her a kindred spirit who loved sweets and laughter as much as she did, while Bonnie, growing up in the rather barren and isolated confines of the island, thought of her aunt as terribly exotic. Bonnie longed to hear tale after tale of what, to her, were the peculiar and far-off people and events of Upton St. Mary.

To the young girl, almost anything beyond the coastline of the island that she had grown up on was the source of mystery, excitement, and intense curiosity. She bombarded her aunt with question after question on the smallest of details. She asked about the types of plants and flowers that surrounded St. Mary's church, the shops that people frequented, and the fashions and foibles particular to those who lived on the south coast. Annabelle indulged her niece's inquisitions, finding Bonnie a rapt audience for her accounts of life as an English country vicar.

Though Annabelle did her best to temper the wide-eyed wonder that accompanied her answers to Bonnie's questions, it often seemed that Bonnie envisioned Upton St. Mary as a bustling metropolis of action and momentum; a place in which the people were determined and always in a hurry; where there was drama and excitement on a regular basis. Whenever Annabelle was tempted to dissuade Bonnie of these notions and convince her that Upton St. Mary was only slightly larger and busier than Blodraigh, she saw her stories through the young girl's eyes and quickly realized that her own life as the Vicar of the village was indeed rather hectic and often full of surprises.

Bonnie loved nothing more than adventure, and she thought constantly of escape from her narrow existence. It was for that reason (as well as a rather obvious hint in one of her letters) that Annabelle had brought with her a special, limited-edition copy of the latest and hottest children's fantasy series, *Celestius Prophesy and the Circle of Doom*. It had been released only a few days prior, and Annabelle had reserved it long in advance, already cherishing the moment she would hand it to her niece.

Annabelle set about wrapping the presents in the paper she had bought during her stopover in London. As she did so, she glanced at the passing lochs and mountains, a sense of satisfaction warming her insides like a glowing hearth. Upton St. Mary may not be a hive of activity and drama, but the persistent requests and quirks of her congregation still kept her busy. It was appealing, exciting, essential even, to squirrel oneself away from those demands every so often. As she always did, she had agreed to give a sermon at the church during her stay on the island, but it would be her only duty. For the rest of her week-long visit, she was determined to enjoy the rest and tranquility that her trip would afford. What could possibly be more pleasing than spending time with her much-loved brother and his daughter amid the serene and beautiful landscape of a Scottish island?

To get your copy of *Horror in the Highlands*, visit the
link below:
http://cozymysteries.com/horror-in-the-highlands

BOOKS BY ALISON GOLDEN

FEATURING INSPECTOR DAVID GRAHAM

The Case of the Screaming Beauty (Prequel)

The Case of the Hidden Flame

The Case of the Fallen Hero

The Case of the Broken Doll

The Case of the Missing Letter

FEATURING DIANA HUNTER

Hunted (Prequel)

Snatched

Stolen

Chopped

Exposed

ABOUT THE AUTHOR

Alison Golden was born and raised in Bedfordshire, England. She writes cozy mysteries and suspense novels, along with the occasional witty blog post, all of which are designed to entertain, amuse, and calm. Her approach is to combine creative ideas with excellent writing and edit, edit, edit.

She is the creator of the Reverend Annabelle Dixon cozy mysteries, a charming, fun series featuring a female vicar ministering in the beautiful county of Cornwall, England. She also produces a Jersey-based detective series featuring Inspector David Graham and the Diana Hunter series, set in Vancouver.

Her books' themes range from the humorous and sweet to harder hitting suspense. They are recommended for readers who like to relax and unwind with their books, who enjoy getting to know the characters, and who prefer the tougher side of life implied.

She is based in the San Francisco Bay Area with her husband and twin sons. She splits her time traveling between London and San Francisco.

For up-to-date promotions and release dates of

upcoming books, sign up for the latest news here: http://cozymysteries.com/annabelle.

For more information:
cozymysteries.com
alison@cozymysteries.com

THANK YOU

Thank you for taking the time to read this box set. If you enjoyed it, please consider telling your friends or posting a short review. Word of mouth is an author's best friend and very much appreciated.

Thank you,